VOODOO RIVER

VOODOO RIVER

ROBERT CRAIS

HYPERION

NEW YORK

Library of Congress Cataloging-In-Publication Data
Crais, Robert.
    Voodoo River / Robert Crais. — 1st ed.
        p.   cm.
    ISBN 0-7868-6076-6
    1. Cole, Elvis (Fictitious character)—Fiction.   2. Private
investigators—California—Los Angeles—Fiction.   3. Birthparents-
-Louisiana—Fiction.   I. Title.
PS3553.R264F67   1995
813'.54—dc20   94-32389   CIP

FIRST EDITION

10 9 8 7 6 5 4 3 2

Designed by Jessica Shatan

FOR STEVE VOLPE,

proprietor of The Hangar,
trusted friend,
and the best slack man in the business.
Semper fidelis.

1

I met Jodi Taylor and her manager for lunch on the Coast Highway in Malibu, not far from Paradise Cove and the Malibu Colony. The restaurant was perched on the rocks overlooking the ocean, and owned by a chef who had his own cooking show on public television. A *saucier*. The restaurant was bright and airy, with spectacular views of the coast to the east and the Channel Islands to the south. A grilled tuna sandwich cost eighteen dollars. A side of fries cost seven-fifty. They were called *frites*.

Jodi Taylor said, "Mr. Cole, can you keep a secret?"

"That depends, Ms. Taylor. What kind of secret did you have in mind?"

Sid Markowitz leaned forward, bugging his eyes at me. "This meeting. No one is to know that we've talked to you, or what we've discussed, whether you take the job or not. We okay on that?" Sid Markowitz was Jodi Taylor's personal manager, and he looked like a frog.

"Sure," I said. "Secret. I'm up to that."

Sid Markowitz didn't seem convinced. "You say that now, but I wanna make sure you mean it. We're talking about a celebrity here." He made a little hand move toward Jodi Taylor. "We fill you in, you could run to a phone, the *Enquirer* might pay you fifteen, twenty grand for this."

I frowned. "Is that all?"

Markowitz rolled the bug eyes. "Don't even joke about that."

Jodi Taylor was hiding behind oversized sunglasses, a loose-fitting man's jeans jacket, and a blue Dodgers baseball cap pulled low on her forehead. She was without makeup, and her curly, dusky-red hair had been pulled into a ponytail through the little hole in the back of the cap. With the glasses and the baggy clothes and the hiding, she didn't look like the character she played on national television every week, but people still stared. I wondered if they, too, thought she looked nervous. She touched Markowitz's arm. "I'm sure it's fine, Sid. Peter said we could trust him. Peter said he's the best there is at this kind of thing, and that he is absolutely trustworthy." She turned back to me and smiled, and I returned it. Trustworthy. "Peter likes you quite a bit, you know."

"Yes. It's mutual." Peter Alan Nelsen was the world's third most successful director, right behind Spielberg and Lucas. Action adventure stuff. I had done some work for him once, and he valued the results.

Markowitz said, "Hey, Peter's a pal, but he's not paid to worry about you. I wanna be sure about this guy."

I made a zipper move across my mouth. "I promise, Sid. I won't breathe a word."

He looked uncertain.

"Not for less than twenty-five. For twenty-five all bets are off."

Sid Markowitz crossed his arms and sat back, his lips a tight little pucker. "Oh, that's just great. That's wonderful. A comedian."

A waiter with a tan as rich as brown leather appeared, and the three of us sat without speaking as he served our food. I had ordered the mahi-mahi salad with a raspberry vinaigrette dressing.

Sid was having the duck tortellini. Jodi was having water. Perhaps she had eaten here before.

I tasted the mahi-mahi. Dry.

When the waiter was gone, Jodi Taylor quietly said, "What do you know about me?"

"Sid faxed a studio press release and a couple of articles to me when he called."

"Did you read them?"

"Yes, ma'am." All three articles had said pretty much the same thing, most of which I had known. Jodi Taylor was the star of the new hit television series, *Songbird*, in which she played the loving wife of a small-town Nebraskan sheriff and the mother of four blond ragamuffin children, who juggled her family with her dreams of becoming a singer. Television. The PR characterized *Songbird* as a thoughtful series that stressed traditional values, and family and church groups around the nation had agreed. Their support had made *Songbird* an unexpected dramatic hit, regularly smashing its time-slot competition, and major corporate sponsors had lined up to take advantage of the show's appeal. Jodi Taylor had been given the credit, with *Variety* citing her "warmth, humor, and sincerity as the strong and loving center of her family." There was talk of an Emmy. *Songbird* had been on for sixteen weeks, and now, as if overnight, Jodi Taylor was a star.

She said, "I'm an adopted child, Mr. Cole."

"Okay." The *People* article had mentioned that.

"I'm thirty-six years old. I'm getting close to forty, and there are things that I want to know." She said it quickly, as if she wanted to get it said so that we could move on. "I have questions and I want answers. Am I prone to breast or ovarian cancer? Is there some kind of disease that'll show up if I have children? You can understand that, can't you?" She nodded hopefully, encouraging my understanding.

"You want your medical history."

3

She looked relieved. "That's exactly right." It was a common request from adopted children; I had done jobs like this before.

"Okay, Ms. Taylor. What do you know about your birth?"

"Nothing. I don't know anything. All I have is my birth certificate, but it doesn't tell us anything."

Sid took a legal envelope from his jacket and removed a Louisiana birth certificate with an impressed state seal. The birth certificate said that her name was Judith Marie Taylor and that her mother was Cecilia Burke Taylor and her father was Steven Edward Taylor and that her place of birth was Ville Platte, Louisiana. The birth certificate gave her date of birth as July 9, thirty-six years ago, but it listed no time of birth, nor a weight, nor an attending physician or hospital. I was born at 5:14 on a Tuesday morning and, because of that, had always thought of myself as a morning person. I wondered how I would think of myself if I didn't know that. She said, "Cecilia Taylor and Steven Taylor are my adoptive parents."

"Do they have any information about your birth?"

"No. They adopted me through the state, and they weren't given any more information than what you see on the birth certificate."

A family of five was shown to a window table behind us, and a tall woman with pale hair was staring at Jodi. She had come in with an overweight man and two children and an older woman who was probably the grandmother. The older woman looked as if she'd be more at home at a diner in Topeka. The overweight man carried a Minolta. Tourists.

"Have you tried to find out about yourself through the state?"

"Yes." She handed a business card to me. "I'm using an attorney in Baton Rouge, but the state records are sealed. That was Louisiana law at the time of my adoption, and remains the law today. She tells me that we've exhausted all regular channels, and recommended that I hire a private investigator. Peter recommended you. If you agree to help, you'll need to coordinate what you do through her."

I looked at the card: Sonnier, Melancon, & Burke, Attorneys at Law. And under that: Lucille Chenier, Associate. There was an address in Baton Rouge, Louisiana.

Sid leaned forward, giving me the frog again. "Maybe now you know why I'm making a big deal about keeping this secret. Some scumbag tabloid would pay a fortune for this. Famous actress searches for real parents."

Jodi Taylor said, "My mom and dad are my real parents."

Sid made the little hand move. "Sure, kid. You bet."

She said, "I mean it, Sid." Her voice was tense.

The tall woman with the pale hair said something to the over-weight man and he looked our way, too. The older woman was looking around, but you could tell she didn't see us.

Jodi said, "If you find these people, I have no wish to meet them, and I don't want them to know who I am. I don't want anyone to know that you're doing this, and I want you to promise me that anything you find out about me or my biological relatives will remain absolutely confidential between us. Do you promise that?"

Sid said, "They find out they're related to Jodi Taylor, they might take advantage." He rubbed his thumb across his finger-tips. Money.

Jodi Taylor was still with me, her eyes locked on mine as if this was the most important thing in the world. "Do you swear that whatever you find will stay between us?"

"The card says 'confidential,' Ms. Taylor. If I work for you, I'm working for you."

Jodi looked at Sid. Sid spread his hands. "Whatever you want to do, kid."

She looked back at me, and nodded. "Hire him."

I said, "I can't do it from here. I'll have to go to Louisiana, and, possibly, other places, and, if I do, the expenses could be consider-able."

Sid said, "So what's new?"

"My fee is three thousand dollars, plus the expenses."

Sid Markowitz took out a check and a pen and wrote without comment.

"I'll want to speak with the attorney. I may have to discuss what I find with her. Is that okay?"

Jodi Taylor said, "Of course. I'll call her this afternoon and tell her to expect you. You can keep her card." She glanced at the door, anxious to leave. You hire the detective, you let him worry about it.

Sid made a writing motion in the air and the waiter brought the check.

The woman with the pale hair looked our way again, then spoke to her husband. The two of them stood and came over, the man holding his camera.

I said, "We've got company."

Jodi Taylor and Sid Markowitz turned just as they arrived. The man was grinning as if he had just made thirty-second-degree Mason. The woman said, "Excuse us, but are you Jodi Taylor?"

In the space of a breath Jodi Taylor put away the things that troubled her and smiled the smile that thirty million Americans saw every week. It was worth seeing. Jodi Taylor was thirty-six years old, and beautiful in the way that only women with a measure of maturity can be beautiful. Not like in a fashion magazine. Not like a model. There was a quality of realness about her that let you feel that you might meet her at a supermarket or in church or at the PTA. She had soft hazel eyes and dark skin and one front tooth slightly overlapped the other. When she gave you the smile her heart smiled, too, and you felt it was genuine. Maybe it was that quality that was making her a star. "I'm Jodi Taylor," she said.

The overweight man said, "Miss Taylor, could I get a picture of you and Denise?"

Jodi looked at the woman. "Are you Denise?"

Denise said, "It's so wonderful to meet you. We love your show."

Jodi smiled wider, and if you had never before met or seen her, in that moment you would fall in love. She offered her hand, and said, "Lean close and let's get our picture."

The overweight man beamed like a six-year-old on Christmas morning. Denise leaned close and Jodi took off her sunglasses and the maître d' and two of the waiters hovered, nervous. Sid waved them away.

The overweight man snapped the picture, then said how much everybody back home loved *Songbird*, and then they went back to their table, smiling and pleased with themselves. Jodi Taylor replaced the sunglasses and folded her hands in her lap and stared at some indeterminate point beyond my shoulder, as if whatever she saw had drawn her to a neutral place.

I said, "That was very nice of you. I've been with several people who would not have been as kind."

Sid said, "Money in the bank. You see how they love her?"

Jodi Taylor looked at Sid Markowitz without expression, and then she looked at me. Her eyes seemed tired and obscured by something that intruded. "Yes, well. If there's anything else you need, please call Sid." She gathered her things and stood to leave. Business was finished.

I stayed seated. "What are you afraid of, Ms. Taylor?"

Jodi Taylor walked away from the table and out the door without answering.

Sid Markowitz said, "Forget it. You know how it is with actresses."

Outside, I watched Jodi and Sid drive away in Markowitz's twelve-cylinder Jaguar while a parking attendant who looked like Fabio ran to get my car. Neither of them had said good-bye.

From the parking lot, you could look down on the beach and see young men and women in wetsuits carrying short pointy boogie boards into the surf. They would run laughing into the surf, where they would bellyflop onto their boards and paddle out past the breakwater where other surfers sat with their legs hanging down, bobbing in the water, waiting for a wave. A little swell would come, and they would paddle furiously to catch its crest. They would stand and ride the little wave into the shallows where they would turn around and paddle out to wait some more. They did it again and again, and the waves were always small, but maybe each time they paddled out they were thinking that the next wave would be the big wave, the one that would make all the effort have meaning. Most people are like that, and, like most people, the surfers probably hadn't yet realized that the process was the payoff, not the waves. When they were paddling, they looked very much like sea lions and, every couple of years or so, a passing great white shark would get confused and a board would come back but not the surfer.

Fabio brought my car and I drove back along the Pacific Coast Highway toward Los Angeles.

I had thought that Jodi Taylor might be pleased when I agreed to take the job, but she wasn't. Yet she still wanted to hire me, still wanted me to uncover the elements of her past. Since my own history was known to me, it held no fear. I thought about how I might feel if the corridor of my birth held only closed doors. Maybe, like Jodi Taylor, I would be afraid.

By the time I turned away from the water toward my office, a dark anvil of clouds had formed on the horizon and the ocean had grown to be the color of raw steel.

A storm was raging, and I thought that it might find its way to shore.

It was just after two when I pulled my car into the parking garage on Santa Monica Boulevard and climbed the four flights to my office there in the heart of West Hollywood. The office was empty, exactly as I had left it two hours and forty minutes ago. I had wanted to burst through the door and tell my employees that I was working for a major national television star, only I had no employees. I have a partner named Joe Pike, but he's rarely around. Even when he is, conversation is not his forte.

I took out Lucille Chenier's business card and dialed her office. A bright southern voice said, "Ms. Chenier's office. This is Darlene."

I told her who I was and asked if Ms. Chenier was available.

Darlene said, "Oh, Mr. Cole. Mr. Markowitz phoned us about you."

"There goes the element of surprise."

She said, "Ms. Chenier's in court this afternoon. May I help?"

I told her that I would be flying in tomorrow, and asked if we might set a time for me to meet with Ms. Chenier.

"Absolutely. Would three o'clock do?"

"Sounds good."

"If you like, I can book you into the Riverfront Howard Johnson. It's very nice." She sounded happy to do it.

"That would be great. Thank you."

She said, "Would you like someone to meet you at the airport? We'd be happy to send a car."

"Thanks, but I think I can manage."

"Well, you have a fine flight and we'll look forward to seeing you tomorrow." I could feel her smiling across the phone, happy to be of service, happy to help, and happy to speak with me. Maybe Louisiana was the Land of Happy People.

I said, "Darlene?"

"Yes, Mr. Cole?"

"Is this what they mean by southern hospitality?"

"Why, we're just happy to help."

I said, "Darlene, you sound the way magnolias smell."

She laughed. "Oh, Mr. Cole. Aren't you the one."

Some people just naturally make you smile.

I dialed Joe Pike's condo and got his answering machine. It answered on the first ring and Joe's voice said, "Speak." You see what I mean about the conversation?

I told him who we were working for and where I would be, and I left both Sid Markowitz's and Lucille Chenier's office numbers. Then I hung up and went out onto the little balcony I have and leaned across to look into the office next door. A woman named Cindy runs a beauty distribution outlet there, and we often meet on the balcony to talk. I wanted to tell her that I would be gone for a few days, but her office was dark. Nobody home. I went back inside and phoned my friend Patricia Kyle who works on the Paramount lot, but she was in a casting meeting and couldn't be disturbed. Great. Next I called this cop I know named Lou Poitras who works detectives out of the North Hollywood division, but he wasn't in, either. I put down the phone, leaned back in my chair, and looked around the office. The only thing moving besides me was this Pinocchio clock I've got. It has eyes that tock side-to-side and it's nice to look at because it's always smiling, but, like Pike, it isn't much when you're trying to work up a two-way conversation. I have figurines of Jiminy Cricket and Mickey Mouse, but they aren't much in the conversing department, either. My office was neat, clean, and in order. All bills were paid and all mail was answered. There didn't seem to be a whole lot of preparation necessary for my departure, and I found that depressing. Some big-time private detective. Can't even scare up a friend.

I shut the lights, locked the door, and stopped at a liquor store on the way home. I bought a six-pack of Falstaff beer from a bald man with a bad eye and I told him that I was going to Louisiana. On business. He told me to have a nice time and to stop in again when I got back. I said that I would, and I told him to have a nice night. He gave me a little wave. You take your friendship where you find it.

At 1:40 the next afternoon I was descending into the Baton Rouge metropolitan area over land that was green and flat and cut by chocolate waterways. The pilot turned over the muddy wide ribbon of the Mississippi River, and, as we flew over it, the bridges and the towboats and the barges and the levee were alive with commerce and industry. I had visited Baton Rouge many years before, and I remembered clear skies and the scent of magnolias and a feeling of admiration for the river, and for its endurance through history. Now, a haze hung low over the city, not unlike Los Angeles. I guess commerce and industry have their drawbacks.

We landed and taxied in, and when they opened the airplane the heat and humidity rolled across me like warm honey. It was a feeling not unlike what I had felt when I stepped out of the troop transport at Bien Hoa Air Base in 1971 in the Republic of South Vietnam, as if the air was some sort of extension of the warm soupy water in the paddies and the swamps, as if the air wasn't really air, but was more like thin water. You didn't walk through the air down here, you waded. Welcome to Atlantis.

I sloshed down to the baggage claim, collected my bag, then

presented myself to a smiling young woman at the Hertz desk. I said, "Pretty hot today, huh?"

She said, "Oh, this isn't hot."

I guess it was my imagination.

I gave her my credit card and driver's license, asked directions to the downtown area, and pretty soon I was driving past petrochemical tank farms and flat green fields and white cement block structures with signs that said things like FREE DIRT and TORO LAWNMOWERS. The undeveloped land gave way to working-class neighborhoods and grocery markets and, in the distance, the spidery structures and exhaust towers of the refineries and chemical plants that lined the river. The chemical plants reminded me of steel towns in the Northeast where everything was built low to the ground and men and women worked hard for a living and the air smelled strange and sulfurous. Most of the men in these neighborhoods would work at the refineries, and they would work in shifts around the clock. The traffic in the surrounding areas would ebb and flow with great whistles announcing the shift changes three times a day, at seven and three and eleven, sounding like a great sluggish pulse, with each beat pumping a tired shift of workers out and sucking a fresh shift of workers in, never stopping and never changing, in its own way like the river, giving life to the community.

The working-class neighborhoods and the refineries gave way to the state's capitol building, and then I was in the heart of downtown Baton Rouge. The downtown area was a mix of new buildings and old, built on a little knoll overlooking the river and the Huey Long Bridge. The river ran below the town, as much as within it, walled off from the city by a great earth levee that probably looks today much as it did over a hundred years ago when Yankee gunboats came down from the north. Even with the commerce and the industry and a quarter million people, there was a small-town southern feel to the place. Monstrous oak trees laden with Spanish moss grew on wide green lawns, standing sentry before a governor's mansion sporting Greek Revival pillars. It made me think of *Gone With the Wind*, even though that was Georgia and this wasn't, and I sort of expected to see stately gentlemen in coarse gray uniforms and women in hoop gowns hoisting the Stars 'n Bars. *I wish I was in the land of cotton . . .*

At six minutes before three, I walked into an older building in the heart of the riverfront area and rode a mahogany-paneled elevator to the third floor and the offices of Sonnier, Melancon, & Burke, Attorneys at Law. An African-American woman with gray hair watched me approach and said, "May I help you?"

"Elvis Cole for Lucille Chenier. I have a three o'clock appointment."

She smiled nicely. "Oh, yes, Mr. Cole. I'm Darlene. Ms. Chenier's expecting you."

Darlene led me back along a corridor that was solid and enduring, with heavily lacquered pecan walls and art deco sconces and framed prints of plantations and cotton fields and portly gentlemen of an age such that they might have shared cigars with old Jeff Davis. . . . *Old times there are not forgotten.* . . . The whole effect was unapologetically Old South, and I wondered what Darlene felt when she walked past the slave scenes. Maybe she hated it, but then again, maybe in a way I might never understand, she was proud the way any person might be proud of obstacles overcome and disadvantages defeated, and of the ties with a land and a people that adversity builds in you. On the other hand, maybe not. Like friendship, you take your paycheck where you find it.

She said, "Here we are," and then she showed me into Lucille Chenier's office.

Lucille Chenier smiled as we entered, and said, "Hello, Mr. Cole. I'm Lucy Chenier."

Lucy Chenier was five-five, with amber green eyes and auburn hair that seemed alive with sun streaks and a wonderful tan that went well with the highlights. She seemed to radiate good health, as if she spent a lot of time outdoors, and it was a look that drew your eye and held it. She was wearing a lightweight tweed business suit and a thin gold ring on the pinkie of her right hand. No wedding band. She came around her desk and offered her hand. I said, "Tennis."

"Pardon me?"

"Your grip. I'll bet you play tennis."

She smiled again, and now there were laugh lines bracketing her mouth and soft wrinkles at the corners of her eyes. Pretty. "Not as often as I'd like. I had a tennis scholarship at LSU."

Darlene said, "Would you like coffee, Mr. Cole?"

"No, thank you."

"Ms. Chenier?"

"I'm fine, Darlene. Thanks."

Darlene left, and Lucy Chenier offered me a seat. Her office was furnished very much like the reception area and the halls, only the couch and the chairs were covered with a bright flower-print fabric and there were Claude Monet prints on the walls instead of the plantation scenes. A blond wood desk was end on to a couple of double windows, and an iron baker's rack sat in the corner, filled with cascading plants. A large ceramic mug that said LSU sat among the plants. The Fighting Tigers. She said, "Did you have a nice flight?"

"Yes, I did. Thank you."

"Is this your first time to Louisiana?" There was a southern accent, but it was slight, as if she had spent time away from the South, and had only recently returned.

"I've visited twice before, once on business and once when I was in the army. Neither was a fulfilling visit, and both visits were hot."

She smiled. "Well, there's nothing I can do about the heat, but perhaps this time will be more rewarding."

"Perhaps." She went to the blond desk and fingered through a stack of folders, moving with the easy confidence of someone who trusted her body. It was fun watching her.

She said, "Sid Markowitz phoned yesterday, and I spoke with Jodi Taylor this morning. I'll bring you up to date on what we've done, and we can coordinate how you'll proceed."

"All right."

She took a manila folder from the desk, then returned to sit in a wing chair. I continued to watch her, and continued to have a fine time doing it. I made her for thirty-five, but she might have been younger. "Yes?"

"Sorry." Elvis Cole, the Embarrassed Detective, is caught staring at the Attorney. Really impress her with the old professionalism.

She adjusted herself in the chair and put on a pair of the serious, red-framed reading glasses that professional women seem to prefer. "Have you worked many adoption cases, Mr. Cole?"

"A few. Most of my experience is in missing persons work."

She said, "An adoption recovery isn't the same as a missing persons search. There are great similarities in the steps necessary to locate the birth parents, of course, but the actual contact is a far more delicate matter."

"Of course." She crossed her legs. I tried not to stare. "Delicate."

"Are you familiar with Louisiana's adoption laws?"

"No."

She slipped off her right shoe and pulled her foot up beneath her in the chair. "Jodi Taylor was relinquished to the state for adoption on an unknown date thirty-six years ago. Under the laws of the state at that time, all details of that surrender and all information pertaining to Jodi's biological parents were sealed. When Mr. and Mrs. Taylor adopted her, their names were entered as parents of record, and Jodi's birth name, whatever that might have been, was changed to Judith Marie Taylor. All records of that name change were also sealed by the state."

"Okay." Maybe I should take notes. If I took notes, she might think me professional.

"Louisiana maintains what we call a voluntary registry of birth parents and adopted children. If birth parents or adopted children wish to contact each other, they register with the state. If both the parent and the child are registered, then, by mutual consent, the records are unsealed and an intermediary working for the state arranges a meeting between the two."

"Did Jodi enter the registry?"

"Yes. That was the first thing we did. Neither of her birth parents are registered. I filed a request for special leave with the state to open the records, but we were turned down."

"So, legally speaking, that was the end of the road and now it's up to me."

"That's right. You'll conduct the actual investigation to try to identify Jodi's birth parents or locate a bio-family member who can supply the information she seeks, but you won't make contact with them. If contact has to be made, that will be my job. Do you understand?"

"Sure." Strong back, weak mind.

She took a folder from the larger file and passed it to me. "These are local maps with directions to Ville Platte, as well as some tourist information. I'm afraid there isn't much. It's a small town in a rural area."

"How far away?" I opened the folder and glanced at it. There was a Triple-A map of the state, a Chamber of Commerce map of Ville Platte, and a typed sheet listing recommended restaurants and motels. Everything the visiting private eye needs in order to swing into action.

"A little over an hour." She closed the larger file and placed it in her lap. "Our firm is very well established, so if there's any way that we can help with research or access to state agencies, don't hesitate to call."

"I won't."

"May I ask how you'll proceed?"

"The only way to ask about a child who was given up for adoption is to ask about a child who was given up for adoption. I'll have to identify people with a possible knowledge of the event, and then I'll have to question them."

She shifted in the chair, not liking it. "What do you mean, question them?"

I smiled at her. "Questions. You know. 'Where were you on the night of the fourth?' Like that."

She nodded twice, then frowned. "Mr. Cole, let's be sure that you appreciate the complexities involved. Typically, the birth parents of a child given for adoption in the nineteen-fifties were young and unmarried, and great pains were taken to keep that birth secret. It's just as typical that, years later, those birth parents are leading lives in which their current friends and families know nothing of that earlier pregnancy and the fact that a child was born. Nothing must be said or done that could possibly give away their secret. It's as much your job to protect the birth parents' confidences as it is to uncover Jodi Taylor's medical history. Jodi wants it that way, and so do I."

I gave her my most winning smile. "I just look stupid, Ms. Chenier. I can actually spell the word 'discretion.' "

She stared at me for a surprised moment, and a trace of color crept onto her cheeks and neck. She was wearing a necklace of large silver shells and they stood out against her skin. "That did sound like a lecture, didn't it?"

I nodded.

"I'm sorry. You don't look stupid at all. Perhaps I should tell you that these issues are important to me. I'm an adopted child myself. That's why I practice this kind of law."

"No apologies are necessary. You just want to make sure I respect everyone's privacy."

She was nodding. "That's right."

I nodded back at her. "I guess that rules out the ad."

She cocked her head.

"Famous actress seeks birth mother! Huge reward."

The laugh lines reappeared at the corners of her mouth and the flush went away. "Perhaps we'd be better served with a more conservative approach."

"I could tell people that I'm investigating an alien visitation. Do you think that would work?"

"Perhaps in Arkansas." Regional humor.

We grinned at each other for a moment, then I said, "Would you join me for dinner?"

Lucy Chenier smiled wider, then stood and went to the door. "It's very nice of you to ask, but I have other plans."

"How about if I sing 'Dixie'? Will that soften you up?"

She opened the door and held it for me. She tried not to smile, but some of it got through. "There are several fine Cajun restaurants listed in the folder. I think you'll like the food."

I stood in the door. "I'm sure I'll be fine. Maybe Paul Prudhomme will see me for dinner."

"Not even if you sing 'Dixie.' Paul Prudhomme lives in New Orleans."

"That makes two fantasies you've destroyed."

"I don't think I'll ask."

"Good night, Ms. Chenier."

"Good night, Mr. Cole."

I walked out singing "The Battle Hymn of the Republic," and I could hear Lucy Chenier laughing even as I rode down in the elevator.

3

I had a fine catfish dinner at a restaurant recommended by Lucy Chenier's office, and then I checked into a Ho-Jo built into the base of the levee. I asked them for a room with a view of the river and they were happy to oblige. Southern hospitality.

I ordered two bottles of Dixie beer from room service and sat drinking the beer and watching the towboats push great strings of barges upstream against the current. I thought that if I watched the river long enough I might see Tom and Huck and Jim working their raft down the shore. Of course, river traffic was different in the 1800s. In the old days, there were just the paddle wheelers and mule-drawn barges. Now, Huck and Jim would have to maneuver between oil tankers and Japanese container ships and an endless gauntlet of chemical waste vents. Still, I trusted that Huck and Jim were up to the job.

The next morning I checked out of the hotel, drove across the river, then turned north and followed the state highway across a wide flat plain covered with cotton and sugarcane and towns with names like Livonia and Krotz Springs. Cotton gins and sugar-processing plants sprouted on the horizon, the sugar plants belching thin smoke plumes that gave the air a bitter smell. I turned on the radio and let the scanner seek stations. Two country outlets, a station where a man with a high-pitched voice was speaking French, and five religious stations, one of which boasted a woman proclaiming that all God's children were born evil, lived evil, and would die evil. She shrieked that evil must be fought with evil, and that the forces of evil were at her door this very moment, trying to silence the right-thinking Christian truths of her broadcasts and that the only way she might stave them off was with the Demon Dollar Bill, twenty-dollar minimum donation please, MasterCard or Visa accepted. Sorry, no American Express. I guess some evils are better than others.

I left the highway at Opelousas, then went north on a tiny two-lane state road following what the map said was Bayou Mamou. It was a muddy brown color and looked more like standing water than something that actually flowed. Cattails and cypress trees lined the far bank, and the near bank was mostly wild grass and crushed oyster shells. A couple in their early twenties poled a flat-bottomed boat along the cypress knees. The man stood in the stern, wearing an LSU T-shirt and baggy jeans and a greasy camouflage ball cap with a creased bill. He pushed the little boat with steady, molasses-slow strokes. The woman wore a pale sundress and a wide straw hat and heavy work gloves and, as the young man poled, she lifted a trotline from the water to see if they had caught fish. The young man was smiling. I wondered if John Fogerty had been thinking of Bayou Mamou when he wrote "Born on the Bayou."

I passed a wooden billboard that said THE KNIGHTS OF CO-LUMBUS WELCOME YOU TO VILLE PLATTE, LA. "HOME OF THE COTTON FESTIVAL," and then the highway wasn't the highway any more. It was Main Street. I passed gas stations and an enormous Catholic church, but pretty soon there were banks and clothing and hardware stores and a pharmacy and a couple of restaurants and a record store and all the places of a small southern town. A lot of the stores had posters for something called the Cotton Festival. I turned off the air conditioner and rolled down the window and began to sweat. Hot, all right. Several people were standing around outside a little food place called the Pig Stand, and a couple of them were eating what looked like barbecued beef ribs. A million degrees outside, and these guys were slurping down ribs in the middle of the day. Across from the Pig Stand there was a little mom-and-pop grocery with a hand-painted sign that said WE SELL BOUDIN and a smaller sign that said FRESH CRACKLINS. Underneath that someone had written *no cholesterol— ha-ha*. These Cajuns are a riot, aren't they?

I drove slowly and, as I drove, I wondered if any of the people I passed were in some way related to Jodi Taylor. I would look at them and smile and they would smile back, and, with a curious feeling, I searched for Jodi Taylor's reflection. Were those the eyes? Is that the nose? If Jodi Taylor were beside me, and were not familiar from being on television, would one of these people catch a passing glance of her and call her by another name? I realized then that Jodi Taylor must sometimes wonder these same things.

If I was going to find Jodi Taylor's birth family, I would have to interview people, but the question was who? I could check with local medical personnel, but any physician who was a party to the adoption would be legally bound to remain silent. Ditto clergy and members of the local legal community. Also, they would ask questions that I didn't want to answer and would probably notify the cops, who would come around to ask similar questions. Small-town cops are notoriously territorial. Therefore, ix-nay the more obvious sources of information. Perhaps I could forgo interviews altogether and use the concept of familial resemblance to find said birth parents. I could post pictures of Jodi Taylor all over town. *Do you know this woman?* Of course, since she was famous, everybody would know her, but maybe there was a way around that. I could have Jodi wear a Groucho Marx nose when I took the picture. That should fool 'em. Of course, then everybody might think she was Groucho Marx. Ix-nay the nose.

Thirty-six years ago a child had been born and its care relinquished to the state. That would not be a common occurrence in a town of Ville Platte's size. People would talk and, quite possibly, people would remember, even thirty-six years later. Gossip is a detective's best friend. I could randomly question anyone over the age of fifty, but that seemed sort of unprofessional. A professional would narrow the field. All right. Who talks about having babies? Answer: mommies. Task at hand: locate women who delivered on or about 9 July, thirty-six years ago. The detective flies into action and it is awesome to behold. A mind like a computer, this guy. A regular Sherlock Holmes, this guy.

I drove back to the little grocery with the "boudin" sign, parked at the curb, and went in. A kid in a gray USL Ragin' Cajuns T-shirt was sitting behind the register, smoking a Marlboro and reading a drag boat magazine. He didn't look up when I walked in. In Los Angeles, you walk into a convenience store and the people who work there reach for their guns.

I said, "Howdy. Is there a local paper?"

He waved the cigarette at a newspaper rack they had off to the side, and I picked up a copy and read the masthead. *The Ville Platte Gazette—established 1908*. Perfect. *Daily*. Even better.

I said, "Do you have a library in town?"

He sucked on the Marlboro and squinted at me. He was pale, with wispy blond hair and caterpillar fuzz above his lip and a couple of primo zits ripening on his forehead. Eighteen, maybe, but he could've been older.

I said, "You got a library?"

" 'Course. Where you think you are, Arkansas?" They're really into that Arkansas thing down here.

"Any chance you'd tell me how to get there?"

He leaned back on his stool and crossed his arms. "*Which* library?" Score one for the yokel.

Six minutes later I circled the town square past a red brick Presbyterian church and parked at the library. An older African-American gentleman was behind the counter, stacking books onto a gray metal cart. A young woman with braided hair sat at a reading table and a kid with a limp shuffled through the stacks, listing to the right so he could read the book spines. I went to the counter and smiled at the librarian. "That air conditioning feels good."

The librarian continued stacking the books. "That it does. And how are you today, sir?" He was shorter than me and thin, with a balding head and a prominent Adam's apple and very dark skin. He was wearing a plaid short-sleeved shirt and a burgundy knit tie. A little nameplate on the counter said MR. ALBERT PARKS.

I said, "Do you have the *Gazette* on microfiche?" I could have gone by the newspaper offices, but newspaper people would ask questions.

"Yes, sir. We do." He stopped stacking books and came over to the counter.

I told him the year I wanted, and asked if he had it.

Mr. Parks grinned broadly, pleased to be able to help. "I think we might. Let me run in the back and see."

He disappeared between the stacks and returned with a cardboard box and had me follow to an ancient microfiche unit on the other side of the card catalogs. He pulled out one of the spools and threaded it into the machine. "There are twenty-four spools in this box, two spools for each month of the year. I put in January. Do you know how to work the machine?"

"Sure."

"If the film gets stuck, please don't force the little crank. These kids from the school use this thing and always tear the film."

"I'll be careful."

Mr. Parks frowned down into the little box and fingered through the spools.

I said, "What's wrong?"

"Looks like we have a month missing." He frowned harder, then arched his eyebrows and looked up at me. "May's gone. Did you need May?"

"I don't think so."

"Maybe I put it in a different year."

"I don't think I'll need it."

He nodded thoughtfully, told me to call him if I needed any help with the little crank, then went back to his book cart. When he was gone I took the January spool out of the microfiche and dug around in the box until I found the two July spools. I threaded in the first and skimmed through until I reached the *Gazette* dated 9 July. The ninth was a Tuesday and had no birth announcements. I searched through the tenth, eleventh, and twelfth, which was the following Friday. Friday's paper had three birth announcements, two boys and twin girls. The boys were born to Charles & Louise Fontenot and William & Edna Lemoine, the twin girls to Murray & Charla Smith. As I was writing their names on a yellow legal pad, Mr. Parks strolled by. "Are you finding everything you need?"

"Yes," I said. "Thank you."

He nodded and strolled away.

I cranked the little spool back to the beginning of July and copied the birth announcements published at the end of every week, and then I did the same for June and August. When I was working through August, Mr. Parks pushed the book cart next to me and made a big deal out of straightening shelves and trying to pretend that he wasn't interested in what I was doing. I glanced up and caught him peeking over my shoulder. "Yes?"

Mr. Parks said, "Heh heh," then pushed the cart away. Embarrassed. They get bored in these small towns.

When I finished with August I had eighteen names. I put the little spools back into their box, turned off the microfiche, and returned the box to Mr. Parks. He said, "That didn't take very long."

"Efficiency. Efficiency and focus are the keys to success."

"I hear that."

I said, "Is there a phone book?"

"On the reference table next to the card catalog."

I went over to the reference table and looked in the phone book for the names I had copied. I was on the fourth name when Mr. Parks said, "Seems to me you appear to be looking for someone."

He was standing behind me again, peering over my shoulder.

I put my hand over the names. "It's rather personal."

He frowned. "Personal?"

"Private."

He peered at my hand as if he were trying to see through it. "You're not from around here, are you?"

"No," I said. "I'm from the government. Central Intelligence."

He looked offended. "No reason to be rude."

I spread my free hand.

He said, "You were copying birth announcements. Now you're looking for those names in the phone book. I think you're trying to find someone. I think you're a private detective." Great. The big-time Hollywood op gets made by the small-town librarian. He started away. "Perhaps we should call the police."

I caught his arm and made a big deal out of looking around. Making sure that the coast was clear. "Thirty-six years ago, the person I'm working for was born in this area and given up for adoption. She has now contracted leukemia and requires a bone marrow transplant. Do you know what that means?"

He answered slowly. "They need a blood relative for those transplants, don't they?"

I nodded. You toss it on the water and sometimes they take it, but sometimes they don't. He was a knowledgeable man. He'd know more than a little about marrow transplants. He could ask to speak with my client or my client's physician, and, if I were legitimate, they'd be more than happy to speak with him. He could ask me if the leukemia was acute or chronic, or he could ask me which type of white blood cells were affected. There were a hundred things he could ask me, and some of them I could scam but most of them could blow me out of the water.

25

He looked at my hand over the list of names, then he looked back at me and I saw his jaw work. He said, "I saw some of your names there. I know some of those folks. This lady, the one you're working for, she gonna die?"

"Yes."

He wet his lips, then pulled over a chair and sat down beside me. "I think I can save you some time."

Of the eighteen names on my list, Mr. Albert Parks knew four, and we found another three listed in the phone book. The rest had either died or moved away.

I copied addresses and phone numbers for the seven still in the area, and Mr. Parks gave me directions on how to find those people who lived in the outlying areas. He offered to phone the four that he knew to tell them that I'd be stopping around, and I said that that would be fine, but that he should ask them to respect my client's privacy. He said that he was certain that they would. He said that he hoped that I could find a donor for my client, and asked me to give her his very best wishes for a complete recovery. His wishes were heartfelt.

Mr. Albert Parks worked with me for the better part of an hour, and then I walked out of the cool quiet of his library into the damp midday Louisiana heat feeling about three inches tall.

Lying sucks.

4

Of the seven names on the list, four lived in town and three lived in the outlying area. I decided to speak with the townies first, then work my way out. Mr. Parks had recommended that I start with Mrs. Claire Fontenot who, as the widowed owner of a little five and dime just across the square, was the closest. He said that she was one of God's Finest Women. I took that to mean that she was kind and caring and probably easy to manipulate. Sort of like Mr. Albert Parks. As I walked over I thought that maybe I should just cut out this manipulation business and proclaim for all the world who I worked for and what I was after. If I did, I would probably feel much better about myself. Of course, Jodi Taylor probably wouldn't, but there you go. Her privacy would be violated and her confidence breached, but what's that when compared to feeling good about oneself? Elvis Cole, detective for the nineties, comforts his inner child.

Going into Fontenot's Five & Dime was like stepping backward in time. Cardboard cut-out ads for things like Carter's Little Liver Pills and Brylcreem—a little dab'll do ya!—and Dr. Tichnor's Antiseptic were taped and retaped to the door and the windows, filling the same spaces that they had filled when they were first put up forty years ago. Some of the cutouts were so faded that they were impossible to read.

An overweight girl in her late teens sat on a stool behind the counter reading a copy of *Allure*. She looked up when I entered.

"Hi. Is Mrs. Fontenot in?"

The girl called out, "Miss Claire," and a stately woman in her early sixties appeared in the aisle, holding a box of Hallmark cards. I said, "Mrs. Fontenot, my name is Elvis Cole. I believe Mr. Parks over at the library might've phoned."

She looked me up and down as if she viewed me with caution. "That's right."

"May I have a few minutes?"

She viewed me some more, and then she put down the box of cards and led me to the rear of the store. She seemed rigid when she moved, as if her body were clenched. "Mr. Parks told me that you want to know something about a baby that was given up for adoption." She arched an eyebrow when she said it, clearly suspicious of the practice and disapproving.

"That's right. Somewhere around the time that Max was born." She had delivered a son, Max Andrew, sixteen days before Jodi Taylor's birth.

"I'm afraid I don't know anything about that. I kept all my children, believe you me." Daring me to deny it. When she spoke, she kept both hands folded together between her breasts, as if she were praying. Maybe you did that when you were one of God's finest.

"Not one of your children, Mrs. Fontenot. Another woman's child. Maybe you knew her, or maybe you just heard gossip."

The eyebrow arched again. "I don't gossip."

I said, "Ville Platte is a small town. Unwed pregnancies happen, but they would be rare, and babies given for adoption would be still more rare. Maybe one of your girlfriends at the time mentioned it. Maybe one of your aunts. Something like that."

"Absolutely not. In my day, that type of thing wasn't tolerated the way it is now, and we would never have discussed it." She clutched her hands tighter and raised both eyebrows, giving me All-knowing. "Now, people don't care about this kind of thing. People do whatever they want. That's why we're in this fix."

I said, "Onward Christian soldiers."

She frowned at me. "What?"

I thanked her for her time and left. One up, one down. Six more to go.

Evelyn Maggio lived alone on the second floor of a duplex that she maintained six blocks south of the five and dime. Her duplex was a big white clapboard monster set high on brick piers in case of flood. Evelyn Maggio herself was a vital woman in her late fifties, twice married and twice divorced, with tiny teeth and too much makeup. She showed me the teeth when she let me in and latched onto my arm and said, "My, but you're a good-lookin' fella." Her words were long and drawn out, sort of like Elly May Clampett. She smelled of bourbon.

I was with her for almost forty minutes and in that time she called me "sugar" eleven times and drank three cups of coffee. She drank it *royale*. She put out a little tray of Nabisco Sugar Wafers and told me that the very best way to eat them was to dip them in the coffee, but to watch because they could get too soggy and would fall apart. She put her hand on my arm and said, "No one likes a limp sugar wafer, honey, especially not lil' ol' me." She seemed disappointed that it wasn't what I wanted to hear, and, when it became clear that she knew nothing about a child being given to the state, she seemed even more disappointed when I left. I took two of the sugar wafers with me. I was disappointed, too.

I spent the next twenty-two minutes with Mrs. C. Thomas Berteaux. She was seventy-two years old, rail thin, and insisted upon calling me Jeffrey. She was quite certain that I had visited her home before, and when I told her that this was my first time in Ville Platte, she asked if I was sure. I said I was. She said she was certain that I had asked her about this adoption business before. I asked if she remembered her answer, and she said, "Why, of course, Jeffrey, don't you? I didn't remember anything then, and I don't now." She smiled pleasantly when she said it and I smiled pleasantly in return. I used her phone to call Mrs. Francine Lyons, who said she'd be happy to see me, but that she was on her way out and could I call later. I said that I could, but then she volunteered that Mr. Parks had mentioned something about a child given for adoption and that she just didn't know anything about that, though, as she'd said, she'd be happy to see me later in the day. I told her that that wouldn't be necessary and scratched her off my list. You either remember or you don't. Mrs. C. Thomas Berteaux, watching from her chair, said, "What's the matter, Jeffrey? You look disappointed."

I said, "Some days are more difficult than others, Mrs. Berteaux."

She nodded sagely. "Yes, Jeffrey. I know that to be true. However, I might suggest that you speak with Mrs. Martha Guidry."

"Yes?" Martha Guidry wasn't on my list.

"Martha was a midwife at that time and, if I remember correctly, quite a well-known busybody. Martha may know." Then she looked thoughtful. "Of course, Martha may be dead."

I let myself out.

Four up, four down, and nary a shred of evidence to show for it. I had three more women to see, and, if the results were the same, it was back to the drawing board. Not good. The key to all this seemed to be the sealed state documents. Maybe I should stop trying to investigate my way to Jodi Taylor's medical history and concentrate on unsealing those documents. I could shoulder my way into the appropriate state agency, pistol whip a couple of civil servants, and force them to hand over the documents. Of course, this method might get me shot or imprisoned, but wasn't that better than questioning women who called me Jeffrey? Of course, thirty-six-year-old documents would probably be buried under thirty-six years of more recent documents in an obscure state building long forgotten by any living person. You'd need Indiana Jones just to find the place.

I decided to think about it over lunch.

The Pig Stand was a white cinder block building with hand-written signs telling you what they offered and a couple of windows to order the food. The people on the sidewalk were mostly thin guys with crepey skin and women with pale skin and loose upper arms from eating too much deep-fried food. Everybody was drinking Dixie beer and eating off paper plates and laughing a lot. Guess if you stand around eating barbecued ribs in this kind of heat you had to have a sense of humor.

An enormously wide black woman with brilliant white teeth looked out of the order window at me and said, "Take ya awdah, please?"

I said, "Do you have *boudin?*" I had wanted to try *boudin* for years.

She grinned. "Honey, we gots the best *boudin* in Evangeline Parish."

"That's not what they say in Mamou."

She laughed. "Those fools in Mamou don' know nuthin' 'bout no *boudin*! Honey, you try some'a this, you won't be goin' back to no Mamou! This magic *boudin*! It be good for what ails you!"

"Okay. How about a couple of links of *boudin,* a beef rib with a little extra sauce, some dirty rice, and a Dixie."

She nodded, pleased. "That'll fix you up jes' fine."

"What makes you think I need fixing?"

She leaned toward me and touched a couple of fingers beneath her eye. "Dottie got the magic eye. Dottie *know*." Her eyes were smiling when she shouted the order into the kitchen, and I smiled with her. It wasn't just the food around here that gave comfort.

Passing cars would beep their horns and diners would wave at the cars and the people in the cars would wave back, sort of like everybody knew everybody else. While I was waiting, a sparkling new white Mustang rag-top cruised past, top up, giving every-body the once-over and revving his engine. The Mustang circled the block, and when he came back around an older guy with a thick French accent yelled something I couldn't understand and the Mustang speeded up. Guess the older guy didn't like all the engine-revving.

A couple of minutes later, Dottie called me back to the window and handed out my order on a coarse paper plate with enough napkins to insulate a house. I carried the food to the street, sat the Dixie on the curb, then went to work on the food. The *boudin* were plump and juicy, and when you bit into them they were filled with rice and pork and cayenne and onions and celery. Even in the heat, steam came from the sausage and it burned the inside of my mouth. I had some of the dirty rice, and then some of the beef rib. The dirty rice was heavy and glutinous and rich with chicken liv-ers. The rib was tender and the sauce chunky with onion and gar-lic. The tastes were strong and salty and wonderful, and pretty soon I was feeling eager to dive back into the case. Even if it meant being called Jeffrey.

The black woman looked out of her little window and asked, "Whatchu say 'bout dat *boudin* now?"

I said, "Tell me the truth, Dottie. This isn't really Ville Platte, is it? We're all dead and this is Heaven."

She grinned wider and nodded, satisfied. "Dottie say it'll fix you up. Dottie know." She touched her cheek beneath her left eye and then she laughed and turned away.

At ten minutes after two, I used a pay phone at an Exxon sta-tion to call the last two women on my list. Virginia LaMert wasn't home, and Charleen Jorgenson said that she'd be happy to see me.

Charleen Jorgenson and her second husband, Lloyd, lived in a double trailer two miles outside of Ville Platte on Bayou des Cannes. The double trailer sat upon cement block piers and looked sort of ratty and overgrown. A small flat-bottomed boat rested on a couple of saw horses in the back yard, and a blue tick hound slept in a tight knot in the shade thrown by the boat. They had a little drive made out of the crushed oyster shells, and when I pulled up, the oyster shells made a loud crunching sound and the blue tick hound charged at my car, barking and standing on its back legs to try to bite through the window. An old guy in his seventies came out on the step yelling, "Heah naow! Heah naow!" and threw a pop bottle at the dog. That would be Lloyd. The bottle missed the dog and hit the Taurus's left front fender. Lloyd said, "Uh-oh," and looked chagrined. Good thing it was a rental.

Charleen Jorgenson told me that she wished she could help, but she just didn't remember anything like I was asking.

I said, "Think hard, Mrs. Jorgenson. Are you sure?"

She sipped her coffee and nodded. "Oh, yes. I thought about it when that other fellow was here."

"What other fellow?"

"Another young man was here a few months ago. He said he was trying to find his sister."

I said, "Do tell."

"He wasn't very nice and he didn't stay long."

"Were you able to help him find his sister?"

"I would've been happy to, but I just couldn't help him. He became very abusive. Lloyd like to threw a fit." She nodded her head toward Lloyd, as if one of Lloyd's fits was quite a spectacle. Lloyd, sitting in a heavy chair that had been covered with a bedspread, had fallen asleep as we talked. She said, "You're trying to find some kind of organ donor, aren't you?"

"Yes, ma'am. A marrow donor."

She shook her head. "That is so sad."

"Mrs. Jorgenson, this guy who was here, was his name Jeffrey?"

She had more of the coffee, thinking. "Well, maybe. He had red hair, all piled up on his head and oily." She made a sour face. "I remember that."

"Ah."

"I've never been comfortable with a red-haired person."

33

People say the damnedest things, don't they?

I left Charleen Jorgenson's home at twenty-five minutes after four that afternoon and stopped at a bait and tackle shop on the road leading back to town. They had a pay phone on the wall under a huge sign that said LIVE WORMS. I tried calling Mrs. C. Thomas Berteaux to ask if Jeffrey's hair had been red, but I got no answer. Probably out. I tried Virginia LaMert again, but also got no answer. Virginia LaMert was the last name on my list, and if she didn't come through it was drawing-board time. I called Information and asked them if they had a listing for Martha Guidry. They did. I dialed Martha Guidry's number and, as I listened to her phone ring, the same white Mustang I'd seen at the Pig Stand turned into the parking lot and disappeared behind the bait shop.

Martha Guidry answered on the sixth ring. "Hello?"

I identified myself and told her that Mrs. C. Thomas Berteaux had suggested I call. I said that I was trying to find someone who was born in the area thirty-six years ago, and I asked if I might pay a visit. She said that would be fine. She told me her address and gave me directions and said that, as old as she was, if I didn't hurry she might be dead before I arrived. I was going to like Martha Guidry just fine.

I hung up and stood at the phone, waiting. A blue Ford pickup pulled in and a young guy with a scraggly beard went into the bait shop. An older man came out of the shop with a brown bag and got into a Chevy Caprice. The young guy came out with a Budweiser Tall Boy and hopped back into his truck. The Mustang didn't return.

I climbed back into my car and followed the directions toward Martha Guidry's house. Maybe this business with the Mustang was my imagination, like the heat.

I had gone maybe three-quarters of a mile when the Mustang swung around a Kleinpeter Dairy milk truck and eased in behind me. He came up so close that I could see the driver in my rearview mirror. He had a scoop-cut pompadour maybe six inches high and long nasty sideburns carved down into points so sharp you could cut yourself.

And he had red hair.

5

The guy in the Mustang wouldn't let anyone get between us, as if he wanted to follow me and thought he had to stay close to do it. He was wearing a short-sleeved shirt with the sleeves rolled, and he drove with his left hand hanging down along the door. One of those.

I turned off the state road and headed back toward town, and the Mustang turned with me. I pulled into an Exxon station and topped off my tank and asked a kid in a grease-stained uniform about the local bass fishing. The Mustang drove past while the kid was telling me, but a couple minutes later it pulled up to a stop sign a block away and sat waiting. Following me, all right.

I took it easy up through town, letting him follow, and twice managed to stop for traffic lights. Each time I stopped he eased up behind me, and each time he made a big deal out of staring off to the side. The ostrich technique. If I don't see you, you can't see me. I had to smile at this guy. He was something. At a four-way stop a kid in a red Isuzu pickup tried to turn in behind me, and the guy in the Mustang jumped the stop sign and blew his horn, cutting him off. Maybe he thought I wouldn't notice.

A set of railroad tracks ran through the center of town. The tracks were prominent and the road was old, so everybody was slowing to ease their cars across the tracks. On the other side of the tracks there were several businesses and a couple of cross streets and, still further down, a little bridge where the road crossed the bayou. Cars were waiting at most of the cross streets, people getting off work.

I eased the Taurus across the tracks, then punched it, putting enough distance between me and the Mustang for a woman in a light blue Acura to get between us. The Mustang came up to her fast, swerving into the oncoming lane, but there was too much traffic for him to pass. I swung to the right onto the shoulder, floored it past six or seven cars, then jerked it back into the traffic lane and then right again around a bread truck and into a Dairy Queen parking lot. He wouldn't have been able to see me turn past the bread truck. I pushed it around the back of the Dairy Queen, threw it into park, then jumped out and ran up the side past a couple of kids sucking malts in a '69 VW Bug. The Mustang was still behind the woman in the Acura, blowing his horn and swerving from side to side, until finally she couldn't take it anymore and pulled to the side. He horsed it past her, giving the finger and screaming that she should get her head out her butt, and then he blasted away up the shoulder, spraying gravel and dust and little bits of oyster shell. I wrote down his license number, went back to my car, and turned again toward Martha Guidry's. I checked the rearview mirror from time to time, but the Mustang didn't reappear. You had to shake your head.

I drove up the center of Evangeline Parish through dense stands of hardwood trees and sweet potato fields, passing small frame houses set near the road, many with rusted cars and large propane gas tanks and chickens in their yards. Martha Guidry lived in such a house across the street from a strawberry stand. She was a small bony woman with skin like rumpled silk and cataract glasses that made her eyes look huge and protruding. She was wearing a thin housedress and socks and house slippers, and when she answered the door she was carrying a large, economy-sized can of Raid Ant & Roach Killer. She squinted out the thick glasses. "You that Mr. Cole?"

"Yes, ma'am. I appreciate your seeing me."

She pushed open the screen door and told me to come in quick. She said if you don't come in quick all kinds of goddamned bugs come in with you. As soon as I was in she fogged the air around the door with the Raid. "That'll get the little bastards!"

I moved across the room to get away from the cloud of Raid. "I don't think you're supposed to breathe that stuff, Ms. Guidry."

She waved her hand. "Oh, hell, I been breathin' it for years. You want a Pepsi-Cola?"

"No, ma'am. Thank you."

She waved the Raid at the couch. "You just sit right there. It won't take a moment." I guess she was going to give me the Pepsi anyway. When she was in the kitchen there was a sharp *slap* and she said, "Gotcha, you sonofabitch!" The thing about this job is that you meet such interesting people.

She came back with two plastic tumblers and a single can of Pepsi and the Raid. She put the glasses on her coffee table, then opened the Pepsi and poured most of it in one glass and a little bit in the other. She offered the full glass to me. "Now, what is it you want to know?"

I lifted the glass but noticed something crusted down in the ice. I pretended to take a sip and put it down. "Mrs. Berteaux said that you're a midwife."

She nodded, eyes scanning the upper reaches of the room for incoming bugs. "Unh-hunh. Not in years, a'course, but I was."

"Thirty-six years ago on July ninth a baby girl was born in this area and given up for adoption. Chances are that the child was illegitimate, but maybe not. Chances are that the mother was underage, but maybe not."

Her eyes narrowed behind the thick lenses. "You think I birthed the child?"

"I don't know. If not, maybe you heard something."

She looked thoughtful. "That was a long time ago."

"Yes, ma'am." I waited, letting her think. Probably hard with all the nerve damage from the Raid.

Martha Guidry scratched at her head, working on it, and then seemed to notice something in the far corner of the room. She put down her Pepsi, picked up the Raid, then crept across the room to peer into the shadows behind the television. I got ready to hold my breath. She said, "Goddamned ugly bugs," but she held her fire. False alarm. She came back to the chair and sat. "You know, I think I remember something about that."

Well.

She said, "There were some folks lived over here around the Nezpique." She was nodding as she thought about it, fingering the Raid can. "They had a little girl, I think. Yes, that's right. They gave her away."

Well, well. "You remember their names?" I was writing it down.

She pooched out her lips, then slowly shook her head, trying to put it together. "I remember it was a big family. He was a fisherman or somethin', but they might've cropped a share. They lived over on the bayou. Right over here on the Nezpique. Wasn't no bastard, though. Just a big family with too many mouths to feed."

"A name?"

She looked sad and shook her head. "I'm sorry. It's right on the tip of my tongue and I just can't remember it. You get old, everything goes to hell. *There's one!*" She raced to a potted plant beneath the window and cut loose with the Raid. Clouds of gas fogged up around her and I walked over to the door, leaned out, and took deep breaths. When she was finished with the Raid I went back to the chair. Everything smelled of kerosene and chemicals. I said, "These bugs are something, aren't they?"

She nodded smugly. "They'll run you out of house and home, let me tell you."

I heard the crunch of a car pulling off the road. Not in her yard, but further away. I went back to the door. The white Mustang was sitting across the street by the strawberry stand. I said, "Ms. Guidry, has someone else approached you about this?"

She shook her head. "Unh-unh."

"A few months ago."

She got the thoughtful look again. "You know, I think a fella did come here." She made a face like she'd bit into something sour. "I didn't like his looks. I won't deal with anybody I don't like the way they look. No, siree. You can tell by a person's looks, and I didn't like that fella, at all. I ran 'm off."

I looked back out the door. "Is that the man?"

Martha Guidry came over next to me and squinted out through the screen. "Well, my goodness. That's him. That's the little peckerwood, right over there!"

Martha Guidry charged through the screen door with her can of Raid as if she'd seen the world's largest bug. She screamed, "Here, you! What are you doin' over there?!"

I said, "Oh, God."

She lurched down the steps and ran toward the highway, and I was wondering if maybe I should tackle her before she became roadkill. Then the Mustang fishtailed out onto the highway and roared back toward Ville Platte and Martha Guidry pulled up short, shaking her fist at him. I said, "Martha, do you remember his name?"

Martha Guidry stalked back up the steps, breathing hard and blinking behind the thick glasses. I was hoping I wouldn't have to dial 911. "Jerry. Jeffrey. Somegoddamnthing like that."

"Aha."

"That rotten sneak. Why do you think he was out here?"

"I don't know," I said. "But I'm going to find out."

She took a deep breath, shook herself, then said, "God *damn,* but I feel like a drink! You're not the kind of fool to let a lady drink alone, are you?"

"No, ma'am, I'm not."

She threw open the door and gestured inside with the Raid. "Then get yer ass in there and let's booze."

At twenty minutes after six that evening I checked into a motel in Ville Platte and phoned Lucille Chenier at her office in Baton Rouge. I only had to wait eight or nine minutes for her to come on the line. She said, "Yes?"

"Guess who?" Martha had been generous with the Old Crow.

"I'm very busy, Mr. Cole. Is there some way I can help you?" Some people just weren't around when they handed out laugh buttons.

"Can your office run a license plate check for me?"

"Of course."

I gave her the Mustang's number and told her about the red-haired man. She said, "He was also asking about a child?"

"Yes."

You could hear her fingernails clicking on her desk. Thinking. "That's odd. I wonder why he would be following you?"

"When he tells me, I'll pass it along."

"It's very important that this not be associated with Jodi Taylor." She sounded concerned.

"I'm telling people that I'm searching for a marrow donor. In a case like this, you have to ask questions. People talk. This kind of thing can be exciting to folks, and they like to share their excitement."

"And people with secrets want to protect them."

"That's the point. But I've no reason to believe that anyone I've yet seen has secrets."

"Except, perhaps, for your red-haired man."

"Well, there is that. Yes."

She told me that she would have the information on the Mustang's owner by ten the next morning, and then she hung up. I stared at the phone and felt strangely incomplete now that the connection was broken, but maybe that was just all the Raid I had breathed. Sure. You spend most of the afternoon breathing Raid and drinking Old Crow, it heightens your sense of dissociation. It also puts you to sleep.

At eighteen minutes after nine the next morning, the phone rang and Lucy Chenier said, "Your Mustang is registered to someone named Jimmie Ray Rebenack." She read two addresses, both in Ville Platte.

"Okay."

"Mr. Rebenack lists his occupation as a private investigator. He was licensed two and a half years ago."

I was grinning. "If this guy's for real, he has to be the world's worst detective."

"Prior to licensing, he was employed as a full-time auto mechanic at an Exxon station in Alexandria. His tax records indicate that he continues to derive the majority of his income from part-time mechanic work."

"Wow. You guys work fast."

"The firm is well positioned. You'll keep me informed?"

"Of course, Ms. Chenier." Elvis Cole, Professional Detective, discourses in a professional manner.

I located Rebenack's addresses on my map of Ville Platte, then went to find him. One was a business address, the other a residence. The residential address put Jimmie Ray Rebenack in a small frame duplex on the east side of town, four blocks north of a switching station for the Southern-Pacific Railroad. It was an older neighborhood, and it wasn't particularly proud, with small unkempt houses and spotty lawns and cars and trucks that were mostly Detroit gas guzzlers in need of paint. Jimmie's Mustang was not in evidence.

I cruised the block twice, then drove to Jimmie Ray Rebenack's office two blocks north of Main above a fresh-seafood market. The seafood market was set between a barber shop and a secondhand clothes store, and there was a little stairwell between the seafood and the clothes, and a black felt and glass directory for the offices up the stairs.

I circled the block, looking for the Mustang, but as with the house the Mustang was not there. I parked around the corner, then walked back to the little directory. There were five businesses listed, and Rebenack Investigations was the third. You had to shake your head. Jimmie Ray Rebenack in his brand-new Mustang, thinking he wouldn't be noticed as he followed me all over town.

I crossed the street to a little coffee shop opposite the fish market. There was a counter and a half-dozen Formica tables spread around the place sporting overweight men in thin cotton shirts drinking coffee and reading the newspaper. A napkin dispenser sat on each of the tables, alongside a bottle of Tabasco sauce. I sat at a table in the window, watching the fish market until a sturdy woman with about a million miles on her clock came over with a coffeepot. She poured without asking, and said, "You wan' some breakfast, sugah?"

"How about a couple of hard poached eggs, toast, and grits?"

"Wheat or white?"

"Wheat."

She walked away without writing anything and left me to sip at the coffee. It was heavy with flavor and about a million times stronger than the coffee people drink in the rest of the world, sort of like espresso that's been cooked down to a sludge. Mississippi mud. I tried to pretend that I enjoyed it, and I think I did a pretty good job. Maybe the Tabasco was on the tables for the coffee. I sneaked glances at the men with their papers. Okay. If they could drink it, I could drink it.

When the waitress brought the food, I said, "Mm-mm, that coffee's some kinda strong!"

She said, "Uh-huh."

I smushed the eggs into the grits and mixed in a little butter and ate it between bites of the toast. The grits were warm and smooth and made the awful coffee easier to drink. I watched the fish market. People came and went, and a couple of times people climbed the stairs, but none of them was Jimmie Ray Rebenack. The front of the fish market was covered with hand-lettered signs saying CATFISH and LIVE CRABS and GASPERGOO $1.89. The people who patronized the fish market came out with brown paper bags that I took to be the catfish and the crabs, and, as I watched them, I wondered what a gaspergoo was and why someone might want to eat it. Another little sign had been painted on the door. WE HAVE GAR BALLS! These Cajuns know how to live, don't they?

I was halfway along my third cup of sludge when Jimmie Ray Rebenack's Mustang rumbled down the street and pulled into a metered spot outside the clothing store. Jimmie Ray fed some money into the meter, then trotted up the stairs. He was wearing blue jeans and a red western shirt and gray snakeskin boots. His pompadour looked a foot high and must've taken most of the morning to shellac into place.

I gave it a few minutes, then paid at the counter, left a hefty tip, and crossed the street to Jimmie Ray Rebenack's office.

The building was dingy and low class, with crummy linoleum floors and water-stained paint. The smell of fish was strong, and seemed a part of the fiber of the building. Three offices overlooked the front street, and three overlooked the alley behind the fish market. Rebenack had the middle office over the alley. I listened for a second, didn't hear anything, then let myself in.

Jimmie Ray Rebenack was sitting behind a plain wooden desk, feet up, staring at some papers when he heard the door. He saw me, then came out of the chair as if somebody had poured hot oatmeal into his lap. "Hey."

"Nice boots, Jimmie Ray. You going for that Joey Buttafucco look?"

"Who?" Out of the cultural loop, down here in Ville Platte. "What do you want?" He slid the papers into his desk drawer. Surreptitious.

Jimmie Ray Rebenack had sharp features and pockmarks on his neck and the pink skin of a natural redhead. Maybe an inch shorter than me, but muscular in a rawboned kind of way. Grease from his part-time mechanic's job was embedded in the thick skin of his knuckles and fingers. He'd tried to wash it off, but the grease was in deep and probably a part of him. A lowboy gray metal file cabinet sat in one corner of the little room, and a couple of padded dinette chairs sat against the wall opposite his desk. Both of the chairs looked like they had been out in the rain, and the padding on one had been patched with duct tape. Classy. Everything in the place looked like it had been picked up at a yard sale, or maybe bought secondhand from the Louisiana public school system. There was a framed picture of Tom Selleck as Magnum sitting on top of the file cabinet.

I said, "I want to know why you're following me, Jimmie Ray."

"Man, what d' hell you talkin' 'bout? I ain't followin' you." The accent was somewhere between Cajun and French Quarter New Orleans.

I crossed his office and looked out the window. He had a view of the dumpster behind the fish market and, beyond that, a back-yard with a little tomato garden. A mayonnaise jar with a two-headed turtle floating in alcohol was on his windowsill. Keepsake, no doubt. I said, "You're Jimmie Ray Rebenack. You drive this

46

year's Mustang, license number 213X455, and you possess Louisiana State investigator's license number KAO154509."

You could see him relax. I hadn't shot him or thrown a punch, so the surprise of my entry was wearing off and he was getting himself together. He put together a pretty good smile, sort of a Jack Nicholson number, part sneer and part smirk. He sat again, leaning back and trying to look expansive. "You made me, huh? You must be pretty good."

"Jimmie, a twelve-year-old could've made you. Why are you following me?"

"I heard you was in town and I wanted to find out why, you know? Like there might be some money in it, thas all."

"Why were you talking to Martha Guidry and Claire Fontenot and Evelyn Maggio last year?"

He frowned and dug at the inside of his teeth with his tongue. Nervous. "I don't know whatchu talkin' 'bout, man."

"C'mon, Jeffrey."

He stared at me like he was trying to think of something to say, but couldn't. I grinned at him. "Gotcha."

He frowned, not happy about it. "They got me confused with somebody else."

"With hair like that?"

He leaned forward. "Hey, podnuh, this is my town. I ain't gotta tell you dick. I know your name is Elvis Cole, and you're from Los Angeles. I know you're stayin' at the motel over here." He pointed his thumb at me and smirked. "You see? I ain't no goddamned slouch in the detectin' department, either."

"Wow. You think we could have a detect-off? You think we could duke it out for the world middleweight detective championships?" I looked at the picture of Tom Selleck. Jesus Christ.

He said, "Maybe my business is knowing your business. Maybe I figured that since you was workin' in *my* town, I could cut myself in." He leaned back again, grinning at me like I was supposed to believe it. "These coonies won't open up to a stranger, and I know my way around. Figured that might be worth some cash. Whatchu think?"

"I think you're full of shit."

Jimmie Ray shrugged like what I thought didn't matter, and then I heard steps coming up the linoleum stairs. The steps came closer and then the door opened and a guy in his mid-forties stepped in. Something large filled the hall behind him.

Jimmie Ray kept grinning at me and said, "This my podnuh, LeRoy." He nodded at the shape in the hall. "That there's René, behind him."

LeRoy's eyes narrowed and he looked at Jimmie Ray as if Jimmie was the world's largest turd. LeRoy was maybe five-eight, with dark weathered skin just beginning to loosen and eyes like a couple of hard black marbles. He was in a thin short-sleeved plaid shirt and worn denim pants, and there was a tattoo on his forearm so obscured by wiry hair that I couldn't make it out. Anchor, maybe. Or a bulldog. He looked surprised to see me, and not particularly happy about it. "Who d'fuck dis?" He said it with a heavy Cajun accent.

Jimmie Ray's smile lost some of its confidence. "Just some guy. He's leaving. Let'm pass, René."

René moved into the room behind LeRoy, and when he did I stepped back the way you might when something large passes very close to you, say a mobile home, or some great African beast. René was only six-three or six-four, but his body possessed size in the way a dirigible possesses size, as if there were a quality to its bulk that could block out the sun. He had a tiny round head and thin, sandy hair and fingers as thick as my wrists. He wore humongously thick glasses that made his eyes seem tiny and far away, and the lenses were speckled with white flecks of matter. There were liver-colored blotches on his forearms and ears that looked like birthmarks, and a large misshapen lump riding the top of his right shoulder like a second head. His skin looked like tree bark. I said, "Jesus Christ."

Jimmie Ray said, "That René is somethin', idin' he? Had him a job in a carnival down 'round Bossier City. Useta bill him d' Swamp Monster." Jimmie Ray liked René the same way he liked the two-headed turtle. Something in a jar.

LeRoy still had the narrow eyes on Jimmie Ray. "Jus' some guy? You callin' names wi' jus' some guy? How goddamn stupid you are?"

Jimmie Ray raised his hands like what's the big deal? "It's nothin', man. Eve'body cool here." The sharp smile fell away and you could see that Jimmie was scared.

LeRoy said something in French.

Jimmie Ray nodded. "Hey, Cole, there's nothin' I can tell ya, all right? Now, I got business. Go on."

LeRoy had put the narrow eyes on me. "Whatchu lookin' at, podnuh?"

Rebenack came around the desk and took my arm. "C'mon, Cole. Out. I gotta go." Now he was trying to get me out of there and damned anxious to do it.

I said, "Are you okay with this?"

Jimmie Ray Rebenack looked at me with wide, surprised eyes. "Hey, yeah, no problem."

LeRoy squinted at me, then at Rebenack. "Who dis guy?" Then back at me. "You his boyfrien', what?"

I said, "If you're in trouble with these guys, Rebenack, don't go with them."

Rebenack waved me toward the door, making a big deal out of showing me that everything was fine. "Hey, these are just a couple of pals. It's not your business, man. Now, c'mon, I gotta lock up."

I let myself get shown out, and then I went down the stairs and back across to the little coffee shop. In a couple of minutes, LeRoy and René and Jimmie Ray came down and climbed into a rusty, gold Polara double-parked at the curb. When René got in, the Polara groaned and settled on its springs. They eased away down the street, did a slow K-turn, then headed back to Main Street and swung left.

I ran hard around the corner to my car, jumped in, pushed it hard through the little alley behind the fish market to Main, then jumped out of the car, climbed onto the hood, and looked both ways to find them. The gold Polara was moving south, just winding a bend in the street maybe three blocks and a dozen cars away. I followed them.

Jimmie Ray might be a turd, but he was my turd.

They were easy to follow. I trailed them south of Ville Platte, staying four to six cars back. LeRoy drove slowly, and a train of cars piled up behind them, unable to pass because of the narrow road.

Six miles south of Ville Platte we crossed a little bayou, and the line of traffic slowed as LeRoy turned west. I didn't turn after him because no one else had, and the land was wide and flat and empty of trees. Sweet potato fields, maybe. I pulled onto the shoulder and waited until the Polara was out of sight, and only then did I turn. If Jimmie Ray was doing the following, he'd be tooling along a couple of car lengths behind, thinking he was invisible because he was playing the radio. Hmm. If I was the world's greatest detective and Jimmie Ray was the world's worst, maybe this was some kind of karmic coming together.

Maybe a mile off the main road another road branched away, this one going through a gate with a big sign that said ROSSIER'S CRAWFISH FARM, MILT ROSSIER, PROP. The farm was hidden from the road by a heavy windbreak of hardwood trees, and I couldn't see beyond the windbreak into the farm. I could see pretty far up the tarmac road, and the gold Polara wasn't visible. No dust trail, either. Hmm, again. I drove a hundred yards past the gate, pulled onto the shoulder, then trotted back into the trees.

The windbreak was maybe a hundred yards deep, with more fields beyond cut through by a regular crosswork of shell roads. The gold Polara was parked on the far side of a large rectangular pond about the size and shape of a football field. There was another pond of identical size and shape beyond it, and another one after that, and a couple of long, low cinder block buildings. The Polara was parked beside a white Cadillac Brougham and an Evangeline Parish Sheriff's department highway car. Jimmie Ray and LeRoy and René were standing at the edge of the pond with a guy in a tan sheriff's uniform. The sheriff was maybe in his fifties, and everybody seemed to be talking to a heavy guy with baggy trousers and a cheap white short-sleeved shirt and a straw field hat on his head. He looked about the same age as the sheriff, but he might have been older, and he carried himself with the unmistakable bearing of an overseer. He gestured out toward the pond, and everybody looked. He gestured in the opposite direction, and everybody looked there, too. Then he leaned against the Cadillac and crossed his arms. Milt Rossier, no doubt. Proprietor.

I watched for another few minutes, and then I made my way back through the trees, drove back to town, and let myself into Jimmie Ray Rebenack's office. It was as we had left it, quiet and smelling of raw shrimp, the sounds of the alley and backyards below drifting nicely through the open window. A lawn mower was growling a few houses away, and the rich smell of cut St. Augustine grass mixed nicely with the shrimp. The two-headed turtle was milky in its jar on the sill, and Tom Selleck looked bored in his frame atop the file cabinet. I could see Jimmie Ray Rebenack, watching *Magnum* reruns, watching Tom Selleck drive the fast car and mug with the beautiful women. Jimmie sitting in his little duplex in Ville Platte, thinking, yeah, I could do that, then taking some mail order course, *How to Be a Private Eye!*

I opened his desk to see what he had been reading, and suddenly the lawn mower sounds faded and the office was very quiet. Jodi Taylor smiled up at me from the cover of *Music* magazine. The cover and an accompanying article had been clipped from the magazine and stapled together. The *People* article was under it. I took a breath and let it out. Sonofagun. I went through the rest of the desk, but the rest of the desk was empty. I moved to the file cabinet. Two cans of Dr Pepper were hiding in the bottom drawer, and a single roll of prank toilet paper, the kind with Jerry Falwell's face printed on each of the sheets. Office-warming gift. The second drawer was empty, and the third was nicely outfitted with hanging file folders in various colors, only the folders were as empty and as clean as the day Jimmie Ray had installed them. There were eight hanging files in the top drawer. One of them held a Polaroid snapshot of a nude woman with a Winn-Dixie shopping bag over her head. A lot of blonde hair peeked out beneath the bag, and she was cheap-looking, wearing rings on her third and fourth fingers. Girlfriend, no doubt. Another held a surveillance report that Jimmie Ray Rebenack had written for a Mrs. Philip R. Cantera, who was convinced that her husband was playing around. Jimmie Ray's report said that he had observed Mr. Cantera in intimate embrace on several different occasions with (a) a young woman who worked at Cal's Road House and (b) another young woman who sold beer at the Rebel Stock Car Oval. The next three files contained case notes from similar jobs, two of them involving suspected infidelity, and the remaining being a grocery store owner who suspected an employee of stealing houseware products. The fifth folder contained more pictures of Jodi Taylor clipped from magazines and newspapers and what looked like studio press release sources, only sandwiched in with the articles were the Xeroxed copies of the first two pages of a document relinquishing the care and trust of one Marla Sue Johnson, a baby girl, to the State of Louisiana from her natural parents, Pamela E. Johnson and Monroe Kyle Johnson, on 11 July, thirty-

six years ago. The document was incomplete and bore no signa-
tures. Jodi Taylor's birth certificate was paper-clipped to the document along with a second birth certificate, this one stating that
Marla Sue Johnson had been born to Pamela E. Johnson and
Monroe Kyle Johnson on 9 July. Jodi Taylor's birthday.

Jesus Christ.

An address had been written in pencil on the back of the birth
certificate: 1146 Tecumseh Lane. I copied it.

I stared at the birth certificate and the relinquishment document for quite a while, and then I put Jimmie Ray's office back as
I had found it, let myself out, and went back through the smell of
wet shrimp to the little diner across the street. The same cook
with the cratered nose was leaning on the counter. The same crinkled old man with the snap-brimmed hat was smoking at the little window table. Dignified. I said, "Use your pay phone?" They
have a pay phone on the wall by the restroom.

The cook nodded help yourself. Watching me gave him something to do.

I fed a quarter into the phone and dialed Martha Guidry, who
answered on the second ring. I said, "Martha, it's Elvis Cole."

"*What?*" The Raid.

I had to yell. "It's Elvis Cole. Remember?" The old man and
the cook were both looking at me. I cupped the receiver. "Her
ears." The cook nodded, saying it's hard when they get like that.

Martha Guidry yelled, "Goddamn bugs!" You could hear the
flyswatter whistle through the air and snap against the wall, Martha cackling and saying, "Gotcha, you sonofabitch!"

"Martha?" Trying to get her back to the phone.

Something crashed, and she came back on the line, breathing
harder from her exertion. "You have a bowel movement yet? I
know how it is when I travel. I cross the street, I don't go potty for
a week." A living doll, that Martha.

I said, "The people you were trying to remember, were their
names Johnson?"

"Johnson."

"Pamela and Monroe Johnson."

There was a sharp *slap*. "You should see the size of this god-damned roach."

"The Johnsons, Martha. Was the family named Johnson?"

She said, "That sounds like them. White trash lived right over here. Oh, hell, Pam Johnson died *years* ago."

I thanked Martha Guidry for her help, then hung up and stared at the address I had copied. 1146 Tecumseh Lane. I fed another quarter into the phone and dialed Information. A pleasant female voice said, "And how are you today?" She sounded young.

"Do you have a listing for a Pamela or Monroe Johnson on Tecumseh Lane?"

She didn't say anything for a moment, and then she said, "No, sir. We've got a bunch of other Johnsons, though."

"Any of them on Tecumseh Lane?"

"I'm sorry, sir. I don't show Pamela or Monroe Johnson, and I don't show a Tecumseh Lane, either."

I hung up.

The cook said, "No luck?"

I shook my head.

The old guy at the window table said something in French.

"What'd he say?"

The cook said, "He wants to know what you want."

"I'm trying to find Monroe and Pamela Johnson. I think they live on Tecumseh Lane, but I'm not sure where that is."

The cook said it in French, and the old man said something back at him and they talked back and forth like that for a while. Then the cook said, "He doesn't know these Johnson people, but he says there's a Tecumseh Lane in Eunice."

"Eunice?"

"Twenty miles south of here." Ah.

I smiled at the old man. "Thank him for me."

The cook said, "He understands you okay, he just don't speak English so good."

I nodded at the old man. *"Merci."*

55

The old man tipped his hat. Dignified. *"Il y a pas de quoi."* You take your good fortune where you find it.

I went out to my car, looked up Eunice on the Triple-A map, and went there. Like Ville Platte, the landscape was flat and cross-cut with bayous and ponds and industrial waterways, mostly sweet potato fields and marshlands striped with oil company pipelines and vent stations. The town itself was bigger than Ville Platte, but not by a lot, and seemed like a neat, self-contained little community with a lot of churches and schools and quaint older buildings.

Tecumseh Lane was a pleasant street in an older residential area with small frame houses and neatly trimmed azalea bushes. 1146 was in the center of the block, with a tiny front lawn and an ancient two-strip cement drive and a big wooden porch. Like every other house in the area, it was set atop high brick pillars and, even though the land was flat, you had to climb three or four steps to enter the house.

I left the car at the curb and went up to the house and rapped at the door. An older black woman in what looked like a white nurse's uniform answered. "May I help you?"

I gave her one of my nicer smiles. "Mrs. Johnson?"

"Oh, no."

"I'm looking for Mr. and Mrs. Johnson. I was told they lived here." The air behind her smelled of medicine and pine-scented air freshener.

She was shaking her head before I finished. "You'll need to speak with Mrs. Boudreaux. I work for her."

"Who's Mrs. Boudreaux?"

"She owns this house." A wet, flapping sound came from deeper in the house, and a raspy old man's voice yelled something about his pears. The black woman took a half-step out onto the porch, pulling the door so I wouldn't hear. "She doesn't live here, though. She only comes by in the morning and the evening."

I let myself look confused. A relatively easy task. "Did the Johnsons move?"

"Oh, Mr. Johnson's her daddy. She used to rent this place out, but now she lets him live here." She pulled the door tighter and lowered her voice, letting me in on the know. "He can't live by himself, and they didn't want to put him in a home. Lord knows he couldn't live with them." She raised her eyebrows. "He's very ill."

I said, "Ah. So Mr. Johnson does live here."

She nodded, then sighed. "He's eighty-seven, poor thing, and he takes spells. He's a devil when he takes a spell." The voice in the house yelled again, something about the TV, something about Bob Barker and the goddamned pears.

I said, "How is Mrs. Johnson?"

"Oh, she died years ago."

Score another for Martha Guidry. "If I wanted to speak with Mrs. Boudreaux, how could I do that?"

"She'll be here in a little while. She always comes around two. Or you could go by her shop. She has a very nice formal wear shop on Second Street by the square. They call it Edie's. Her first name is Edith, but she goes by Edie."

"Of course."

She glanced back toward the house. "Twice a day she comes, and he don't even know it, most days. Poor thing."

I thanked her for her time, told her I'd try to stop at the house again around two, then drove back to the square. Edith Boudreaux's boutique occupied a corner location next to a hair salon, across from a little square filled with magnolia trees. I parked on the square, then walked back and went inside. A young woman in her early twenties smiled at me from a rack of Anne Klein pants suits. "May I help you, sir?"

I smiled back at her. "Just sort of browsing for my wife."

The smile deepened. Dimples. "Well, if you have any questions, just ask."

I told her I would. She finished racking the Anne Kleins, then went through a curtained doorway into the stockroom. As she went through the curtains, an attractive woman in her late forties came out with an armful of beige knit tops. She saw me and smiled. "Have you been helped?"

The similarities to Jodi Taylor were amazing. The same broad shoulders, the good bone structure, the facial resemblance. They were, as the saying goes, enough alike to be sisters. We would have to unseal the sealed documents to be sure. We would have to compare the adoption papers from the Johnson family to the Taylor family to be positive, but Edith Boudreaux and Jodi Taylor were clearly related. Maybe Jimmie Ray Rebenack wasn't the world's worst detective, after all. I said, "Are you Ms. Boudreaux?"

"Why, yes. Have we met?"

I told her no. I said that her shop had been recommended and that I was browsing for something for my wife, but if I had any questions I would be sure to ask. She told me to take my time and she returned to her stock. I browsed around the store another few minutes, then let myself out, walked to a pay phone on the other side of the square, and dialed Lucy Chenier. I said, "Well, I've done it again."

"Tied your laces together and tripped?" Maybe she had a laugh button, after all.

I said, "I have found a gentleman named Monroe Johnson. Thirty-six years ago on Jodi Taylor's birthday, his wife, Pamela Johnson, delivered a baby girl. They gave the child up for adoption. I saw his adult daughter, a woman named Edie Boudreaux, and she is Jodi's spitting image."

Lucy said, "You've done all this in two days?"

"It is not for nothing that I am the World's Greatest Detective."

"Perhaps you are." She sounded pleased.

"Also, Rebenack found them for me." I told her what I had found in his office.

"Oh." She didn't sound as happy about that.

I said, "I still don't know what Rebenack's interest in all this might be, but if these people are, in fact, Jodi's biological family, Edie Boudreaux should be able to provide whatever medical information Jodi wants." I gave her Bogart. "So it's all yours, shweetheart."

"Was that Humphrey Bogart?"

Some people are truly cold.

She said, "The next step is to approach these people. Perhaps we can figure out a plan of action over dinner."

I said, "Is this an invitation, Ms. Chenier?"

"It is, Mr. Cole, and I advise you to accept. There may not be another."

"Dinner sounds very nice, thank you."

"Where are you?"

"Eunice. The family lives here."

She said, "Can you be back at the Riverfront and ready to be picked up by six-thirty?"

"I think I can manage." If I grinned any wider I'd probably split my gums.

"Good. I'll see you then." She paused, and then she said, "Good work, Mr. Cole."

I hung up, went to my car, and sat there with the grin until a guy in a Toyota flatbed yelled, "Hey, pumpkinhead! You're gonna catch bugs that way!"

Southern humor.

8

I went back to the motel in Ville Platte, showered, shaved, then drove back across the Atchafalaya Basin to Baton Rouge. It seemed a lot faster than when I had driven from Baton Rouge to Ville Platte, but maybe that was because I was looking forward to getting there. I am nothing if not goal oriented.

I checked into the Riverfront again and was nursing a Dixie beer in the lobby bar at six-thirty when Lucy Chenier walked in wearing a rose blazer over a clay-colored blouse and tight jeans. Two businessmen at a little round table watched her walk in. So did the bartender. She smiled when she saw me and her eyes seemed to fill the room. She offered her hand. "Did you satisfy your urge for local cuisine, or are you still feeling adventurous?"

I said, "Adventure is my middle name."

She smiled wider, and her teeth and eyes sparkled, but maybe that was just me. "Then you're in for a treat."

Lucy waited while I paid the bar bill, then we went out to her car. She was driving a light blue Lexus 400 two-door coupe. The sport model. It was clean and sleek and had been freshly washed. There was an AT&T car phone, and the small backseat was littered with CDs, mostly K. D. Lang and Reba McEntire. She looked good behind the wheel, as if she and the car were comfortable together. "Nice," I said.

She flashed the laugh lines, pleased. Lucy Chenier drove cleanly and with authority, very much the way I imagined she practiced law or played tennis, and pretty soon we turned into a great warehouse of a building with streams of people going in and coming out. Ralph & Kacoo's. She said, "Let me warn you. The decor is kind of hokey, but the food is wonderful."

"No problem," I said. "I go for that Barnacle Bill look."

Ralph & Kacoo's made an airplane hangar look small. It was festooned with fishing nets and cork buoys and stuffed game fish and mutant crab shells the size of garbage can lids. There must have been seven hundred people in the place. A lot of families, but a great many couples, too. All it needed was Alan Hale in a yellow slicker greeting everyone with a hearty "Ahoy, matey!" I said, "Kind of?"

Lucy Chenier nodded. "We're big on hoke down here."

A young woman who looked like a college student seated us and asked if we'd care for a drink. I said, "Shall we order a bottle of wine?"

"Never with Cajun food." Lucy grinned, and now there was a glint of fun in her eyes. "You're going to think it's hokey again."

"What?"

She looked at the waitress. "Could we have two Cajun Bloody Marys, please?"

I raised an eyebrow. "Cajun Bloody Marys?"

"Don't laugh. They're made with cayenne and a hint of fish stock. You said you're adventurous." She turned back to the waitress. "And we'll have an appetizer of the alligator sausage."

The waitress went away.

I said, "First, it's dinner at Gilligan's Island, now it's alligator sausage. What could be next?"

Lucy looked at her menu. "The best is yet to come."

The waitress came back with Bloody Marys that were more brown than red, with a ring of lemon floating in them. I tasted. There was the hint of fish, and the flavors of Tabasco and pepper and cayenne were strong and tingly, and went well with the vodka.

Lucy said, "Well?"

"This is good. This is really very good."

Lucy smiled. "You see?"

The waitress returned with the alligator sausage and asked if we were ready to order. I tried the sausage. It could have been chicken or pork, but the texture was interesting.

Lucy said, "If you really want to taste Louisiana, I'd suggest any of the crab dishes, or the crawfish. The crab dishes tend to be fried; the crawfish boiled or made in a soup."

"Sounds good."

Lucy Chenier ordered the crawfish étouffée, and I ordered the crawfish platter. With the platter I would get a bowl of crawfish bisque, as well as boiled crawfish and fried crawfish tails. The fried tails were called Cajun popcorn. We finished the first Bloody Marys and ordered two more. The waitress brought our salads, and I watched Lucy eat as, in her office, I had watched her move. To watch her was a singular, enjoyable occupation. She said, "To be honest with you, when Jodi told me that she was bringing in an investigator from California, I tried to discourage it. I didn't think you'd be as effective as a local investigator."

"Reasonable."

She tipped her glass toward me. "Reasonable, but clearly misplaced. You're good."

I tried to sit straighter in the chair. "You're making me blush."

She sipped the Bloody Mary. She didn't seem too interested in the salad. "What did Mr. Rebenack have to say for himself?"

I went through it for her. I told her that Jimmie Ray Rebenack had approached at least two of the women I interviewed and presented himself as someone seeking to find a sister, and that when I questioned him about this, he denied it, and also denied approaching the women. I told her that I had taken the opportunity to enter his office, and that when I did I discovered what appeared to be Louisiana State adoption papers and a birth certificate for a girl child born to Pamela and Monroe Johnson on the same day as the day of Jodi Taylor's birth. When I said that part of it, Lucy Chenier put down her Bloody Mary and held up a hand. No longer smiling. "Let me stop you. You broke into this man's office?"

"Yes."

She shook her head. "Breaking and entering is a crime. I will not be a party to criminal behavior."

I said, "What office?"

She sighed, still not liking it.

I said, "The state papers were standard stuff, showing that the Johnsons remanded all rights and claims on the child to the state. Someone had written the Johnsons' address on back of the birth certificate. It could be coincidence, but if it is, it's a big one."

"Were the Taylors mentioned anywhere on the papers?"

"There was a copy of Jodi's birth certificate. That's all."

"Do you think this man Rebenack is related to Jodi Taylor or to the Johnson family?"

"I have no way to know. He denied all knowledge, yet he had the file. He's interested in Jodi Taylor, and he's linked her to the Johnsons. He had Monroe Johnson's address, so he may have approached them, but I don't know that."

Lucy Chenier stared into midspace, thinking. Now that we were on the serious stuff, she seemed intent and focused and on the verge of a frown. Her court face, I thought. A mix of the tennis and the law. I had more of the Bloody Mary and watched her think. Watching her think was as rewarding as watching her move, but maybe that was just the vodka. My mouth tingled pleasantly from the spices, and I wondered if hers was tingling, too.

She said, "The documents you're describing are part of the files sealed by the state. The biological parents would've been given a copy, what you might call a receipt for the child, but there's no way Mr. Rebenack should have a copy."

"Only he has it." I wondered what it would be like to kiss someone with a tingling mouth.

She said, "Still, that document doesn't prove that Jodi Taylor is in fact the child given up by the Johnsons. We'll have to open the state files for that. We'll have to approach Edith Boudreaux to confirm that what you've found is correct. If her father is incapacitated and her mother is dead, then it falls to her to give the state permission to open the files. That's the only way to officially confirm that Jodi Taylor was born to Pamela Johnson."

"And that we'll do tomorrow."

She nodded. "Yes. I think it's best if we approach her at the boutique. We'll make contact there, on ground where she's comfortable, and ask to speak with her in private. That should be me, because I've done it before and because women are less threatened by other women."

"You mean, we don't just walk up and say, hey, babe, how'd ya like to meet your long lost sister?"

Lucy Chenier smiled, and had more of her drink. "Perhaps in California."

I said, "Is your mouth tingling?"

She looked at me.

"From the spices."

"Why, yes. It is."

I nodded. "Just wondering."

The waitress took the salad plates away and came back with the étouffée for Lucy and the crawfish platter for me. A bowl of bisque was in the center of my plate, surrounded by a mound of boiled crawfish on one side and the fried crawfish tails on the other. The fried tails looked like tiny shrimp, curled tight and lightly breaded. I forked up several and ate them. They were hot and tender and tasted in a way like sautéed baby langostinos. "Good."

Lucy said, "The bisque is like a soup that's been enriched with

crawfish fat. The heads have been stuffed with a mixture of crawfish meat and bread crumbs and spices. You can pick it up, then
use your spoon to lift out the stuffing."

"Okay." The bisque was a deep brown, and several stuffed
crawfish shells bobbed in it. I did as she said and dug out the
stuffing and tasted it. The stuffing tasted of thyme. "This is terrific. Would you like one?"

"Please."

I spooned out one of the stuffed shells and put it on her plate.
She said, "Here. Try the étouffée."

The étouffée was a rich brown sauce chunky with diced green
bell peppers and celery and crawfish tails over rice. She forked
some onto one of the little bread plates, then passed it to me. I
tasted it. These people have redefined the word *yummy*.

She said, "Does the étouffée you get in California taste like
this?"

"Not even close."

Lucy Chenier picked up the stuffed shell I had given her and
spooned out the filling. As she did, a brown drop of the gravy ran
down along the heel of her hand toward her wrist. She turned up
her hand without thinking about it and licked off the drip. I felt
something swell in my chest and had to swallow and then had the
rest of the Bloody Mary. I said, "Would you like another?"

Nod. Smile. "Maybe one more. I have to drive."

I flagged at the waitress and showed her two fingers. *Two bags
of ice and a cold shower, please.* Lucy said, "You eat the boiled crawfish by breaking the tails out of the body, then pinching the tail
so that the shell cracks and you can get out the meat." She took
one of my crawfish and demonstrated. "You see?"

"Unh-hunh." Maybe if I concentrated on the food. The food
could save me.

"Then you put the head in your mouth and suck it."

I blinked at her as she put the head in her mouth and sucked it.
She smiled simply. "Gets out the juice."

I coughed and covered my mouth. I drank some water. Think

about the food. The food. The waitress brought our drinks and I drank mine without stopping. Lucy looked concerned. "What's wrong?"

"Nothing." I shook my head. "Not a thing."

She sipped her new drink and ate some more of her étouffée. I noticed that most of my food was gone and most of hers was still on her plate. I hope she didn't think me a glutton. "Are you from Baton Rouge?"

"That's right."

"Your accent is softer than the others I hear."

She smiled. "I'm not the one with the accent, Mr. Cole."

I spread my hands. Busted.

"I went to LSU for prelaw, but I attended law school in Michigan. Living with yankees can devastate your accent."

"And you returned home to practice."

"My boyfriend was here, working, and we wanted to be married. He was a lawyer, too. He still is."

"How about that."

"We were divorced four years ago."

"That happens." I tried not to beam.

"Yes, it does." It seemed as if she was going to say more, but then she went back to the étouffée. "Now tell me about you. Do you have a background in law enforcement?"

"Nope. I've been licensed for twelve years and, before that, I apprenticed with a man named George Fieder. George had about a million hours of experience and was maybe the best investigator who ever lived. Before that, I was in the army."

"College?"

"University of Southeast Asia. The work-study program."

She shook her head, smiling. "You look too young for Vietnam."

"I looked older then."

"Of course."

"May I ask you a personal question, Ms. Chenier?"

She nodded, chewing.

"Have you sought out your birth parents?"

"No." She shook her head, then used the back of her wrist to move her hair from her eyes. Fingers still sticky from the crawfish. "The vast majority of adopted children don't. There may be a minor curiosity from time to time, but your mom and dad are your mom and dad."

"The people who raise you."

"That's it. A long time ago a woman gave birth to me, and gave me over to the state because she felt it best for both of us. She now has her life, I have mine, and my birth father his. I can appreciate on an intellectual level that they birthed me, but emotionally, my folks are Jack and Ann Kyle. Jack helped me ace algebra and Ann drove me to the court every day after school to practice tennis. Do you see?"

"Sure. They're your family."

She smiled and nodded and ate more of the étouffée. "Just like yours."

"Yet you've devoted your career to this kind of work."

"Not really. Most of my practice is in the area of divorce and custody disputes. But I don't have to want to recover my birth parents to appreciate that need in others. All of us should have access to our medical histories. Because I feel the weight of that, and because I'm in a position to help those with the need, I do."

"You share a mutual experience with other adopted children and you feel a kinship. All brothers and sisters under the skin."

She seemed pleased. "That's exactly right." Amazing how a little vodka can dull the senses, isn't it? She put down her fork and crossed her arms on the table. "So, Mr. Adventure, tell me what you think of our Louisiana crawfish. Is it the most incredible thing you've ever eaten?"

"I ate dog when I was in Vietnam."

Lucy Chenier's smile vanished and she looked uncertain. "How . . . adventurous."

I shrugged and finished off the crawfish tails.

She said, "Arf."

I looked up.

Lucy Chenier's face was red and her mouth was a dimpled tight line. She opened her mouth and breathed deep and blinked to clear her eyes. "I'm sorry, but the idea of it." She covered her face with her napkin. "Was it a poodle?"

I put down my fork and folded my arms on the table. "Oh, I get it. Humor."

"I'm sorry. It's just so funny."

"Not to the dog."

Lucy laughed, then motioned to the waitress and said, "I really do have to be going."

"Would you like coffee?"

"I would, but I can't. I have another appointment with a very special gentleman."

I looked at her. "Oh."

"My son. He's eight."

"Ah."

The waitress brought us Handi Wipes. Lucy paid, and then we drove back to the hotel. I suggested that we go together to Edith Boudreaux's shop the next morning, but Lucy had two early meetings and thought it better if we met there. I told her that that would be fine. We rode in silence most of the way with an air of expectancy in the car that felt more hopeful than uncomfortable, as if the night held a kind of static charge waiting to be released.

When we stopped at the Ho-Jo's front entrance, it was almost ten.

She said, "Well."

"I had a very nice time tonight, Lucy. Thank you."

"Me, too."

We sat in the neon light another moment, looking at each other, and then I leaned across to kiss her. She put her hand on my chest and gently pushed, and I backed up. She looked uncomfortable. "You're a neat guy, and I had a good time with you, but we're working together. Do you see?"

"Sure." I swallowed and blinked, and then offered my hand. "Thanks for dinner. I enjoyed myself."

She took my hand, eyes never leaving mine. "Please don't take this wrong."

"Of course not." I tried to smile.

We shook, and then I got out of Lucy Chenier's car and watched her drive away.

The night was balmy and pleasant, and I walked along the levee and up the little hill and along the nighttime Baton Rouge streets, drunk not from the vodka but with the joyful awareness that tomorrow I would see her again.

9

The next morning I left the hotel just before eight, drove across the Huey Long Bridge, and, one hour and five minutes later, parked in a diagonal spot beneath the Eunice town clock just across the square from Edith Boudreaux's clothing store. A CLOSED sign hung in the window, and the red and white store hours sign said that they opened at ten A.M. It was twelve minutes after nine.

I went into a coffee shop, bought two coffees to go, and brought them and a handful of sweetener and creamer packs out to my car. I sat there with the windows down, sipping the coffee and watching the store. At twenty-six minutes after nine Lucy Chenier's Lexus came around the square and parked four spaces down from me. I got out with the coffees, walked over, rapped on her fender, then opened her passenger-side door, slid in, and handed her a coffee. "There's sweetener and creamer. I didn't know what you take."

"This is so thoughtful. Thank you."

"We're a full-service operation, ma'am." She popped the plastic top off the Styrofoam cup, blew on the coffee, then sipped it black. Even watching her sip was an adventure.

She said, "Is that the store?"

"Yes. Edie's. They open at ten."

Lucy Chenier sipped more of the coffee and watched the store. When she sipped, the steam from the coffee brushed over her face like a child's fingers. The amber-green eyes seemed darker today, almost brown, and I wondered at their change. She was wearing a crushed linen jacket over a white blouse and baggy camel pants, and she smelled of buttermilk soap. If I stared at her any more I'd probably reveal myself to be the world's largest doogie. I forced myself to look at the store.

At fourteen minutes before ten, Edith Boudreaux walked around the corner and came down the block and let herself in through the shop's front door. I said, "That's her."

"My God, she does look like Jodi, doesn't she?"

"Yep."

Lucy finished her coffee, then said, "Let's go see her."

We walked across the square and went in. The same little bell rang when we entered, and the air was as chill today as I remembered it. Edith Boudreaux looked up at us from the cash register where she was loading a fresh tape. She said, "Sorry. We're not open yet." She hadn't yet turned around the CLOSED sign.

Lucy smiled pleasantly and stepped into the store as if they were old friends. "I know, but I was hoping we might spend a few minutes now. My name is Lucille Chenier. I'm an attorney from Baton Rouge." Lucy crossed with her hand out and Edith Boudreaux took it without thinking. She seemed sort of puzzled, and then she recognized me.

"You were in yesterday."

"That's right."

She brightened and glanced at Lucy. "You brought your wife this time."

Lucy gave a friendly laugh. "No. Mr. Cole and I work together." She patted Edith Boudreaux's hand, calming her, telling her that we were good people and there was nothing to be frightened of. Friendly people come to change your life. Lucy said, "I know you need to ready for opening, but it's better that we're alone."

"What are you talking about?" Looking at me. "Why alone?"

Lucy said, "I practice civil law, and part of my practice involves adoption recovery. It's a sensitive, private matter, and I treat everyone's confidence with the utmost respect."

Edith Boudreaux's face darkened and she took a single step back. Jimmie Ray had been to see her, all right.

Lucy went on, "Birth parents who want to find their children or adoptees who want to find their birth parents or learn something about their biological relatives employ me to help make those connections. I'm working for such a person now, and Mr. Cole and I have come across something that we need to check."

Edith Boudreaux glanced from Lucy to me and back to Lucy. Her mouth opened slightly, then closed, and her hands came together beneath her breasts. Lucy said, "Mrs. Boudreaux, I hope this won't come as a shock to you, but it may. This isn't bad news in any way. It is very, very good news. Were you aware that your mother gave birth to a child on July 9, thirty-six years ago, and then gave that child up for adoption?"

The eyes flicked again. Me to Lucy. Lucy to me. "Why did you come here? Who sent you here?" Jimmie Ray, all right.

The bell tinkled again and the young blond clerk came through the door. Edith Boudreaux clutched at Lucy and said, "Please don't say anything."

She went to the young woman and said something so softly that we could not hear. Lucy looked at me and lowered her voice. "Why's she so scared?"

I shook my head. Edith Boudreaux returned and said, "That's Sandy. Sandy helps out. We can go in back." She hustled us through the curtained doorway and into the stockroom. Racks of plastic-covered clothes filled most of the floor space, and blue and white garment boxes were stacked against the walls and on cheap shelves. An Arrowhead water cooler stood outside what I guessed was a restroom. Edith pulled the curtain and wrung her hands. "I don't know what you want of me."

Lucy's voice was calm and measured and soothing, an FM disc jockey playing easy listening after midnight. She said, "My client may be the child that your mother gave away. Your sister, Edith. She wants nothing of you, or anyone else in her biological family, except to learn her medical history."

Nodding now. Squinting like all of this was going by very fast and it was difficult to contain. I wondered what Jimmie Ray had told her. I was wondering where he'd gotten the money to buy the Mustang. She said, "I don't know."

Lucy said, "The only way we can be sure that my client is the child that your mother gave away is if both parties submit to the state's adoption registry search so we can see if there's a match. If there is a match, the state will unseal the records and confirm the identity."

Edith Boudreaux was nodding, but I'm not sure the nods meant anything. She said, "You think your client is that baby?"

"We believe she is, yes."

"That's who sent you here? The baby?" She was so nervous she was rocking, swaying back and forth as if in time with a heartbeat.

"My client is thirty-six years old. She's a woman now."

"That was all so long ago."

"She doesn't want anything from you, Mrs. Boudreaux. She simply wants to know the particulars of her medical heritage. Does breast or uterine cancer run in the family? Is the family long-lived? That kind of thing."

"My mother's dead."

"We know. And we know that your father is ill. That's why we came to you. Won't you help us?"

She was still making the little rocking moves, and then she said, "I have to call my husband. I need to speak with him."

She went out through the curtain without looking at us. Lucy blew out a loud sigh and took a cup of water from the cooler. "What's wrong with this picture?"

"Somebody scared her. Probably Jimmie Ray."

Lucy crumpled the cup, didn't see any place to toss it, put it in her pocket. "With what? All we're talking about here is an adoption."

It didn't take long for Edith Boudreaux to talk to her husband, and it didn't take long for him to arrive on the scene. We waited maybe eight or nine minutes, and then the outer bell tinkled and a tall, florid man about Edith's age came through the curtain ahead of her. He was thick across the shoulders and butt, with small eyes and a sun-reddened face and large hands that looked callused and rough. He was wearing a crisp khaki Evangeline Parish sheriff's uniform open at the collar, and he was the same cop I'd seen with Jimmie Ray Rebenack at the crawfish farm.

He said, "My name's Jo-el Boudreaux. I'm the sheriff here in Evangeline Parish. Could I see some identification, please?" As he said it he looked over Lucy and then he looked over me. His eyes stayed with you without blinking. Cop eyes.

Lucy showed her driver's license and gave him a business card. When he looked at my investigator's license he said, "California."

I nodded.

"You carrying?"

I shook my head. "Nope. Not licensed in Louisiana."

"Why don't we see?"

He pointed at the wall and I assumed the position and he patted me down. Lucy Chenier looked surprised and then angry. She said, "There's no need for that. I'm an attorney, this man is a licensed investigator. This is a legitimate inquiry." She was breathing quickly, confused by his manner. Everything had suddenly risen to a level she wasn't used to.

I said, "It's okay."

The sheriff copied some information off the license into a little notepad. After that he flipped back the license, and he didn't much care if I caught it or not. He said, "Yeah, well, we'll check on that. We'll see. Now that we know where we stand, why don't you tell me what you're after." He squared himself off at us, the way he'd front a kid he'd stopped for driving too fast on a back road.

Lucy didn't like it, but she went through it again for Jo-el Boudreaux, telling him about the sealed state documents, about the possibility that our client was the child given away by Pamela Johnson, about our client's desire not to contact her long lost family but simply to establish her medical history.

Jo-el Boudreaux was shaking his head before she finished. "You got any proof that this baby and your client are the same person?"

Lucy said, "No, sir. But they were born on the same day, and they're both female, and they were both given up to the state. That's why we need the records opened."

He was shaking his head again. "Not interested. I want you people to leave my wife alone. Whatever you're selling, we don't want any."

Edith Boudreaux looked like she wasn't as sure. She said, "Jo-el, maybe we should—"

He cut her off. "Edith, what's there to say? The past is the past, isn't it?"

Lucy said, "Our client doesn't want anything from you, Mr. Boudreaux. She simply wants to know her medical history. You can understand that, can't you?"

He said, "I understand that a lot of my wife's family's dirty laundry is going to be stirred up again. You people go around town spreading crap about my wife's family, it'll go hard on you."

Lucy stiffened and the court face appeared. "Is that a threat, Sheriff?"

"Yes, ma'am. I've just threatened legal action. As an attorney, I'm sure you understand that." He handed back her card. "We've got nothing to say to you."

Lucy looked at Edith Boudreaux. She was small behind her husband. Her eyes looked hurt. "Is this what you want?"

Edith repeated it. "What's past is past. Let's not stir things up." Nervous.

Lucy stared at the other woman for a time, then carefully put her business card on a stack of Anne Klein boxes. "I can appreciate your confusion. If you change your mind, please call me at this number."

Sheriff Jo-el Boudreaux said, "There's no confusion, counselor. If you leave the card, I can cite you for littering."

Lucy picked up the card, thanked Edith for her time, and walked out.

I said, "A litter bust. That'd probably make your month."

The cop eyes clicked my way. "You wanna push for the prize, podnuh?"

I said, "How'd a guy like Jimmie Ray Rebenack get you so scared?"

The big sheriff looked at me, and a single tic started beneath his left eye. The blocky hands flexed, and Edith Boudreaux touched her husband's arm, and it was suddenly still in the little room. Outside, the doorbell tinkled, and I wondered if it was Lucy leaving. Edith said, "Jo-el?"

Boudreaux went to the curtained door and pulled the curtain aside and held it for me. "You'd better leave now, podnuh. That'd be best for you. That'd be best for everyone."

I wished Edith a good day and then I walked out past the blond clerk. She smiled brightly and told me to have a good day. I told her I'd try. When I got to the door I looked back, but the curtain was drawn again and Jo-el Boudreaux and his wife were still in the stockroom. I thought I heard a woman crying, but I could have imagined it.

It was supposed to be a simple case, but cases, like life, are rarely what they seem. I walked out of Edie's Fashion Boutique wondering at the pain I'd seen in their eyes.

Lucy was waiting on the sidewalk, her arms crossed and her face set. A couple of teenagers were behind her, looking at the sheriff's shotgun through the driver's side window of his highway car, the older of the two sneaking glances at Lucy's rear end. He cut it out when he saw me approach. Lucy said, "I've been doing this for almost eight years and I've never had a reaction even close to that. Something's wrong."

"They're scared. Him, maybe more than her."

As we walked back to our cars, I told her about Jimmie Ray Rebenack and the two goons who'd come to his office. "I followed them to a place called Rossier's Crawfish Farm. Boudreaux was there, and some older guy with a Panama hat who was probably Milt Rossier. Boudreaux didn't look thrilled to be there, but he and Rebenack are connected."

"Do you think that Rebenack has seen these people about Jodi Taylor?"

"Looks that way."

"Maybe he's working for them, just like we're working for Jodi."

"Maybe."

When we reached the cars, Lucy leaned against her Lexus and shook her head. "I don't believe it, but even if he were, so what? All we're talking about is a child who was given away for adoption. It's a simple matter to unseal the files and confirm the biological link. It's done all the time."

I looked at her. "Maybe the problem is coming from an altogether different place."

She squinted at Edith Boudreaux's dress shop, thinking about it. Frustrated. "Well, it can't just end here. They say no, thanks, so that's the end of it. Jodi still has a right to find out about herself, and I'm still going to help her do that."

"All right."

Jo-el Boudreaux came out of his wife's store, got into his highway car, and roared away. He didn't look at us, but perhaps he didn't know that we were across the square. I said, "Does Sonnier, Melancon practice criminal law?"

"Yes."

"Have someone run a check on Rebenack and also on that guy LeRoy Bennett. I don't know René's last name, but he might be listed as a known associate if Bennett has a sheet. And run the paper on Milt Rossier, too." I thought about it. "And Edith Johnson."

Lucy said, "I guess you're serious."

"While you're doing that, I'll look up Jimmie Ray again."

She crossed her arms at me. "What does that mean?"

"We were interrupted last time, and Jimmie didn't have a chance to answer my questions. Maybe I'll go see him again and see if he's more forthcoming."

She held up a hand. "If you do anything illegal I don't want to know about it."

I grinned. "You won't."

Lucy made a big deal out of sighing, then got into her car and drove away.

The trip from Eunice to Jimmie Ray's office in Ville Platte took thirty-six minutes, but when I got there Jimmie Ray's Mustang was not in evidence and neither was Jimmie Ray. I double-parked behind the fish market and ran up to see, but the office was empty. I could have rifled his files again, but I didn't expect that there would be anything different in them from yesterday.

I drove to Jimmie Ray's duplex, circled the block, then eased to a stop. No Mustang here, either.

Jimmie's duplex was a shotgun with two doors coming off a common porch and the whole thing sandwiched on a long, narrow lot that was overgrown and kind of crummy beneath a dense oak canopy. I went to Jimmie Ray's door and pressed the bell. I pressed the bell again and knocked loudly, and again no one answered. No sounds came from the adjoining apartment. I went around the side of Jimmie Ray Rebenack's house as if I had been doing it every day for the past ten years and let myself in through his kitchen door. I called, "Hey, Jimmie, what's going on, man?"

Silence. Just think of all the fun Lucy Chenier was missing. And I couldn't even tell her about it.

Jimmie Ray's home smelled of fried food and dust. The kitchen was small. There were dishes piled in the sink and on the tile counter, and the grout between the tiles looked like it hadn't been scrubbed since 1947. A Formica dinette set with mismatched chairs filled the dining area, and a monstrously large overstuffed couch took up most of the living room. The couch was uphol-stered in a kind of black and white cowhide fabric, and there was a single matching chair and a square glass coffee table. The couch and the chair and the coffee table were too big for the room and ended up jammed together. A Sony home entertainment unit was stacked in the corner, and there wasn't enough room for that, ei-ther. Everything except the Sony looked low-end and cheesy, as if the local discount store had run a clearance sale: COMPLETE BACHELOR PAD—ON SALE NOW!!! "Taste," I said. "You can't develop it; you have to be born with it."

There were two rooms on the second floor, along with a bath and a linen closet. Jimmie Ray Rebenack was using the front room for his bedroom and the back room for a study. I went into the back room first. Two cardboard cartons sat against one wall, and a flimsy red card table with a single folding chair stood in the center of the room. A poster of the Bud Light models was pinned to the wall along with a couple of posters of bikinied women dressed up like commandos and holding machine guns. Ah, the bachelor life. One of the cardboard cartons held old copies of *Penthouse* and *Sports Illustrated* and a single VHS videotape called *Seymore Butts and The Love Swing*, but the other was where Jimmie Ray kept his bills and receipts. I lifted the stuff out, turned the stack upside down, and went through it back to front, returning the items to the box so that they'd be in their original order. I didn't think Jimmie Ray would be able to tell, but you never know. Guys like Jimmie Ray can surprise you.

There were Visa card bills going back eight months, and receipts for his office rent and the rent he paid on the duplex. The Visa charges were incidental. Most of the paperwork in the box had to do with buying the Mustang. He had purchased it used for $29,000 three months ago from an outfit called High Performance Motors in Alexandria, Louisiana. It had 8200 miles on the odometer at the time of purchase, and he had made the purchase for cash with a check drawn on his personal account. Three months ago, exactly two days before he bought the Mustang, he deposited $30,000 into his checking. Prior to that he held a balance of $416.12. Makes you wonder, doesn't it? Further on in the box there was warranty information and auto insurance papers and phone and utility bills. I didn't bother with the utilities. The phone bills went back five months, and during that time he had made seven phone calls to Los Angeles, California, at two different numbers. Two of the calls were lengthy.

I went out past the bathroom and into the front room and looked out at the street. Still clear. The front bedroom was as well appointed as the rest of the place, with an unmade oversized futon against the wall opposite a yard-sale dresser and a couple of lamps. Two thin pillows had been used as a backrest at the head of the futon, and a black sheet and a quilted spread were kicked to the side. The black sheet highlighted the hair and the lint and the crud in the bed nicely. That Jimmie Ray.

There was a closet beside the dresser, but I didn't have to go into the closet or look through the dresser or dig around under the futon to find what I was looking for. Jimmie Ray had what looked like the entirety of the sealed state files on the relinquishment of Marla Sue Johnson and the adoption of Judith Marie Taylor, and he had left them scattered on the bed. There were nine separate documents, at least two of which appeared to be originals, and all of the documents were complete. They were mixed with more articles and clippings about Jodi Taylor, and with yellow legal pages of what were probably Jimmie Ray Rebenack's handwritten notes. I whistled between my teeth and knew that I could not leave it here. Oh, Jimmie. How'd you get this stuff?

Maybe Jimmie Ray Rebenack wasn't the world's worst private investigator after all.

I gathered everything together, went back into the other room for the phone bills, then let myself out and drove back to the motel. Jimmie would know that someone had been in his house and he would probably know it was me, but if things played out the way I thought they might, Jimmie and I would be discussing these things soon enough.

I phoned Lucy Chenier at her office, but she wasn't back yet. I told Darlene to have her call me as soon as she returned, and Darlene said that she would. I hung up and went through what I'd found. As near as I could tell, everything was there. All of the documents were either original or were new clean copies of the originals. The original birth certificate showing Pamela Johnson as the mother of Marla Sue Johnson was attached to the complete original document showing that the Johnsons had relinquished all rights to the child to the state of Louisiana. A Louisiana State Department of Social Services document showed that Steven Edward Taylor and Cecelia Burke Taylor, lawfully wedded man and wife, were adopting the child known as one Marla Sue Johnson. A Louisiana juvenile-court document showed that Marla Sue Johnson's name was henceforth changed to Judith Marie Taylor. Each of the documents had a file and case number. The handwritten notes were mostly about Jodi Taylor and were probably culled from magazine articles: where she was born, her birth date, the name of her studio and agency and personal manager. Edith Boudreaux's name and address and phone were written on the back of one of the sheets. Jimmie Ray had been to see her, all right. On another sheet the name LEON WILLIAMS was written in big block letters and was the only name I didn't recognize. Six phone numbers were scrawled in no particular order on two of the sheets, two of them with Los Angeles area codes. The name "Sandi" had been written a half dozen times around the page. I checked the numbers against the numbers from the phone bill, and the numbers matched. I picked up the phone and dialed one of the Los Angeles numbers, thinking maybe I'd get someone named Sandi. A young man answered, "Markowitz Management. May I help you?"

"Jesus Christ."

"Pardon me, sir?"

"Is this Sid Markowitz's office?"

"It is, sir. May I help you?"

I didn't know what to say.

"Sir?"

"Does someone named Leon Williams work there?"

"No, sir."

"How about someone named Sandi?"

"No, sir. Who's calling, please?"

I said, "Tell Sid it's Elvis Cole, the Lied-to Detective."

"Pardon me?"

I hung up and dialed the other L.A. number. A young woman's voice said, "Jodi Taylor's office."

I went through it again. No Leon Williams. No Sandi. I hung up.

In the past three months, Jimmie Ray Rebenack had made seven calls to Sid Markowitz, one of the calls lasting almost an hour and one of the calls lasting thirty-five minutes. They were lengthy calls implying meaningful conversation. The longest call was made just three days before Jimmie Ray Rebenack deposited $30,000 in his checking account. My, my.

I put down the phone and stretched out on the floor and thought about things. A large monetary payoff seemed to imply the "B" word. But if Jodi Taylor was in fact being blackmailed, why not tell me that and hire me to find out who was doing it? Of course, since Sid had spent so much time on the phone with Jimmie Ray, it looked as if they already knew who was doing it and, besides that, what was there to blackmail her with? That she was adopted? That had already been in *People*. Jodi Taylor spoke of it publicly and often. Maybe they wanted me to get their money back. That seemed reasonable. Then again, it would seem even more reasonable if they had told me the score. I went back to the phone and called Sid Markowitz again. The same young man answered. I said, "This is Elvis Cole. May I speak with Sid?"

"I'm sorry, Mr. Cole, but he's not in." Great.

"Would you have him call me, please?"

"Of course."

I left the motel number and I called Jodi Taylor again, but she, too, was unavailable. I was getting angry at having been lied to and I wanted to know what was going on. I got up and paced around the room, and then I called Lucy's office again. Still not in. Nobody was in. Maybe I should leave and then I wouldn't be in, either. I looked up Jimmie Ray's office number, dialed, and hung up on the twenty-sixth ring. Another one. I decided to go back to Jimmie Ray's house and wait for him.

I gathered together the documents and the articles and hid them between the mattress and box spring. The Dan Wesson was too big to wear at my ankle, so I clipped the holster on the inside of my waistband and pulled out my shirt to hang over it. Neatness counts, but bullets often count more.

I had locked my room and was getting into my car when LeRoy Bennett and his sidekick René drove up. LeRoy showed me a Colt Government .45. "Get in," he said. "We goin' f' a little ride."

I guess Jimmie Ray would have to wait.

I said, "Well, well. Bill and Hillary."

LeRoy lowered his gun. "Knew we'd see you again, podnuh." He tilted his head toward the backseat. "C'mon. Don't make ol' René have to get out."

René was in the backseat. His eyes were filmy and moved independently of each other, and I was struck again with the sense that maybe he was here with us, but maybe not. I said, "What if I won't go?"

LeRoy laughed. "Knock off da bullshit and les' go."

I said, "Tell me something, is René for real or did someone build him out of spare parts?"

René shifted and the Polara squeaked on its springs. He had to tip in at close to four hundred pounds. Maybe more. LeRoy said, "Get in front wi' me. René, he won't fit up front. He ride in back."

I got in and they brought me south through Ville Platte and down along the highway to Milt Rossier's Crawfish Farm. We drove slowly up between the ponds and along the oyster shell road past a couple of long low cinder block buildings. The buildings had great sliding doors and the doors were open and you could see inside. Hispanic men driving little tractors towed open tanks alive with wiggling catfish into the near building. There, Hispanic women working at large flat tables scooped up the catfish, lopped off their heads, then gutted and skinned them with thin knives. Other men drove trucks filled with crawfish into the far building where women washed and sorted and bagged the crawfish in heavy burlap bags. With the windows down and no air conditioning, the crunching oyster shells were loud in the car and sounded like breaking bones. Jimmie Ray Rebenack's Mustang was parked on the far side of the processing sheds, and Jimmie Ray was standing with Milt Rossier at one of the ponds. LeRoy parked by the nearest building and said, "Here we go."

We got out and went over to them.

Milt Rossier was in his early sixties, with blotched crepey skin and cheap clothes and a gut that hung well out over his belt. The short stub of a cigar was fixed in one side of his mouth, and his hands were pale and freckled with liver spots. He wore a long-sleeved shirt with the sleeves down and cuffed at his wrists, and he was wearing the Panama hat again. Sensitive to the sun, no doubt. Milt said, "My name is Milt Rossier. They tell me you're some kinda private investigator."

"Did they?" René walked past us to the edge of the pond and stared into the water.

"Mm-hmm." The cigar shifted around in the side of his mouth. "What you doin' heah?"

"LeRoy brought me."

Rossier frowned. "I don' mean heah, I mean in my town. You been makin' waves in my town, and I want it to stop. You got no bidniss heah."

I said, "Wrong, Milt. I do have business here."

Jimmie Ray said, "He was with some woman, Milt. Some kinda attorney." I looked at Jimmie Ray and grinned. He couldn't have known that unless Sheriff Jo-el Boudreaux had told him.

I said, "I've been trying to find you, Jimmie Ray. I've been in your house."

Jimmie Ray looked at me as if I'd just shot him in the foot, but then he turned a very bright red. He said, "Well, we'll see about that. That ain't why you're here."

René suddenly dropped to his knees at the edge of the pond and reached into the water. He moved faster than I would have thought possible for such a large man. One moment out of the water, the next in. He lifted out something black and wiggling and bit it. The wiggling stopped.

LeRoy yelled, "Goddammit, René. You stop that!"

René dropped what was left back into the pond.

"Spit it out."

René spit something red and black and glistening into the grass. He walked a few feet away and sat down. LeRoy squinted after him, then hurried over for a closer look. "Goddammit, he's sittin' in red ants. Get up, *fou!*" René lumbered to his feet, and LeRoy brushed at his pants. *"Fi de chien! Emplate!"*

Milt Rossier shook his head, then took out a handkerchief and wiped his brow. It had to be a hundred degrees in the sun, and the sweat seeped out but had nowhere to go with the humidity. He said, "That boy is a trial."

"I'll bet."

He looked back at me. "You know anythin' about me, son?"

"I can guess."

"Don't let's guess. I got business interests all over this parish, and I have to protect those interests. It's the dollah, you see?"

"Sure."

"Someone from outta town comes in, diggin' aroun', that can push things outta kilter." He took out the cigar, examined it, then put it back in his mouth. "Why you heah, son?"

"I'm here because you're blackmailing my client."

He stared at me, and when he did I could tell that he didn't know. I looked at Jimmie Ray, who was squirming like something from one of the ponds. It wasn't Rossier; it was Jimmie Ray, all by his lonesome. I said, "I'm here because this asshole is black-mailing a woman in California."

Jimmie Ray shrieked, "That's a goddamned lie!" He waved a hand at Milt Rossier. "That's pure bullshit, Milt! He's makin' this shit up!"

"No," I said. "I'm not." I looked at Jimmie Ray. "Three hours ago I broke into your house and found documents there relating to the birth of my client. I also found evidence linking you to a series of conversations with my client, predating a thirty-thousand-dollar deposit into your checking account." I glanced back at Milt Rossier. "I don't know what this has to do with whatever you've got going, but I don't give a damn. All I care about is how it affects my client."

Jimmie Ray said, "Oh, man, what a bare-faced liar!" Laughing like he couldn't believe these lies.

Milt Rossier swiveled the Panama toward Jimmie Ray, his eyes hard black dots. "I thought you were workin' for me, son. You out on your own?"

"This is bullshit, Milt. Who you gonna believe, me or this turd?"

Rossier squinted harder. "You bring me something and I pay for it, it's mine."

Jimmie Ray looked greasy and he kept shooting glances at René. "Hell, yes, it's yours. This sumbitch is jus' tryin' to wea-sel!"

Rossier shook his head and sighed. "Goddammit."

"I swear, Milt. I'm tellin' you the truth."

LeRoy came back and slapped Jimmie Ray on the back of his head, knocking the pompadour sideways. *"Emplate!"*

Jimmie said, "Hey!"

Milt Rossier spit at the weeds, then headed for the near build-ing. "Y'all c'mon. Bring'm, LeRoy. René! You, too, now."

We followed Rossier between the two buildings and out to a small circular pond surrounded by a low wire fence. LeRoy picked up a two-by-four as we walked. The banks of the pond were muddy and scummed with something green and slimy, probably runoff from the processing sheds. Rossier got there first and waited impatiently for the rest of us to catch up. He gestured at the pond with his cigar. "René. You get Luther. Be careful, now."

I said, "Luther?"

Jimmie Ray shook his finger at me and laughed. "Yo' ass is grass now, boy."

René stepped over the fence, knelt at the edge of the little pool, and slapped the water. He slapped three or four times, and then something moved beneath the surface and the water swirled. René jumped in up to his knees and his hands plunged down and caught something that made him stagger. He found his balance and then his face went red with strain and he lifted out a snapping turtle that had to be three feet across and weigh almost two hundred pounds. It was dark and primordial with a shell like tank armor and a great horned head and a monstrous beak. The head twisted and snapped and tried to reach René, but couldn't. Its mouth was almost a foot across, and every time it snapped there was a sharp clicking sound, like a ruler rapping on a desk. René trudged up out of the water, stepped across the fence, and put Luther down. When he did, the turtle pulled its feet and head up under its shell. The head was so big it didn't fit and its snout was exposed. LeRoy was grinning like a jack-o'-lantern. He waved the two-by-four in front of the turtle. The big head flashed out and the big jaws snapped and the board splintered. LeRoy beamed. "That Luther's somethin', huh?"

Jimmie Ray shook his finger at me some more. "We'll see who's lyin' now."

Milt Rossier said something in French, and René grabbed Jimmie Ray and jerked him toward the turtle. Jimmie Ray said, "Hey!"

Jimmie Ray tried to pull away from René, but he didn't have any better luck than Luther. René carried him by the back of the neck and the belt, and pushed him down on the ground just outside of Luther's range. You could see the beady turtle eyes following the action from up under the shell. Jimmie was yelling, "Goddamn, Milt, stop it! Please!" His eyes were big, and he had gone as white as typing paper.

René let go of Jimmie's belt and grabbed his right forearm and forced his right hand toward the turtle. Jimmie Ray screamed.

Milt said, "Now you tell me true, son. You using my information to blackmail this gal?"

"I swear I ain't, Milt. I swear."

"René."

René forced the hand closer. Luther's eyes blinked, and the big jaws parted.

Milt said, "Try again, son."

I took a half-step forward. "That's enough, old man. Make him stop."

Milt said, "LeRoy," and LeRoy pointed the big .45 at me. LeRoy was grinning. Milt shook his finger at me. "You jes' sit tight." He stepped closer to Jimmie Ray and squatted beside him. "Ol' Luther looks like he's anxious, boy. You better tell me."

Jimmie Ray was babbling. "I didn't see what it'd hurt. It didn't have nothing to do with you or us and I thought I could just make a little extra cash please Milt please make'm stop I never woulda done it if I thought you'd be mad I swear to Christ!"

"All right, René. He's done." Jimmie Ray Rebenack had peed his pants.

René lifted Jimmie Ray out of harm's way. The wet stain spread across the seat of his pants and down his legs. Milt chewed on the cigar and stared toward the buildings. His eyes were small and hard and not a great deal different from the turtle's. He moved the cigar at me. "The only reason you're heah is because of this blackmail thing?"

"That's it."

Milt chewed on the cigar some more. "René, put ol' Luther back."

René put Luther back in the pond. Luther slipped beneath the water, and the water grew still. Milt said, "We feed ol' Luther there catfish heads. Had a fella from LSU out here once said Luther might be better'n a century old."

Jimmie Ray was on his knees with his face in his hands. I felt embarrassed and ashamed both for him and for me. Milt Rossier went over to Jimmie and patted his shoulder. "You see what dishonesty gets fo' ya? You go behin' my back, now this fella's heah. You see where ya get?"

"I'm sorry, Milt. I swear to God I am."

Milt Rossier looked over at me with the Luther eyes. He stared at me, thinking, until LeRoy said, "He was with some woman, Milt."

Milt spit. "Yeah. I guess so." Disappointed, as if he had come to a serious decision about something, only now to change his mind. He patted Jimmie Ray's shoulder again, then helped him up. "C'mon, now, Jimmie Ray. Get up and stop blubberin'. You get yourself on outta heah."

Jimmie Ray said, "I didn't think I was doin' anythin' wrong, Milt. I swear to Christ."

"We'll jus' forget about it. Go on, now."

Jimmie Ray looked like a man who'd just won Lotto, like he couldn't believe that Milt Rossier was giving him a pass on this one. Milt Rossier said, "Goddammit, get outta my sight."

Jimmie Ray scrambled back to his Mustang, and the Mustang's rear end fishtailed hard as he drove away.

Milt shook his head, then turned back to me. "You go on back where you come from and tell your woman everythin's over with. What we got down here, it don' have nothin' to do with her, and nothin' to do with you, either. You understand that?"

"Sure. You want me to go home. You want me to stop stirring things up?"

He nodded, looked at the cigar again, then tossed it in the pond. It floated for a second, sending out perfect circles, and then the water exploded and the cigar was gone.

Milt Rossier made a little dismissive gesture and walked away. "LeRoy, you see this fella gets back real safe, you hear?"

LeRoy said that he would.

René and LeRoy brought me back to the motel in the gold Polara and let me out in the parking lot. I watched them leave, then went to my room and tried to let myself in, but I couldn't get the key in the lock. I tried as hard as I could, and then I sat on the sidewalk with my hands between my knees and pressed my knees together to try to make myself stop shaking. I pressed for a very long time, and finally the shaking stopped.

I double-locked the door and showered, letting the hot water beat into me until my skin was red and burning and I began to feel better about things.

I was out of the shower and getting dressed when Lucy Chenier returned my call. She said, "Sorry it's taken so long. I was trying to find out about Milt Rossier."

"I just came back from Milt's. Before that, I broke into Jimmie Ray Rebenack's home and found what I believe to be the entire state file on Jodi's adoption. I found other things, too, and I learned some things at Rossier's that we need to talk about." Maybe there was something in my voice that the shower hadn't washed away. She didn't say anything about the break-in.

"Can you drive back to Baton Rouge this evening?"

"Yes."

"I have to leave the office soon to be home for Ben, but you could meet me there and we could have dinner. Is that all right?"

"That would be fine."

Lucy gave me directions to her home and then we hung up. I dressed, then got the papers together from under the mattress, and drove back to Baton Rouge. I brought flowers.

The late afternoon was clear and bright when I found my way through a gracious residential area east of Louisiana State University to Lucy's home. The streets were narrow, but the houses were large and set back on wide rolling lawns amid lush azaleas and oaks and magnolia trees, worthy digs for doctors and lawyers and tenured professors from LSU. I slowed several times for families on bicycles and young couples with strollers or elderly people enjoying a walk. Two girls and their dad were on one lawn, trying to launch a blue kite with no breeze; on another, an elderly man sat on a glider, gently swaying in the evening shade beneath an oak tree. Everything seemed relaxed and wonderful, the ideal environment in which to escape the realities of lying clients, enraged snapping turtles, and the loneliness of being far from home. Maybe I should move here.

Lucy Chenier lived in a brick colonial with a circular rock drive and a large pecan tree in the front yard. A knotted rope hung from the tree and, higher in the branches, several boards were nailed together into a small platform. Somebody's treehouse.

I crunched into the drive, got out with the flowers and the documents, and went to the front door. When I had stopped for the flowers I had picked up a folder in which to hide the documents. Can't very well be seen sneaking stolen documents into an attorney's home. Might get her disbarred. The door opened before I reached it and a boy with curly brown hair looked out. He said, "Hey."

"Hey. My name's Elvis. Are you Ben?" He was looking at the flowers.

"Yes, sir. My mom's on the phone, but she says you can come in."

"Thanks."

He opened the door wider and let me in. He was still with the flowers. Suspicious. "Are those for my mom?"

"Unh-hunh. Think she'll like 'm?"

Shrug. "I dunno." Can't give stray guys too much encouragement, I guess.

From somewhere in the house Lucy called, "I'm on with the office. I'll be off in a minute."

I called back. "Take your time."

Ben stood straight and tall in cut-off jeans shorts and a gray LSU Athletic Department T-shirt. Every kid in Louisiana was probably issued an LSU T-shirt at birth. He led me through a spacious home that was neat and orderly, but still lived-in and comfortable and clearly feminine, with plenty of photographs in delicate frames and pastel colors and plants. The entry led into the family room and the kitchen. Everything was open and casual, with the family room flowing into the dining area, which looked out French doors across a brick patio and a large backyard. Tennis trophies filled the shelves of a wall-sized entertainment center in the family room, but pictures of Ben and books and ceramic animals were crowding out the trophies. I liked that. Balance.

Ben leaned against the counter that separated the kitchen from the family room, watching me. I said, "You play tennis like your mom?"

He nodded.

"She's pretty good, huh?"

He nodded again.

"Can you beat her?"

"Sometimes." He cocked his head a little bit to the side and said, "Are you a detective?"

"Doesn't it show?"

He shook his head.

"I left my trench coat at the motel."

"What's a trench coat?"

Times change.

He said, "Is it fun?"

"Most of the time it's fun, but not always. You thinking about becoming a detective?"

He shook his head. "I want to be a lawyer like my dad."

I nodded. "That'd be good."

95

"He practices corporate law in Shreveport. He really goes for the jugular." I wondered where he'd heard that.

Lucy came through the family room and smiled at me. "Hi."

"Hi, yourself." I held out the flowers. Mr. Charming. "I didn't want to come empty-handed."

"Oh, they're lovely." Her eyes crinkled nicely when she took the flowers, and I flushed with a kind of pleasure that made me return her smile. She was wearing khaki hiking shorts and a loose white cotton top and sandals, and she seemed relaxed and comfortable in her home. Looking at her made me feel relaxed, too. "Let's put them in water."

Ben said, "Can I set the coals?"

"Not too many."

Ben ran out the back, slamming through the French doors. Someone had set up a Weber grill on the patio, and he went to work with the coals. Lucy said, "I picked up potato salad and cole slaw from the market. I thought we'd grill hamburgers since we're going to work. Something simple."

"Hamburgers are great."

"Would you like a glass of wine?"

"Please. That would be nice."

She took an unopened bottle of Sonoma-Cutre chardonnay from her refrigerator, offered it to me with a corkscrew, and asked if I'd mind opening it. She put out two wineglasses, then used kitchen shears to trim the flowers before placing them in a simple glass vase. I poured the wine. When the flowers were finished, she said, "They're absolutely lovely."

"Drab. Drab and plain next to you."

She laughed. "Tell me, do all men from Los Angeles come on this strong?"

"Only those of us with an absolute confidence in our abilities."

The laugh became a smile, then she put on the red reading glasses and motioned at the folder, jammed with the documents and handwritten notes and phone bills. "Why don't you tell me what happened while I see what we have?"

I went through everything that had happened since I'd last seen her, up to where René and LeRoy brought me to Milt's farm. I had arranged the papers with the state documents on top, so she saw those first. As I spoke, a vertical frown line appeared between her eyebrows and she no longer looked happy and relaxed. She said, "These are real. These are court-sealed documents. How could he get these?"

"I don't know."

"Illegally possessing these is a felony under state law. They're numbered and referenced, and I can have their authenticity checked, but these are real. These papers do in fact show that Jodi Taylor was born Marla Johnson. I can't believe he has these."

"Had."

Ben came in to tell us that the coals were ready to be fired and Lucy went outside to make sure he did it safely. I sat at the counter with my wine, watching them, and found myself smiling. Ben struck the big safety matches and tossed them on the coals while Lucy supervised. They looked comfortable and at ease with each other, and you could see Lucy in his features and in the confident way he carried himself. Reflections. When the flames were rising and the grill was in place, Lucy returned and smiled at me smiling at her. She said, "What?"

"You guys look good together. Happy. I like that."

She turned and looked at her son. He had left the grill and was climbing into a pecan tree. A knotted rope hung from the limbs, just like the tree in the front yard, but he didn't use the rope. She said, "You seem to have passed the test."

"What test?"

"He's leaving us alone. He's very protective of me."

"Does he have to guard you often?"

She looked smug. "Often enough, thank you." She took two plates from the Sub-Zero, one with hamburger patties and the other with sliced onions and tomatoes and lettuce, both covered with Saran Wrap, and put them out to warm. She returned to the file, now skimming Rebenack's handwritten notes. "Who's Leon Williams?"

"I don't know, but you can tell from what's written that these are the notes Rebenack made when he was digging into Jodi's past, so Williams might be significant."

Lucy made a note on the legal pad. "I've got a friend at the Baton Rouge Police Department. I'll see if they have anything."

"Okay. Here's where it gets worse." I showed her Jimmie Ray's phone bills. I pointed out the long distance calls. "Do you recognize these phone numbers?"

She shook her head. "They're calls to Los Angeles."

"This is Sid. This is Jodi. Rebenack had at least seven conversations with Sid Markowitz over the past five months."

Lucy didn't move for a very long time, and then she left the kitchen. She came back a few minutes later with a leather datebook jammed with notes and papers and business cards. She opened it to a phone index and compared the numbers she found there with the numbers on the phone bill. She shook her head. "Sid never mentioned this to me."

"Nor to me." I pointed out the longest call. "Three days after this call Rebenack deposited thirty thousand dollars into a checking account. He used the money to buy a car."

"Do you think he's blackmailing them?"

"He admitted it." I told her about Jimmie Ray and Milt and Luther.

"But blackmail doesn't make sense. Jodi's never kept her adoption a secret, and even if she had, so what? What could he blackmail them with?"

I spread my hands. "I guess that's what we still have to figure out, and it doesn't end with Jimmie Ray Rebenack. Milt has something going on, too, and I'm also guessing that it involves the Boudreauxs. That's why the sheriff was out at the crawfish farm. That's why the Boudreauxs are scared."

Lucy brought her address book to the kitchen phone and stabbed in a number. She puffed out her cheeks and blew a hiss of breath while she waited. "This is Lucille Chenier calling for Mr. Markowitz. May I speak with him please?" She walked with the phone in a small circle. "You must have him call me as soon as possible. It's urgent. Let me give you my home number." She left the number, then hung up and went through it again with Jodi Taylor. No luck there, either.

I said, "I phoned them too. They haven't gotten back to me."

She shook her head. "I can't believe they didn't tell us. We've got an Evangeline Parish sheriff involved with a convicted felon and possible blackmail, and no one tells us. Were we hired to uncover information that was already known?"

"Looks that way."

She took off her glasses, rubbed at her eyes, then assembled the papers and put them aside. "Enough work, Mr. Cole. More wine."

She held out her glass, and I poured.

When the coals were ready we brought out the burgers and put them on the grill. They hissed nicely, and soon the silky twilight air was filled with the smell of cooking meat. She had mixed ground sirloin with Worcestershire sauce, and it smelled wonderful. Somewhere a dog barked, and cicadas were making their buzz-saw racket. Ben was still in the tree, hanging upside-down. Lucy called, "Ben, it won't be long. Wash your hands."

Ben dropped out of the tree, but didn't go in. "Can I have a cheeseburger?"

Lucy nodded. "Sure. Elvis?"

"You bet."

She handed me the spatula and went in for the cheese. When she was gone I looked at Ben and caught him grinning at me. I said, "What?"

"She likes you."

"She does?"

He nodded. "I heard her talking to her friend, Marsha. She called you Studly Do-Right." He giggled.

I looked in at his mother and then I looked back at the hamburgers. "She probably wouldn't like it that you told me."

"Why not?"

"Women tell other women things that they don't tell men. It's a law they have."

He giggled some more.

Lucy came back and put cheese on the hamburgers, then covered the grill so that the cheese would melt. Ben and I stood with straight faces until Ben couldn't stand it anymore and giggled. I concentrated on the burgers, hoping that they wouldn't overcook. Ben giggled harder. Lucy said, "What?"

I said, "Nothing." Ben giggled harder.

Lucy smiled. "Hey! What were you guys saying?"

Ben giggled louder and I looked at Lucy. "Studly?"

Lucy turned a deep rich red. "*Ben!*"

Ben howled. I said, "It wasn't Ben. I am Elvis Cole, the world's greatest detective. I know all and see all, and there can be no secrets from the All-Seeing Eye."

Lucy said, "I hate you both."

Ben put out his hand and I gave him a low-five. Masculine superiority strikes again.

Lucy said, "Benjamin. *Wash.*"

Ben ran into the house, cackling, and Lucy shook her head. "That little traitor."

I said, "Studly."

She waved the spatula at me. "I was just being cute. Don't get any ideas."

"I won't."

"Fine."

"But what do I do with the ones I've got?"

She closed her eyes, maybe envisioning the line we shouldn't cross. "You're really quite something, aren't you?"

"Most people think so."

She opened her eyes and looked at the sky. "Oh, God."

"Well, no. But close."

Lucy laughed, and I laughed, too.

When the cheese was melted we brought the burgers inside and ate them with the potato salad and cole slaw and the rest of the Sonoma-Cutre. Ben ate quickly, then asked to be excused and raced to the TV so that he could watch *Star Trek—The Next Generation*. Lucy called after him, "Not too loud!"

I said, "Won't bother me. I like *Star Trek*."

Ben yelled, "Cool!"

Lucy shook her head and rolled her eyes. "Oh, Studly." She tilted her glass toward me. "Pour."

So we watched *TNG*. It was the one where you follow the android, Data, through a twenty-four-hour period in his life, most of which is spent attempting to comprehend the vagaries of the humans around him. The fun comes in watching the logical, emotionless Data try to make sense of the human condition, which is akin to trying to make sense of the senseless. He never quite gets it, but he always keeps trying, writing endless programs for his android brain, trying to make the calculus of human behavior add up. When you think about it, that is not so different from what I do.

When *Star Trek* was over I said that I had better be going. I told Ben good night, and Lucy walked me out. I thought that she'd stop at the door, but she didn't. It was a clear night, and pleasant. She said, "Will you drive back to Ville Platte tonight?"

"Yes. There are still plenty of questions and Jimmie Ray might be willing to answer them."

She nodded. "Okay. I'll call you there tomorrow as soon as I have something."

"Great." A man and a woman and an Akita walked past. The Akita was a big brindle pinto, and watched me suspiciously as his people nodded hello. I said, "Good-looking dog."

The man said, "Thanks."

Lucy and I stood silently until they were gone, vanishing gently in the humid dark.

We looked at each other. "This is the second time you've fed me. Thanks again."

"It's an ugly job, but somebody's gotta do it."

We both grinned. I said, "Oh, man. Dueling comedians."

She looked at me carefully and said, "I have a good time with you."

I nodded. "Me, too."

Then she said, "Oh, damn." She leaned forward, kissed me, then pulled away. "I've just kissed a man who ate dog. Yuck."

She ran back into her house.

I guess there are lines, but sometimes lines bend.

The night canopy above the Atchafalaya Basin was velvet black as I drove through the sugar cane and the sweet potato fields and the living earth back to Ville Platte. A woman I had known for approximately four days had given me what was maybe the world's shortest kiss, and I could not stop smiling about it. A lawyer, no less.

I folded up the grin and put it away and rolled down the window and breathed. Come to your senses, Cole. The air was warm and rich and alive with the smells of water and loam soil and blossoming plants. The sky was a cascade of stars. I started singing. I stopped singing and glanced in the mirror. Smiling, again. I let the smile stay and drove on. To hell with senses.

When I got back to Ville Platte there was a message from Jimmie Ray on the motel's voice mail system, his voice tight and sounding scared. "This is Jimmie Ray Rebenack and you really put me in a world of hurt, podnuh." You could hear him breathing into the phone. The breathing was strained. "It's twenty after six right now, and I need to talk to ya. I'm at home." He said the number and hung up.

ROBERT CRAIS

It was now ten fifty-two, and there were no other messages in the voice mail.

I dialed his number and got a busy signal. I took off my shirt, then went into the bathroom to brush my teeth and wash my face. I dialed his number again and again got a busy signal. I dialed his office, got his answering machine, and hung up without leaving a message. I redialed his home. Busy. I called the operator. "I need an emergency break-in."

"Number, please?"

I gave her the number. She went away for a little bit and then she came back. "I'm sorry, sir, but that number seems to be off the hook."

"He's not on the line?"

"No, sir. The phone's probably just off the hook. It happens all the time."

I put my shirt back on and drove once more to Jimmie Ray's house. A couple of houses on his street were still bright with life, but most of the street was dark and still. Jimmie Ray's Mustang was parked at the curb in a dapple of moonshadows, and the front upstairs window of his duplex was lighted. The bedroom. Probably with a woman. They had probably been thrashing around and had knocked the phone out of its cradle. I left my car on the street, went to his front door, and rang the bell. I could hear the buzzer go off inside, but that was it. No giggles. No people scrambling for their clothes. I rang the bell twice more, then went around the side of the house and let myself in through the back exactly as I had twelve hours ago.

The ground floor was dark, and the kitchen still smelled of fried food, but now there was a sharp, ugly smell beneath it. I moved across the kitchen and stood in the darkness, listening. Light from the upstairs filtered down the stairwell and put a faint yellow glow in Jimmie Ray Rebenack's bachelor-pad living room. I said, "Oh, Jimmie. You goof."

The imitation zebra skin couch was tipped over on its back and

104

Jimmie Ray Rebenack was lying across it, head down and arms out, Joey Buttafucco boots pointing toward the ceiling. The living room phone had been knocked off its hook when the couch went over. I took out the Dan Wesson, held it along my thigh, and went past Jimmie Ray to the stairs and listened again. Nothing. I went back to Jimmie Ray and looked without touching him. His neck was bent at a profound and unnatural angle, as if the vertebrae there had been separated by some tremendous force. His neck didn't get that way by tripping over the couch or by falling down the stairs. It took a car wreck to do that to a neck. Or a four-story fall. His face was dark with lividity, and the big, stiff pompadour was crushed and matted on one side, the way it might be if someone with large hands had grabbed his head and pushed very hard to make the neck fail. René.

I went upstairs and looked in the two rooms, but everything was pretty much as it had been twelve hours ago, the magazines and posters still in their places in the back room, the bed still rumpled in the front room. The pants he had worn at Rossier's crawfish farm were soaking in the upstairs lavatory. Getting out the pee stains. The front bedroom's light was on, and the room showed no evidence of a search or other invasion. No one had come to search. No one had come to steal. Whoever had been here had come only to murder Jimmie Ray Rebenack, and they had probably done it not so very long after he'd called me. Maybe Jimmie Ray had finally realized that he was in over his head and had called for help. That was possible. A lot of things are possible until you're dead.

The message counter on Jimmie Ray's answering machine showed three messages. The first was a young woman who did not identify herself and who said that she missed Jimmie Ray and wanted to speak with him. The second message was from a guy named Phil who wanted to know if Jimmie Ray would like to pick up a couple of days' mechanic work. Phil left a number and said he needed to hear by Friday. The third message was the young woman again, only this time she sounded irritated. She said she thought that Jimmie Ray was rotten for not calling her, but then her voice softened and said she really did wish he'd call because she really, really missed him. She whispered, "I love you, Jimmie," and then she hung up. There were no other messages. So long, Jimmie Ray.

I left the upstairs light on and the rooms as I'd found them and Jimmie Ray Rebenack's body in its frozen position across the overturned couch. I wiped the kitchen doorknob and the places on the jamb I might have touched, and then I let myself out and went around to the front porch and wiped the doorbell button. I called the police from a pay phone outside a Winn-Dixie supermarket. I gave them Jimmie Ray's address twice, then said that there was a body on the premises. I hung up, wiped the phone, and went back to the motel where I called Lucy Chenier. Two hours ago I'd been feeling pretty good about things.

Lucy answered on the second ring, her voice clear the way it might be if she were awake and working. I said, "Rebenack's been murdered."

"Oh, Jesus God. How?"

"I think it was Rossier, but I can't be sure. I think he paid off Jimmie for the double-dealing."

She blew a loud breath. "Did you call the police?"

"Yes, but I didn't identify myself."

"They'll want to speak with you."

"If I talk with them I'll bring in Jodi Taylor, and I don't want to do that. Do you see?"

She said, "Oh, my God."

"Do you see?"

It took her a few seconds to answer. "I understand. What are you going to do?"

"Wait for you to find out about Leon Williams."

She paused again. "Are you all right, Elvis?"

"Sure."

"You sound upset."

"I'm fine."

"If you want to talk, I'm here."

"I know. Call me when you find out about Leon Williams."

We hung up, and in that moment my little motel room there in Ville Platte, Louisiana, became more empty than any room I have ever known. There were the sounds of crickets and frogs and the rumble of a passing truck, but the sounds seemed to heighten the emptiness rather than fill it. The cheap motel furniture stood out in a kind of stark clarity, as if everything were magnified through some great invisible lens, and the emptiness became oppressive.

I turned off the light and went out into the parking lot and breathed the warm air. I had come two thousand miles believing that I had been hired to uncover a woman's medical history, and now a man was dead. He was a goof and an extortionist, but somewhere near his final moment a young woman had called and said that she loved him. I wondered if he had played back the message. Jimmie Ray Rebenack was just the kind of guy who would have missed the message, or, if he'd heard it, wouldn't have listened. Guys like Jimmie Ray never quite learn that love doesn't visit often, and that even when it comes, it can always change its mind and walk away. You never know.

I went back inside and double-locked the door and wedged one of the flimsy motel chairs under the knob. The locks and the chair wouldn't keep out a guy like René, but there was always the Dan Wesson.

I lay on the bed and tried to sleep, but sleep, like love, is not always there when you want it.

14

The phone in my room rang at 9:14 the next morning as I stepped out of the shower. I had been up early, eating breakfast at the diner across from what used to be Jimmie Ray's office and waiting for the morning paper. A couple of police cars had been outside the fish market, but when the paper came there was nothing in it about Jimmie Ray's murder. Not enough lead time, I guess. When I answered the phone, Lucy Chenier said, "I spoke with my friend at BRPD."

"Could he identify Leon Williams?" I toweled off as I listened.

"Yes. Leon Williams was killed by a single gunshot to the head on May 12, thirty-six years ago, in Ville Platte."

"Sonofagun."

"There was an investigation by the Ville Platte police and the Evangeline Parish Sheriff's Department, but there were no suspects and no one was arrested for the crime. The case currently resides in the unsolved homicide file."

"My first move in Ville Platte was to scan through the microfiche at the local library. The May films were missing."

"Do you think it's connected?"

"Maybe. Maybe there's something in the local news coverage that someone didn't want us to see."

She didn't say anything for a time. "There's LSU. The School of Journalism keeps an extensive library of state papers. You might be able to find it there."

"That sounds good. I'll check it out."

She paused again. "Have you heard anything about Mr. Rebenack?"

I told her about the cops at his office and the local papers. I left out the part about wedging the chair against the door because I was scared.

She said, "Is there any way they can connect you to him?"

"I move with the silence of a stalking leopard. I leave less evidence than a passing shadow. I am invisible as is the breeze."

She sighed. "Yes, well, we have an able staff of criminal attorneys should you need us."

"Hey, the fragile male ego needs constant reinforcement, not cheap humor."

"My rates are anything but cheap, Mr. Cole, I assure you." Then she said, "I enjoyed myself last night, Elvis. I hope we can get together again."

"I could probably be there in thirty minutes. Faster, if I run down the highway naked."

She laughed. "That would probably be worth seeing, but I think you should concentrate on Leon Williams."

" 'Probably'?"

"Ah, the male ego is indeed a fragile beast."

Lucy hung up. I got the LSU School of Journalism's number from Information, called, and spoke with a woman who sounded to be in her fifties. I explained what I wanted and she told me that she'd have to connect me with the journalism library. A man came on the line. "May I help you?"

"I'm looking for the Ville Platte *Gazette*." I told him the year and the month. "Would you guys have that on microfiche?"

"Can you hold while I check?"

"Sure."

He came back on the line maybe thirty seconds later. Fast checker. "We have it. Would you like me to put it aside?"

"Please." I gave him my name and told him that I was coming from Ville Platte but that I would be there directly. He said fine. Maybe things were looking up. Maybe I was getting to the bottom of this and, once reaching the bottom, would bounce over the top. Of course, reaching the bottom can sometimes be painful, but we try not to think of that. Imagine an egg.

One hour and ten minutes later I drove through a wide gate that said Louisiana State University. A young guy in an information kiosk gave me a map of the university, pointed out the journalism building, then told me to park in a big lot by the football stadium. I left the car where he told me, then walked back between Tiger stadium and the basketball arena where Pistol Pete Maravich used to rack up forty-four points a game. The House that Pete Built. It was a pretty campus with green lawns and curved walkways, and I remembered once hearing the radio broadcast of an LSU basketball game in which Maravich scored fifty-five points against Alabama. It was in 1970, and I was in the army at Fort Benning, Georgia. Ranger School. A guy in my platoon named James Munster was from Alabama and loved basketball. His parents had recorded the game and sent it to him and six of us listened to the tape on a Saturday night. Jimmy Munster loved the Crimson Tide and he hated LSU, but could only shake his head at the miracle that was Pistol Pete Maravich, saying, "What can you do? That guy owns the basket. What can you do?" Seven months later Specialist Fourth Class James Munster died in a VC ambush while on a long-range reconnaissance patrol just south of the Cambodian highlands. He was eighteen years old. I still remember the score of that game. LSU 90, Alabama 83.

A clutch of coeds in biking shorts and T-shirts cut so that you could see their midriffs passed and smiled at me, and I smiled

back. Southern belles. A little sign saying TENNIS STADIUM
pointed past the arena, and I thought maybe it'd be fun to see
where Lucy had played, but then I thought it might be more fun
if she were with me to give me the tour. Have to ignore the coeds,
though.

I walked up a little hill and past a couple of stately buildings
and into Memorial Hall, also known as the School of Journalism.
The kid in the kiosk had told me that the journalism library was
in the basement, so I found the stairs, went down, and wandered
around for twenty minutes before I located the right door. Professional detection at its finest.

A bald guy in his early thirties was sitting with a placard that
said RESEARCH. He looked up from a textbook and said, "May I
help you?"

I told him that I had called a little while ago. I told him it was
about the Ville Platte *Gazette.*

He said, "Oh, yeah. I've got it right here." He had a little box
on his desk. "You a student?"

"Nope."

"I'll need your driver's license, and I'll need you to sign right
here. You can use any of the cubicles down that aisle."

I gave him my driver's license, signed where he wanted, then
took the single spool of microfiche film to the first cubicle and
threaded it into the projector. On May 13, there was a short article on page 6 stating that a male Negro named Leon Cassius Williams, age 14, had been found floating at the south bank of Bayou
Maurapaus by two kids fishing for mudcats. Sheriff Andrus Duplasus stated that the cause of death was a single .38 caliber gunshot wound to the head, and that there were no leads at present.
The article ended by saying that Leon Cassius Williams was the
son of Mr. and Mrs. Robert T. Williams, of Ville Platte, and that
services were scheduled at the African Methodist Episcopal Zion
Church. The entire article was four inches long, and set between
an ad for Carter's Little Liver Pills and an article about a guy

who'd caught an eight-pound large-mouthed bass in Bayou Nez-pique.

On May 17, another short article appeared on page 4, this one reporting that Leon Cassius Williams, 14, found murdered the week before, had been laid to rest. An obituary included within the article said that Leon was survived by his mother and father and three siblings, all of whom were listed, along with their ages. I copied the list. Sheriff Duplasus was quoted as saying that there were no new developments in the case. The last article relating to Leon Williams appeared on page 16 of the May 28 paper. Sheriff Duplasus reported that investigations within the Negro community had led him to believe that Leon Williams was murdered by a Negro transient seen earlier that day, and that the murder very likely resulted from a dispute over a gambling debt. Duplasus said that he was continuing to compile evidence, and had issued a description to state police authorities, but that the chances for an arrest were minimal. None of Leon Williams's survivors were referred to except for a single quote from Mrs. Robert T. Williams, who said, "I feel like they robbed my heart. I pray the good Lord watches after my baby."

When I reached the end of the film I turned off the projector and thought about what I had found. Leon Williams, a fourteen-year-old African-American male, had been murdered, and the murder was unsolved. Nothing in the articles indicated a connection to the Johnson family, or to any other principal in my investigation. I had thought there might be, but there you go. *Nada.* Jimmie Ray Rebenack was very likely the guy who had stolen the May microfiche film from the Ville Platte Library. I didn't know that, and I hadn't found it at his home, but it made sense. Jimmie Ray had found some significance in Leon and had made note of him. Since Jimmie Ray had done all right with the other stuff, further investigation was in order.

I brought the film back to the bald guy, then went to a bank of pay phones at the side of the building. There were three names on the list of Leon Williams's siblings: Lawrence, 17; Robert, Jr., 15; and Chantel Louise, 10. Thirty-six years later, Lawrence would be fifty-two and Chantel Louise forty-six. Chantel Louise would very likely have a different last name. I called Ville Platte Information and asked for numbers and addresses for Lawrence Williams and Robert Williams, Jr. There was no listing for a Robert Williams, Jr., but they had Lawrence. I copied his number and address, thanked the operator, then dialed Lawrence Williams. On the third ring, a woman with a precise voice answered. I said, "May I speak with Mr. Lawrence Williams, please?"

There was a pause, and then she said, "I'm sorry, but Mr. Williams is deceased. May I help you?" Deceased.

"Is this Mrs. Williams?"

"Yes, I am Mrs. Lawrence Williams. Who is calling, please?"

I told her my name. "Mrs. Williams, did your husband have a younger brother named Leon?"

"Why, yes. Yes, he did. Leon died, though, when they were boys. He was murdered." Maybe this was going to work out after all.

"That's why I'm calling, Mrs. Williams. I'm a private investigator, and I'm looking into the murder. Did Mr. Williams speak about it with you?"

"Mr. Williams did not. I'm afraid I can't help you."

"There was another brother and a sister."

"Robert, Jr., died in 1968. Over in that war."

"How about the sister? Do you know how I might reach her?"

Her voice became crisp. "She's working right now. She works for a Jew in that damned sausage factory, and you shouldn't be calling her there. When you call, that Jew answers the phone and he doesn't like that. You'll get her in trouble."

"Please, Mrs. Williams. It's important."

"Feeding her five children is important, too. That job is all she has, working for a Jew." Oh, man.

"I promise I won't get her in trouble, Mrs. Williams." Like a kid, *cross my heart and hope to die.*

"How do I know you're who you say you are? You might be up to no good. I assure you that I am not to be trifled with."

"There's an attorney in Baton Rouge named Lucille Chenier. I can give you her number and you could call her office and speak with her about me."

That seemed to mollify her. "Well, perhaps that won't be necessary. I take pride in knowing a sincere voice."

"Yes, ma'am."

"Chantel lives right over here in Blue Point. She has lunch soon. Why don't you see her at lunch. Her name is Chantel Michot now, and she always goes home for lunch. She has to put dinner on for those little ones."

I looked at my watch. "That's fine, Mrs. Williams. I'm coming from Baton Rouge." It was a quarter before eleven. I could get there by twelve-thirty.

"Well, then, I guess this must be important, all the way from Baton Rouge."

"Yes, ma'am, it is."

"We'll be expecting you." We.

"Yes, ma'am, I'm sure you will."

I copied the directions as she gave them, and then I went to see Chantel Michot, Leon Williams's younger sister.

B lue Point, Louisiana, was a wide spot in the road five miles south of Ville Platte at the tip of Bayou des Cannes. You had to go to Ville Platte first, then take a little state road that wound its way over narrow steel bridges and sluggish channels of water and sweet potato fields. It was rural country, with a lot of barbed wire fences and great live oaks bearded with Spanish moss, and the air was heavy with pollen and bees and moisture.

Chantel Michot lived in a clapboard shotgun house at the edge of the road that backed upon a wide green pasture. The pasture was fenced and the fence ran behind her house as if a little square had been cut from the owner's pasture so that the Michot family might live there. The house looked old and poorly kept, with peeling paint and a green shingle roof that was missing tiles and a wooden front porch that was cracked and splintered. There was a screen door like every other house in Louisiana, but the screen was cruddy and stretched, and little wads of pink Kleenex had been stuck into holes to keep out the mosquitoes. Martha Guidry would have a field day. Tire ruts ran down from the road past the house and the rusted chassis of a very old Dodge and across the pasture. Maybe a dozen chickens pecked in the dirt around the chassis. Yard birds. A late-sixties Bel Air sedan was parked beneath an elm tree, and a newer Pontiac Sunbird was parked behind the Bel Air. I pulled in behind the Sunbird and got out. The engines of both the Bel Air and the Sunbird were still ticking. Couldn't have gotten here more than ten minutes ago.

The screen door opened and a little boy maybe four years old came out and looked at me from the lip of the porch. He was barefoot in shorts, with a little round belly and a runny nose and an ocher complexion. Hair more curly than nappy. His left index finger was stuffed up his nose to the first joint. I said, "My name's Elvis. What's yours?"

He pushed the finger in deeper and didn't answer. I often have that effect on people.

The door opened again and a light-skinned woman in her forties came out, followed by an older, heavier woman with skin the color of burnished walnuts. The younger woman was wearing a thin cotton smock over faded Bermuda shorts and open-toed sandals. Her hair was piled on her head and held there with a broad purple band. It wasn't particularly neat, but she didn't have it like that for style; she had it like that for work. Keep the hair out of the sausage. The older woman was in a light green rayon suit with a little white hat and white gloves and a crocheted purse the size of a grocery bag. All dressed up to meet the detective. The older woman said, "I am Mrs. Lawrence Williams. Are you Mr. Cole?"

"Yes, ma'am. I appreciate you and Ms. Michot agreeing to see me."

Chantel Michot said, "I got to see about these children and I got to get back." Not exactly thrilled to meet the detective. She was holding a filter-tipped cigarette and kept one arm crossed beneath her breasts. I offered her a card, but Mrs. Lawrence Williams took it. "Ada say this about Leon." Ada was Mrs. Williams.

"That's right. I know you were only ten when he was killed, but I thought we might speak about it."

"Why?"

"I'm working on something and Leon's name came up, and I don't know why. Maybe you can help me with the reason."

Chantel Michot sucked on the cigarette and blew smoke. Trying to figure me. There were children's voices behind her in the house, and another little boy came to the door, this one maybe five. He pressed against the screen and looked out. She said, "Anthony, get on in there and eat that lunch." Anthony disappeared. "Ada, would you make Lewis sit at that table, please?"

The little boy with his finger up his nose said, "No."

Mrs. Lawrence Williams pulled the big purse in closer and raised her eyebrows. Not liking the idea of being inside with the children and left out of all the great stuff on the porch. "Well, if I must." Snooty. She took Lewis by the arm and brought him inside. Lewis yelled bah bah bah bah as loud as he could.

I said, "They never caught Leon's killer. No arrest was made."

"You the police?"

"No."

"All these years, you gonna find the guy done it?"

"That's not what I'm after."

"But maybe?" All these years, she was still hopeful.

"I don't know, Chantel. I found Leon's name in a place it doesn't fit and I want to find out why it was there. I don't want to lead you on. I know you've got to get back to work."

"Least you ain't lyin' about it." She stared at me a minute, motionless, a thin trail of smoke drifting from her cigarette, barely moving in the still air, and then she made up her mind. "You want some lemonade? I put some up this morning."

I smiled at her and she smiled back. "That'd be fine. Thanks. If you've got the time."

"I got a few minutes."

We sat in the shade of the little porch on a sofa that was covered with crocheted bedspreads. Mrs. Lawrence Williams came to the door every few minutes, still pissed about being inside, always with the big purse. She probably had something in there in case I decided to trifle with them. "This is good lemonade."

"I put honey in with the sugar. That's clover honey. A man down the bayou keeps a hive."

I said, "The newspaper reports said that the sheriff believed that Leon was killed by a transient over a gambling dispute."

"Leon was fourteen. What he know about gamblin'?"

"What'd your parents think?"

"Said it was silly. Said it was just the sheriff's way of shinin' us on. A black man gets killed, they don' care."

"Did your parents have an idea of what happened?"

She squinted out at the road. Trying to remember. A truck pulling a natural-gas tank rumbled past and made the thin glass in the windows rattle. "Lord, it's been so long. Daddy died in seventy-two. Mama went, oh, I guess it was eighty-one, now."

"How about Lawrence or Robert, Jr.? Did they ever say anything?"

She thought harder. "Lawrence didn't really have nothin' to do with Leon, but Leon and Junior were close. I remember Junior sayin' somethin' 'bout some gal. I guess there coulda been some gal mixed up in there."

"Like maybe Leon got killed over a girl?"

"Well. I guess." Chantel pulled deep on the cigarette, then flicked the butt out into the yard. A skinny Rhode Island Red hen picked it up, ran a few feet, then dropped it, squawking. The other chickens circled it, cocking their heads for a better look, then ignored it. Chantel said, "The gals did flock around Leon, let me tell you. He was a beautiful boy, and, my, he could talk. Charmin'? I was just a baby and I remember that. Robert used to get *jealous*! Oo!" She crossed her arms and leaned forward on her knees, enjoying the memories. "You know, I haven't thought about that in years. Here it is, sometimes I can't even remember Leon's face, but I remember that."

Mrs. Williams came to the door, still with the big purse, still with the pissy expression. "You don't have time for all this, now, girl. You have to get back to work."

Chantel nodded without looking.

"You late, that Jew'll get after you."

Chantel closed her eyes. *"Ada!"*

"Well, he's a Jew, isn't he?"

"Ada. Please."

Mrs. Williams harumphed and stalked back into the house. Chantel Michot said, "That woman is such a trial."

I said, "Think about Leon. Maybe you'll remember something else."

She stood up. "I may have something. You wait here." She went into the house and came back a few minutes later with a King Edward cigar box and sat with it on her knees. "This is mostly Robert's things, but there's some stuff from Leon in here, too. Lord, I haven't looked in here in years."

She opened the box and stared down at the contents, as if the letters and snapshots and papers within were treasures awaiting discovery. "You see Leon? Here's Leon right here. That's Lawrence and that's Junior and that's Daddy."

She handed me a yellowed Kodak snapshot with a little date marker on the white border: 1956. An older man was standing in front of an enormous Chevrolet roadster with three boys. Mr. Williams and his sons. Lawrence and Junior and Leon. They were light-skinned men with delicate features. Leon was the smallest, with large expressive eyes and long lashes and an athlete's carriage. He would have been twelve. She said, "We had some good-looking men in this family, but that Leon, he was plain pretty."

"He's handsome, all right."

She fingered through handwritten notes and birthday cards and a couple of elementary school report cards and tiny black-and-white snapshots of older black men and women, all neatly dressed and stiffly formal. "My momma gave me these things. She said these were the little bits of us that she held dear. This is me. This

119

is Robert and Lawrence. Oh, my God, look how young." She smiled broadly and the smile made her seem younger and quite pretty, as if for a moment she was free of the weight of the five children and the crummy job at the sausage factory. "Robert was killed in the army," she said. "He died in that Tet thing." That Tet thing.

"Uh-huh."

She lifted out a white government envelope, its edge ragged from being torn, now yellow and flat from the years in the box. *We regret to inform you . . .* There were spots on the envelope. I wondered if they were tears. "They gave him a medal. I wonder where it is."

I shook my head.

Mrs. Williams reappeared at the door. "You are going to be *late* now."

"I am busy, Ada." Sharp.

Ada shook her finger at me. "You are going to get her in trouble with that Jew."

"*Ada!*"

Mrs. Williams stalked away.

She said, "Oh, here's some of Leon's things." She lifted out two brown newspaper clippings, the originals to the articles I'd read on the LSU microfiche, brittle and brown and very likely untouched since the day her mother had cut them from the Ville Platte *Gazette* and put them in the King Edward box. She took out more bits of paper and photographs and passed them to me. Leon sitting on a tractor that looked a million years old. Leon and a swaybacked mule. There were a couple of Mother's Day cards drawn in a child's hand and signed "Leon," and a poem he had written. She handed me things as she found them, and she was still fingering through the box when I opened a piece of yellowed notebook paper filled with the doodles you make when you're bored in class. Most of the page was class notes about the Louisiana Purchase, but in the borders there were finely detailed pencil drawings of Sherman tanks and World War II fighter planes and the initials EJ EJ EJ. LW+EJ.

I was wondering about EJ when I saw a little heart at the bottom right-hand corner of the page. The kind kids draw when they have a crush on someone. And that's when I knew about EJ, and all the rest of it, too.

Inside the heart Leon Williams had printed I LOVE EDIE JOHNSON.

Edie Johnson. Edie Boudreaux.

Edith Boudreaux wasn't Jodi Taylor's sister. She was Jodi Taylor's mother. And Jodi's father was Leon Williams.

16

I folded the paper and handed it back to her and twice she spoke and both times I had to ask her to repeat herself. *I love Edie John-son*. When we had gone through the rest of the things, she said, "Does any of this help?"

"Yes. I believe it does."

She nodded, pleased that her effort was of value. "You wanna take any of these things, you may."

I smiled. "No. These are your precious things. Keep them safe."

She put the papers back in the King Edward box and closed it. "I wonder if they'll ever catch that man who killed Leon."

"I don't know."

"It's been so long now. I can't imagine anyone would care."

I patted her hand and then I stood. "Somebody cares, Chantel. Somebody somewhere cares. I've always believed that."

She gave me a nice smile and we finished our lemonade and then I left. I followed the back roads north to Ville Platte, checked out of the motel there, then stopped by the Pig Stand and bought a link of *boudin* for the road. I told Dottie that my business here was finished, and that this would be our last time together. She laughed and told me that I'd be back. She touched the place beneath her eye as she had done before and said she had the second sight. I wished that she would have used it earlier. Jimmie Ray might still be alive.

I ate the *boudin* as I drove back to Baton Rouge and listened to the same female radio evangelist screaming about plague-carriers from abroad and once more crossed the big Huey Long Bridge and arrived back at the Riverfront Ho-Jo at 1:40 that afternoon.

I didn't bother trying to call Sid Markowitz or Jodi Taylor. I booked the first available flight back to Los Angeles, checked out, then phoned Lucy Chenier's office from the lobby. Darlene said that Lucy was in and asked if I wished to speak with her, but I said no, that I was at the Riverfront and would walk over. Ten minutes later I rode the elevator to the Sonnier, Melancon, & Burke offices. Lucy's smile was wide and bright, and she seemed glad to see me. Something ached in my chest when I looked at her, and the ache increased when I took her hand. I said, "I think I've come to the end of the line on this and there are some things we need to talk about. I'm going back to Los Angeles."

She stopped smiling, and said, "Oh."

We sat on the flower-print couch and I showed her the copies I'd made of the articles reporting Leon Williams's murder, and as she read them I told her about Mrs. Lawrence Williams and Leon's sister, Chantel Michot, and the little heart that said *I LOVE EDIE JOHNSON*. She finished reading before I finished talking, then sat quietly, watching me with sharp lawyer eyes until I was done with it. "Jodi told me none of this."

"I didn't think that she had."

"And you believe she knew all of this? She knew that Leon Williams was her father."

"I think that's how Jimmie Ray bought his Mustang. I think he went to them with the documentation, and they paid to have him sit on it."

She placed both hands in her lap, one atop the other, then stood and went to the window, and then she came back around her desk and leaned against the front of it. "This is silly. It's the nineties. What does she think will happen?"

I shrugged.

She waved her hand. Adamant. "It isn't even compelling evidence. 'Edie Johnson' is hardly an uncommon name. The possibility of coincidence is large."

"Maybe she didn't see it that way."

She shook her head again. "But why hire us to find out something she already knew? Why lie to us about it? She had to believe that we'd find out."

"I'm going to ask her."

Lucy pursed her lips and stared at the floor. She took a breath, let it out, then looked up at me. "So you're going back."

"I don't think I was hired to learn anything about her medical history. They knew Jimmie Ray was blackmailing them, so they didn't hire me to uncover his identity. I think she just wanted to know if it was real."

Lucy sighed again and stared out the window. Maybe she, too, was looking for Huck and Jim.

"Also, I don't like being lied to. I like it less because the lying may have had something to do with getting Jimmie Ray Rebenack killed."

Lucy came over and sat beside me. "I know you're angry, but may I offer something?"

"Always."

"Adopted people often wonder at their histories, but there are more obvious traits by which we define ourselves. How tall we are. The color of our hair. I want you to consider that the entirety of Jodi Taylor's identity has been called into question. Not just her name, but what she sees when she looks in the mirror." Lucy's face was softer now, and I wondered if she were putting herself in Jodi Taylor's place. "She has a career and friends, and she is probably wondering if everyone in her life will see her differently. Do you understand?"

"You're making it hard to stay mad."

She smiled, but it was sad. "Mad is always easier, isn't it?"

I nodded. "Are you going to call them?"

"Of course. I don't like being lied to, either, and if my employment is at an end, then we have to terminate the file."

Termination. There didn't seem to be a whole lot left to say. "I guess that's it."

"I guess so."

I nodded at her. "I'm glad we had a chance to meet."

She nodded back. "Yes. I am, too."

We stared at each other. The Lawyer and the Big Time Op, not knowing what to say. She stood and I stood with her. "Well. I hope we stay in touch."

"Christmas. We can do cards."

"That would be nice."

"I write very funny cards."

"I'm sure you do."

We stood like that for a time, and then she put out her hand and I took it. "Tell Ben I said 'bye."

"I will."

"I'll see you, Lucy."

"Good-bye, Elvis."

Lucy went back to her desk and I rode the elevator down to my rental car, and four hours and twelve minutes later I was descending through the haze into midafternoon Los Angeles.

It was ten minutes after three, L.A. time, and I was home. There had been no significant earthquakes in my absence, and the temperature was a balmy eighty-four, the humidity twenty-nine percent, winds out of the northwest. Home. The freeways were jammed, the smog was a rusty shade of orange, and Lucy Chenier was two thousand miles away. On the other hand, we didn't have hundred-year-old snapping turtles and mutant Cajuns. Also, I wasn't very likely to get anyone else murdered in the foreseeable future. If I could keep myself from strangling Sid Markowitz, I might even be able to drink enough beer to stop seeing Jimmie Ray Rebenack's body. That's the great thing about L.A.—anything's possible. Portrait of the detective looking on the bright side of life.

I phoned Sid Markowitz's office from the terminal. His secretary said, "I'm sorry, but Mr. Markowitz is unavailable."

"This is Elvis Cole. Do you know that I'm working for him?"

"Yes, sir. I do."

"It's important that I speak with him."

"I'll give him the message when he checks in, Mr. Cole. He's at the studio now, with Ms. Taylor."

I hung up and dialed Jodi Taylor's number on the General-Everett lot. A man's voice answered. "Ms. Taylor's office."

"This is Elvis Cole. Is Ms. Taylor or Mr. Markowitz available?"

"Oh, hi, Mr. Cole. Jodi's on the set, now. May I take a message and have her get back to you?"

"Nope."

I rode the escalator down to baggage claim where a representative of the airline informed me that my bag had been misrouted to Kansas. They said that they would be very happy to deliver it to my home upon its recovery, and they smiled when they said it. I said fine. I caught the airport shuttle to long-term parking to pick up my car. The shuttle bus was jammed with Shriners from Orange County, and I had to stand. No problemo. A fat guy with breath like a urinal stood in front of me. Every time the shuttle hit a bump he lost his balance and stepped on my toes. Every time he stepped on my toes he would excuse himself and burp into my face. Sour. We were on the shuttle bus for twenty-two minutes, and most of that time I was trying not to breathe. Looking on the bright side. When I got to my car, the top had been slashed and my CD player stolen. A Blaupunkt. I tried to file a report, but the parking attendant didn't speak English. Hey, that's L.A. It took forty-five minutes to get out of the airport and onto the freeway, only to find that the freeway was gridlocked. A bald guy in a deuce-and-a-half truck cut me off in a sprint to the exit ramp. He called me an asshole, but he was probably having a bad day. At the bottom of the ramp he squeaked through on the yellow, but I got caught by the red. No big deal. Look at the bright side. A homeless woman wearing a garbage bag spritzed oil on my windshield and told me Jesus was coming. She said that in the meantime she'd be happy to clean my windshield for a dime. I paid her, and said that if Jesus didn't get here soon I was going to stop looking on the bright side and kill somebody. Welcome home.

I sat at the light and thought about Christmas.

At Christmas, I could send Lucy Chenier a card.

Songbird kept its standing sets on Stage 12 at the rear of General-Everett Studios. I parked at a Shell station across from the front gate, called a friend of mine on the lot, and had them send down a pass.

Much of the time when you walk along the back streets of a movie studio, you see Martians and Confederate soldiers and vehicles of strange design and other magical things. I have visited the different studios maybe a hundred times, and I have never grown tired of that little-boy surprise at seeing the strange and unexpected. But not this time. This time, the magic had been put away and the walk to Stage 12 seemed somehow oppressive and unwelcome.

The little streets around Stage 12 were alive with activity. Big eighteen-wheelers were wedged against the soundstage walls, belly to butt with costume trailers and makeup trailers and a honeywagon. Econoline vans and station wagons were parked between the larger vehicles, all of which had little cards with the *Songbird* logo displayed in the windshields. Burly men wearing ball caps sat in the station wagons reading newspapers or Dean

Koontz novels. Teamsters. Sid Markowitz's Jaguar XJS convertible was parked behind a full-sized motor home near a door in the side of the soundstage with a red light over it. The red light was on, and a couple of people who looked like grips were watching it. I walked up like I had business there, and we stared at the light together. When the light went out, a loud buzzer rang inside the soundstage and we went in. I followed the two guys along a stream of heavy electrical cables between false walls and through dark sets: Jodi Taylor's bedroom in the series, her family's kitchen, the big bedroom where all four of her tiny blond children lived. Welcome to Oz, the Land of Make Believe where the nation's favorite family drama comes to life.

I came out at the roadhouse set where Jodi Taylor sang every week in *Songbird,* chasing her character's dream of becoming a star. Maybe forty people were setting up for a shot: the camera crew positioning the camera on its dolly and gaffers rigging lights and stand-ins and extras waiting for their call to the set. A woman in an L.A. Raiders cap and baggy bush pants was with Jodi and the actor who played Jodi's husband, framing a shot with her hands. She would be the director. A guy with a walkie-talkie and a guy with long gray hair were watching, the guy with the hair suggesting something every once in a while and whispering to the camera crew. The guy with the hair would be the director of photography. Sid Markowitz was talking to a woman in a business suit by a coffee machine in the shadows to the side of the set. I went over and said, "Hi, Sid."

Sid Markowitz's face turned the color of fresh clams. "It's you."

I held up two fingers. "Two words, Sid. Leon Williams."

The fresh clam color went fishbelly white and Sid Markowitz pulled me away from the woman in the business suit. "Jesus Christ, keep your voice down. Whattaya doin' here, f'christ's sake? All this is confidential."

"That was before I found out you lied to me, Sid."

I stepped away from him into Jodi Taylor's line of sight and crooked my finger at her. She looked at me as if she wasn't quite sure who I was, and then she recognized me and her face shut down into a grim chalk mask. Now you're smiling, now you're not. Sid hurried up behind me and took my arm again. "C'mon, Cole, don't make a scene here, okay?"

I said, "If you don't stop touching me, I'm going to break off your hand and stuff it up your ass."

Jodi Taylor left the woman in the Raiders cap and came up to me as if we were the only two people in the soundstage, as if everyone else were only shadows flickering on the wall, cast by a tree through an unseen window. She said, "Leon Williams is my father, isn't he?"

"Yes."

Sid Markowitz had Jodi by the arm, now, trying to move her away from me. "Jesus, would the two of you keep it down? Let's go outside." Then he was back with me again. "We had our reasons for not coming clean, all right? What's the big deal?"

"Jimmie Ray Rebenack is dead. A human being died, and now it's time to tell the truth because I have to decide what to tell the police."

Neither Jodi Taylor nor Sid Markowitz said anything for several heartbeats, and then Sid Markowitz said, "I'm gonna call Bel, kid. Bel needs to know." Beldon Stone was the president of General-Everett Television.

I said, "Other people know about this?"

"About *this*, but not about you. We hired you without telling anybody."

We went out to the motor home, Jodi moving as if she were numb and Sid Markowitz fluttering like a moth around a Bug-Zapper. The motor home was the full-size luxury model, with a bedroom and a bath and a kitchenette with a dining table. Last week's Nielsen ratings had been push-pinned to a little corkboard in the kitchenette, along with a couple of clippings from the *Hollywood Reporter* and *Daily Variety*: HIT SERIES!!, SONGBIRD

SCORES AGAIN!. A teamster was sitting in the driver's seat, listening to the afternoon race report and reading the paper. Sid said, "Eddie, we need a little privacy here, okay?"

The teamster left without a word. Jodi Taylor curled up on the motor home's couch, and folded her hands in her lap while Sid went to the phone. Jodi looked small and frightened.

A few minutes later a studio limo double-parked next to the motor home, and two men in suits and a woman in a short skirt got out. One of the men was in his fifties, and the other was in his thirties. The woman was in her twenties, but she looked older. Sid Markowitz saw them and said, "Oh, Christ, Beldon's gonna be pissed." He shook his head and chewed at his lip and went into the Bug-Zapper routine again. "I told you, Jodi. Didn't I tell you?"

Jodi pulled herself tighter and nodded without looking at him. On TV, Jodi Taylor was strong and resilient and exuded confidence. But that was TV, and this was real. I guess they don't put you on the cover of *People* for being real.

They came into the motor home without knocking, Beldon Stone first and his two assistants in trail. Beldon Stone had a great hawk nose and tiny eyes, and he looked like he wanted to swoop down and eat someone. Sid plastered on a big smile and said, "Hey! Bel!" and offered his hand, but Beldon Stone ignored him. Stone looked first at me, then at Jodi, and then at Sid, and you could tell that he read it before the first word was spoken. "Well," he said, "it seems someone else is in on our little secret."

Jodi said, "I'm sorry, Bel." A voice like a child.

I said, "Okay, Markowitz, the gang's all here. Knock off the bullshit and tell me what's going on."

Beldon Stone said, "Yes, Sid." His voice was resonant and smooth and filled with authority. "Tell us how this gentleman comes to know our secret." He said it to Sid Markowitz but his eyes never left me, as if I were a potential adversary and might attack him.

Sid identified me as a private investigator who had been recommended by Peter Alan Nelsen. He used Peter's name at least six times in the telling, as if that might take the edge off. He said, "Jodi couldn't just let it hang there, Bel. She had to know if all this stuff Rebenack was saying was true. You can understand that, can't you? She hired this guy to find out if it was true."

Everything was Jodi, even the business about not telling me the whole story. Putting the blame on her. When Markowitz was finished weaseling to Beldon Stone, he looked back at me. "Rebenack was threatening to sell the stuff to the tabloids. Hey, all the guy wanted was thirty grand and thirty grand's nothing to keep the lid on something like this, so we paid him. Everybody agreed." He glanced at Beldon Stone like he expected Stone to chime in with how much he agreed, but Stone was silent. Markowitz said, "I don't see what you're so pissed about, Cole. We were paying this guy, and we wanted to find out if what he had was really real." Really real. "We didn't wanna stir the water, so we didn't hip you to the whole deal. So sue us. We wanted you to go into this with a fresh eye. That makes sense, doesn't it? We wanted to see if you'd get to the same place as the goof with the hair. If he had bupkis, you didn't need to know. If it was emmis, then you'd confirm it and we'd know it's real. Okay, it's real. We know what we wanted to know and you got paid. Whattaya makin' a case for?"

"The goof with the hair was found murdered two days ago. He was probably murdered because I was in something that I should've known about but didn't."

Sid Markowitz rolled his eyes. "Oh, a fuckin' blackmailer was murdered! What a loss!"

I grabbed Sid Markowitz and pushed him against the table and the woman in the short skirt made *ee-ee* noises and the younger guy tripped over himself trying to get out of the way. Markowitz tried to back away from me, but there was no place to go. "Lemme go! Lemme go! There's witnesses here!"

Everything seemed to slow and grow silent. My eyes felt large and dry, and my shoulders felt swollen. The woman in the short skirt kept making the noises, and I pressed Markowitz back into the table, but once he was there I didn't know what to do with him, as if he was suddenly beside the point. Jodi Taylor said, "I'm sorry we lied to you. I didn't know what else to do and I'm sorry."

I let go of Markowitz and stepped away from him. I was breathing hard and blinking, but my eyes still felt dry. I said, "Maybe it hasn't dawned, genius, but when an extortionist turns up dead, they always suspect the extortee."

Markowitz said, "Hey, we didn't even know!"

Beldon Stone had not moved. I guess people at his level grab each other all the time. He said, "The gentleman who was extorting Ms. Taylor is dead?"

"Yes."

"And his documents?"

"I have them."

He nodded. "And what do you want?"

"I don't know." My head began to ache, and that made me even more angry. I thought I had known why I was coming back, but now I didn't. Maybe I was expecting to find some great evil, but instead there was only a frightened woman and the greedy men around her.

Beldon Stone settled onto the couch beside Jodi Taylor and patted her leg. Reassuring. Fatherly. He reached into his jacket and came out with a slender cigar, looked at it for a moment, then ran it beneath his nose. He neither put it in his mouth nor lit it, but the smell seemed to comfort him. "I realize you're upset, Mr. Cole, but would you do me the courtesy of telling me if Mr. Rebenack's assertions were correct?"

"Yes."

"And how do you know this?"

I blinked at him.

He made a small gesture with the cigar. "You were paid for your services, were you not?"

Sid Markowitz said, "Goddamn right he was. Three grand."

Stone made the gesture again. "Then please tell these people what you found."

I didn't give them all of it, but I gave them enough. I told them about finding the woman who I believed to be Jodi Taylor's birth mother, and I told them about Leon Williams. As I told it, Jodi Taylor watched me as if she were peering out from a cave. When I finished, she said, "You found my birth mother?"

"Yes."

Stone patted her knee again. He was larger and older, and his touch cut her off. He said, "And no one else knows these things, or suspects?"

"The man responsible for Rebenack's death probably knows, but he's not interested in Jodi Taylor. He probably killed Rebenack because this business with the blackmail put some other crime he's got going in jeopardy."

Jodi Taylor peered out from the cave again. "Crime involving my birth mother?"

Beldon Stone patted her knee again, again cutting her off. *There, there, little girl.* "The important thing is that the information is contained." As if he couldn't care less what Jodi Taylor was feeling or what she wanted to know.

I said, "Are you people crazy? Who cares if Leon Williams was Jodi Taylor's father?"

Beldon Stone looked at me with great empathy. "Well, certainly none of us, Mr. Cole. But perhaps not everyone is as generous as we."

The younger guy said, "*Songbird*'s a solid hit. We're looking at a five-year run and a potential back-end profit exceeding two hundred million dollars."

Sid Markowitz nodded. "Fuckin' A."

Stone said, "Jodi Taylor has been given a gift that many dream of but few are granted. She's a star." He patted her knee again, and she stared at the floor. "Our audience sees her every week, mother to four adorable blond children, wife to a blond Nordic husband. Would that audience accept a person of color in the role?"

"Jesus Christ, Stone."

"Our series has built its popularity on traditional family values. Our advertisers pay for that popularity and expect us to protect it. We have enemies, Mr. Cole. Every left-wing, ultraliberal reviewer and special interest group has taken shots at this series since the beginning. They make fun of us. They criticize us. They condemn us for portraying a white, middle-class nuclear family in a fragmented multicultural world. Wouldn't they love to learn that our star is not only part African-American, but illegitimate?"

Jodi Taylor sat with her head down, as if she were shrinking away from what he was saying, as if she could just make herself small enough the words would pass by and be gone and her life would continue on its way.

Stone said, "I regret that you were brought into this matter, Mr. Cole, but considering the way things have worked out, I think some sort of bonus is in order."

"I didn't come sucking around for a payoff."

Stone raised an eyebrow. "No?"

"I have information pertaining to a homicide, and by withholding that information I am violating the law. I don't like that."

Sid Markowitz said, "Jesus Christ, Cole, I'm sorry Rebenack died and I'm sorry you feel bad about it. You want an apology? I apologize. The guy was puttin' it to us, all right? He was trying to ruin Jodi Taylor. Who'd Jodi Taylor ever hurt? Huh? Answer me that?"

"Tuck in your shirt, Markowitz. Your ten percent is showing."

Beldon Stone smiled the fatherly smile at me. "It seems that everyone is sorry, Mr. Cole. I am certainly sorry that you were brought into this, and I am also sorry that a man has died, even a man such as Mr. Rebenack."

"Sure."

He patted Jodi again. "But now it appears the ball is in your court. If you wish to go to the police, I suppose you can do that." The pat again. "We didn't want Jodi hurt." Leaving it on me, saying do what you do and bring it down on Jodi Taylor. Elvis Cole, Bad Guy. My head was splitting, and it felt like a couple of steel rods had been jammed into my neck.

I said, "Fuck you."

Beldon Stone smiled and stood. It was over, and he knew it. I knew it, too. He paused at the door to the motor home and fixed the hawk eyes on Sid Markowitz. The warm, fatherly expression was gone. "I'm disappointed that you went behind my back, Sid. We'll have to speak about this again."

Sid Markowitz looked as if he'd just received a positive biopsy. "You gotta understand, Bel. Hey, we hadda know."

Beldon Stone stayed with the killer eyes another moment, and then he left, the younger guy and even younger woman after him.

It was quiet in the motor home except for the air conditioner and the generator and the sound of Jodi Taylor crying. They were small sounds, pained and somehow distant.

Sid Markowitz brightened, coming up with the big idea. "Hey, how 'bout that bonus? You came through. You're playin' it straight. We'll give you a fat bonus. You deserve it."

I said, "Sid?"

"Yeah, a bonus. We'll treat ya right. Whaddaya say?"

I shook my head and then I walked out. If I had stayed any longer, I was afraid that I'd kill him.

18

It was twenty minutes after six when I left the General-Everett lot, picked up my car from the Shell station, and drove to the Lucky Market on Sunset. The traffic was heavy, with plenty of horn-blowing and fist-shaking, but I drove without a sense of personal involvement, as if I were somehow apart from the world around me. I parked in the Lucky's lot, went inside, and selected two baking potatoes, green onions, a very nice Porterhouse steak, and three six-packs of Falstaff beer. Nothing like a well-balanced meal after a hard day at the office.

I pushed my cart to the registers and stood in line behind an overweight woman with a cart filled with Dr Pepper, chicken parts, and jumbo family packs of Frosted Flakes and Cocoa Puffs. The Cocoa Puffs were open, and the woman was eating them dry. She would reach into the box and pluck out a handful and put them into her mouth and then repeat the process. The woman stared blankly into a huge display of Purina Dog Chow, and the process seemed without conscious thought or direction. Automatic eating. A little girl maybe two years old stood in the cart surrounded by the Frosted Flakes and the Cocoa Puffs, bouncing up and down and going *ga-ga-ga-ga*. The overweight woman ignored her. Maybe that's what I needed to do. Ignore what went on around me. Maybe I could become Elvis Cole, Zen Detective, and let the ugly realities of life flow around me without affect, like water passing over a stone. *A client hires you under false pretenses? No problem! Withholding evidence from the police during a homicide investigation? No big deal! A guy gets zapped because you shoot off your mouth? Those are the breaks!* The road to inner peace through Cocoa Puffs was sounding pretty good. Of course, you probably had to eat Cocoa Puffs to achieve this state of grace, and I didn't know if I was up to that.

When I got closer to the cashier there was a little four-pocket *TV Guide* rack above the Certs and the chewing gum, and Jodi Taylor was staring at me from the covers. She was sitting on one of the *Songbird* kitchen stools, surrounded by the guy who played her husband and the four kids who played her children, and everyone was smiling. The slug line on the top of the picture said "America's Favorite Family." Funny. I had just left Jodi Taylor, and she had looked small and frightened and nauseous. Amazing how pictures lie, isn't it? The overweight woman was already gone, else I would've asked to try the Cocoa Puffs.

I drove home and let myself into the kitchen. It was just before eight and the house was quiet. I opened a Falstaff, put the others in the refrigerator, and left the meat and the potatoes and the onions on the counter. I brought my suitcase upstairs, put the dirty things in the hamper and the clean things away, and then I changed out of the travel and client clothes and into something more suitable for a gentleman of leisure: sweatpants and a Bullwinkle T-shirt. No maiden to save, no dragon to slay, no client to serve. There would also be no money coming in, but what's that to a tough guy like me? Maybe Pike and I would go river kayaking in Colorado. Maybe we'd run with the bulls in Pamplona. Why not? When you're between jobs, you can do things like that.

Halfway through the sorting and changing I discovered that

most of the Falstaff was gone. Leaky can. I went back downstairs, opened another Falstaff, then got KLSX on the radio for Jim Ladd, the best disc jockey in the universe. Jim was playing George Thorogood. What could be better than that? I went out onto the deck and stoked the Weber. The sun was down and the air was cool and smelling of mint and honeysuckle. George finished, and Jim put on Mick Jagger singing about his lack of satisfaction. I layered mesquite charcoal into the kettle, splashed on the starter fluid (EPA approved), and fired up. The flames rose tall and orange and a wave of heat rolled over me, and in that moment of warmth I wondered what Lucy Chenier was doing. I had more of the Falstaff and thought that it might be pretty nice if Lucy were out here on the deck with me. Maybe we'd spent the day at Disneyland, and now we were back and feeling good about it. We'd be a little bit sunburned and a little bit tired, but Lucy would be smiling. She'd stand at the rail and think the view was fine, only she'd find the desert nights chilly and I'd put my arms around her to ward off the cold. I had the rest of the Falstaff. Funny. Thought I'd just opened the can.

I washed the potatoes, slit the tops, and wrapped them in foil. I put them in the oven at five hundred degrees. They were small and wouldn't take long. I took the steak out of its package, stabbed it with a fork a zillion times on each side, then sprinkled it with pepper and garlic powder and soy sauce. I washed the green onions, chopped them, then mixed them with a container of non-fat yogurt. Everything was ready to cook. Your basic fast meal. Of course, since I was unemployed, fast wasn't a requirement. A nine-course Julia Child extravaganza would have been appropriate. Goose in aspic, perhaps. Or oyster-stuffed quail in chili poblano sauce. Maybe Pike and I should head down to Cabo San Lucas and go after billfish. Our friend Ellen Lang might like to go. So might my friend, Cindy, the beauty-supplies distributor. I opened another Falstaff.

The cat came in while I was thinking about it, and hopped up onto the counter the way he does when he's hoping I won't notice. You could see his nostrils working, smelling the steak. I said, "Bet you missed me, huh?"

He made a little cat nod.

I carved a piece of steak, then put the cat and the steak on the floor. He sniffed once, then went to work on the meat. I said, "I missed you."

I was sitting on my kitchen floor, drinking beer and petting the cat when the doorbell rang, and there was Jodi Taylor. She was wearing a gray sweatshirt over jeans, and no makeup. Her hands were in her pockets, and she looked closed and pensive, not unlike she had in the motor home. Awkward. I said, "Well, well. The TV star." It was only my fourth beer, wasn't it?

She said, "I hope you don't mind."

"Why should I mind? It beats getting lied to." Maybe my fifth. I held up a hand, shook my head, and stepped back. "Forgive me for saying that. I'm feeling sorry for myself, and I've been drinking. It's a boy thing."

She nodded.

"Please come in." I showed her in, only moderately embarrassed by the Falstaff and the Bullwinkle shirt. "Have you eaten?"

She kept her hands in her pockets. "I'm not hungry. I feel bad about what happened and I wanted to talk about it."

"Okay. I was just about to put a steak on the grill. Do you mind talking while I eat?"

She said of course not and followed me to the kitchen. "Oh. You have a cat."

The cat looked up from his piece of steak, lowered his ears, and growled. "Don't try to pet him. He doesn't care for people and he bites."

She moved away. The cat stopped growling and went back to work on the meat. I said, "Would you care for a drink?"

"That might be nice. Do you have scotch?"

"I do." I put ice in a short glass, then dug around for the Knockando.

"Do you live here alone?"

"Yep. Except for this cat."

"You're not married?"

"No."

She looked around at my home. "This is very nice." Like she wanted to talk but didn't know how to begin.

I held out the glass and she took her hands from her pockets to accept it. I went back into the kitchen, opened the oven, and squeezed the potatoes. They were soft. I put them on a wooden trivet on the counter, then removed the little bowl of yogurt and green onions from the fridge. I brought the steak and the steak tongs outside to the grill. Jodi Taylor watched me do these things and followed me out onto the deck without speaking. Her face was creased and intent and I hoped that she wasn't thinking me a drunk. She said, "I love the way barbecues smell. Don't you?"

She held the glass with both hands, and I saw that the glass was already empty. Nope. She wouldn't be thinking me a drunk. I brought out the bottle of Knockando, refreshed her drink, then put the bottle on the deck rail. "Your mission this evening, Ms. Taylor, is the care and handling of this bottle. You are to replenish your drink at your discretion without asking for my permission or awaiting my action in same. Is this clear?"

She giggled. "I can do that."

I smiled back at her. "Fine."

I put the steak on the grill. The coals were a fierce, uniform red, and the meat seared nicely with a smell not unlike the hamburgers we'd cooked at Lucy Chenier's. *Put her out of your head, Elvis.*

Jodi said, "I'm sorry about what happened."

"Forget it."

"I want to apologize."

"Accepted, but forget it. It's over. It's time to move on." Would Lucy like Cabo? *Stop that!*

The canyon was quiet except for a couple of coyotes beyond the ridge. Below us, a single car eased along the road, its headlights sweeping a path in the darkness. The sky was clear and black, and the summer triangle was prominent. Jodi said, "This isn't easy for me."

I turned the steak and prodded it with the tongs so the fat would flame on the coals.

"My dad died in 1985. My mom died two years after that. They were everything to me."

"Uh-huh."

"I know who my mom and dad were. My dad was Steve Taylor. My mom was Cecilia Taylor. Do you see?"

"Yes."

"I loved them more than anything. I still do."

Something dark flicked by overhead. An owl gliding along the ridge. Jodi Taylor had more of the scotch and stared at the flames licking the meat. "There are things about Louisiana I want to ask." Her voice was soft, and her eyes never left the flames.

"All right."

"Do I look like her?" We both knew who she meant. Jodi sighed when she said it, as if, in the saying, she had started down a path she had long avoided.

"Yes. You could be sisters."

"And my birth father is dead?" Her eyes never left the flames, never once looked at me as if, by refusing human connection, the questions were unreal and of no more substance than those questions you speak to yourself in the moments before sleep.

"Yes. I spoke with his younger sister."

"My aunt."

I nodded.

"Do I look like her?"

"No." The steak was done but Jodi Taylor seemed poised upon some internal precipice between painful things, and I didn't want to upset her balance.

"But you saw a picture of my birth father?"

"You don't look like him. Your birth father's family is light-skinned, with fine features, but you look like your birth mother."

I flipped the steak again. "Are you sure you want to hear these things?" In the restaurant she had said no; in the restaurant she had been adamant.

Jodi Taylor blinked hard several times and had more of the scotch. The cat crept out onto the deck and sat downwind, barely visible in the dark. Watching. I often consider, *Does he wonder at the human heart?* Jodi said, "I feel like I'm being pulled apart. I feel guilty and ashamed, as if I'm betraying my mom and dad. I never so much as thought of my birth parents, and now I feel that if I can't find some peace with this it's going to get larger and larger until it's all that I am and I won't be me anymore. Do you understand that?"

I took the steak off the grill. I put it on a plate and stood in the night, looking at her.

She said, "I didn't want to pay that man. I said it doesn't matter. I said no one will care about these things." Her eyes were filling again.

"But Beldon and Sid convinced you."

She nodded.

"They frightened you, and they made you ashamed."

She blinked harder. "God, I'm scared. I don't know what to do."

"Sure, you do."

She looked at me and took more of the scotch.

I said, "Why did you come here, Jodi?"

"I've got two days off before we start shooting the next episode. I want to hire you again. I want you to take me down there. I want to see where I come from, and see who I am. Will you do that for me?"

Lucy Chenier.

"Yes."

She nodded, and neither of us spoke again.

We went inside with the steak. I guess Cabo San Lucas and the billfish would have to wait. The human heart bears greater urgency.

19

Jodi Taylor and I flew to Louisiana the next day, catching the seven A.M. flight through Dallas/Fort Worth and arriving in Baton Rouge just before noon. We rented a gray Ford Thunderbird in my name and drove to Lucy Chenier's office. Jodi wanted to apologize, and I didn't argue. I phoned Lucy's office from the airport and told her assistant that we were on our way. Darlene said, "I didn't think we'd see you again."

"Miracles happen."

Darlene said, "Unh-hunh."

Lucy greeted us pleasantly at the door, offering her hand first to me, then Jodi. I was grinning as wide as a collie in a kibble factory, but Lucy seemed cool and somehow distant, and her handshake was professional. "Hello, Mr. Cole. Hello, Ms. Taylor. Please come in." Like that.

We sat, and Lucy told us that Sid had phoned and that they had discussed what had happened and why, and she said that she would certainly be happy to continue assisting Jodi in whatever way possible. She said it to Jodi and did not once look at or speak to me. I said, "Hi, remember me?"

"Of course. It's nice to see you again." Professional. Lawyerly. She refocused on Jodi.

Jodi said, "I knew Sid was going to phone, but I wanted to personally apologize for what happened. I should've been honest with you, and feel ashamed of myself."

Lucy stood and came around her desk. "Please don't be. Are you going to introduce yourself to Edith Boudreaux?"

Jodi Taylor shook her head and also stood. It seemed as if we had just arrived. "I don't want to meet these people, and I don't want to know them. I guess I just want to see them. Can you understand that?"

Lucy took her hand. "Of course, I can. We all have that curiosity. Seeing her is a way of seeing a part of yourself, even if you have no wish to know her."

Jodi said, "Yes. That's it."

Lucy said, "If there is any way I can help you, even if you just want to talk, don't hesitate to call."

"Thank you."

I told Jodi that I would be along in a moment, and she left. Lucy was standing at the door, still not looking at me. I said, "Is there something here that I'm missing?"

"I don't think so."

"Would you join me for dinner tonight?"

"That's very nice, but I can't."

"We could bring Ben."

She shook her head.

"Are you angry?"

"Of course not. I think Jodi is waiting for you."

"You sound angry."

She raised her eyebrows. "If Jodi requires my assistance she may call any time. She has the number."

"I'll tell her. Thank you."

I walked out of the office, and Jodi and I went down to the car. I got in behind the wheel and she climbed into the passenger seat, neither of us speaking. Jodi sat with her knees up and her hands clasped between her legs, staring out the window. She said, "What's wrong with you?"

"Nothing. Nothing is wrong with me."

She frowned at me and then she went back to staring out the window.

We crossed the Mississippi River, and pretty soon Baton Rouge was behind us. We made good time past Erwinville and Livonia and Lottie, and, at 1:36 that afternoon, we neared the exit for Eunice. I said, "Edith Boudreaux lives here with her husband and her family. She's married to a man named Jo-el Boudreaux. He's the sheriff. She has a dress shop in the center of town. Her father lives here, too. Leon Williams's sister is a woman named Chantel Michot. She lives fourteen miles north of here. You were born in a private home thirty miles north of here, above Ville Platte. What do you want to see first?"

"I want to see the woman." The woman. You knew she didn't mean Chantel Michot. You knew she meant Edith Boudreaux.

We left the highway, and Jodi put both hands on the dashboard and held herself with an expectancy that was a physical thing within the car.

I brought her to Edith Boudreaux's home first. Edith and her husband lived in a well-kept brick colonial ringed with azaleas bright with flowers and a large, neat yard. The street was quiet and slow; warm, with the smell of fresh-cut St. Augustine grass and scores of great black and yellow bumblebees lumbering around the azaleas. A shirtless black teenager pushed a mower along the side of the street, and nodded at us when we passed. I let the Thunderbird slow, and we stopped at the mouth of the drive. Jodi twisted in the seat, eyes wide. Neither the sheriff's highway car nor Edie's Oldsmobile Eighty-eight was present. Jodi said, "Is that where she lives?"

"Yes. She drives an Oldsmobile, and it's not here. She's not home."

"She's married to the sheriff?" She already knew that.

"Yes. His name is Jo-el." She already knew that, too.

"Does she have children?"

"She has three children, all in their twenties. I don't know if any of them live here."

"What are their names?"

"I don't know."

"Are they boys or girls?"

"I'm not sure."

She stared at the house as we spoke, tracing its lines with her eyes as if she was trying to read some truth there. When she had enough of the house we drove first to the small home where Monroe Johnson was waiting to die, and then to Edith Boudreaux's dress shop. Edie's car was neither at her father's nor at the dress shop. Jodi seemed uninterested in the old man, but when we cruised the dress shop she asked me to see if Edie was inside. I parked along in the square and looked in the window but there was only a dark-haired woman I hadn't seen before. I went back to the car. "What next?"

"The Michot woman." Jodi was frowning and her eyes were hard.

I said, "It's almost two. Would you like something to eat?"

"No."

"Do you need a bathroom?"

"Show me the Michot woman."

"She works. We won't be able to see her now." I hadn't eaten since the airplane, and my head was throbbing.

"Then show me where she lives."

I stopped at a 7-Eleven for two Slim Jims and a bag of peanut M&M's. Lunch. We took the old road north to Point Blue and Chantel Michot's shotgun house. Lewis and Robert were chasing each other around the Dodge, and an older girl was sitting on the porch, very near where I had sat, doing homework. I drove past, found a place in the road to turn around, then came back and pulled off onto the grass across from them. The older girl looked up from her homework and stared at us. I said, "The little guy's name is Lewis. The other boy is Robert. I don't know the girl. Chantel is Leon Williams's baby sister."

Jodi Taylor leaned forward in the seat again, eyes wide. "These are her children?"

"Yes."

"They're so poor."

I nodded. The girl had gone back to her homework, but kept glancing up at us, unable to concentrate. A fat Rhode Island Red hen stepped out from beneath the house, pecking at the dirt. The rest of the chickens followed her. Jodi said, "This is overwhelming. I can't believe this."

I didn't answer.

"These people are related to me."

I nodded. Robert ran in a circle around Lewis and Lewis tripped, bumping his head on the Dodge. He landed on his bottom and rubbed at his head, crying. Robert ran back to make sure his little brother was all right. The chickens scratched around them, undisturbed.

Jodi Taylor took a deep breath and let it out. The girl was staring at us again. She put her book aside and came to the edge of the porch and called to the little boys and all three of them went inside. An older boy maybe a year or two younger than the girl came to the door and looked out at us. Jodi said, "I want to see the woman." Edith, again.

"It's late, Jodi. We should head back to the city. We can come back tomorrow."

"I didn't come here to sit in a goddamned hotel. I want to see that woman." She was out at the edge, now, strung tight and fraying. Cheeks the color of milk.

I looked at her.

"Please." Her face softened and she took my arm. "Let's try her shop again. If she's not there, we'll go to the hotel."

I took her back to Eunice.

We got there just before four, and again I had to get out and look in the window, and again Edith wasn't there. I went back to the car, and got in shaking my head. Jodi said, "What do you have to do to get a break around here?"

We were just pulling away when Edith Boudreaux's metallic blue Oldsmobile passed us and parked at the curb and Edith got out. Jodi and I saw her at the same time. I said, "That's her."

Jodi came erect and stiff in the seat, her face almost to the windshield, both hands on the dash. Her lips parted, and there seemed a kind of electrical field flooding the car. I looked from Jodi Taylor to Edith Boudreaux and back again. Looking at Edith was liking looking at an older, softer version of Jodi.

It took Edith maybe fifteen seconds to move from her car to her shop and then she was gone.

I said, "Are you okay?"

Jodi stared at the closed door. Her breasts rose and fell, and a pulse hammered in the smooth skin beneath her jaw.

I said, "Jodi?"

Jodi blinked twice and looked at me, and then she shook her head. She said, "I was wrong. I can't leave now. I have to go in there."

The sun was high and bright, and the sky was a deep, rich blue, and maybe I hadn't heard her correctly. Maybe she wasn't talking about Edith Boudreaux. Maybe we had taken a wrong turn coming back to town and we weren't even in Eunice, Louisiana, anymore. Maybe we were in Mayberry, and she had seen Aunt Bea slip into this dress shop and she wanted to meet the old gal. Sure. That was it. I said, "I thought you didn't want to meet her."

"I've changed my mind." She didn't look at me when she said it. She was looking past me, at the dress shop, as if Edith might suddenly make a break for it and disappear.

I said, "Are you sure you want to do this?"

She shook her head.

"The smart thing is to bring in Lucy Chenier. Lucy knows about this."

Jodi shook her head again. "I might chicken out."

"If you're not sure, maybe you should chicken out."

"Why are you trying to talk me out of this?"

"Because you were adamant about not meeting her. Once you meet her you can't take it back, either for you or for her. I want you to be sure."

She kept her eyes on the store, drumming her fingers on the dash.

I said, "At the very least I should go in first and prepare her."

She said, "Let's just get this over with." Jodi pushed out of the car the way you come off the high board, all at once so that you don't give yourself time to reconsider. The way you do when you're not sure you want to go, but you're going to go anyway.

I got out with her and we crossed the street and went into Edith's place of business, me in trail and Jodi ahead, plowing on come hell or high water. Two women in their sixties were browsing through a rack of summer frocks to our right, and the young blond sales clerk was talking with a red-haired woman who was looking at herself in one of those three-sided mirrors in the rear of the place. Edith was standing at the register, frowning at a sales receipt. She looked up when the little bell chimed and smiled automatically, and then she saw me and her smile froze with the abruptness of a stopping heart. Her eyes went to Jodi for a moment, held there, then came back to me. Jodi froze in the center of the store as if she'd been spiked to the floor. Up close is different than out in the car. I said, "Hi, Mrs. Boudreaux. I hope this is a good time."

She wasn't liking it that I was back. "Well, it isn't really." She looked at Jodi again. She knew that this wasn't the same woman who was with me before. Jodi was still in the dark glasses and ball cap, with her hair pulled back and a shapeless cotton top and big dangly earrings and no makeup. She didn't look the way she did on television.

I went to the counter, trying to act as if this was the most mundane visit in the world. "Mrs. Boudreaux, could we speak with you in private?"

She glanced at Jodi again, and this time the look was curious. "Why?"

"Because we want to discuss something personal, and it's better if we don't do it here." I kept my voice low, so that only Edith could hear.

She shot another glance at Jodi, and now she looked nervous. "My husband spoke quite clearly for us the last time. I don't have anything to say and I'd rather you leave."

Jodi took off the sunglasses. Her eyes hadn't left Edith since we entered, and now Edith was staring back at her.

Edith said, "You look familiar."

Jodi opened her mouth to say something, then closed it. She came closer and stood next to me, so close that her shoulder was touching my arm. She didn't look full-steam-ahead now. Now, she looked the way you would look after you leaped off the board, and realized the pool was empty. She said, "My name is Jodi Taylor."

Edith seemed confused, then nodded and gave a little smile. "You're on television. We see you all the time."

Jodi moved toward Edith Boudreaux. "Mrs. Boudreaux, I believe that you and I are related. State records indicate that I was born to your mother, Pamela Johnson, thirty-six years ago. But I don't believe that. I believe that you gave birth to me. Is that true?"

The color drained from Edith Boudreaux's face, and her lips parted and she said, "Oh my God."

The two women in their sixties turned toward us, one of them holding a rust-colored dress that had to be four sizes too small. "Edie, do you think this works for me?"

Edith didn't hear them. She took a half-step back and then stepped forward again, gripping the Formica counter to steady herself. I smiled at the two women. "I'm sorry, but Mrs. Boudreaux is busy, now."

The woman with the rust dress made a face and said, "I don't think anyone asked *you*."

Edith blinked six or eight times, then said, "Jill, will you help Maureen, please?" You could barely hear her.

The blond clerk went over to the two women, but Maureen wasn't happy about it.

Jodi said, "There are some questions about myself that I'm hoping you will answer." She said it without emotion or intimacy, as if she had no more stake in the answers than a census taker.

Edith reached out as if to touch Jodi, but Jodi took a half-step back, her hands at her side. I said, "Why don't we go for a walk?"

Edith told the clerk that she had to go out for a while, and the three of us walked across to the square, me telling Edith what we knew and how we knew it. I thought she was going to deny it, but she didn't. I thought she might evade us, or start screaming for her husband, or make a big deal about how dare we invade her life like this, but she didn't do any of that. It was as if she had been waiting thirty-six years for Jodi to walk through the door, and now Jodi had and Edith couldn't stop looking at her. They walked on either side of me, keeping me between them, Jodi with her hands in her pockets, staring straight ahead, Edith anxious and staring at Jodi, as if Jodi might suddenly disappear and Edith wanted to have her committed to memory. When I finished, Edith said, "I can't believe how much she looks like me. She looks more like me than the children I raised." She said it to me, as if Jodi was a dream, and not really there.

I said, "If the state papers Rebenack had were legitimate, then Jodi is the child that Pamela Johnson handed to the state welfare authorities. There aren't any papers that indicate that the child was born to you. Nor are there documents that establish fatherhood."

She shook her head. "No. No, there wouldn't be."

Jodi said, "Then you don't deny that you're my birth mother?"

Edith seemed surprised. "No. No, of course not. Why would I?"

"You denied it thirty-six years ago."

"Oh."

I said, "Well, now that we're all together, maybe I should wait in the yogurt shop and let you two talk."

They both said, "No!" and Jodi grabbed my hand. She said, "I want you to stay. This won't take long."

We walked past a couple of wrought iron benches to a little gazebo in the square. An older man in coveralls and a red engineer's cap was on one of the benches, head back, mouth open, eyes closed. Sleeping. He had a tiny dog on a leash with him, the leash tied to the bench. The dog sat in the shade beneath the man and whined when we passed. The little dog was black and shaggy and its hair was matted. I thought it must be hot, with all the hair. We walked up the steps onto the gazebo and stood there in the shade. It was still hot, there in the shade.

Jodi stood well away from Edith, still holding my hand. She said, "So."

Edith uncrossed her arms, then recrossed them. She started to say something, then stopped. The little dog crept out from under the bench and tried to follow us up onto the gazebo, but reached the end of its leash and cried. Both Edith and Jodi looked at it.

I said, "Don't everybody talk at once."

Jodi frowned. "That's not funny."

"Nope. I guess not."

We stood there some more. The gazebo was sort of nestled in a stand of three mature magnolia trees, and the air was heavy with their scent. The big bumblebees zigged in and around the gazebo like police helicopters on patrol.

Edith said, "I'm sorry. I don't know what to say. I always thought you might come back to me. I would think of you, sometimes, and try to imagine what this moment would be like, and now here we are."

Jodi frowned, and her face pulled into a tight, uncomfortable knot. "Mrs. Boudreaux, I think I should make something clear."

"All right."

"I haven't come here to find my mother. I have a mother. She's the woman who raised me."

Edith glanced at the little dog again. "Of course."

"Just so we understand."

Edith nodded. "Oh, yes." She pooched out her lips, and then she added, "I hope the people who got you were good to you."

"They were. Very."

Edith nodded again.

Jodi said, "Was Leon Williams my father?" She said it abruptly, the same way she had gotten out of the car when she decided to go into Edith's store, like she had to do it that way or it wouldn't get done.

Edith's eyes flagged. Knew it was coming and here it was. "Yes. Leon was your father."

Jodi drew a slow breath, her mouth still the tight knot. "All right," she said. "All right."

Edith uncrossed her arms and cupped her right hand in her left at her breast. She looked at me, and then she looked back at Jodi. "That is what you wanted to know, isn't it?"

Jodi nodded.

Edith again took a single step toward Jodi, and Jodi lifted her free hand, stopping her. She still held onto me. "Please don't."

"Does it bother you that your father was a black man?"

Jodi's face tightened even more. "It seems to bother a great many people."

"It always has," Edith said. "I was just a girl, and Leon wasn't much older. We were children, and we were friends, and it became more than that." Her eyes grew wet and she blinked several times. "I hope you don't hate me for all of this."

Jodi stared at the little dog, and then she leaned against the gazebo rail. Even in the shade it was hot, and a single line of perspiration ran down the side of her face in front of her left ear. She didn't say anything for a while, maybe trying to put it in a kind of order. A couple of flies buzzed around the old man's face and he swatted at them without opening his eyes. She said, "Of course, I don't hate you. Don't be silly."

Edith was blinking harder. "Someone was blackmailing you with this, weren't they?"

"That's right."

155

Edith smiled softly, but there was no pleasure in it. Just a kind of acknowledgment of shared experience. "Yes, well, I know about that, too. When they say getting in trouble, they really mean it, don't they? It looks like you get everybody in trouble."

Jodi looked at me, embarrassed, as if she suddenly regretted being here and speaking with this woman and witnessing her pain. Edith said, "You've grown into quite a beautiful woman. I'm very proud of you."

Jodi said, "How did Leon Williams die?"

Edith drew breath and closed her eyes. "My father murdered him."

"Because he was black?"

Edith wet her lips and thought for a moment, and I found myself wishing that I were not present. I had no right to what was happening, and no place in it, and the sense of alienness made me feel large and intrusive, but Jodi still gripped my hand, and seemed to be holding on all the tighter. Edith said, "I think he shot Leon because he couldn't bring himself to shoot me."

Jodi said, "Jesus Christ."

Edith leaned back against the gazebo rail and told Jodi how Jodi came to be. Jodi hadn't asked that Edith tell her these things, but it seemed important to Edith, as if she needed to explain herself to Edith as much as to Jodi. She described an impoverished home dominated by rage and a brutal father who beat wife and children alike. She sketched herself as a shy, fearful girl who loved school, not so much for learning but simply because school allowed brief escape from the numbing despair of her home, and that after school she would buy yet more moments of peace by walking along the levees and the bayous, there to read or write in her journal, there to smell the air and enjoy the feeling of safety that being anyplace other than home allowed her. The Edith Boudreaux she described did not seem in any way like the person in the gazebo, but then, of course, she wasn't. She described a day on the bayou, her feet in the water, when Leon Williams had come upon her, an absolutely beautiful young man with a bright, friendly smile, who asked what she was reading (*Little Men,* she still remembered) and made her laugh (he asked how tall they were) and who, like Edith, dreamed of better things (he wanted to own an Esso station). When Edith spoke of Leon, her eyes closed and she smiled. She said that they had run into each other again the following week, very much by accident, and that Leon had again made her laugh and how, after that, the meetings were planned and no longer left to chance. As Edith went through it you could see the old emotions play across her face, and after a while it was like she wasn't with us anymore. She was with Leon, sitting in the warm shade, and she told us that it was she who had first kissed him, how she had thought about it for weeks and wanted him to do it but that all he did was talk until she finally realized that he wasn't going to cross that line, her being white and him not, and that she finally said, oh, to hell with it, and she took the bull by the horns, so to speak, and kissed him, and when she said it you knew that she was seeing his face as plain and clear before her as if it were happening now. She said the meetings became more frequent and frenzied and then she missed her period and then another, and she knew she was pregnant, thirteen and white and pregnant by Leon Williams, he of the African-American persuasion (no matter how watered-down that might be). She had been terrified to tell her mother and then she grew even more terrified not to, until finally she had, and then, of course, her parents demanded to know the identity of the father. Edith stopped abruptly, as if she realized that she wasn't Edith Johnson anymore, but was now Edith Boudreaux. She grew very quiet, and her face darkened. She said, "My father wanted me to name the boy. He kept after me for weeks, and I wouldn't tell them, and then one night he was drunk and he was beating me, and my mother was screaming you're going to make her lose that baby, and I didn't want to tell him but I was so scared that I would lose you . . ." She shook her head and crossed her arms again and began to blink back tears.

I said, "It's okay, Edith. You were a child. You were scared."

She nodded, but she didn't look at us, and the tears came harder. "He went out after Leon and he shot him. Just like that." A whisper.

Jodi said, "My God."

Edith wiped at her eyes, smearing the tears and her mascara and the mucus running from her nose. She gave a weak smile. "I must look like such a fool. I'm sorry."

Jodi said, "No."

Edith was getting control of herself. "Would you come back to my house? I could make coffee. There's so much more I'd like to tell you."

Jodi looked uncomfortable. "I really don't think I can." She looked at me like she wanted me to say something, like maybe we had someplace to go and I should check my watch and get her away from there.

Edith's eyes grew panicky. "You have three sisters, did you know that? I could show you their pictures." Pleading.

Jodi said, "I'm sorry. I have to get back to Los Angeles."

Edith shook her head and her face seemed to close and grow fearful. She said, "I didn't want to tell. I have cursed myself every day for it, but I just wasn't strong enough to save him." She put her face in her hands. "I want you to know that I would have kept you if I could. I want you to know that I've wondered about you, and prayed for you. God forgive me, I wasn't strong enough to save either one of you. Please forgive me for that. Please please please forgive me." Her shoulders heaved and she turned away and put her hands on the rail and wept.

The old man on the bench opened his eyes and sat up and looked at us. He said, "What in hell's going on over there?"

I leaned toward him. "Shut up or I'll kick your ass."

The old man untied the little dog and hurried away. I was blinking fast. Dust in the air. Damn dust is something.

Jodi said, "Edith?"

Edith shook her head.

Jodi said, "Edith, I forgive you."

Edith shook her head again, and her body trembled.

Jodi looked at me, and I said, "Whatever you want."

Jodi pursed her lips and blew a stream of air and stared at the rough board deck of the gazebo. She said, "Edith, I need to know one more thing. Did you love my father?"

Edith answered in a voice so small that we could barely hear her. Maybe we imagined it, hearing only what we wanted to hear. She said, "Oh, God, yes. I loved him so. God, how I loved him."

Jodi went to Edith and put her hands on her shoulders, and said, "Maybe we could stay for a little while, after all."

The two of them stood like that, Edith crying, Jodi patting her shoulder, together in the heat of the day.

21

We drove to Edith Boudreaux's house, parked in the drive, then went inside so that she could share her life with her long-lost daughter.

It was a nice house, furnished in Early American and smelling faintly of Pine-Sol. Everything was clean the way a home can be clean only after the children are older and have moved out. A grandfather clock stood in the entry, and a Yamaha piano was against the wall just inside the door. A cluster of family photographs sprouted on top of the Yamaha. Edith and Jodi moved together ahead of me, and there seemed a careful distance between them, each overly polite, each watchful and uncertain. Jodi said, "You have a lovely home."

"Thank you."

"Have you lived here for very long?"

"Oh, yes. Almost fifteen years, now." You see? Like that.

I sat in a wing chair at the end of the couch as they moved around the room examining the artifacts of Edith's life, as if we had stumbled upon a long-sealed chamber beneath the great pyramid. *This is my husband, Jo-el. This is when we were married. These are our daughters.* Pictures of the three grown daughters were spotted around the living room and hanging on the walls. Red-letter stuff: the graduation, the marriage. *That's Sissy, our oldest; she has two boys. That's Joana and Rick, they live in New Orleans. Barb's the baby, she's at LSU.* Jodi followed Edith from picture to picture with her hands clasped behind her back, unwilling to touch anything. She didn't seem particularly happy to be there, but maybe it was just me.

After a little bit of that, Edith said, "Would you like coffee? Coffee won't take but a minute." Nervous, and anxious to please.

Jodi looked at me, and I said, "That would be very nice. Thank you."

When Edith was gone, I lowered my voice. "How are you doing?"

Jodi made a little shrug. "It feels creepy."

"We can leave whenever you want."

She shook her head. "I'm here. I might as well learn whatever I can learn."

"Sure."

"I won't be coming back."

I spread my hands.

Jodi frowned. "Well, I can't very well be rude."

"Absolutely not."

When Edith came back with the coffee, Jodi was looking at the pictures on the piano. Edith had bypassed the Yamaha before, and didn't seem thrilled when she saw Jodi over there. Jodi said, "Are these your brothers and sisters?"

Edith poured the coffee, then handed me a small plate with three pecan pralines. I hadn't had pralines in years. She said, "Some of them." Not looking that way.

Jodi said, "Show me who's who."

Edith made a little frown as she joined Jodi at the pictures. "This is my mother, standing with my aunt. That's Jo-el when he was a boy. And these are my brothers and sisters. That's me. I was sixteen."

Jodi nodded and leaned closer to the pictures. "Which one is your father?"

Edith seemed to pull herself in. "I don't keep a picture of my father here."

"Elvis says you take care of him."

"Yes, that's true."

Jodi stared at Edith for a moment, then looked back at the pictures. "How do you and they live with it?"

Edith started to speak, stopped, then found some words. "Families keep secrets. We've never once spoken of it in all this time. My brother Nick was closest to my age. He was twelve, but he's dead. Sara was ten, and the others even younger. I don't know if they know or not."

Jodi made a whistling sound through her teeth. "He murdered a child and he got away with it. Just like that."

Edith crossed her arms again, as she had at the gazebo. "A man named Duplasus was the sheriff back then. He came to the house, and my father told him exactly what happened and why." She pulled her arms tighter, protection from the cold. "I'm sure Mr. Duplasus felt that my father's rage was justifiable, a white girl being ruined by a colored."

Jodi said, "Jesus Christ."

Edith came back to the couch. "Yes. Well. Things like this used to be called crimes of passion. Would you like more coffee, Mr. Cole?"

"Yes, ma'am. That would be nice."

Jodi turned away from the piano and stood in the center of Edith's living room. "You could've said something. You still can." She looked at me. "There's no statute of limitation on murder, is there?"

"Nope."

Edith said, "My father is eighty-six years old. He's incontinent and he talks to himself, and much of the time he's incoherent. I care for him now in ways that he doesn't always like, but I'm the only one to do it." She shook her head. "I'm not as angry as I used to be. Leon's been gone a very long while."

Jodi's jaw worked.

Edith made a little shrug, and seemed profoundly tired. "It's just the way we feel about it. I guess that's why we have this trouble."

I said, "Milt."

Edith looked at me. "My, but you must be a good detective."

Jodi said, "Who's Milt?"

Edith looked at her. "He didn't tell you what's going on?"

Jodi was frowning. "What didn't you tell me?"

Edie said, "Some of the same people who were blackmailing you are blackmailing us, too."

Jodi looked at me. "What?"

I said, "I told you what was relevant to you. Edith's business is Edith's business."

"Jesus Christ, but you're a tight-lipped sonofabitch."

I shrugged. "Privacy is my middle name." Jodi wanted me to fill her in and Edith said it was all right with her. I said, "Rebenack was working for a man named Milt Rossier. As near as I can figure it, Rebenack uncovered Leon Williams's murder and sold it to Rossier so that Rossier would have leverage over Edith's husband. Rebenack double-crossed Rossier by going behind his back to blackmail you. Rebenack thought he was being sharp, but that brought me into it and focused attention on Rossier." I looked at Edith. "You know Rebenack is dead."

She looked confused. "No. Jo-el hasn't said anything."

Jodi said, "Jesus Christ. Is everything in this family a secret?"

I said, "After Lucy Chenier and I came to see you, Rossier's goon picked me up and brought me out to the crawfish farm. There's no way that Rossier would've known that I came to see you unless your husband told him. Rebenack was out there, too.

Rossier wanted to know why I was digging around, and he became upset when I told him that Rebenack was putting the twist on Jodi. He didn't know that, and I suspect he killed Rebenack because of it."

Edith shook her head. "Jo-el wouldn't murder anyone. I don't believe that."

I shrugged.

Edith put down her coffee cup and said, "I told Jo-el that thirty-six years is enough lying. I said that I didn't want him to do anything wrong, and he said what was he supposed to do, go arrest my father?" She shook her head again and rubbed at her eyes. "This is a nightmare."

I looked at Jodi Taylor. "Sound familiar?"

"What?"

"You didn't want to pay extortion, either."

Jodi pursed her lips, then leaned toward Edith. "Can't your husband do something?"

"He wants to, but he doesn't know what. This is killing him." The skin around her eyes and mouth was tight, and showing the strain.

Jodi said, "I think it's killing both of you."

A car turned into the drive and Edith went to the door. "That will be Jo-el. I want you to meet him."

The front door opened and Sheriff Jo-el Boudreaux walked in, campaign hat in one hand, a rolled copy of *Sports Illustrated* in the other, looking the way you look when you're calling it quits after a long day. He stopped when he saw us, and said, "What's going on here?" Calm and reasonable, like you walk in every day to see a detective and a TV star sitting in your living room. Only not. His eyes flicked to Jodi, then came to me, and the calm look was the kind guys get when their hearts are pounding, but they know they've got to cover. Every cop I ever knew could get that look.

Edith stood. "Jo-el, this young lady is named Jodi Taylor." She wet her lips. "She's my daughter."

Jodi stood and offered her hand. "Hello, Mr. Boudreaux."

Edith said, "She's the one on TV, Jo-el. She's the little girl I gave away."

Jo-el Boudreaux took Jodi's hand without apparent feeling, shaking his head and making out as if all of this was sort of benignly confusing. "I don't understand, hon. Your mother gave away a baby." Like she had made a mistake recalling which day she'd gone to the market.

"We don't have to pretend, Jo-el." Edith put a hand on his arm. "They know. Those people were blackmailing her, too, just like they're doing to us."

Jo-el's eyes got wide and he wet his lips and his eyes flicked nervous and frantic. One minute you're coming home to take it easy with the new *Sports Illustrated*, the next you're watching your life go down the toilet. "No one's blackmailing us."

I said, "We're not going to hurt you, Jo-el. It's okay."

Sheriff Jo-el Boudreaux waved the *Sports Illustrated* at me. "I don't know what you think you've dug up, but we don't want any part of it." He squared himself toward me, making himself large and threatening. Cop technique. "I think you should leave."

Edith jerked at his arm. "You stop that! We need to talk about this. We need to start dealing with this."

Jo-el was frantic now and didn't know what to do. He said, "There's nothing to deal with, Edie. Do you understand me? There's nothing to talk about here, and they should leave."

Edith's voice grew harder. Insistent. "I want to know what's going on. I want to know if you're involved in a murder."

Jo-el Boudreaux's left eye ticked twice, and he took a single step toward me and I stood. Edith was pulling at his arm, her face red. I said, "I saw you with Milt Rossier. We know about Leon Williams and Edith's father. Rebenack was extorting Jodi and her studio, and Rossier is extorting you."

Boudreaux's eye ticked again and he shook his head. "No."

Edith said, "He says that Rossier killed that redheaded man. Do you know about that? Are you covering up for him?"

Boudreaux blinked hard, and he looked at his wife. "You know better than that." He squinted at me to stop the blinking. "If I knew who murdered Jimmie Ray Rebenack I would make an arrest. Maybe you did it. Maybe I should take you in for questioning."

I said, "Sure. That would look good in the local papers."

He shook his head again, and now the eye was ticking madly, like a moth caught in a jar. "I don't know what Edie's been saying to you, but she's been confused. She's not making sense."

Edith made a sudden, abrupt move and slapped her husband on the side of the face. There wasn't a lot on it, but the sound was sharp and clear, and Jo-el stepped back, surprised. Edith grabbed his arm and shook him. "Don't you dare speak about me that way! We have been living in a way that makes me ashamed, and I want it to stop. I want it to stop, do you hear?"

Jo-el took his wife by her upper arms. You could barely hear him. "You want me to go arrest your father? That's what will happen, and won't that be fine? You can even testify at his trial."

Edith was crying.

Jodi said, "We're on your side. Maybe we can help you. Maybe we can work together."

Jo-el Boudreaux said, "There's nothing to talk about. I don't know anything about this, so you take care of your business and let me worry about mine."

Edith was crying harder. "I want to stop lying. I want this to end."

Jo-el said, "Edie, Goddammit. *There's nothing to talk about.*" Denying it to the end.

Edith pulled away from him and ran back through the house, and a door slammed. For a long moment no one moved, and then Boudreaux went to the front door and held it open. He was breathing hard, and it took him a minute to control it. He looked at me and said, "Do you have a statement that you wish to make in the murder of Jimmie Ray Rebenack?"

"Let us help you, Jo-el."

He looked at Jodi. "I'm glad Edie had a chance to meet you,

but there's just been a misunderstanding here. We don't know anything about Milt Rossier, or about the murder of Leon Williams."

Jodi said, "You're being a fool."

Boudreaux nodded and looked back at me. "Where's it go from here?"

I said, "Jesus Christ, Boudreaux."

He blinked hard once. "I want to know." I thought he was about to cry.

I took a deep breath. "It starts here, it stops here. We won't give you up."

Sheriff Jo-el Boudreaux stood at the door, the big hand holding it open, the soft sounds of the neighborhood drifting in with the moist scent of cut grass, and then he simply walked away, back across the living room and through a door and after his wife.

Jodi and I went out through the door, closed it behind us, and drove away. The late afternoon had given way to the evening, and the sky in the east was beginning to purple. Fireflies traced uneven paths in the twilight.

Jodi huddled on her side of the car, arms crossed, staring out the window and chewing her lip. The lip started bleeding so she stopped with the lip and chewed at a nail. We drove in silence.

I said, "So say it."

"They're good people. He thinks he's protecting her because he's a big dumb goober, but he's making it worse for both of them."

"Uh-huh."

She glanced at her watch and her right knee began bouncing. Nervous energy. "I have to go back to L.A. to finish the show, but I can't just walk away. I want you to stay here and find out what's going on and see if you can help them."

The air had cooled, and smelled sweet, but I didn't know from what. "I have found that, in cases like this, the only way to escape the past is to confess it. They don't seem anxious to do that."

"I want you to try. Will you?"

"What about you?"

She looked at me. "What does that mean?"

"Who are you, Jodi? Do you want these people in your life?"

She stared at me for what seemed like years, and then she crossed her arms and settled back into the shadows. "I don't know what I want. Just help them, okay?"

"Okay."

22

We drove directly to the airport. Jodi bought the last remaining first class seat on a flight readying to leave the gate. They held the plane. Can't just fly away and leave America's sweetheart holding her bag.

Jodi said, "Call me whenever you want. The pickups should only take a few days, and then I'll come back."

"Sure."

She gave me a kiss, and then she was gone. A businessman with a receding hairline watched Jodi get on the plane. "Say, podnuh, that who I think it is?"

"Who'd you think it was?"

"That one on TV. The singer."

I shook my head. "Nope."

As I walked back through the terminal, I felt alone and at loose ends and overly aware that Lucy Chenier was only a short drive away. Of course, Lucy didn't seem particularly interested in my proximity, but that didn't make it any easier. I tried not thinking about her. I thought, instead, that perhaps I should do something exciting to clear my head. With a clear head, I could probably think of a way to help Edith Boudreaux, which was, of course, what I was being paid to do. Also, something exciting would probably make it easier to not think about Lucy.

It was twenty-three minutes after seven, and there were exactly six people in the terminal besides me. A man of action is ever resourceful, however, and one's options are limited only by one's imagination. Hmm. I could hike up to the levee and shoot rats, but that would be noisy and one probably needed a rat-shooting permit. Difficult to obtain. Okay, I could scale the outside of the state's thirty-two-story capitol building then paraglide onto the Huey Long Bridge, but where would I get the parasail? Rent-a-chute was probably closed, too. *Elvis Cole, this is your life!*

I drove to the Riverfront Ho-Jo, checked in yet again, then ordered a turkey sandwich from room service, and went up to my room. Twenty minutes later I was eating the sandwich when the phone rang. I said, "Diminished expectations. Elvis Cole speaking."

Lucy Chenier said, "If that was a play on *Great Expectations,* it's too obscure."

I said, "Hi." My heart speeded up and my palms went damp. We are often not as tough as we make out to be.

Lucy said, "I want to apologize for the way I acted. I'd like a chance to explain."

"It's not necessary."

"Jodi phoned me from the plane. She told me a little of what's going on, and, as before, she asked me to assist you in any way possible." She sounded mechanical, as if she were nervous.

"All right."

Lucy didn't say anything for a moment, and I wondered if the line had gone dead. Then she said, "I'm making dinner. If you'd like, you could join me and we could talk about these things."

"That would be very nice. Thank you."

"Do you remember the way?"

"Of course."

There was another pause before she said, "Then I'll see you soon."

"Yes."

"Good-bye."

I hung up and stared at the phone. Well, well. I threw away what was left of the turkey, took a quick shower, then talked the bartender in the hotel bar into selling me a bottle of merlot and a bottle of chardonnay for three times what they were worth. I made it to Lucy's in fourteen minutes. Try getting across Los Angeles in fourteen minutes. You'd need a Klingon battle cruiser.

Lucy's neighborhood was quiet, and her home was well lit and inviting. The same man and woman were walking the pinto Akita. I parked in the drive behind Lucy's Lexus, and nodded at them. The woman said, "It's such a lovely night."

I said, "Yes. It is, isn't it?"

Lucy answered the door in jeans and a soft red jersey top and dangling turquoise earrings, and I thought in that moment that I had never before been in the presence of a woman who looked so lovely. My heart pounded, hard and with great intensity. She said, "I'm glad that you could come."

I held up the bottles. "I didn't know what we were having."

She smiled and looked at the labels. "Oh, these are wonderful. Thank you."

She showed me into the kitchen. The kitchen was bright, but only a single light burned in the family room, and Janis Ian was on the stereo. Lucy and her home and the atmosphere within it seemed to have a kind of hyperreality, as if I had stepped into a photograph featured in *Better Homes & Gardens,* and I wondered how much of it was real and how much was just me. I said, "It smells terrific."

"I have *rumaki* in the oven for an appetizer, and I'm making roast duck with black cherry sauce for dinner. I hope that's okay."

I said, "Wow."

"I was having a glass of wine. Would you join me?" A bottle of

Johannesburg Riesling was on the counter near a mostly empty wineglass. The bottle was mostly empty, too.

"Please."

"Why don't we save your wine for dinner and have the Riesling now."

"Sounds good." She seemed to be moving as carefully around me as I was around her.

I opened the merlot to let it breathe while she brought out another glass and poured. I said, "Is there anything I can do to help?"

"Everything's done except for the cherry sauce. Why don't you sit at the counter and bring me up to date about Jodi while I do that."

Lucy opened a can of black pitted cherries and poured them into a saucepan with lemon juice and port and a lot of sugar, and then put the pan over a low fire. I told her how I had given Jodi the tour of Eunice and Ville Platte and how Jodi had introduced herself to Edith Boudreaux and what had happened when they met. Lucy nodded every once in a while and frowned when I got to the part about Jodi steaming into Edith's dress shop while there were customers, but mostly she sipped at her wine and concentrated on her cherry sauce. Nervous, I thought. Distracted. She finished her glass of wine and refilled it and added a drop to mine. The Riesling bottle was empty, and I'd only had one glass. I wondered how long she'd been working at it. I said, "I think the rumaki's burning."

She said, "Oh, damn," and took the rumaki from the oven. The rumaki were little bits of water chestnut wrapped in bacon and held together with toothpicks. The toothpicks were black and smoking, and a couple of the rumaki were overdone, but mostly they were fine. She put them on the stove.

I said, "I like them like that."

She smiled lamely and had another belt of the wine.

I said, "Are you okay?"

She put down the wineglass and looked at me. She'd been working at it, all right. "I really like you."

Something clutched in my stomach. "I like you, too."

She nodded and looked at the rumaki. She began taking them off the cooking pan and arranging them on a serving plate. I was breathing faster, and I tried to take it easy and slow the breathing. "Lucy?"

She finished arranging the rumaki and put the little plate on the counter between us. She said, "Would you please eat one of these things and tell me that it's wonderful."

I ate one. "They're wonderful."

She did not look happy.

"They're great. I mean it."

She drank more wine. I was breathing so fast that I thought my head might fill with blood and explode. I put my hand across the counter and she put her hand into mine. I said, "It's okay."

She shook her head.

I said, "It's going to be fine."

She took her hand back and walked across the big kitchen, and then she came back again. She put both hands flat on the counter and looked directly at me and said, "I'm drunk."

"Big secret."

She frowned. "Don't laugh at me."

"If I don't laugh at something I'm going to have a stroke."

She said, "When you went back to Los Angeles I realized how much I was liking you. I don't want to be involved with a man who lives two thousand miles away. I was mad at you for going. I got mad at you for coming back. Why'd you have to come back?"

The blood seemed to be rushing through my head, and my ears were ringing and I was blinking.

She said, "I have this rule. I don't get involved with people I work with. I'm feeling very confused and stupid and I don't like it."

I got a handle on the breathing, but I couldn't do anything

about the ears. I looked at the table in the dining area. Candles. Elegant seating for two. I said, "Where's Ben?"

"I sent him to sleep over at a friend's."

I stared at her and she stared back.

She said, "Jesus Christ, what kind of lousy detective are you? Do I have to draw you a map?"

I looked at the table and then I looked at the wine and then I looked at the rumaki. I went around the counter and into the kitchen and I said, "Help me detect some coffee." I started opening cabinets.

She waved her arms. "I just offered myself to you and you want coffee?"

I found a jar of Folger's Mountain Grown. I started looking for cups. "We're going to have coffee. We're going to eat." I found cups. I looked for a spoon so I could fix the goddamned coffee. "I do not want you to go to bed with me if you have to get drunk to do it!" I stopped all the slamming around and looking and turned back to her. "Do you understand that?"

Lucy opened her mouth, then closed it. She put one hand to the side of her head, then lowered it. She nodded, then thought for a moment, and then she shook her head, confused. "Is this some kind of male power trip or something?"

"Of course. Isn't that why men do everything?" I think I was yelling.

Lucy grew calm. "Please don't yell."

I felt the way I had when I'd lied to the Ville Platte librarian.

She crossed the kitchen and took my face in both her hands. She said, "I think the coffee is a good idea. Thank you."

I nodded. "You are absolutely beautiful."

She smiled.

"You are all that I think about. You have filled my heart."

She closed her eyes, and then she put her head against my chest.

We had the coffee, and then we had the duck. We sat on the couch in the dim family room and we listened to Janis Ian and we held hands. At a quarter to ten she made a phone call and asked how Ben was doing and then she wished him a good night. When she hung up she came back into the family room and said, "Watch this."

She stood with her feet together, held out her arms, then closed her eyes and touched her nose with her right index finger. She giggled when she did it, then opened her eyes. "Do I pass, officer?"

I picked her up and carried her to her bedroom. I said, "Ask me that in the morning."

"Studly, you probably won't last until morning."

23

I woke the next morning relaxed and warm and at peace, with Lucy snuggled beside me in her king-sized bed, small beneath light gray sheets and a comforter. Her breathing was even, and when I burrowed under the sheet and kissed her back, she said, "Mrmph."

I touched my tongue to her skin, and she said, "Sleepin'."

Her back was salty with sweat dried from the hours before. The bed and the room smelled of us and our lovemaking and the warmth of our bodies, and under it was the sweet smell of her fragrance and shampoo and soap. I lay there for a time, enjoying the warmth of her and the memories that the smells triggered, and after a while I could smell the food from the night before and the jessamine that grew around her home. Lucy's bedroom was large, her bed facing toward double French doors that opened toward the backyard. There were drapes, but the drapes were open so that I could see the used-brick patio and the Weber where we'd grilled the hamburgers. Three or four cardinals and maybe a half dozen sparrows were clustered around the bird feeder, chirping and scratching at the seed. We had cardinals in L.A., but you rarely saw them. The patio and the yard beyond it were filled with bright light, and somewhere there was the two-cycle whine of a lawn mower. It seemed as if there was always the sound of a lawn mower in Louisiana. Maybe that was the nature of this place, that the land was so fertile that life grew and expanded so quickly that a never-ending maintenance was in order, and without it the people who lived here would be overcome. I wondered for an instant if it could be that way with love, too, but then the thought was gone.

I eased out of the bed, careful not to wake her, then pulled on my underwear and went into her bathroom. I brushed my teeth with my finger, then went out to the kitchen. We had probably burned twenty thousand calories last night, and it was either make breakfast or fall upon Lucy and end up arrested for cannibalism.

I washed the dishes from the night before, then searched through her cupboards and fridge until I found Bisquick and frozen blueberries and some low-fat cottage cheese. There was a pancake griddle in a tall drawer beside the dishwasher, but I found a large skillet instead. Old habits. I poured a cup of the blueberries into a little bowl and covered them with water, then found a larger bowl and made a batter with the Bisquick and the cottage cheese and some nonfat milk. I sprayed the pan with butter-flavored Pam, then put it on a medium fire. While it was heating I ran out into the garden, clipped a pink rose, then ran back inside. I drained the blueberries and was mixing them in the batter when Lucy Chenier squealed, "Somebody help! There's a strange man in my house!"

She was standing on the other side of the counter, wrapped in a sheet. I gave her Groucho. "Don't be scared, little girl. That's not a chain saw. I'm just happy to see you."

"Ho, ho. Keep dreaming."

I held out my hand, fingers spread. She laced her fingers between mine. Her fingers were warm and felt good. I said, "Good morning."

"Good morning." We grinned at each other. She made a big

deal out of looking around and shook her head. "You cleaned up. You're making breakfast."

I turned back to the berries. "We're a full-service agency, ma'am."

She let the sheet drop and came around the counter and snuggled against me. "You can say that again, trooper." She looked out from under my arm at the batter. "Pancakes. Yum. What can I do?"

"Find me a spatula?"

She did.

I gave her a kiss. "Will you go in today?"

She snuggled against me again. "Maybe after lunch. I can barely walk, you animal."

I increased the heat under the pan, then spooned in four equal amounts of batter, making sure each pancake had a like number of berries. I made the batter dry so that the cakes would be thick and fluffy. I said, "A woman of your advancing years needs regular workouts, else she gets out of shape."

"Pig." She dug her thumb between my ribs, then hugged me again and widened her eyes. "Hmm. I could think of something to eat besides pancakes."

I adjusted the heat down. When they're thick like that you have to be careful with the heat, hot at first to set the cake and keep it from spreading, then low so that it will cook through without burning. "A man of my advancing years needs enormous sustenance to even pretend to keep up with a woman of your years."

"I guess that's right. Female superiority."

"Tell me about it." I put down the spatula, touched the tip of her nose, then her lips. I said, "You are devastatingly beautiful."

She nodded. "Um-hm."

I ran my finger down between her breasts and along the flat plane of her belly. "Perfect in all discernible ways."

She made a purring sound. "Ah."

"And a pretty fair lay." I turned back to the pancakes.

"That's not what you said last night, big guy." She pressed her breasts into my back, and then she stepped back and touched the places on my lower back and side. "What are these?"

"I caught some frag in Vietnam."

I felt her fingers move from scar to scar. They're little scars. "How did that happen?"

"I was trying to hide in the wrong place at the wrong time."

She bent low and kissed one of the marks and then she touched the puckered scar high on the top of my left trapezius. "What happened there?"

"A hood named Charlie DeLuca shot me."

She ran her finger along the scar. It's a little crater shaped like an arrowhead. She said, "Do you get shot often?"

"Only the once."

She came around in front of me and pulled my face down and looked deep into my eyes, frowning. "Do me a favor and don't get shot anymore, okay?"

"Aw, shucks. Not even a little bit?"

She shook her head. Slow. "Uh-uh."

When the pancakes were done we heaped them with sliced bananas and maple syrup, then sat at the counter with our knees touching. She said, "These are wonderful."

I nodded. "Old family recipe. Ideal for restoring one's energy reserves and reinvigorating the libido."

"Ah. Something to look forward to."

I wiggled my eyebrows.

She said, "So are you going to be able to help the Boudreauxs?"

"I don't know. Jo-el isn't going to cooperate, so I'll have to figure out what Milt has going and how to make him back away. I'll probably need help to do that, so I'll have my partner come in."

"You have a partner?"

"An ex–police officer named Joe Pike. He owns the agency with me."

She ate a piece of the pancake, then a slice of the banana. "Do you have any leads?"

"Sandi."

"The name in Jimmie Ray's papers?"

I nodded and kept eating. I was getting close to the end of the pancakes and was thinking I should make a couple more. "I found two messages on his answering machine from a woman who implied some sort of romantic relationship. If that's Sandi, maybe Jimmie Ray told her what was going on."

"And maybe she'll tell you."

"Maybe." I finished my plate and frowned at the batter. Enough for one more, maybe two.

Lucy split what was left on her plate and pushed the larger piece onto mine. Mind reader. "I won't be able to finish."

"Thanks." I dug in.

She took a last bit of pancake, then set her fork onto her plate. "How will you find her?"

"Shouldn't be hard. If they were close, they would've talked often. I'll go back through his phone bills and try the most frequently dialed local numbers. I'll dial them and hope that someone named Sandi answers."

Lucy leaned forward on her elbows and grinned. "You make it sound easy."

"Private detecting has very little in common with multidimensional calculus, Lucille." I finished the last of the pancake and touched my napkin to my lips. "Also, it is only easy if the call from Jimmie Ray's to Sandi's was a toll call. If she lived across the street, her number won't show up on the bills and we're screwed."

Lucy grinned wider and looked devilish. "There's no way I'm going to work without knowing this." She slid off the stool and came back with her briefcase and we went through the papers I had taken from Jimmie Ray Rebenack. It didn't take long. We had four phone bills stretching back five months, the two most recent, then a missing bill, and then the two earlier bills. We started with the earliest bill and found fourteen calls to the same number in Baton Rouge. This was during the same month in which he'd made the calls to Jodi and Sid. The next month showed twelve calls to that number, and the two most recent bills showed six calls and two calls respectively. Lucy said, "Do you think it's her?"

I used Lucy's kitchen phone and dialed the number. It rang four times, and then a woman's voice said, "Hi! I can't come to the phone right now, but please leave your message and I'll get back to you! Promise!" The voice was bright and cheery, and was exactly the same voice I'd heard on Jimmie Ray Rebenack's machine.

I hung up and spread my hands. *"Voilà."*

Lucy said, "You sonofagun."

I tried to look modest. "The kid's a pistol."

Lucy wrote down the number and made a note beside it. "I can run the number through our office and get a name and address. Would that help, oh great seer, or can you just sort of infer those things from the way her phone rang?"

"It's important for the little people to feel helpful. You can take care of it."

She put the note and the papers into her briefcase, then put the briefcase aside and leaned close to me. "The pancakes were wonderful, Elvis. Thank you."

"Darlin', you ain't seen nothing yet."

She slid off the stool and patted my arm. "Perhaps I'll see it this evening. I've got a one o'clock that I can't miss and I smell. I'm going to take a shower."

I watched her disappear into the rear of her home, put the dishes into the sink, and then I used her kitchen phone to call Joe Pike. He answered on the second ring and said, "It's you." That Pike is something, isn't he?

"How did you know it was me?"

He didn't answer.

I gave him the short version on Edith and Jo-el Boudreaux and Milt Rossier and what we wanted to do. I told him about Sandi. When I was done he said, "I can come in tonight or tomorrow."

I said, "Tomorrow's fine. Tonight I have plans."

He said, "Uh."

I said, "Call Lucy Chenier's office with your arrival time. I'll pick you up."

Joe hung up without another word. Some partner, huh?

I put the dishes in the sink, then walked back to Lucy's bedroom and into her bath. The water was running, and the steam from the water had fogged the mirror. I peeled off my underwear and let myself into the shower and ran my hands over her back and down along her sides and across her belly. She was slick and glistening, and her flesh was firm. Her hair was white with bubbles. She said, "Well, I guess the old family recipe is working." She turned and pressed into me. "Let's not forget my one o'clock. I don't have very much time."

"Efficiency," I said. "Efficiency is the key to all happiness." I worked my fingers into her hair.

"Perhaps I could be ravished and cleaned at the same time. Do you think?"

I worked the soap down along her neck and shoulders. "I think I'm up for the try."

She smiled and sank down to her knees. "You are," she said. "But not for long."

24

The next morning, Lucy and I were in the Baton Rouge Airport at 11:40, waiting for Joe Pike. We had been together twenty-eight minutes and had done a fine job of keeping our clothes on. I was pleased with my self-control. I had cramps, but I was pleased.

When Pike's plane taxied in, she said, "How will I recognize him?"

"He's six-one and he weighs right at one-ninety. He has short brown hair and large red arrows tattooed on the outside of each deltoid. He'll be wearing jeans and a gray sweatshirt with the sleeves cut off and dark glasses."

"How do you know what he'll be wearing?"

"It's what he wears."

"All the time?"

"If it's cold, he wears a Marine Corps parka."

She smiled. "And if the occasion were formal?"

"Think of it as consistency. Joe Pike is the most consistent person I know."

"Hm."

"And if he speaks, he will be direct. He won't say much. That's just his way."

"It sounds like you're warning me."

"Preparing. Preparing is a better word."

Joe Pike materialized in the file of passengers as if he were there yet not there, as separate from them as one photograph superimposed upon another. He came to us, and we shook. I said, "Lucy Chenier, this is Joe Pike. Joe, Lucy."

Lucy put out her hand and said, "It's a pleasure, Mr. Pike."

Pike's head swiveled toward her and he gave her the full focus of his attention. He is like that with people. You are either there to him, or you are not. If you are there, he gives you all of himself. He said, "Joe." He took her hand, held it for a moment, then kissed it. Gracious.

Lucy beamed. "Why, thank you."

"You're a couple."

That pleased her, too. "Is it that obvious?"

Joe nodded.

I said, "You can let go of the hand, now, Joe."

Joe's head swiveled my way, his eyes hidden and secret behind the black lenses of his glasses. His mouth twitched, and he let go of Lucy's hand. Joe will never smile, but his mouth will twitch, so you know he found this funny. He looked at Lucy again, then came back to me. The mouth twitched a second time. A riot, for Joe. Absolute insane hysteria. He said, "I've got a bag."

We collected an olive green duffel bag from the claim area, then picked up the car, and drove cross town toward Lucy's office. Pike rode in the back and Lucy was in the front. She sat sideways so that she could see him. "Have you been to Louisiana before, Joe?"

Pike said, "Uh-huh."

"When was that?"

"A while back."

"Did you enjoy yourself?"

Pike didn't answer.

She twisted more in her seat to get a better look at him. "Joe?"

Pike was staring out the window, the passing scenery racing across the dark lenses. Immobile.

Lucy looked at me and I patted her leg. You see?

As we drove I brought Joe up to speed on Milt Rossier and Jodi Taylor and what Jodi wanted us to do. I told him what I had uncovered about Leon Williams, and how Rossier was using it against the Boudreauxs, and I told him about Jimmie Ray Rebenack and Sandi. "Lucy ran a DMV check on Sandi through her firm and got us a name and an address."

Lucy said, "Sandi's last name is Bergeron. She's twenty-eight years old, unmarried, and she works in the Social Services Department here in the capitol building."

I said, "A guy like Jimmie Ray couldn't get sealed state documents without help, so maybe that's Sandi."

Pike said, "Um." It was the first sound he'd made in fifteen minutes. "What about Rossier?"

Lucy took a 9 by 12 manila envelope from her briefcase and passed it to Pike. "My friend in the attorney general's office gave me a printout of Rossier's file. Rossier ran prostitution and intimidation rackets through the sixties and seventies until he was convicted of supplying methamphetamines to a local motorcycle gang in nineteen seventy-three. He pulled twenty-four months in Angola, then went into the fish farm business. The fish farm is legitimate, but its primary purpose is to launder money. He was indicted as a co-conspirator in two drug-related murders, and suspected of involvement in six additional homicides."

Pike looked through the file as they spoke. "So how come this guy's walking around?"

"Action was dropped on the indictments when the state's witnesses disappeared. They don't think Rossier pulled the trigger, but they believe he ordered it. They think LeRoy Bennett did the shooting, or a man named René LaBorde."

Pike offered the file back, but Lucy shook her head. "You can keep it if you'd like. Just be careful with it. My friend could get in trouble if anyone found out he'd given it to me."

I said, "He?"

Pike tapped my shoulder. Getting my attention. "You think Boudreaux is involved with Rossier in some kind of crime?"

"I don't think so. I think he's just looking the other way so that Rossier can do whatever he's doing."

Pike said, "But we don't know what that is."

I shook my head. "Not yet, but maybe Sandi Bergeron can tell us."

Pike went back to staring out the window. "Some great gig, helping people who don't want to be helped."

Lucy twisted around to again look at Pike. "Mrs. Boudreaux wants the help. She'd like to put this behind her. Jodi Taylor hired us to do that."

Pike said, "Us."

Lucy said, "Do you have a problem with that?"

Pike's mouth twitched. "Not at all." He squeezed her arm. "Thanks for the help."

I frowned. "What's your relationship to this guy in the A.G.?"

Lucy made a big sigh. "I love a man with raging hormones."

We dropped Lucy at the curb outside her office. She gathered her things and offered her hand to Joe Pike. "It was a pleasure, Joe. You're an interesting man."

Pike said, "Yes."

Lucy gave me a kiss, then let herself out and went into her building. I twisted around in the seat and looked at Joe. "She says you're interesting and you say yes?"

Pike got out of the back and into the front. "Did you want me to lie?"

We drove to the capitol building and parked in the shade of an enormous oak near the banks of a lake. The Louisiana State capitol building is thirty-four stories of art-deco monolith rising above the Mississippi River, sort of like the Empire State Building in miniature. It's the largest state capitol building in the nation, and looks like the kind of place that Charles Foster Kane would call home. Huey Long was assassinated there.

A tour group of retired people from Wisconsin were filing through the lobby, and we filed with them, slipping past a couple of guards who were laughing about the New Orleans Saints, and taking an elevator to the sixth floor. The Social Services Department was on the sixth floor. We could have phoned ahead and asked to speak with Sandi Bergeron, and Sandi might have been willing to talk with us, but you never know. Surprise is often your only recourse.

We went through a door marked Social Services and up to an older African-American woman sitting behind a high counter. You had to pass her if you wanted access to the rest of the social services offices, and she didn't look like she'd be easy to pass. I said, "I'd like to see Sandi Bergeron, please." Lucy's DMV check said that Sandi was something called an associate claims monitor, and that she worked in this office.

The woman said, "Is she expecting you?"

I gave her one of my nicer smiles. "It's kind of a surprise. Tell her it's Jimmie Ray Rebenack." She would either know he was dead, or she wouldn't. If she knew, she'd call security. If she didn't, she'd come out to see him.

The woman picked up her phone and punched some numbers. I said, "We'll wait outside in the hall."

The woman covered the receiver and said that that would be fine, and Pike and I went out into the hall.

We were there no more than thirty seconds when a woman in her late twenties hurried out. She had teased blond hair and thin shoulders and rings on both the third and fourth fingers of her right hand, just like the woman in the photograph I'd found at Rebenack's office. Sandi Bergeron, letting Jimmie Ray put a bag on her head and snap a nudie shot. She wore too much makeup, and her nails were the color of Bazooka bubble gum.

She glanced at me and Pike, then looked past us, first one way down the hall and then the other. Looking for Jimmie Ray. She frowned when she didn't see him and started back inside. I said, "Ms. Bergeron?"

She stopped. Confused. "Are you here with Jimmie Ray?" She didn't know he was dead.

"I've got some bad news, Ms. Bergeron. Is there someplace we can talk?"

She looked from me to Pike and back again. She looked nervous. "Are you the police?"

I shook my head. "No, ma'am."

"Where's Jimmie? They said he was here."

"He couldn't make it. Is there someplace we can talk?"

You could see the world slow down for her. You could see the ceiling lower and the end of the hall recede and the pounding of her pulse grow to mask all lesser sounds. She seemed to sway, the way a reed might in a soft breeze, and then she shook her head. "I'm sorry. I don't know you, and I don't think I have anything to say to you."

She turned back to her office. I took her arm and quietly said, "Jimmie's dead. Milt Rossier had him murdered."

In that instant she tried to pull away from me, but I held on, and, just as quickly, she stopped pulling. Tears welled and she blinked frantically, and pretty soon the tears were gone. People moved along the hall, in and out of offices, in and out of the elevators. I let go of her and stepped back.

I said, "We're not the police, and we're not from Milt Rossier. We won't hurt you."

She nodded.

"I'm a private investigator, and I'm not after you. I'm after Milt. He's the guy I want to hurt. Do you understand?"

She nodded again. Getting her breath under control. "He killed Jimmie Ray?"

"I believe so. Yes."

"It's about those files, isn't it?"

"We shouldn't talk in the hall."

She brought us two flights down to an employees' cafeteria that smelled of hamburgers and lima beans. We sat at a table with a view across the city and drank coffee while Sandi Bergeron told us that she had met Jimmie Ray ten months ago when he had come to her office to ask for Jodi Taylor's adoption records. Just like that, he had walked in and asked if he could have a copy. They'd told him no, of course, and turned him away, but Jimmie Ray had hung around out in the hall by the Coca-Cola machine, stomping about and fuming and convinced that "the Boss Bitch," as he'd called Mrs. Washington, was just looking for a payoff. Sandi had gone out for a Dr Pepper and had met Jimmie there when he'd asked her if she had change of a dollar. She was surprised when he'd phoned a few days later, tracking her down by calling the Social Services Department and saying that he'd like to speak with "the pretty blond girl." They had connected him with two other women before they put on Sandi Bergeron, who was not pretty, and never would be, and would always feel bad about it.

Three weeks later, when they were lying in bed, he'd asked what was the big deal with these sealed documents, did they keep 'em in a goddamned vault or somethin'?

Two weeks after that, when they were lying in bed, he'd asked if she'd ever *seen* one of these sealed documents and, if she hadn't, how did she know they were really there?

One week after that, when they were lying in bed, he'd asked if she could get her hands on Jodi Taylor's adoption records, and, if she could, would she give it a quick read and tell him Jodi's bio-mama's name?

He hadn't asked her to steal the file, she said, but by the time she had it in her hands she was just so gol-darned nervous that it was just easier to steal it than to stand there reading the thing. So she had.

I said, "Did you know that Jimmie Ray was working for Milt Rossier?"

"Not then he wasn't. He was just lookin' for somethin' he

could sell to the *National Enquirer* or one of those magazines. Only he found that thing about Leon Williams and that sheriff over there, and he took it to Milt Rossier."

"You knew about the blackmail?"

She looked defensive. "Jimmie Ray said Mr. Rossier was gonna put him on retainer. He said he wouldn't have to work as a mechanic anymore. Jimmie didn't want to be a nobody all his life."

Pike said, "He doesn't have to worry about it any more, does he?"

Sandi Bergeron stared at him, and then had some of her coffee.

I said, "Did Jimmie Ray tell you why Milt was blackmailing the sheriff?"

She shook her head.

"Did he tell you anything about Rossier's business?"

"I'm sorry."

"Please try to remember."

She put down the coffee cup and picked at the table. The bubble-gum nails were long and French-tipped and probably false. She made a little shrug. "Jimmie didn't know everything that old man had going, and Jimmie Ray had spent a lot of time trying to find out. He told me so himself. He said that Mr. Rossier was so careful about all these things that he'd never get caught. He said he learned a lot from that old man."

"Like what?"

You could see her work to try to remember. "He said the old man never got involved himself. He had this other guy do that."

"LeRoy Bennett."

"Jimmie Ray called him a stooge. He said that if there was ever any trouble, it would all go back to the stooge."

"What else?"

She chewed at her lips, thinking harder. "He told me about this place called the Bayou Lounge."

"Uh-huh."

"Mr. Rossier owns it. Jimmie Ray said that the old man

bought it so he wouldn't have to bring any of his bad business home. Jimmie thought that was just the smartest thing. He said the old man's stooge would go to the Bayou Lounge to take care of business. That way they didn't have to bring it home. You see?"

I glanced at Pike, and Pike nodded. He said, "If we're looking for something, maybe we should look there."

Sandi Bergeron crossed her arms over her middle. She said, "Am I going to get in trouble?"

I looked at her. "Maybe, but not because of us. The cops are going to investigate Jimmie's murder, and they may find you the way we found you, but it won't be because we told them. We won't."

She nodded and looked at her coffee. "I know that what I did was wrong. I'm really sorry."

"Sure."

"I think I'm going home. I don't feel well."

We walked to the elevator with her. She pressed the button for *up.* We pressed for *down.* The *up* elevator came first, but she didn't get on right away. She stopped in the door and said, "I know what you're thinking, but it's not so. Jimmie Ray didn't use me. He loved me. We were goin' to get married." She stood straight when she said it, as if she were challenging me to disagree.

I said, "Sandi?"

She stared at me.

"I got to know Jimmie Ray a little bit before he died. You were all he talked about. He did want to marry you. He told me so."

She blinked hard twice and her eyes filled. She stepped backward into the elevator, the doors closed, and she was gone.

We stood in silence for a moment, and then Pike said, "Is that true?"

The *down* elevator came. We got aboard, and I did not answer.

25

We drove back to the Riverfront Ho-Jo, checked out, then called Lucy at her office and told her that we were on our way to Ville Platte. She said, "Do you know what you're going to do when you get there?"

"Sit on the Bayou Lounge and establish a pattern for Rossier and his people. It could take a while."

She didn't say anything for a moment. "Yes. I guess it could."

"I'm going to miss you."

"Me, too, Studly. Try not to get shot."

At a little bit before two o'clock that afternoon, Pike and I took the same room I had used before in Ville Platte and unloaded our things. I changed into waterproof Cabela boots and a black T-shirt. Pike stayed in the same clothes, but took a Colt .357 Python out of his duffel and put it under his sweatshirt. I put my Dan Wesson into a clip-on holster, put the clip-on on the inside of my waistband, and left the T-shirt out to cover it. My T-shirt didn't hide the Dan Wesson as well as Pike's sweatshirt hid the Python. People would probably think I was wearing a colostomy bag.

We went down to the Pig Stand for a couple of catfish poboys, then walked across to the little superette, bought a cheap Styrofoam ice chest, ice, and enough Diet Coke, Charmin, and sandwich stuff to last a couple of days. Pike went for the cheese and peanut butter, I went for the pressed chicken and Spam. Pike shook his head when he saw the Spam. He was shaking his head about the Spam even before he was a vegetarian. The woman at the register thought we must be going fishing, and we said sure. She said the *sac-à-lait* were biting real good. She said her husband went out just last night and got a couple dozen on the bayou just over there by Chataignier. We thanked her and said we'd give it a try. Walking out, Pike said, "What's a *sac-à-lait*?"

"I think it's a kind of white perch. Like a crappie."

Pike grunted.

I said, "They eat gar balls down here, too."

Pike gave me a look like, yeah, sure.

Lucy had provided us with a current address for LeRoy Bennett. We got the Bayou Lounge address from Information. Pike and I decided to split our time between LeRoy's and the crawfish farm during the day, then watch the lounge together at night. We went to LeRoy's first.

LeRoy Bennett lived on a narrow residential street on the west side of Ville Platte in a tiny clapboard house that was dusty and dirty and overgrown by weeds. All of the houses on the street were small, but most were well kept with neatly trimmed lawns and edged walkways. The St. Augustine at LeRoy's place had to be a good eight inches tall, the crabgrass and weed sprouts even taller. Twin tire ruts were cut into the yard, with great black dead spots between them where LeRoy had parked the Polara and the engine had dripped. There was a drive, but why use the drive when you can park on the grass? I was hoping that LeRoy and his car would be there so that Pike could see them, but they weren't. Of course, maybe they were hidden behind all the foliage. I said, "That's LeRoy's place."

Pike shook his head. "No self-esteem."

I stopped at the mouth of LeRoy's drive. "He drives a gold Polara with a lot of sun damage." I looked up and down the street. Cars were parked along both sides of the street. "Best place for a stake would be on the next block, under that oak."

Pike looked and approved. Next door to LeRoy's, a man in his mid-sixties was working Bond-o into the side of a beige '64 Chevelle. His home and his lawn were immaculate, but the weeds from LeRoy's crappy yard hung over onto his property like shaggy hair curling over a collar. He looked at us, taking a break from the Bond-o, and we drove away.

We went to Milt Rossier's crawfish farm. I cruised the front gate to let Pike have a look, then parked the car on a little gravel road maybe a quarter mile away. We worked our way through the trees to the edge of Milt's property and crouched by a fallen pine. We could see pretty much everything, from the ponds and the processing buildings on our left up to Milt's home on the little knoll to our right. When we were in position and looking, I said, "Well, well. The gang's all here."

LeRoy Bennett was talking to a heavyset woman by the processing buildings and Milt Rossier was driving a little golf cart between the ponds with one of his skinny foremen. LeRoy's Polara was parked up by the house, and René LaBorde was at the house, too, sitting in a white lawn chair, either sleeping or staring at his crotch. Pike squinted when he saw René. "This is some operation."

"Uh-huh."

We watched as people waded into ponds, scattering what was probably crawfish food and pulling weeds and keeping the bottoms stirred. In other ponds, people used trucks with winches to seine out slick gray catfish or dark red crawfish, emptying filled nets into little trailers with open tops. Some of the people working the ponds were African-American women, but most of them were short, blocky Hispanics. A couple of older, skinny white guys in wide-brimmed straw hats moved between the pools, telling everybody else what to do. Upper management. I said, "Seen enough?"

Pike nodded.

We made our way back to the Thunderbird, then drove to the Bayou Lounge, just west of Ville Platte off the State 10 near Reddell. It was a small, white building set back from the road in a little clearing carved into the woods. An abandoned bait shop sat nearby, its windows boarded over, painted ground to roof with ICE and WORMS in ten-foot letters. Both buildings were surrounded by crushed oyster shells and little patches of grass and weeds, and felt sort of like LeRoy Bennett's place. Crummy. A rusted steel pole jutted up from the side of the bar with a sign that said SCHLITZ. The Bayou Lounge didn't look like a hotbed of criminal activity, but you never know.

We eased off the road past the bait shop, stopped, and looked back. It was thirty-six minutes after three. A blue Ford Ranger was parked on the side of the lounge and a Lone Star truck was parked out front. If there was a bayou around, you couldn't see it from the road. A guy in a blue-and-white Lone Star uniform pushed a hand truck out the door, followed by a woman with a clipboard. The woman with the clipboard had a lot of bright red Clairol hair piled atop her head and red nails and red lipstick. Thin in the shoulders and wide in the butt, with white denim pants that were ten years and fifteen pounds too tight. She talked with the guy as he loaded the dolly onto his truck, then watched him drive away before she went back inside. Pike said, "I make it for her Ford. You want to check it, or me?"

"Me."

We pulled around to the front of the lounge and parked by the Schlitz sign, and I went in. Six cases of Lone Star were stacked at the end of the bar, and the woman was frowning at a thin Hispanic guy as he lugged them one at a time behind the counter. Eight or nine small square tables were scattered around the place, all with upended chairs on top of them, and a Rockola jukebox was against the back wall beside a door that said RESTROOMS. An industrial wash bucket was by the jukebox, and the back door was open for the breeze. The woman looked over at me and said, "Sorry, sugah. We closed."

"I'm supposed to meet a guy here. What time you open?"

" 'Bout five, give or take. Who you lookin' by?" She gave me a loose smile. She was maybe forty-five, but looked older, with rubbery skin pulled tight by all the smiling. The Hispanic guy stopped working to look at us.

"Oh, just a friend." Mr. Mysterious.

"You keepin' it a big secret or what, sug? I'm here all the time." When she said it she noticed the Hispanic guy and snapped at him. "Don't just stand there, goddammit! Put that stuff away! *Endelay!*" The Hispanic guy spun back to his work with a vengeance. I wasn't sure if he understood what had been said to him, but he understood that she was pissed. The Clairol Queen flipped her hand at him, disgusted. "These spics are somethin'. Gimme a good nigger any day."

I said, "A guy named LeRoy Bennett said I could find him here."

She went back to the smiling and folded herself against the bar. It was probably a pose that played well with the older guys after a dozen or so beers. "Oh, yeah. LeRoy's here all the time. I can take a message, you want."

"Nah. I'm on my way to Biloxi. I'll catch him on the way back."

I went back to the car and climbed in beside Pike. "They open at five. LeRoy's here all the time."

"Who could blame him?"

We drove up the road for a mile and a half, then turned around and went back. One hundred yards past the bait shop I eased onto the shoulder, and Pike got out with his duffel and moved into the trees. I drove on for maybe another four hundred yards until I found a gravel timber road running across a plank bridge, and pulled off. I locked the car, then trotted back to the bait shop. By the time I got back Pike was inside and set up, watching the bar through a clean spot he'd made on the dusty plate glass.

The Bayou Lounge might have opened at five, but no one showed up until six, and then it was mostly younger guys with deep tans and ball caps, looking like they had just gotten off work and wanted to have a couple of cold ones before heading home. Someone cranked up the Rockola at nine minutes before seven, and we could hear Doug Kershaw singing in French.

Pike and I made cold sandwiches and drank Diet Coke and watched the people come and go, but none of them were Milt Rossier or LeRoy Bennett or even René LaBorde. Crime might have been rampant, but if it was, we didn't see it.

The bait shop was an empty cinder-block shell containing the remnants of a counter and a couple of free-standing shelves and a cement floor. We sat on the floor, surrounded by the odd-cut piece of plywood and about a million rat pellets. Everything was covered with a thick layer of heretofore undisturbed dust, and everything smelled of mildew. "Just think, Joe, some guys have to wear a tie and punch a time clock."

Pike didn't answer.

At 8:15 that night, seven cars were parked in the oyster shell lot and maybe a dozen people were inside the Bayou Lounge, but Milt Rossier and LeRoy Bennett were not among them. Pike rarely spoke, and there wasn't a great deal to do in our watching, and I found myself thinking of Lucy, wondering where she was and what she was doing, seeing her in her office, seeing her on the couch in her family room, seeing her snuggled with Ben watching *Star Trek*. After a while I got tired of all the thinking about it and tried to stop, but then I thought that maybe I could walk across to the Bayou and use the pay phone to call her. Of course, if I did, ol' Milt and LeRoy would probably amble in at exactly that time. It's one of those laws of nature. Pike said, "You deserve someone."

"What are you talking about?"

"Ms. Chenier."

I stared at him. Do you think he reads minds? "We enjoy each other's company."

He nodded.

"I like her and she likes me. It's nothing more or less than that."

He nodded again.

By 9:15 we were down to two cars, and by ten the lot was empty except for the blue Ford Ranger. Pike said, "This place is a gold mine."

At twenty minutes before eleven, a beat-up Mercury station wagon bumped into the lot and sat with its engine running. The little Hispanic man and a Hispanic woman I had not seen came out, got in, and the wagon lurched away. The woman was carrying what looked like a brown paper grocery bag. Pike said, "Latin guy driving."

I squinted, but couldn't be sure. "Joe? Do you find it odd that there are so many Latin people down here on the bayou?"

Pike shrugged.

At ten minutes after eleven, the Bayou Lounge went dark, and the woman who ran the place got into her Ford and drove away. Pike and I gathered our things, walked up the road to our car, then returned to the motel. I wanted to phone Lucy, but it was just before midnight, and I thought I might wake her or, if not her, Ben.

The last thing I remember that night was the sound of Lucy's laugh and the smell of her skin, and the deep, hollow feeling of her absence.

26

At eighteen minutes after five the next morning, Joe Pike slipped into the woods fronting Milt Rossier's crawfish farm. I went back to Ville Platte and parked beneath the oak tree one block down from LeRoy Bennett's house. The sky began to lighten at twenty minutes after six, and by 7:30 the old man who lived next to LeRoy was again working at the beige Chevelle with the Bond-o and the putty knife. A fluffy white cat strolled up to the old man, shoulder bumped against his legs, and the old man scratched at the cat's head. The old man and the cat seemed to be enjoying each other when LeRoy Bennett came out with a little green towel, hawked up a lugey, and let'r fly into the overgrown front lawn. The old man stopped with the cat and scowled at Bennett. Bennett had to see him but pretended he didn't, and neither of them spoke to the other. LeRoy wiped the dew off his front and back windshields, then tossed the wet towel up onto his front steps, climbed into the Polara, and drove away. The old man watched him drive off, then looked at the towel and at LeRoy's crummy yard. The towel looked like hell, just thrown there. The old man looked at his own immaculate yard and shook his head.

Probably wondering why he should bother with all the yard work if LeRoy was going to let his place look like a shit hole, probably thinking that all the stuff you hear on the talk radio was right; America was going to hell in a handbasket and he was stuck with living proof of it.

The plan had been for me to stay on LeRoy until four, whereupon I would break contact and pick up Pike to return to the Bayou Lounge. We hoped that LeRoy would, in his capacity as Milt Rossier's right-hand man, have a variety of important errands to accomplish through the day, perhaps one or more of said errands providing a clue as to Milt Rossier's criminal operation. When LeRoy Bennett cleared the corner, I pulled a quick U-turn, took it easy going around the corner to make sure he wouldn't see me, then followed him directly to the Ville Platte Dunkin' Donuts. LeRoy stoked up on crullers with sprinkles, then bought four dollars of gas at the Sunoco self-serve and tooled directly to Rossier's place. By 8:36 that morning, LeRoy was sitting in the white lawn chairs outside Rossier's main house, flipping through a magazine, and I was crouching behind the fallen pine tree with Joe Pike. So much for clues. I said, "Some operation."

Pike was watching him through a fine pair of Zeiss binoculars. "He's not reading. He's just looking at the pictures."

I nodded. "Geniuses rarely go into crime."

We sat on plastic poncho liners amid the sumac and the small plants of the forest's floor and let the day unfold. The heat rose, and with the heat the air grew heavy and damp, and a thick gray buildup of rain clouds appeared overhead. The woods were alive with the sounds of bees and lizards and squirrels and swamp martins, and only occasionally did we catch the voices of the people before us, moving through their labors in the ponds and pools of the fish farm. It was ordinary business and none of it appeared illegal or suspicious, but maybe all of it was.

About midmorning Milt Rossier came out of his house, and he and Bennett strolled down past the ponds to the processing sheds.

Milt stopped and spoke with each of the foremen, nodding as they spoke and once taking off his hat and mopping his brow, but that was probably not an actionable offense. René LaBorde came out of the processing shed and lurched his way over to them and followed them around, but no one spoke to him. I hadn't seen him arrive, and Pike hadn't mentioned him, so maybe he had been in the processing shed all along. Maybe he lived there.

The guy who bossed the processing shed came out when Rossier and Bennett got down there, and the three of them spoke. René stood outside their circle for a time, then walked to the turtle pond and waded in up to his knees. The straw boss saw him first, and everybody got excited as LeRoy ran over to the edge of the pool, yelling, "Goddammit, René, get outta there! C'mon, 'fore Luther bites you!" René came back to the shore but stared down at the murky water, his shoes and pants muddy and dripping. He didn't seem to know what he had done or to understand why he'd been made to stop. Pike shook his head. "Man."

After a while, Rossier and LeRoy started back to the main house and everyone went back to work. René continued staring down at the water, his large body giving the occasional lurch as if his synapses had misfired. Halfway up to the house, Rossier saw that René wasn't following, slapped at LeRoy, and LeRoy trotted back for René. René followed LeRoy back to the main house, and the two of them sat in the white chairs, passing the day, the water and mud drying on René's pants, LeRoy looking at the pictures in his magazine.

The clouds continued to build, and by three o'clock the sky was dark. Lightning arced somewhere in the trees behind us, producing a deep-throated rumble, and it rained, slowly at first but with increasing intensity. LeRoy and René went into the main house and, one by one, the people working the ponds sought shelter in the processing sheds. Pike and I pulled on ponchos and made our way out to the car. We were leaving earlier than we had planned, but with everyone hiding from the rain the possibility of crime seemed remote. We stopped at an AM/PM Minimart on the state road to Reddell, and I used a pay phone to call Lucy at her office. She was with a client, and Darlene asked if I wanted to leave a message. I said to tell her that I had called and would call her again when I had the chance. Darlene said that that wasn't much of a message, considering. I said considering what? Darlene laughed and hung up. Do women always tell each other everything?

The sky was the color of sun-bright tarmac, and forks of lightning were dancing along the horizon when Pike and I again moved into the bait shop across from the Bayou Lounge. The rain hammered down in a steady, thunderous assault, and leaked in tap-water streams through the roof, but it was better than standing in the woods. By seven that night, the only people in the place were a couple of old codgers who'd come in a white Bronco. By eight they were gone, and by nine the same green wagon once more came around for the Hispanic couple. By 9:30 the Bayou Lounge was closed. Maybe the rain had kept people away. Maybe if it rained all year round, the crime rate would be zero.

Pike and I went through it again the next day and the day after, with no great variety of pattern. Every morning I would wait for LeRoy Bennett outside his house, and every morning he would beeline first to the Dunkin' Donuts and then to the crawfish farm where he would sit and wait and page through his magazines. Working off the sugar high, no doubt. Once Milt Rossier came out at midday and said something to LeRoy, and LeRoy hopped into his Polara and brodied away. I ran back through the woods to the car in time to see LeRoy hauling ass up the road toward town. I followed him directly to the Ville Platte McDonald's where he loaded up on a couple of bags worth of stuff, then hauled ass back to Rossier's. I guess even criminals like Big Macs.

If the days were bad, the nights were worse. We would sit in the dust on the bait shop floor, watching the cars come and go, and noting the people within them, but the people within them were never LeRoy Bennett or Milt Rossier, nor did anything happen to point to or indicate illegal activity. Once, a fat man in a cheap suit and a thin woman with Dolly Parton hair had sex in the backseat of a Buick Regal, and two nights later the same woman had sex with a skinny guy with a straw Stetson in the back of an Isuzu Trooper, but you probably couldn't indict Milt Rossier for that. Another time, three guys staggered out of the bar, laughing and hooting, while a fourth guy in a white ball cap stumbled out into the center of the road, dropped his pants, and took a dump. He lost his balance about midway through and fell in it, and the other three guys laughed louder and threw a beer can at him. Nothing like a night out with the boys.

Over the next three days I had exactly two opportunities to call Lucy, and missed her both times, once leaving a message on her home answering machine and once again speaking with her assistant. Darlene said that Lucy very much wanted to speak with me and asked if couldn't we prearrange a time when I might call. I told her that that would be impossible, and Darlene said, "Oh, you poor thing." Maybe Darlene wasn't so bad after all.

We had two dry days and then another day of rain, and all the watching without getting anywhere was making me cranky and depressed. Maybe we were wasting our time. Maybe the only illegal stuff was the stuff behind closed doors, and we could sit in the woods and the bait shop until the bayous froze and we'd never quite make the link. Pike and I took turns exercising.

At 8:22 on the fourth night in the bait shop, the rain was tapping the roof and I was doing yoga when Pike said, "Here we go."

LeRoy Bennett and René LaBorde pulled in and parked next to the blue Ford. Six cars were already in the lot, four of them regulars and none of them suspicious. LeRoy climbed out of the Polara and swaggered into the bar. René stayed in the car. Pike said, "I'll get the car."

He slipped out into the rain.

At 8:28, a dark gray Cadillac Eldorado with New Orleans

plates pulled in beside the Polara. A Hispanic man in a silver raincoat got out and went into the bar. At 8:31, Pike reappeared beside me, hair wet with sweat and rain. Maybe two minutes later, the Hispanic man came out again with LeRoy Bennett. The Hispanic man got into his Eldo and LeRoy got into his Polara, and then the Polara moved out with the Eldo following.

Pike and I hustled out to our car and then eased onto the road after them. As I drove, Pike unscrewed the bulb in the ceiling lamp. Be prepared.

No one went fast and no one made a big deal out of where they were going, as if they had made the drive before and were comfortable with it, just a couple of guys going about their business. Traffic was nonexistent, and it would have been better if we'd had a car or two between us, but the steady rain made the following easier. We drove without lights, and twice oncoming cars flicked their headlights, trying to warn us, the second time some cowboy going crazy with it and calling us assholes as he roared by. If the guy in the Eldo was watching the rear he might have seen all the headlight switching and wondered about it, but if he was he gave no sign. Why watch the rear when you own the cops and you know they're not looking for you?

We turned onto the highway leading to Milt Rossier's crawfish farm, and I thought that was where we were going, only we came to the gate and passed it, continuing on. I dropped further back, and Pike leaned forward in his seat, squinting against the rain and the windshield wipers to keep the red lights in sight. Maybe a mile past Rossier's gate, the Eldo's taillights flared and Pike said, "They're turning."

The Polara grew bright in the Eldorado's headlights as it turned onto a gravel feeder road forking off into the marsh through a heavy thatch of wild sugarcane and bramble. We waited until their lights disappeared, then closed the distance and turned across a cow bridge. An overgrown cement culvert thrust up from the earth by the cow bridge, ringed by chain link to protect pipes and fittings and what looked in the darkness to be pressure gauges. Abandoned oil company gear. I said, "If this was anymore nowhere, we'd be on the dark side of the moon."

The little road narrowed and followed the top of a berm across the marsh, moving in and out of cane thickets and sawgrass and cattails, occasionally crossing other little gravel roads even more overgrown. We had gone maybe half a mile when a wide waterway appeared on the left, its banks overgrown but precise and straight and clearly manmade. I said, "Looks like an industrial canal."

Pike said, "They turn and head back on us, we've got a problem."

"Yeah." When we came to the next crossing road, we stopped and backed off the main road, far enough under the sawgrass to hide the car, then went on at a jog. Once we were out of the car we could hear the rain slapping the grass and the water with the steady sound of frying bacon. We followed the little road for maybe another quarter mile and then an enormous, corrugated tin building bathed in light rose up from the swamp like some incredible lost city. It stood on the edge of the canal, a huge metal shed, maybe three stories tall, lit with industrial floodlamps powered by a diesel generator. Rusted pipes ran in and out of the building, and some of the corrugated metal panels were hanging askew. The isolation and the technology lent a creepy air to the place, as if we had stumbled upon an abandoned government installation, once forbidden and now best forgotten.

The Polara and the Cadillac were at the foot of the building, along with a couple of two-and-a-half-ton trucks. Both of the trucks were idling, their exhausts breathing white plumes into the damp air like waiting beasts. Pike and I slipped off the road and into the sawgrass. I said, "Pod people."

Pike looked at me.

"It's like the nursery Kevin McCarthy discovers in *Invasion of the Body Snatchers*. The one where the pod people are growing more pods and loading them onto trucks to be shipped all over the country."

Pike shook his head and turned back to the building. "You're something."

A huge, hangarlike door was set into the side of the building. Three guys in rain parkas climbed out of the trucks, opened it, then climbed back into the trucks, and drove them inside. A couple of minutes later, the steady burping of a diesel grew out of the rain and a towboat came up the canal, running without lights and pushing a small barge. It reduced speed maybe a hundred meters from the mouth of the big shed, and the Hispanic guy walked to the water's edge and waved a red lantern. The towboat revved its engines, then came forward under power and slipped inside the building. LeRoy and René and the guy from the Cadillac hurried in after it. Pike and I skirted the edge of the lighted area until we could see through the truck door. I had thought that we'd see people loading bales of marijuana onto the barge or maybe forklifting huge bricks of cocaine off the barge, but we didn't. Inside, maybe three dozen people were climbing off the towboat and into the trucks. Many of them looked scruffy, but not all. Many of them were well dressed, but not all. Most of them were Hispanic, but two were black, three were white, and maybe half a dozen were Asian. All of them looked tired and ill and frightened, and all of them were carrying suitcases and duffel bags and things of a personal nature. Pike said, "Sonofabitch. It's people."

When the trucks were full, the guys in the parkas pulled down canvas flaps to hide their cargo, climbed back into the cabs, pulled out of the building, and drove away into the rain. When the trucks were gone, a couple of hard-looking guys came up out of the barge dragging a skinny old man and carrying something that looked like a rag doll. The old man was crying and pulling at the hard guys, but they didn't pay a lot of attention to him. The old guy went over to the guy from the Eldorado with a lot of hand-waving, and then fell to the ground, pulling at the Eldorado's legs. The guy from the Eldorado kicked at the old man, then pulled out a small revolver, put it to the old man's head, and we heard a single, small *pop*.

My breath caught and I felt Pike tense.

The guy from the Eldo kicked the old man's body away, then said something to LeRoy Bennett, and Bennett nodded. The guys from the towboat climbed back aboard, and LeRoy and the guy with the gun walked out to the Eldo. The shooter opened the Eldo's trunk, took out a small handbag, and gave it to LeRoy. LeRoy brought it to his Polara. The towboat's engines revved, it backed from the shed, spun slowly into the canal, then eased back the way it had come, still without lights, the low gurgle of its engines fading into the mist. The shooter got into his Eldo and followed after the trucks. Now there were only four of us. Pike said, "Too late for the old man. What do you want to do?"

"Let's see what happens."

LeRoy took a shovel from the Polara, then he and René dragged the old man and the rag doll along a little trail into the weeds. Pike and I crept after them, moving closer. René dug a small depression in the wet earth, dumped in the bodies, covered them, then went back to their car. LeRoy turned off the generator, and the swamp was suddenly dark. He and René got into their car, and then they, too, were gone.

I said, "Okay."

Pike and I moved to the shallow grave and pushed the mud away with our hands and found the old man and a little girl. The girl was maybe five. She was small and thin, and perhaps she might have been ill, but maybe not. Her face was dark with the rich earth, but as the rain kissed her skin the dirt washed away. I stroked her hair and felt my breath slow and the muscles along my neck and back and across my ribs tighten. She might have been the old man's granddaughter, but maybe not. Maybe she was alone, and he had befriended her. Maybe he just cared, and in the caring expressed his outrage at her death, and for his outrage he'd been killed. We went through his pockets hoping for some sort of identification, but there was none. There was only a small photograph, bent and water-stained, of the man and a group of people who may have been his family. The man was smiling. I put the photograph in my pocket. I said, "Let's get them out of here."

Pike touched my arm. "We can't, Elvis."

I looked at him.

"If we move them, Rossier will know. We have to wait. We have to know more before we help them."

I breathed deep in the wet air, and then I nodded. I didn't like it, but there you are.

We sat in the rain with the old man and the little girl, and after a while we left.

27

We returned to the motel at a little before two the next morning, driving slowly along roads that were glassy with rain, through a town so still that it seemed as lifeless and empty as the bodies we'd left in the mud and the sawgrass. We were all that moved in Ville Platte, Joe and I, neither of us speaking, lit only by flashing yellow signal lights that whispered *caution.*

We showered and changed, Joe going first, and when we were done and the lights were out, I said, "Joe?"

I heard him move on the floor, but it took him several seconds to answer. "Yes."

"Oh, Jesus, Joe."

Pike might have slept, but I did not. I was in the dry room, yet not. I was with the old man and the girl, yet not. I crouched in the sawgrass beside them, the night air dank and muggy, the rain running out of my hair and down my back, the great fat drops falling on the faces below me, washing circles of perfect clarity on the muddy skin, but a clarity that did not maintain and soon faded, obscured by more drops, as if every new truth clouded an old.

The rain stopped falling a few minutes after four, and at 7:05 we called Lucy at her home and told her what we had seen. She said, "Do you think these people were illegal aliens?"

"We counted thirty-five people climbing onto the trucks, but there could've been more. A few Asians, a few whites and blacks, but the majority were Hispanics." I told her about the old man and the girl.

Lucy said, "Oh, my God."

"We left them in place. Rossier wasn't at the scene, and I'm not certain we can tie this to him. We'd get Bennett and LaBorde for sure, but maybe not Rossier."

She said, "Did you get the Cadillac's license number?"

I gave it to her.

Lucy said, "Stay where you are. I'll call you as soon as I have something."

"Thanks, Luce."

She said, "I miss you, Studly."

"I miss you, too, Luce."

One hour and thirteen minutes later Lucy called back. "The Eldorado is registered to someone named Donaldo Prima from New Orleans. He's thirty-four years old, originally from Nicaragua, with three felony convictions, two for dealing stolen goods and one firearms violation. There's nothing in his record to link him to illegal immigration, but the feds are out of the loop on most of this stuff. I've got a friend here in Baton Rouge you can talk to. She works for an alternative weekly called the *Bayou State Sentinel,* and she's done some pretty good work covering the immigration scene. She might be willing to help."

"Might."

"You'll see." Lucy gave me directions, hung up, then Pike and I drove to Baton Rouge.

The *Sentinel* had their offices in a little clapboard house on a street just off the LSU campus that was mostly rental houses for students and people who enjoyed the student lifestyle. Some of the houses had been converted to businesses, but the businesses were all places like used-CD stores and grunge shops and a place that sold joss sticks and papier mâché alligators. Alternative. A couple of mountain bikes and a Triumph motorcycle were chained to a bikestand in front of a house with a little sign that said BAYOU STATE SENTINEL—THE LAST BASTION OF TRUTH IN AMERICA. I guess being a bastion of truth didn't prevent people from stealing your bicycles.

Pike and I parked at a meter, and Pike said, "I'll wait in the car." Pike's not big on alternative.

I went up a little cement walk and in through the front door to what had probably been the living room when people were living here instead of working here. Now, five desks were wedged into the place, along with a coffee machine and a water cooler and a lot of posters of Kurt Cobain and Hillary Clinton and framed *Sentinel* covers. The covers had headlines like LIFE SUX and FIVE REASONS TO KILL YOURSELF NOW. Alternative. A couple of African-American women in their late twenties were working at Macintosh computers further back in the room, one of them on the phone as she typed, and an athletic white guy with short red hair was at a desk just inside the door. A parrot sat on a perch in the waiting area, copies of the *New York Times* and the New Orleans *Times-Picayune* spread on the floor beneath it. The parrot flapped its wings when it saw me, then lifted its tail feathers and squirted a load of parrot shit onto the *New York Times*. I said, "Man, this parrot is something."

The red-haired guy smiled over at me. "That's Bubba, and that's what we think of the mainstream press. What can I do for you?"

I gave him one of my cards. "Elvis Cole to see Sela Henried. Lucille Chenier called her about me."

He looked at the card and stood. "I'll go see. You want some coffee or something?"

"No. Thanks."

He disappeared into a little hall, then came back a couple of minutes later with a tall woman who didn't look thrilled to see me. She said, "You're the guy Lucy called about?"

I said, "Is it that disappointing?"

She frowned when I said it, then went to the windows and peered out at the street, like maybe there would be a horde of FBI agents in my wake. "Lucy said there were two of you."

"He's waiting in the car."

She looked back at me, and her eyes narrowed as if it were somehow suspicious that Pike would wait in the car. "Well. Okay. Come back to my office."

Sela Henried had a long face and short blond hair that had been bleached white and cut into spikes, and a row of nine piercings running up along the edge of her left ear. A small blue cross had been tattooed on the back of her right hand between the thumb and forefinger, and she was wearing cheap silver rings on most of her fingers. I made her for her mid-thirties, but she could have been older. Her office had once been a bedroom at the front of the house. She went to the windows, looked out at Joe Pike again, then put her hands on her hips. "I don't like him sitting out there."

"Why not?"

"He looks like a cop. So do you." She turned back to me and crossed her arms. "Perhaps you are." Suspicious, all right.

I said, "Ms. Henried, did Lucy explain to you what this is about?" Maybe I should turn on the old charm. The old charm might be just the ticket.

"Yes, or I wouldn't be seeing you. I've known Lucy Chenier for a very long time, Mr. Cole. We played tennis together at LSU, but this is a very controversial newspaper. Our phones have been tapped, our offices have been searched, and there is a damn long list of agencies that would like to see us out of business." She sat and stared at me. "This interview will not take place unless you agree to be searched."

"Searched?" Maybe the old charm wasn't going to do much good, after all.

"I trust Lucy, but for all I know you've duped her to take advantage of me."

I spread my hands. "Are we talking a strip search or just your basic frisk job?"

She yelled, "Tommy!" The red-haired guy came in. "Would you see if he's wearing a wire, please?"

Tommy smiled shyly at me. "Sorry."

"No problem."

Tommy patted me down, moving his hands up under my arms and down the hollow of my back and around my waist. Professional. Like he'd done it before, and like he'd had it done to him. When he reached the Dan Wesson he looked up, surprised. "Hey, he's got a gun."

She frowned at me. One of the posters over her desk showed a pistol with a big red slash across it and the words STOP THE HANDGUN MADNESS. She said, "May we see your wallet?"

"Sure." I took out my wallet and gave it to Tommy. He looked through everything the way a kid might, sort of curious but without any real involvement. "It says he's a private investigator from California. There's a license for the gun."

"All right, Tommy. Thanks."

Tommy handed my wallet back and left. Polite. Another day at the truth factory.

Sela Henried went around behind her desk, and sat. She leaned back and put a foot up on the edge of her desk. Doc Martens. "Lucy says you have questions about the immigration scene in Louisiana."

"That's right. We're trying to find out about a guy named Donaldo Prima. We think he's running illegal aliens, but there's no record of it."

"She mentioned Prima." Sela Henried picked up a plastic pencil and tapped it against her knee. "I looked through my notes and I can't find Prima mentioned, but that doesn't mean anything. We have what the mainstream press likes to call an 'immigration problem' down here. New Orleans is a main entry port for people entering the country through the Gulf, and dozens of coyotes work the coast."

"If you can't help us, maybe you know someone who can."

She shook her head. "I'm sorry." She knew something, she just didn't want to talk about it.

"It's important, Ms. Henried."

She jabbed the pencil at me. "I've covered the victimization of those trying to enter our country for years. The *Sentinel* supports the concept of open borders and the activities of those who circumvent our country's racist and exclusionary immigration policies."

"Ms. Henried, I work for some people who are being victimized in a pretty big way themselves. If I can find out about Donaldo Prima, I may be able to stop their own little slice of the victimization. It ain't saving the world, but it's what I can do."

She said nothing.

"At a little bit after midnight last night, I saw Donaldo Prima shoot an old man in the head with a .32 caliber revolver. I think he shot the old man because the old man was making a stink about a little girl who died in the hold of the barge bringing them into this country. I saw both bodies. I touched them. Is that the kind of activity you support?"

She hissed out a little breath, then dropped her foot from the desk and leaned forward. "Is that bullshit?"

"It's the truth."

"Will you show me the bodies?"

"No."

"Why not?"

"Because to do so might compromise my clients."

"Maybe this issue is larger than your clients."

"Then I'll have to live with it."

She frowned at me some more, then got up, and went to the window to see if Pike was still there. She came back to her desk. "Maybe I know someone. His name is Ramon del Reyo, and he could probably help you out. He wouldn't speak over the phone, though. He's helped a lot of people into the country and the feds just about live up his ass."

"Okay."

She let out another long breath. "I want you to know how much I'm putting at risk, here. I believe in what Ramon's doing. He's a tough little sonofabitch, and everybody's after him, all the way from the feds to the goddamned hoods down in Nicaragua, and I'd hate like hell for anything to happen to him. Do you understand that?"

"I just want Prima, Ms. Henried. Will your guy speak with me?"

She said, "I have to make a call, and I won't do it from here. You can wait, or you can come along." She stood again. "Which is it?"

We walked up the street to a pay phone outside of a Subway Sandwich shop, and Sela Henried placed one call, using her body to block the phone so that I could not see the number she dialed. She spoke for maybe two minutes, then she hung up, keeping her hand on the receiver. "Someone will call back."

I nodded.

Nine minutes later the pay phone rang, and Sela Henried picked up before the first ring had finished. She spoke for a few minutes, this time writing something in a small reporter's notepad. When she hung up she gave me what she had written. "This is in New Orleans, okay? It's a storefront. You have to be there at one o'clock, but you've got plenty of time."

"Thanks, Sela. I appreciate it."

She put the pad in her pocket, then looked at Pike. You could see him sitting in the car down the block, but you couldn't tell where he was looking or what he was thinking. She said, "Ramon will be there, and he'll be with people who can protect him. Do you understand what I'm telling you?"

"Sure. Don't do anything stupid."

She nodded. "I wouldn't bring the gun. It will only make them nervous, and they will probably take it away from you, anyway."

"Okay."

She nodded again, then looked in my eyes the way you do when you want to make sure the person you're talking to doesn't just understand you, but actually gets it. She said, "I'm trusting you with a very great deal, Mr. Cole. Ramon is a good man, but these are dangerous people with a very great deal to lose. If they think you pose a threat to them, they will kill you. If they think that I set them up, they very well might kill me. I hope that matters to you."

I looked at the pay phone, and then I looked back at the offices of the *Bayou State Sentinel.* "If the feds want you enough to tap the phones in your office, they'll tap all of the nearby pay phones, too."

She nodded, and now she looked tired, as if all the years of paranoia and fear were getting to be a little too heavy to bear. "Like you, we do the best we can. I hope this helps, Mr. Cole."

Sela Henried walked back to the *Sentinel,* and Joe Pike and I drove to New Orleans. The drive took a little less than an hour and a half, through forests and swamps so thick they looked like jungle. As we drove I told Pike what Sela Henried had said about Ramon del Reyo and the people around him. Pike listened quietly, then said, "I know guys from down south. They're dangerous people, Elvis. They've grown up with war. To them, war is a way of life."

"Maybe we should split up. Maybe I should meet Ramon, and you should hang back and walk slack for me." Slack was having someone there to pull your ass out of the fire if things went bad. Joe Pike was the best slack man in the business.

Pike nodded. "Sounds good."

The freeway rose the last twenty miles or so, elevated above swamp and cypress knees and hunched men in flat-bottomed boats. Lake Pontchartrain appeared on our left like a great inland sea, and then the swamps fell behind us and we were driving through a dense collar of bedroom communities, and then we were in New Orleans. We took the I-10 through the heart of the city past the Louisiana Superdome, which looked, from the freeway, like some kind of Michael Rennie *The Day the Earth Stood Still* spaceship plunked down amid the high-rises. We exited at Canal Street and drove south toward the river and the Vieux Carré.

At twenty minutes before one, we parked the car in a public garage on Chartres Street and split up, Pike leaving first. I put the Dan Wesson under the front seat, waited ten minutes, and then I followed.

I walked west on Magazine into an area of seedy, rundown storefronts well away from Bourbon Street and Jackson Square and the tour buses. The buildings were crummy and old, with cheesy shops and Nearly-Nu stores and the kinds of things that tourists chose to avoid. I found the address I'd been given, but it was empty and locked. A For Lease sign was in the door, and the door was streaked with grime as if nobody had been in the place for the past couple of centuries. I said, "Well, well."

I knocked and waited, but no one answered. I looked both ways along the street, but I couldn't see Joe Pike. I was knocking for the second time when a pale gray Acura pulled to the curb and a thin Hispanic guy wearing Ray-Bans stared out at me. A black guy was sitting in the passenger seat beside him. The black guy looked Haitian. I said, "Ramon?"

The Hispanic guy made a little head move indicating the backseat. "Get in."

I looked up and down the street again, and again I saw no one. I took a step back from the Acura. "Sorry, guys. I'm waiting for someone else."

The Haitian pointed a fully automatic Tec-9 machine pistol at me across the driver. "Get in, mon, or I'll stitch you up good."

I got in, and we drove away. Maybe splitting up hadn't been so smart, after all.

28

We drove four blocks to the big World Trade Center at the levee, then swung around to Decatur and the southern edge of the French Quarter. We parked across from the old Jackson Brewing Company, then walked east toward Jackson Square past souvenir shops and restaurants and a street musician working his way through "St. Vitus Day March." He was wearing a top hat, and I pretended to look at him to try to find Joe Pike. Pike might have seen our turn; he might have cut the short blocks over and seen us creeping through the French Quarter traffic as we looked for a place to park. The Haitian pulled my arm, "Le's go, mon."

The air was hot and salty with the smell of oysters on half shell and Zatarain's Crab Boil. We walked beneath the covered *banquette* of a three-story building ringed with lacy ironwork, passing souvenir shops and seafood restaurants with huge outdoor boilers, wire nets of bright red crawfish draining for the tourists. Midday during the week, and people jammed the walk and the streets and the great square around the statue of Andrew Jackson. Sketch artists worked in the lazy shade of magnolia trees and mules pulled old-fashioned carriages along narrow streets. It looked like Dis-

neyland on a Sunday afternoon, but hotter, and more than a few of
the tourists looked flushed from the heat and shot glances at the
bars and restaurants, working up fantasies about escaping into the
AC to sip cold Dixie.

I followed the guy with the Ray-Bans and the Haitian across
the Washington Artillery Park to a long cement promenade overlooking the river, and then to a wide circular fountain where another Hispanic guy waited by a Popsicle cart. He had a rugged
bantamweight's face, and he was slurping at a grape Popsicle. I
said, "You Ramon?"

He shook his head once, smiling. "Not yet, podnuh." No accent. "You carrying anything?"

"Nope."

"We gonna have to check." First the red-haired guy, now this.

"Sure."

"Just do what I tell you, and everything'll be fine. Ramon's
nearby."

"I'm Mr. Cooperation."

"Piece a' cake, then." He sounded like he was from Brooklyn.

He told me to stand there like we were having a grand little
time, and I did. Ray-Ban and the Haitian laughed it up and patted me on the shoulders like we were sharing a laugh, their fingers
dancing lightly beneath my arms and down along my ribs. The
new guy yukked it up, too, but while he was yukking he dropped
his Popsicle, then felt my calves and ankles as he picked it up.
Like the red-haired guy, they had done it before. He tossed the
Popsicle away and smiled. "Okay. We're fine. Let's see the man."

We walked to the other side of the fountain where Ramon del
Reyo sat on a little bench beside a couple of sculpted azalea
bushes. The azaleas were in profuse bloom, their hot pink flowers
so dense and pure that they glowed in the blinding sun and cast a
pink light. Ramon stood as we approached and offered his hand.
He was about my height, but thin and scholarly, with little round
spectacles and neat hair. Academic. He was smoking, and his thin

cotton shirt was damp with sweat. He said, "My name is Ramon del Reyo, Mr. Cole. Let's walk along, shall we?"

He started off and I went with him, the others following along-side, some closer, some farther, and everybody keeping an eye out. I had seen presidential Secret Service bodyguards work public places, but I'd never seen anyone work a place better than these guys. You'd think we were in the middle of the cold war some-place, but then, maybe we were. Del Reyo said, "Sela Henried is my friend and so I will speak with you, but I want you to know that there is a man near here with a rifle in the seven millimeter Magnum. He is very good with this thing, you see? He can hit the running deer cleanly at five hundred meters."

I nodded. "How far away is he now?"

"Less than two hundred." Del Reyo looked at me with a stud-ied air. "If anything happens to me, you will be dead in that in-stant."

"Nothing's going to happen, Mr. del Reyo."

He nodded. "Please look here. On your chest."

He gestured to the center of my chest, and I looked. A red dot floated there, hard and brilliant even in the bright sun. It flick-ered, then was gone. I looked up, but could not find the rifleman. I said, "Laser sight."

"Just so you know." He made a dismissive wave. "Please call me Ramon." A guy tells you you're a trigger pull from dead, then says please call me Ramon.

"Who is Donaldo Prima?"

Ramon took a deep pull on the cigarette, then let the smoke curl out of his mouth and nostrils. "He is dog shit."

"Seriously, Ramon. Tell me what you really think."

Ramon del Reyo smiled gently and ticked ash from the ciga-rette with his thumb. A couple of beat cops strolled by, grinning at some college girls from Ole Miss. The cops were wearing shorts like the tourists, and short-sleeved shirts with epaulets and knee socks like they were on safari. Del Reyo said, "He is trying to be the big gangster, you see? *El coyote.* Someone to whom people go when they wish to enter our country."

"Like you."

Ramon del Reyo stopped smiling and looked at me the way he'd look at a disappointing student. "Donaldo Prima is a smuggler. Automobiles, cocaine, farm equipment, people is all the same, to be bought and sold, you see? To be taken advantage of if possible. I am a political activist. What I do I do for free, because I care about these immigrants and their struggle to reach our country."

"Sorry."

He shrugged, letting it go. "It is a nasty business. He is having problems."

"What kind of problems?"

"He used to work for a man named Frank Escobar. You know Escobar?"

I shook my head. "I don't know any of this, Ramon. That's why I'm talking to you."

"Escobar is the big criminal, the one who controls most of what is smuggled into and out of the port of New Orleans. *El coyote grande.* He, too, is very bad. From the military in El Salvador. The truth squads." Great.

"A nut."

Del Reyo smiled slightly. "Yes. A killer, you see? He make much money sending stolen American automobiles to Central America when the boat go south, then bringing drugs and refugees here for even more money when the boat comes north. You see?"

"How much profit can there be in smuggling poor people across the border?"

"It is not just the poor who wish to come here, Mr. Cole. The poor crawl under the fence at Brownsville and work as day laborers picking vegetables. The upper classes and the educated wish to come here, also, and they wish to bring their lives and professions with them. That is much more difficult than crawling under a fence."

"They want to buy an identity."

"*Si*. Yes. The coyote, he tells them that they are buying citizenship, you see? They will be given birth certificates, a driver's license, the social security card, all in their own names and usually with their actual birth dates. This is what they pay for, and they pay a very great deal. With these things they can bring the medical degree, the engineering degree, like that."

"And do they get what they pay for?"

"Almost never." We walked to the edge of the promenade. The river was below us, cutting a great brown swath through the city, flat and wide and somehow alive. The river's edge was prickly with loading cranes and wharfs and warehouses. He glanced at the Haitian and lowered his voice. "Four months after he came, seven members of his family also bought passage through Frank Escobar. They were put in a barge out in the Gulf, fifty-four people put into a little space ten feet by eight feet, with no food and water, and the barge was set adrift. It was an old barge, and Escobar never intended to bring them ashore. He already have his money, you see, paid in full? A tanker reported the abandoned barge, and the Coast Guard investigated. All fifty-four men, women, and children had died. It got very hot in the hold of the barge with no openings for the ventilation and no water to drink. The hatch had been dogged shut, you see?" The Haitian's skin was a deep coal black, greasy with sweat. "His father was a dentist. He wishes to be a dentist, also, but we see." He let the thought trail away and looked back at me. "That is the way it is with men like Escobar and Prima, you see? They get the money, then *fft*. Life means nothing. This is why I have so much protection, you see? I try to stop these men. I try to stop their murder."

Neither of us spoke for a time. "So what about Prima?"

"I hear that he has gone into business for himself, undercutting Escobar's price."

I said, "Ah."

Del Reyo nodded.

I said, "If Prima has set up a competing business, Escobar can't like it."

He sucked on the cigarette. "*Sí.* There is trouble between them. There is always trouble between men like this." The smoke drifted up over his eyes, making him squint. "You say you know nothing about the coyotes, yet you ask about Donaldo Prima. You say you know that he is a bad man. How do you know these things?"

"I saw his people bring a dead child off a barge sometime around eleven-thirty last night. There were other people, but only the child was dead. An old man was making a deal about it, and I saw Prima shoot the old man in the head."

Ramon del Reyo did not move. "You saw this thing?"

I nodded.

"You have proof?"

"May I reach into my pocket?"

"Yes."

I showed him the old man's picture. He held it carefully, then took a deep breath, dropped the cigarette, and stepped on it. "May I keep this?"

"The cops might need it for the identification."

He stared at it another moment, then slipped the picture into his pocket. "I will return it to you, Mr. Cole. You have my word."

I didn't say anything.

"I tell you something, and if you are smart you will listen. These men come from places of war where life has no value. They have executed hundreds, perhaps thousands. This man Frank Escobar, he has murdered many and he murders more every day. Prima himself is such a man." He seemed to have to think about how to say it. "There is so much murder in the air it is what we breathe. The taking of life has lost all meaning." He shook his head. "The gun." He shook his head again, as if in saying those two words he had summed up all he was about, or ever could be about.

I said, "What about the feds?"

Ramon del Reyo rubbed his thumb across his fingertips and said nothing.

I said, "If I wanted to take down Donaldo Prima, how could I do it?"

He looked at me with steady, soft brown eyes, then made a little shrug. "I think that by asking these things, you are looking to do good, but you will not find good here, Mr. Cole. This is a God-less place."

"I don't think you are without God, Mr. Del Reyo."

"I am afraid I will not know that until the afterlife, no?" We reached the little bench by the azaleas. Ramon del Reyo sat, and I sat with him. "We have talked enough, now. I will leave, and you will sit here for exactly ten minutes. If you leave before then, it will be taken the wrong way and you will be killed. I am sorry to be rude in this way, but there we are."

"Of course." I imagined the man with the rifle. I imagined him watching for the sign, and I wondered what the sign might've been. A yawn, perhaps. Perhaps wiping the brow. The sign, the trigger, history.

Ramon del Reyo said, "If the man who is with you approaches, have him sit beside you and he will not be harmed."

I said, "What man?"

Ramon del Reyo laughed, then patted my leg and moved away, del Reyo and the guy with the Ray-Bans, then the others, and finally the Haitian. The Haitian made a pistol of his right hand, pointed it at me, and dropped the hammer. Then he smiled and disappeared into the crowd. What a way to live.

I sat on the lip of the bench in the damp heat and waited. My shirt was wet and clinging, and my skin felt hot and beginning to burn. Joe Pike came through the crowd and sat beside me. He said, "Look across the square, corner building, third floor, third window in."

I didn't bother looking. "Guy with a rifle."

"Not now, but was. Did you make him?"

"They told me. They made you, Joe. They knew you were there."

Pike didn't move for a while, but you could tell he didn't like it, or didn't believe it. Finally he made a little shrug. "Did we learn anything?"

"I think."

"Is there a way out for the Boudreauxs?"

I stared off at the river, at the steady brown water flowing toward the Gulf, at the great ships headed north, up into the heart of America. I said, "Yes. Yes, I think there is. They won't like it, but I think there is." I thought about it for a time, and then I looked back at Joe Pike. "These are dangerous people, Joe. These are very dangerous people."

Pike nodded and watched the river with me. "Yes," he said. "But so are we."

29

A hot wind blew in off Lake Pontchartrain. The last of the clouds had vanished, leaving the sky a great azure dome above us, the afternoon sun a disk of white and undeniable heat. We drove with the windows down, the hot air roaring over and around us, smelling not unlike an aquarium that has been too long uncleaned. We reached Baton Rouge, but we did not stop; we crested the bridge and continued west toward the Evangeline Parish Sheriff's Substation in Eunice, and Jo-el Boudreaux. He wouldn't be happy to see us, but I wasn't so happy about seeing him, either.

It was late afternoon when Pike and I parked in the dappled shade of a black-trunked oak and walked into the substation. A thin African-American woman with very red lips and too much rouge sat at a desk and, behind her, a tall rawboned cop with leathery skin stood at a coffee machine. The cop looked over when we walked in and watched us cross to the receptionist. Staring. I gave the receptionist one of my business cards. "We'd like to see Sheriff Boudreaux, please. He knows what it's about."

She looked at the card. "Do you have an appointment?"

"No, ma'am. But he'll see us."

The rawboned cop came closer, first looking at Pike and then looking at me, as if we had put in a couple of job applications and he was about to turn us down. "The sheriff's a busy man. You got a problem, you can talk to me." His nametag said WILLETS.

"Thanks, but it's business for the sheriff."

Willets didn't let it go. "If you're talkin' crime, it's my business, too." He squinted. "You boys aren't local, are you?"

Pike said, "Does it matter?"

Willets clicked the cop eyes on Pike. "You look familiar. I ever lock you down?"

The receptionist said, "Oh, relax, Tommy," and took the card down a short hall.

Willets stood there with his fists on his hips, staring at us. The receptionist came back with Jo-el Boudreaux and returned to her desk. Boudreaux looked nervous. "I thought you were gone."

"There's something we need to talk about."

Willets said, "They wouldn't talk with me, Jo-el."

Boudreaux said, "I've got it now, Tommy. Thanks."

Willets went back to the coffee machine, but he wasn't happy about it. Boudreaux was holding my business card and bending it back and forth. He looked at Joe. "Who's that?"

"Joe Pike. He works with me."

Boudreaux bent the card some more, then came closer and lowered his voice. "That woman is back and she's been calling my wife. I don't like it."

"Who?"

He mouthed the words. "That woman. Jodi Taylor." He glanced at Willets to make sure he hadn't heard.

"Sheriff, that's just too damn bad. You want to talk out here?"

Willets was still staring at us from the coffee machine. He couldn't hear us, but he didn't like all the talking. He called out, "Hey, Jo-el, you want me to take care of that?"

"I've got it, Tommy. Thanks."

Boudreaux took us to his office. Like him, it was simple and functional. Uncluttered desk. Uncluttered cabinet with a little TV. A nice-looking largemouth bass mounted on the wall. Boudreaux was big and his face was red. A hundred years ago he would have looked like the town blacksmith. Now, he looked awkward in his short-sleeved uniform and Sam Browne. He said, "I want you to know I don't appreciate your coming here like this. I don't like that woman calling my wife. I told you I'd handle my troubles on my own, in my own way, and there's nothing we got to say to each other."

"I want to report a crime. I can report it to you, or to the clown outside."

He rocked back when I said it. He was a large-boned, strong man and he'd probably fronted down his share of oilfield drunks, but now he was scared and wondering what to do. I wasn't supposed to be here. I was supposed to have gone away and stayed away. "What do you mean, 'crime'? What are you talkin' about?"

"I know what Rossier's doing, Sheriff. You're going to have to put a stop to it."

He put his hand on the doorknob like he was going to show us out. "I said I'll take care of this."

"You've been hiding from it for long enough, and now it's gotten larger than you and your wife and your father-in-law."

He said, "No," waving his hand.

"I'm showing you a courtesy here, Boudreaux. Neither your wife nor Jodi Taylor knows about this, though I will tell them. I'm giving it to you first, so that we can do this in private, where you want to keep your fat-ass troubles, or we can do it in front of your duty cops."

Pike said, "Fuckin' A." Pike really knows how to add to a conversation.

Boudreaux stopped the waving.

I said, "At eleven-thirty last night we saw a man named Donaldo Prima shoot an old man in the head at an abandoned pumping station a mile south of Milt Rossier's crawfish farm. They were bringing in illegal immigrants. Rossier's goons were there when it happened."

Jo-el Boudreaux stopped all the twitching and waving as completely as if he had thrown a switch. His eyes narrowed briefly, and then he put his palms flat on his desk and wet his lips again. When he spoke I could barely hear him. "You're reporting a homicide?"

"It's not the first, Jo-el. It's been going on, and it will keep going on until it's stopped."

"Rossier was there?"

"Prima met LeRoy Bennett at Rossier's bar, the Bayou Lounge. Bennett and LaBorde were at the pumping station, but Rossier's the guy who's in business with Prima."

His fingers kneaded the way a cat will knead its paws, only without satisfaction. "Can you prove that?"

"They buried the old man and a little girl. Let's go see them."

He came around the desk and put on his hat. "God help you if you're lyin'."

Tommy Willets was gone when we walked out through the substation and climbed into Jo-el's car.

The sheriff drove. I spoke only to give directions, and a little less than twenty minutes later we turned across the cattle bridge and moved into the marsh and the cane fields. The rain had left the road pocked with puddles, but the ruts from the big trucks were still cut and clear. Everything looked different during the day, brighter and somehow magnified. Egrets with blindingly white feathers took dainty steps near thickets of cattails, and BB-eyed black birds perched atop swaying cane tips.

We parked alongside the pumping station. The sun was cooking off the rain, and, when we left the car, it was like stepping into a cloud of live steam. We moved north along the edge of the waterway for maybe eighty yards until we came to the little grave. The rain had washed away some of the soil, and part of the old man's arm was visible. There was a musty smell like sour milk mixed with fish food, but maybe that was just the swamp.

Jo-el Boudreaux said, "Oh, my Lord."

Boudreaux bent down, but did not touch the earth or what was obscured by it. He stood and turned and looked out across the waterway, shaking his head. "Jesus, ain't this a mess."

I said, "It isn't just you and your wife anymore, Boudreaux. Rossier isn't just selling meth to crackers. He's in business with animals, and people are getting hurt. You can't ignore that."

He wiped at his forehead with a handkerchief. "Oh, holy Jesus. I didn't know about any of this. I never knew what he was doing. That was the deal, see? I just stayed away. That's all there was to it. I just let him go about his business. I never knew what he was doing out here."

"This thing is going to end, now, Jo-el. You're going to shut Rossier down."

He looked confused. "What do you mean?"

"I mean that I can't walk away and let it go on. If you don't stop it, I'll give you up."

He blinked hard and looked from me to Joe Pike, then back to me. His face was bright pink in the sun, and slicked with sweat. "You think I'd let someone get away with this? You think I'd just turn away?"

I pointed at the grave. "That old man and that little girl are dead because you turned away."

The pink face went red, and in that moment he wasn't the scared blacksmith; he was the leather-tough farmer he'd had to be when he was fronting down Saturday-night drunks waving broken Budweiser bottles. He said, "I've got a wife to protect. I had to look out for her goddamned daddy."

Pike moved to the side, and I stepped into Jo-el Boudreaux's face and said very softly, "It was almost forty years ago. Edith was a child, forty years ago. You went along because you didn't want anyone to know she'd been with a black man. It's the race thing, isn't it?"

Jo-el Boudreaux threw a fist the size of a canned ham at me with everything he had. It floated down through the thick air and I slapped it past, stepping to the outside. He threw the other hand, this time crossing his body and making a big grunt with the effort. I slapped it past the same way and stepped under. He was big and heavy and out of shape. Two punches and he was breathing hard. Pike shook his head and looked away. Boudreaux lunged forward, trying to wrap me up with the big arms, and I stepped to the side and swept his feet out from under him. He rolled sideways in the air, flaying at nothing, and hit the muddy ground. He stayed there, crying, hurting for himself but maybe hurting for the old man and the little girl, too. I thought Jodi Taylor was right. I thought that he was a good man, just stupid and scared, the way good men sometimes are. Somewhere nearby a fish jumped, and tiny gnats swarmed around us in great rolling clouds. Boudreaux got control of himself and climbed to his feet. He said, "I'm sorry about that."

I nodded. "Forget it."

He looked down at his pants. "Jesus, I look like I wet myself."

Pike handed Boudreaux a handkerchief.

Boudreaux wiped at his hands and his face, then blew his nose. "I ain't cried like that since I was a kid. I'm ashamed of myself."

I said, "You ready to talk about this?"

He offered the handkerchief back to Pike but Pike shook his head. Boudreaux shrugged. "Jesus, I don't know what to do. If I knew what to do, I wouldn't be in this fix." He blew his nose into the handkerchief again, then put it into his pocket. "I gotta talk with Edie."

"Your choices are limited, Jo-el. The one choice you do not have is inaction. Inaction has led to this, and I will not allow this to continue."

He nodded and looked at the water. It was muddy and still and probably didn't offer much in the way of advice to him. He said, "Man, isn't this a mess. Isn't this a goddamned mess." He looked at the shallow grave and what was in it. "Shit."

Pike said, "There's a way to survive this."

When he said it something cold washed down my spine. I said, "Joe."

Jo-el Boudreaux squinted at Pike, his eyes curious and hopeful. "What?"

Pike said, "Prima's at war with another coyote named Frank Escobar. Escobar's been trying to take out Prima because Prima's cutting into his trade. If he knew that Rossier was in business with Prima, and he knew how to get to them, he might take them out."

Jo-el Boudreaux's left eye began ticking. He stared at Pike, and then he looked at me. "That's murder."

I said, "I don't know if this is helping, Joe."

Pike said, "We could make it happen. Rossier's gone. Prima's gone. You bust Escobar." He cocked his head, and the hot Louisiana sun gleamed off his glasses. "No one ever has to know what Rossier knows." He cocked his head the other way. "You see?" The world according to Pike.

Jo-el Boudreaux wet his lips and looked shaken. "Jesus Christ, I don't know."

I said, "There are a couple of ways to go with this, but what you can't do is nothing. Doing nothing is why those people died." I pointed at the little grave. "If Jodi Taylor's back, I'll have to see her. I have to see Lucy Chenier. You have until tomorrow, Jo-el. Talk about all of this with Edith and decide. We'll call you tomorrow."

He was nodding again. "Okay. Yeah. Sure. Tomorrow." He wet his lips again, then looked again at the little grave and shook his head. He said, "Those poor folks. Those poor folks." He started back toward the highway car.

"Where are you going?"

He answered without looking back at me. "Gotta get the coroner's people out here and recover these bodies. Can't just let these folks stay like that."

He vanished behind the emerald green cane and the sawgrass.

Pike said, "What do you think he'll do?"

I shook my head. "I don't know, but I hope he does something."

We waited beside the little grave, the two of us staring down at the old man's arm, reaching up out of the earth, reaching as if he was trying to find his way back from darkness.

30

Two Evangeline Parish sheriff's cars and a gray van from the parish coroner's office came out to disinter the bodies. A powder blue Buick sedan arrived a few minutes later, driven by a man named Deets Boedicker. Boedicker owned a Dodge-Chrysler dealership and had been elected coroner, a job that mostly consisted of overseeing the technicians from Able Brothers Mortuary to make sure they didn't screw up any evidence until the police had finished with the scene. Able Brothers had a contract with the parish. When the police had finished with their photographs and measurements, Boedicker asked how the bodies were discovered, and Sheriff Boudreaux said that a couple of kids fishing for channel cats in a *bateau* had found them and phoned it in. Boedicker said, "Looks like a couple of Mexes to me. Ain't that just the thing? Sure been a lot of Mexes around here lately." I guess that was the extent of his expertise.

Sheriff Boudreaux told a young black deputy named Berry to finish up with the mortuary people, and then he drove us back to the Eunice substation. None of the cops or coroner's people had asked who we were or why we were on the scene. I guess they had grown used to not asking questions, and the thought of that bothered me, but perhaps it should have bothered me more.

We reached the hotel in Baton Rouge at eight minutes after seven and went to our rooms to shower and change. I asked the front desk people if Jodi Taylor had checked in, and they said she had, but when I called her room she wasn't there. I called Lucy at home, and asked if Jodi was with her.

"Yes, she is. She flew in yesterday."

"Good. I found out what's going on. I spoke with Boudreaux, and I should tell Jodi about it. Things are going to happen, and they'll probably happen quickly, and she might be affected."

"We've already eaten, but you and Joe could come over for dessert and we can discuss it."

I told her that that would be fine, and then I showered and changed and rapped on Joe Pike's door. He didn't answer, so I let myself in, thinking he might be in the shower. He wasn't. There was a haze of fog on the bathroom mirror, but all water had been wiped from the tub and the damp towels had been folded and rehung on their racks. The room was immaculate, the bedspread military tight, the magazines squared on the table by the window, the chairs undimpled by the weight of a reclining body. The only sign that he was here or ever had been was the olive green duffel on the closet floor. It was zipped shut and locked with a tempered steel Master Lock. Now you see him, now you don't. Off doing Pike things, no doubt.

At ten minutes before eight, Lucy let me into her home with a smile that was as warm as the sun glittering off dew-covered grass. I said, "Hi."

She said hi back. The master and mistress of restraint.

Jodi Taylor was standing behind her in the entry with a glass of red wine, clearly expectant. But where it was easy to look at Lucy, it was hard for me to look at Jodi. It would be harder still to tell her the things I would tell her. Jodi said, "Did you find out what's going on?"

"Yes. We need to talk about it."

Lucy led us to the kitchen. The lights in the backyard were on, and Ben and another boy were using the rope to climb into the pecan tree. A black-and-white dog ran in frantic circles around the base of the tree, its rear end high and happy.

Lucy said, "I have a key lime pie. Would you like coffee?"

"How about a beer?"

She took a bottle of Dixie from the Sub-Zero and opened it for me. I drank some. The key lime pie was sitting on the counter beside a little stack of glass dessert plates and forks and cloth napkins. Two pieces of the pie were missing, and I deducted that the two boys in the yard had probably already had their dessert. I am a powerhouse of deduction. A veritable master of the art.

Jodi said, "What's wrong? Why aren't you saying anything?"

I had more of the beer and watched Lucy cut equal slices of the pie and put the pie on the plates.

Jodi pulled at my arm. "Why do I think that something's wrong?"

"Because something is. Rossier and a guy named Donaldo Prima bring in illegal aliens, and sometimes it works out but sometimes it doesn't, and they don't much care." I went through everything. There was a kind of comfort in the telling, as if with each telling the memory of it would become less clear, the sharp lines of the old man and the young girl less distinct.

When I told the part about Donaldo Prima killing the old man, Jodi said, "Waitaminute. This man *murdered* someone?"

"Yes."

"You actually saw a *murder*?"

I said yes again.

Jodi looked at her wineglass. Lucy caught the look, and refilled the glass. Jodi said, "I can't believe this. I'm an actress. I sing, for God's sake." She shook her head and looked at the two boys. Outside, Ben was hanging upside down on the rope, and the other boy was pushing him. Moths and June bugs swarmed around the patio lights. The black-and-white dog danced happily. Inside, the adults were discussing murder and human degradation. Just another day in middle-class America.

Lucy said, "Did you find a way to help the Boudreauxs?"

I shook my head. "No."

Jodi looked back at me. "What do you mean no?"

"I had hoped to find a way to force Rossier out of the Boudreaux's lives so that they could keep their secret, but there doesn't seem a way to do that. Rossier has no family and no known associates other than Donaldo Prima, and their association seems one of convenience. Like all criminal activities, it is a cash business, and Rossier has carefully laundered all the money through his crawfish farm. Milt Rossier answers to and depends on no one. He's safe."

Jodi said, "Well, there must be something."

"We can kill him or arrest him."

She flipped her hand. "Oh, that's silly."

"Prima used to work for another coyote named Frank Escobar. Prima wanted to go into business for himself, but needed a safe and reliable way to move people up from the coast. That's Rossier. Without Rossier, Prima's out of business. Escobar would very much like Prima to be out of business, also. If Escobar knew how to get to Rossier and Prima, he might take care of our problem."

Lucy was not moving. Her hands were on the counter. "You're talking about arranging a murder."

"I am talking about sharing information with Frank Escobar, then letting nature take its course."

Jodi crossed her arms, then uncrossed them. "Are you serious?"

Ben and the other boy came in through the French doors, slick with sweat. Ben was barefoot, and his knees were grass-stained and dirty. The other boy was wearing a Wolverine T-shirt. Ben said, "MomI'mgonnagoovertoGary'sokay? Hi, Elvis."

"Hi, Ben." I guess the other boy was Gary.

Lucy glanced at the clock on the wall above her sink. "I want you home by nine."

Both boys sprinted away before she finished. "ThanksMom."

After the front door crashed, the house was silent. Lucy went to the sink, ran a glass of water, and drank it. Jodi shook her head. "Well, that killing thing is silly. You can't just kill someone. And the Boudreauxs can't arrest him. If they arrest him, he'll tell."

"The sheriff has no choice. I am not going to allow things to continue."

Jodi put her hands on her hips. "What does that mean?"

Lucy turned back from the sink.

I said, "An old man got shot in the head because Jo-el Boudreaux is scared of something that happened thirty-six years ago. This is not acceptable." My neck felt tight. "If things continue as they have, more old men will be shot and more little girls will die of heatstroke, and that is also not acceptable." The tight neck spread to my scalp, and my voice felt hard and far away. "I have told Jo-el these things, and now he must do something, even if it means giving up his secret, because I will not allow any more old men or little girls to die. I will act if he doesn't." My temples were pounding.

Jodi's eyes flicked to Lucy, then came back to me. "What does that mean? What will you do?"

"I'll go to the Justice Department and give them the case against Rossier and Prima."

Her eyes flicked to Lucy again. "But Rossier will tell on the Boudreauxs." *Tell on the Boudreauxs.* Like he might *tattle.*

"I know."

Jodi took one step closer to me, her eyes wide. "But then they'll know about *me.*"

"I know that, too. I'm sorry."

Jodi walked out of the kitchen and into the dining area. She raked her fingers through her hair and looked at herself in the window overlooking Lucy's backyard. It was now dark out, and the glass was a mirror to the room. We weren't talking about the Boudreauxs anymore; we were talking about her. She said, "What happened to confidential? What happened to protecting my interests? You promised me, remember?"

I didn't answer. Her eyes were red-rimmed and filling. I wanted to comfort her and tell her that everything would be fine, but I could not lie to her.

I said, "I saw Boudreaux earlier today. He's going to talk about all of this with Edie tonight, and we'll see how they want to play it tomorrow. I'm sorry, Jodi."

Jodi Taylor walked out. Lucy went after her, and I heard them at the front door, but I could not make out their words. I put my palms on the counter and stared between them. The Corian was flat and gray and seemed of great depth. It was a lovely surface, and I pressed against it and wondered how much pressure it could take. I thought about hot frying pans being placed upon it, and I wondered how often the pans might be placed and how hot they might be before the Corian would be forever changed.

Lucy was gone for a long while, and then there were footsteps and she was standing beside me again, leaning with her back to the counter, her arms crossed. She said, "You look like hell, Studly."

"Thanks."

Lucy took a deep breath, then said, "I know you were in Vietnam, but I have to ask this. Have you killed men in the course of your job?"

"Yes."

"Have you committed murder?"

"No. Each time, I was threatened. Each time, I was trying to help an innocent person whose life was in imminent danger."

"Have you acted to create those moments?"

I thought about it. There have been so many moments. Freckles on the arm of a man who works in the sun. "When you involve yourself in these things, you assume a measure of risk. There always comes a point when you can turn it over to the police, but at that point the risk expands. Will the police blow it? Will the client be helped or harmed? Will justice be served? There are always questions. The answers are not always clear, and are often unknown even after the fact."

She let the breath out. "In a given moment you opt to trust yourself."

"Yes," I said. "Always."

She said nothing for several moments, then she turned sideways and reached up to touch my hair. "Well. At least you're honest."

"As the day is long." I tried to smile, but it wasn't much.

"I'm having trouble with this."

"I know."

"The framework of the law is how we define and protect justice. If everyone were to subjectively define justice, order and law would cease and there would be no justice. There would be only anarchy."

"Easy for you to say."

She frowned. Humor often fails when we need it most.

"But you're right. Of course."

She said, "You don't have to do this. You could just walk away, or you could act unilaterally and go directly to the Justice Department to give them Rossier, but you haven't. You're still in it, even though it troubles you."

I looked at her and tried to frame how I felt. "I help people. I work with their problems and try to stay within the parameters that they set and bring them to a conclusion that is just. Their confidence is sacrosanct to me. Do you see?"

"You define yourself through your service to your clients."

"In a way."

"And you've never breached that confidence, or that service."

I shook my head.

"And now you might, for a justice that you see as greater than your client."

"Yes." My voice was phlegmy.

Lucy pulled me around to face her. She gripped each of my biceps and looked up at me. I watched her look at the different parts of my face and head and ears and hair. Her eyes drifted lower, glancing at my chest, maybe the buttons there, maybe the folds of my shirt, as if whatever answers she sought might be in the fabric. She closed her eyes and snuggled into me. "You're a good man, Elvis. You're a very good man."

She went to the kitchen phone, pressed a speed dial button, then asked someone if Ben could stay over. She said that she would be happy to drive car pool in the morning if he could. The someone must have agreed. Lucy said thank you, hung up, then came back to me and took my hand. She gave me one of the gentlest smiles that I have ever seen. She said, "Did you hear?"

"Yes."

"Will you come to the bedroom with me?"

"Can I think about it?"

Her smile got wider and she squeezed my hand.

"Well. Okay."

She hooked her arm in mine and walked me to her bedroom, but this night we made a different kind of love. We lay upon her bed, still in our clothes, and held each other until dawn.

31

Lucy was driving car pool the next morning when her office called, telling her phone machine that Jo-el Boudreaux had phoned, looking for me. I picked up the phone midmessage and Darlene said, "Well, well. Fancy meeting you there."

"You'll probably be a riot in the unemployment line, too."

"Oh, we're testy in the morning." These assistants are something, aren't they? "May I speak with Ms. Chenier?"

"She's unavailable. What did Boudreaux want?"

"There were two messages on the machine and he sounded anxious. He left a number." She gave it to me and then she hung up.

I called the number, got the Evangeline Parish Sheriff's office, Eunice Substation, and then I got Boudreaux. He said, "I can't just murder somebody. Jesus Christ. I can't do anything like that."

"All right. But doing nothing is no longer an option. So what are you going to do?"

You could hear background noise and the squeaks a chair makes when someone large shifts position.

I said, "Talk to me, Jo-el."

"Edie says you're right. She says it's time to stop hidin' from yesterday. She said that from the beginning, but I guess I was too scared to listen." He was working his way through the guilt, and not just the guilt about his wife. He'd probably seen the old man and the little girl a thousand times last night. He said, "I'm gonna arrest the sonofabitch. I should've arrested him six months ago. I should've arrested him when he came to my house with this stuff and started his blackmail."

I said, "It's the right thing, Jo-el."

"It's not just that old man. It's the whole operation. Prima. The poor bastards they been sneaking in through my parish. I can't get that little girl out of my head."

I said, "You want it to stop."

"Yes. Hell, yes. I don't want any more little girls like that. Oh, hell, yes." His voice sounded thick when he said it. "Jesus Christ, I'm just a hick cop. I don't know how to do this stuff."

"Jo-el, have you spoken with the parish prosecutor about this?"

"Unh-unh. Edie and I want to talk to the kids. We want to let'm know about us and their grandfather before they hear it in the news. I pop Rossier and he'll be screaming."

"Maybe there's a way to put this together, Jo-el."

"You mean get 'em all?"

"Maybe. Let me talk to Lucy about it. We'll need to know the legal end because we'll want to avoid entrapment, but maybe there's a way."

I hung up, then showered and dressed and was standing on the patio with the black-and-white dog when Lucy returned from car pool. She was carrying a wax-paper bag and two large containers of coffee. She offered one of the coffees. "Good morning again."

"Darlene called with a message from Jo-el Boudreaux. I'm afraid I've compromised our liaison."

"Oh, don't worry. She's used to it." These dames.

I told her about the call to Jo-el and asked her opinion. Lucy took a single plain donut from the bag and held it for me to take a bite. I did. Tender and light and still warm from the frying. Not too sugary. She took a bite after me and shook her head. "I have no experience in criminal law, Studly, but there are several ex-prosecutors at the firm."

"Think we could round one up for a quick trip to Eunice?"

She had more of the coffee and fed a small piece of the donut to the dog. "It's possible. After this donut, I'll make some calls."

"Great."

She sipped the coffee and ate a bit of the donut and stared at the camelia bushes that separated her backyard from her neighbor's. The bright morning sun painted their leaves with an emerald glow. She said, "You should tell Jodi. If it's going to come out, you should give her as much warning as possible."

"Of course."

She held out the donut again for me, but I shook my head no. She gave the remainder to the dog. "It won't be easy for you, will it?"

"You helped last night, Lucy. Thank you."

She smiled and patted my arm. "Let me make those calls."

It took about twenty minutes. A senior partner named Merhlie Comeaux agreed to drive to Eunice with Lucy and give an opinion based on his experiences both as a criminal defense attorney and the sixteen years he'd spent as an East Baton Rouge Parish prosecutor. Lucy would pick him up, and the two of them would meet Pike and me at Jo-el Boudreaux's office. I called Jo-el to see if this was agreeable, and he said that it was. He sounded nervous, but he also sounded relieved that someone who knew what they were doing was willing to advise him. When I hung up, I called Jodi Taylor at the hotel. She answered on the sixth ring, her voice puffy with sleep.

I said, "I spoke with Jo-el this morning, and I'm going to drive over there. He's going to arrest Milt Rossier."

She didn't say anything.

"I thought you should know. You want to talk about any of this?"

She said, "I wouldn't know what to say." Her voice sounded hollow, and I didn't know what to say either. She hung up. Another satisfied customer.

I called Joe Pike, told him the plan, then picked him up at the hotel and we went to Eunice.

The drive across the Atchafalaya Basin went quickly, the waterways and sugarcane fields and great industrial spiderworks now familiar. Men and women worked the fields and fished the waterways and sold burlap sacks of live crawfish for fifteen cents per pound. Some of their faces seemed familiar, but maybe that was my imagination. I tuned in to the radio evangelist to learn the topic of the day, and this morning it was the liberal plot to destroy America by breaking down the nuclear family. She said that the liberals had already accomplished this in the Negro community, but that the Negroes were getting wise, which explained the rise in popularity of the black "Musluns." She concluded, inevitably, with warnings of the coming race war, which was not part of the liberal plot but which was clear proof that the liberals were not as smart as they thought they were, since the liberals thought they could use the "blacks" to distract Christian America from their "true plan." Pike said, "Turn it off."

"Aren't you interested in learning about the 'true plan'?"

"No."

I turned it off, wondering how many of the people in the fields and on the water and in the houses were listening to this. Maybe none. Maybe Pike and I had been the only ones because everyone else had long since turned her off. Maybe, now that we had turned her off, too, she was broadcasting into dead air, just another noodle-brain with an eight-thousand-watt transmitter and nothing much to do all day except smoke cigarettes and rail into the microphone about how crummy things were, a voice alone in the dark, her signal spreading like silent ripples in a pond, unheard on the earth but traveling ever outward into space, past the moon and Mars, past the asteroids and Pluto, on into eternity. I hoped the people on Alpha Centauri were smart enough to turn her off, too.

Twenty minutes later we parked next to Lucy's Lexus outside the Eunice substation. The same woman was at the same desk, and the same pristine magnolia was in its little jar. She smiled when she saw me and said, "They're in with the sheriff. They're expecting you."

Lucy and Jo-el were sitting with a great, broad African-American man with white hair and a gut the size of a fifty-five-gallon oil drum. Merhlie Comeaux. Lucy made the introductions, then looked back at Jo-el. "Sheriff, before we begin this we need to establish the ground rules. Merhlie is a former EBR prosecutor, but he is now a partner in the firm of Sonnier, Melancon, & Burke, for private hire. As such, anything said by you in this room is subject to the attorney-client privilege. Is that understood?"

Jo-el looked confused. "But I didn't hire you."

"We are under agreement with Jodi Taylor to work in your best interests. If you are so informed and agree to that arrangement, then we are, de facto, your attorneys."

Jo-el looked at me. "Do I need lawyers?"

I said, "Just listen to her, Jo-el."

He frowned and nodded and looked back at her. Lucy said, "We are about to discuss your awareness of and involvement in activities that may, in the future, result in criminal charges being filed against you. We don't want anything said by you today to prejudice your case at that time."

Jo-el looked embarrassed. "I'm not going to try to get out of anything."

Lucy spread her hands. "That is your choice, of course. You may feel differently at some later date. Also, we may discuss issues of a personal and potentially criminal nature as regards other members of your family. By accepting the attorney-client privilege with us, you also serve to protect them. Do you understand that?"

Jo-el nodded. "Protect them."

"Do you accept this arrangement?"

Jo-el said, "Yes."

Lucy nodded, then glanced at Merhlie Comeaux. "We have prior consent from Jodi Taylor to discuss her affairs openly with the Elvis Cole Detective Agency." She looked back at Jo-el. "As we discussed, Mr. Comeaux is here in an advisory capacity in the criminal apprehension of Milt Rossier. He can't speak for the state, but he can provide his opinion and guidance in the building of such a case. Do you understand that, too, Sheriff?"

"Yes. I need all the help I can get."

Merhlie Comeaux said, "Why don't you gentlemen give me what you have?"

Jo-el raised his eyebrows at me, and I told Comeaux everything that I knew. I started at the head of it with Jimmie Ray Rebenack and what happened at Rossier's crawfish farm, and I brought it up through the meeting between Rossier and Donaldo Prima at the Bayou Lounge and what I had seen at the pumping station. When I told him about the old man's murder and the bodies we recovered from the grave, Comeaux asked for the police report. Jo-el showed him the file and Comeaux stared at the pictures. He said, "Did you get an ID?"

"Not yet. We're running it through New Orleans."

Comeaux shook his head and sighed. "You got any coffee around here?"

Jo-el asked the receptionist to bring in coffee. After she had, I went through the rest of it, describing my meeting with del Reyo and what I had learned about Donaldo Prima and Frank Escobar and how Prima was using Rossier to move illegals up through the Gulf Coast waterways. When I was finished with it, Merhlie Comeaux nodded like he was thinking, then looked at the sheriff. "Do you have anything to add to that?"

Jo-el said, "Unh-unh. No, sir."

Merhlie looked back at me and laced his fingers across his

ample belly. He had clear, hard eyes, and the eyes made me think
he had been an aggressive prosecutor. "Let's go back to what happened at the pumping station. You saw this Prima pull the trigger?"

"Yes."

He looked at Joe Pike. "You saw it, too?"

Pike nodded.

"Where was Rossier?"

"He wasn't there."

"How about those two boys who work for him?"

"Bennett and LaBorde were inside with Prima."

"You get IDs on any of the illegals who came in?"

"No."

"Can you produce any of these people?"

"No."

Merhlie Comeaux pursed his lips and sipped at the coffee.
When he lifted the cup his little finger stuck out at an angle.

Lucy said, "What do you think, Merhlie?"

Comeaux made a shrug, like he would do the best he could
with what he had to work with. "It's not a lot, Lucille. You have
Mr. Prima all right, but you don't have a thing on this Rossier."

Boudreaux said, "Well, hell."

Comeaux spread his hands. "He holds a lease on the land,
maybe the state could file on an accessory, but it's junk. You want
him, you gotta get him at the scene."

I said, "What about on the illegals?"

"*What* illegals? If you can't produce them, you cannot, in fact,
prove that these people are aliens."

Lucy said, "Oh, come on, Merhlie."

He spread his hands again. "That's my opinion. If you think
you can get more, go to the state and see what they say."

Jo-el said, "If we go in now that sonofabitch will know we're
onto him." He chewed at his lip, then went to the window before
turning back and staring at the largemouth on his wall. He stared

at it, but I'm not sure he was seeing it. "Goddammit, me and my family are gonna do something pretty goddamn hard here. Maybe we shoulda done it a year ago, but if we're gonna do it now I want that sonofabitch to pay for his pleasure. I want him in jail. I don't want any more little girls like that." He jerked an angry gesture toward the case file. The one with the pictures.

I said, "So you'll have to bust him in the act."

They looked at me.

I said, "That wasn't the first time Prima brought up a load of people. We just have to be there the next time. And we have to make sure that Rossier is there to take delivery."

Comeaux was shaking his head. "Go easy with that, son. If he's entrapped, you've got nothing."

I was thinking about Ramon del Reyo. "All we have to do is give him a strong enough reason to be there. It won't be easy, but it might be possible."

Comeaux said, "Tell me what you have in mind."

I did. It didn't take very long, and then he got up and Lucy got up with him. The last thing he said was, "It's your neck, podnuh. Go with God."

A frown line had appeared between Lucy's eyebrows. "Can you pull something like that off?"

I looked at Pike. "Can we pull this off, she asks."

Pike was frowning, too. I guess he had his doubts.

I used Jo-el's phone to make some calls, and when I was finished Lucy and Merhlie were gone. Jo-el stood in his office window, passing his palm across his hair and staring down along the street of his town. Maybe at the rows of buildings, maybe at the cars and the people walking on the sidewalks. He said, "I should've done this six months ago. When that bastard came to my house and started all this, I should've dropped the hammer on him then and goddamned there."

"You were caught off guard, and you were scared. People get scared, they don't think straight."

"Yeah." He didn't look convinced. He glanced at the floor, and then he looked up at me. "I appreciate this. So will Edie."

Pike said, "Buy us a beer if we live through it."

That Joe. He's a riot, isn't he?

We went out to our car and drove to New Orleans.

The Haitian was waiting for us at a beignet shop on South Rampart Street along the northern edge of the French Quarter. He hung there just long enough to make eye contact, then started walking without waiting for us. We went west to Canal, then south, and after a couple of blocks, Pike said, "Across the street and half a block behind."

I glanced back and saw the guy with the Ray-Bans. I nodded. "Security conscious."

Pike said, "Creepy."

Ramon del Reyo was waiting in the front passenger seat of a Yellow Cab a little bit down from Carondelet, where the old green streetcars make their turnaround from St. Charles and the Garden District. The cab's Off Duty light was on. The Haitian opened the back door for us, then got in behind the wheel. He didn't start the engine. Ramon smiled at Pike. "So. You are with us this time, señor."

"With you last time, too." Pike tilted his head. "Guy with the glasses across the street. Another guy to our left by the horse carriage. I haven't made the rifle."

Ramon made a little shrug. "But you know he's there. The man with the rifle is always there, you see?"

Pike's mouth twitched.

I said, "I can take Donaldo Prima and Frank Escobar off the board. How badly do you want it to happen?"

The Haitian twisted in his seat to look at me, but Ramon del Reyo did not move.

I said, "I know how and where Prima gets people into the country, and I've got a parish sheriff who is willing to make the case."

Del Reyo wet his lips. "It is a Justice Department case."

"My guy will make the bust and collect the evidence. Justice comes in after the fact, everything laid out and undeniable." I leaned toward him. "It's solid. My guy just wants to clean up his place of business."

The Haitian looked at del Reyo. Del Reyo said, "There is more than that, my friend."

I said, "Yes, but I'm not going to tell you."

Del Reyo said nothing.

"All you need to know is that if we can set it up well, both Escobar and Prima are over."

The Haitian said something in Spanish, but del Reyo did not respond. The Haitian said it again, and this time del Reyo snapped something angrily. He frowned at me. "What is it you want?"

"I need Escobar to make the case. That means I need to learn about the coyote business. I need to know how much it costs and how much people get paid and how Escobar works and how Prima works. I want to make Escobar think I'm in the business, and that I'm trying to cut a deal with him, so I have to know what I'm talking about. If I don't have Escobar, I can't make it happen."

Ramon del Reyo laughed. "You're a fool."

"I think you've got someone inside with Escobar. I think that's how you keep tabs on him. Help me inside, Ramon. Come on."

The Haitian said something else, and this time Ramon nodded. He didn't seem to be liking it a whole lot, but he was going along with it. He said, "Why would Frank Escobar want to see you?"

"Because he hates Prima, and I can give him Prima. And if he wants Prima dead, I can give him that, too."

Ramon smiled at me.

"We haven't identified the old man, Ramon. I want the picture."

Ramon smiled some more and shook his head. He got out of the cab and walked south on Canal. He was gone for the larger part of an hour, and when he returned there was a middle-aged Asian guy with him. The Asian guy was slight and dark and looked Cambodian. The Cambodian leaned in to look at me and Pike, then he and del Reyo stepped away from the cab to talk. After maybe ten minutes the Cambodian walked away, and Ramon came back to the cab. He spent a little less than thirty minutes with us, first describing Escobar's setup, and then Prima's. He told us how much a guy like Escobar charged to sneak someone into the country and how much a guy like Prima paid to use Milt Rossier's pumping station. Everything was related to some sort of by-the-head payment. Escobar charged so much per head to get people in. Prima paid so much per head to use Rossier's waterway. Like we were talking about cattle. Something less than human.

Del Reyo gave me a slip of paper with a phone number. "We have a man on very good terms with Escobar. He is arranging the meeting. Should anyone need a reference, have them call this number."

I put it away without looking at it.

"I will leave you now. Jesus will take you there." I guess the Haitian was Jesus. "He will drop you off and leave, and you will be alone. If something happens, we will not be there to help. Do you understand this?"

"Sure."

Ramon del Reyo walked away without another word and without looking back. No "I'll be seeing you." No "good luck." No "win one for the gipper." Maybe he knew something we didn't.

We drove north across the city toward Lake Pontchartrain, and soon we were out of the business district and driving along narrow residential streets with high curbs and plenty of oak and magnolia and banana trees, and old people in rockers on front veranadas. We seemed to just sort of drive around, turning here and there, taking our time without any clear destination. Killing time. The air was warm and moist and oily like air that was vented from a low-class kitchen, and the cab smelled of sweat and body odor. Maybe the cab smelled like fear, too, but I was trying not to think of that part of it. Elvis Cole, Fearless Detective. I glanced over at Pike and he appeared to be sleeping. Passed out from fear, no doubt.

Pretty soon the neighborhoods became nicer, and we were driving along a beautiful emerald golf course and a sculpted canal, and then we were at the lake. The levee was lush and well maintained, and Jesus wound through streets now lined with mansions, some behind walls and gates but most not. We turned into a cul-de-sac fronting the levee and stopped at an enormous two-story brick home with oak trees in the front and along the sides. A couple of Japanese mountain bikes were lying on the lawn, and a Big Wheel was in the drive. You could look down the drive and see a four-car garage in the back, along with a pool house and a pool, but it seemed pretty quiet. Jesus stopped the car and said, "Just go to the door and knock. It's set up."

"Thanks, Jesus."

Jesus said, "You got a gun this time?"

"Yeah."

He nodded. "Good."

Pike and I got out of the cab, and Jesus drove away. Amazing how alone you can feel in somebody's front yard. I looked at the bikes and the Big Wheel. "Helluva house for a hood."

Pike grunted.

The door opened before we reached it, and an attractive dark-haired woman smiled at us. She was wearing a tasteful one-piece swimming suit with a towel wrapped around her hips like a skirt. She was barefoot, and her hair was wet as if she'd just gotten out of the pool. She said, "Are you Mr. Cole?"

"Yes, ma'am."

Beaming, she offered her hand. "I'm Holly Escobar. Please come in. Frank's in back."

Pike offered his hand and introduced himself. Holly Escobar said that she was happy to meet us. A little boy maybe five years old raced out between us, hopped aboard the Big Wheel, and roared around the cul-de-sac, blurrping his lips to make engine noises. He was as brown as a walnut, and wearing only baggy red swimming trunks. Holly Escobar closed the door. "He's all right out there. We don't have any traffic."

She brought us through a house that looked like anyone else's house, past family photographs and a very fine collection of riding trophies (which I took to be hers) and two older boys planted in front of a television and into a bright, homey island kitchen where a man in baggy plaid shorts was stacking sandwiches on a plastic tray. He was about my height, but younger, with heavy muscles and slicked hair and blunt fingers. He looked at us when we walked in and Holly Escobar said, "Ronnie, these are the men Frank's expecting. Why don't you take them out and I'll finish here." She smiled back at us. "Everybody's in back."

Ronnie led us out through a couple of French doors. Three men were sitting at a round table by the pool, drinking, and a woman was on a chaise longue, sunning herself. Like Holly Escobar, she wore a one-piece, and she looked like somebody's wife. No bimbos at the house. Two of the men were wearing baggy shirts over their shorts, probably to cover weapons, but one of the men was shirtless. Ronnie said, "Frank?"

Frank Escobar was shirtless. He was short and wide and maybe in his early fifties, with a powerful, thick-bodied build. The hair on his head was streaked with gray, but his chest hair had already gone over, a thick gray thatch. He looked over at his name, and stood up when he saw us. "Oh, yeah, hey, let's go in the pool house for this." There was a slight accent, but he'd been trying to lose it. He held up a short glass. "We're doing gin and tonics. You guys want one?" The gang lord as host.

"No. Thanks."

He said, "C'mon. We'll have some privacy in here."

He staggered when he got up, and one of the shirted guys had to catch him. Middle of the day and he was zorched. The gang lord as lush.

We filed into the pool house. Pool table. Bar. Couple of slot machines and video games. A life-sized portrait of Frank Escobar from the old days, wearing an officer's uniform in some Central American jungle, close-cropped hair and bandito mustache. The real Frank Escobar slumped into a tall chair and waved his hand at Ronnie. "Check these guys, huh? See what they got."

I held my arms out. "It's on my right hip."

Ronnie took it, then gave me a quick pat. When he was done with me he moved to Pike, but Pike said, "No."

Frank Escobar frowned and said, "What do you mean no?"

Pike held his hand palm out toward Ronnie. "You want me to wait outside, fine. But he's not going to touch me, and I'm not going to give up my gun."

Escobar rubbed at his eyes. "What the fuck." He finished the rubbing. "You wanna keep your gun, tha's fine. We'll do it another way." Frank Escobar reached under one of the shirts and came out with a little Beretta .380 and pointed it at my head. He said, "Keep your fuckin' gun, you want. We'll do it like this." He waved at the shirt. "Leon, hold on this guy, okay, this other asshole wants to keep his gun." Leon took the .380 and held on me, and Frank Escobar glared at Pike. "There. You happy now, you with your gun?"

Pike nodded. Some friend.

Escobar looked back at me. "Okay. What do you have for me?"

"Donaldo Prima."

Escobar's left eye narrowed, and he didn't seem drunk anymore. Now, he seemed as dangerous as the man in the life-sized picture. "What do you know about Prima?"

"I know how he's getting his people in, Frank. He's working with a friend of mine. My friend provides the transportation and the secure location, but the money's not there."

"Who's your friend?"

"A guy named Rossier. He's got the land and the water. A very secure location for delivering goods. Prima approached him and set up the deal, but now we're dissatisfied. You know what I mean?"

Escobar said, "How much he gettin'?"

"Grand a head."

Escobar laughed. "That's shit." Exactly what del Reyo had said.

"We think so."

"Why doesn't your friend just go into business for himself?"

"Prima has the goods, Frank. Like you. Two grand a head and Prima's out. We've got people coming in now, and we'd like to increase our take."

"Just like that? It's that easy?"

"Whatever you want."

Frank Escobar wet his lips, thinking. He had some of the gin and tonic. A drop of it ran down from the corner of his mouth to his chin. He said, "Prima."

"That's it, Frank. You want to think about it and ask around, fine. We've been in business with Prima maybe six months. He brings up the money personally with every shipment. Like that." Giving him Prima. Saying, here, take him.

Frank Escobar nodded at me.

I said, "Think about it, Frank. You want to get me, I'm staying at the Riverfront in Baton Rouge. You want to give me a number I can call you, that's fine, too." I spread my hands. "Whatever you want. What *we* want is two grand a pop."

Holly Escobar stepped in out of the sun with the tray of sandwiches, smiling the pretty smile, saying, "Would you guys like a sandwich?" She froze in the door when she saw the guy in the baggy shirt pointing the gun at me, and the smile fell away. "Frank?" The guy lowered the .380.

Frank Escobar lost the grip on his drink, and it fell. His face went as purple as overcooked liver and he came off the chair. "Didn't I tell you never walk in on me?"

She took a single step back, trying to rebuild the smile, but the smile was clouded with fear. "I'm sorry, Frank. I'll wait outside."

The guy with the shirt whispered, "Oh, shit."

Frank Escobar rushed at his wife and yanked her back into the pool house. The big plastic plate and the sandwiches spun up and over and sandwiches rained down on the pool table and out onto the patio. Holly shrieked at the pain of his grip, saying, "That hurts!" and then he slapped her twice, first with the palm of his left hand and then the back of his right. She fell over sideways, through the door and out onto the patio. The man and the woman at the pool stood.

I felt Pike move beside me, but it was over. As quick as it had come, it was gone. Escobar pulled his crying wife to her feet, saying, "You gotta listen to me, Holly. You gotta mind what I say. All right? Don't never walk in like that." He brushed at her hair and wiped at her face, but all he did was smear the blood. He said, "Jesus, look at what you made me do. Go get your face, will you?"

Holly Escobar ran toward her house, and Frank wiped blood from his right hand onto his shorts. "Go with her, Ronnie. Make sure she's okay."

Ronnie set off after Mrs. Frank Escobar.

The guy with the shirt said, "You all right, Frank?" Like it was Frank doing the bleeding.

"I'm fine. Fine." Escobar picked up his glass and seemed almost embarrassed. "Jesus. Fuckin' stupid women." Then he looked over at us and must've seen something in Pike's face. Or maybe in mine. He said, "What?" Hard, again. A flush of the purple, again.

Pike's mouth twitched.

Escobar stared at Joe Pike another few seconds, and then he waved his hand to dismiss us. He said, "I'll think about it, okay? I know where to reach you." He motioned toward the guy in the shirt. "Call these guys a car, huh? Jesus, I gotta get another drink."

He walked out and went back to the little round table and picked up someone's glass and drank. Nothing like a gin and tonic to take off the edge after tossing a fit, nosireebob. I stared at him.

The guy in the shirt said that he'd call a cab, and we could wait out front. He said the cabs never took long, Frank had a deal. He said we could take a sandwich, if we wanted. Joe Pike told him to fuck himself.

We walked out past the pool and down the drive and into the street. The little boy was riding the Big Wheel round and round in circles, looping up into one driveway then along the sidewalk and then down the next drive and into the street again. He looked like a happy and energetic child.

Pike and I stood watching him, and Pike said, "Be a shame to drop the hammer on his old man."

I didn't answer.

"But it wouldn't be so bad, either."

33

We were stopped for speeding outside St. Gabriel, Louisiana, and again outside Livonia, but we passed under Milt Rossier's sign at just after five that evening as the air was beginning to lose the worst of the day's heat. The people who worked the ponds were trudging their way toward the processing sheds and the women who worked the sheds were walking out to their cars. Quitting time. Everybody moved with a sort of listless shuffle, as if their lot was to break their backs for Milt Rossier all day, then go home and break their backs some more. It wasn't the way you walk when your body has failed you; it was the way you walk when you've run out of heart, when the day-to-day has worn away the hope and left you with nothing but another tomorrow that will be exactly like today. It would be the way Holly Escobar would walk in another few years.

We drove up past the processing sheds like we owned the place and headed toward the house. The women on their way home didn't look, or, if they looked, didn't care. It's not like we had a big sign painted on the car, THE ENEMY. Pike said, "This is easy."

"What'd you expect, pill boxes?"

We could see the main house from between the processing sheds, and the little figure of Milt Rossier, sitting out on his lawn furniture, still wearing the sun hat. René LaBorde was standing out between the ponds, staring at their flat surfaces, and didn't seem to notice us, but LeRoy Bennett was coming out of the processing shed with one of the skinny foremen when we passed. He yelled something, then started running after us. He'd have a pretty long run. His Polara was parked at the house.

We drove the quarter mile or so up to the house and left our car on the drive by LeRoy's Polara. The house looked pretty much deserted except for a heavyset black woman we saw in the living room and Milt Rossier back on the patio. We were going around the side of the house when Milt met us, coming to see who we were. He was in overalls and the wide hat, and he was carrying a glass of iced tea. I said, "Hi, Milt, remember me?"

Milt Rossier pulled up short, surprised. He knew me, but he'd never seen Pike before, and when Pike took out his .357 and let Rossier see it, the old man said, "Well, goddamn."

Pike said, "Let's go back to the patio. Comfortable there."

Rossier looked back at me. "We ran you outta here. I thought you left."

I said, "Everybody always thinks that, Milt, and everybody's usually wrong."

Pike said, "The patio." Down below us, LeRoy Bennett was yelling for René to get his ass up to the house. René looked our way, but you couldn't be sure what he saw or what he was thinking.

Rossier frowned at Pike's gun and then we went back to the patio. I said, "Sit down, Milt. We've got a business proposition."

Milt Rossier eased his bulk down into one of the white lawn chairs, and Pike lowered the gun. Rossier said, "Somebody got to old Jimmie Ray. I told you he'd stop messin' with that little gal, and he has. I thought we were shut of that." He tried looking at me, but he kept glancing at Pike and the gun. Nervous.

I smiled. "Not that kind of business, Milt." LeRoy Bennett was a white midget down between the ponds, arms and legs pumping as he ran toward us. René LaBorde was finally headed our way, walking with a stiff-legged lumbering gait like Frankenstein's monster. I said, "Milt, here's the word. You're gettin' screwed by Donaldo Prima, and we can double your money."

When I said Donaldo Prima the old man's face tightened and he tried to put down the iced tea, but he missed the little table and it shattered on the patio. Just like Frank Escobar. Maybe poor hand-eye went with a life of crime. He said, "I don't know what you're talking about."

I looked at Joe Pike. "Man, these guys come up with the good lines, don't they, Joe?"

Pike didn't move. LeRoy was closer, and Pike was watching him. René was still down between the ponds, but he was getting up a head of steam. I guess Pike was thinking about having to shoot them.

I said, "You and Donaldo are moving illegal aliens upriver through bayous upon which you hold the leases. Donaldo deals with the people down south and contracts with the illegals, and you provide intercoastal transportation and a secure location through which they can enter the country."

Rossier was waving his hands, feeling panicked and trying to push up out of the chair. "I don't know any of that. I don't know what in hell you're talking about." Pike leaned forward and shoved him back. Rossier swatted at Pike's hand the way you would swat at an aggravating gnat, and Pike palmed him hard once on the top of the head. Milt stopped the swatting. "I don't know any Prima or illegal alien nonsense or anything else. You'd better get out of here right goddamn now 'fore I call the law!" Giving us an old man's outrage.

I held up two fingers. "Two words, Milt. Frank Escobar."

He stopped sputtering, and his eyes focused on me.

"Escobar controls the coyote scene through the port of New Orleans and the intercoastal region. We left him a couple of hours ago. Prima used to work for Escobar, but now he's gone into business for himself with you, and Escobar doesn't like it that Prima's taking his business. Prima's getting the business because he's cutting prices, and Escobar likes that even less. You following me with this, Milt?"

Milt was squinting at me big time now.

"And because Prima's charging less, *you* are getting less. Do you see? You're getting, what, a grand a head for your end?"

Now Milt wasn't bothering with the denials. We were with the money, and when you're with the money you have their attention.

"Frank will give you two grand apiece, Milt. Double your money. If you're getting one load of illegals a week, thirty people on average, that's thirty thousand a week, one hundred twenty thousand a month from Mr. Prima. But Frank doubles it. The thirty becomes sixty. The one-twenty becomes two hundred forty thousand per month, every month, just for using Escobar and cutting out Prima. Are we talking about the same thing, now, Milt?"

LeRoy Bennett chugged up to the patio, winded and barely able to keep his feet. He saw the gun in Pike's hand and clawed under his shirt, trying for his own piece. Pike punched him once in the side of the face. Bennett dropped. Pike bent over and disarmed him. Pike said, "Some muscle."

Rossier stared at LeRoy thoughtfully and said, "I am surrounded by dunces."

I made a little shrug.

Rossier shook his head and settled back into the lawn furniture. "Well, I guess you're the new Jimmie Ray Rebenack, aren't you? He thought he tripped over Easy Street, too. Look where he is."

"Milt, Jimmie Ray and I aren't even from the same planet. Don't forget that and we'll be okay."

René lumbered up and stopped at LeRoy, and then he looked at Joe Pike, and the big body gave a shudder. His eyes focused, and he stepped across LeRoy and Pike brought up the Python. "I'll kill him."

Milt Rossier screamed, "René! Goddamn it, you stop right there, René." The old man's face was mottled, and he looked close to apoplexy.

René looked confused. LeRoy moaned, then rolled over and saw René staring down at him. "Don't just stand there, you dumb fuck, help me up."

René picked up LeRoy as if he were made of air. LeRoy hobbled to one of the lawn chairs, holding his side. "Got a goddamned stitch from d' run."

Pike said, "Exercise."

Bennett scowled. "You fuck. We'll see 'bout it, sometime, heh?"

Pike said, "Unh-hunh."

Rossier said, "Forget all that right now. We're talkin' business." He looked back at me. "What do you get out of this?"

"We get what Escobar pays you for the first delivery. Call it sixty thousand." Big lies are always easier.

"Bullshit."

"What's the bullshit, Milt? I'm brokering the deal. You would've kept going with Prima because you don't know any better, with him laughing behind your back. I've figured it out for you, and I've set it up. Your money doubles right away, and for this service, Joe and myself get exactly one week's take. After that it's all yours. You recoup in two weeks over what you were making from Prima." I gestured to Joe Pike. "Seems fair to me, Joe. How about you?"

Pike nodded. "Fair."

You could see Milt Rossier working it through, thinking about all that free money just for giving the spics a place to dock their boats. Convincing himself. That's the way the best cons work, they convince themselves. He said, "Frank Escobar, huh?"

I said, "Let me give you a couple of pointers, Milt. Two a head is top end, so don't start thinking you can get Prima to pay more.

Frank is looking for what we call exclusivity here, and he will want to make sure that Donaldo is permanently out of the picture. Do we understand each other?"

"Unh-hunh."

"Frank wants you to let Prima bring in another load, only this time we'll all be out there at the pumping station together. Prima won't know about Frank and Frank's people, of course, because if he did, he wouldn't show. When he shows, Frank wants to pay him back personally, you see?"

Milt Rossier was shaking his head. "He don't need me there for that."

"Yeah, Milt, he does. Frank figures that if you'll sell out Prima, you'll sell out him, too, so you guys are going to have to make a marriage out there. No marriage, no two grand per. Two hundred forty thou every month, Milt. Prima won't be going home, but everybody else lives happily ever after."

Milt Rossier was thinking about it.

I gave him the phone number that Ramon del Reyo had given me. "I'm giving you a number to call. Call it if you want, or not. Up to you. It's not Escobar, but it's his people. If you're interested, check out if the deal is real. If not, blow it off. Your choice."

He took the little slip and looked at it. "What's to keep me from cutting you out?"

"Milt, you don't live in a fortress. You cut us out, you're over."

Pike twitched the .357.

LeRoy Bennett said, "Oh. Yeah."

Milt Rossier stared at Pike for a time, then glanced over at LeRoy. LeRoy was feeling a little better, but his eye was swelling where Pike had hit him. It probably didn't inspire confidence. Rossier said, "I've gotta think on it. How can I let you know?"

I told him where we were staying in Baton Rouge, and then Pike and I started back around the house. Milt Rossier called after us. "Hey."

We turned back.

Rossier said, "Podnuh, if either of you ever pull a gun on me again, you'd best use it."

I smiled at him. "Milt, if we pull a gun on you again, we will."

34

When we got back to Baton Rouge I called Jodi Taylor's room from the lobby and got no answer. The desk clerk told me that she had checked out sometime in the early afternoon and that she had left neither note nor message. He said that she seemed distraught. Hearing that she had gone created an empty feeling in my chest, as if I had somehow left a job unfinished and, because of it, had performed beneath myself. I said, "Well, damn."

Pike said, "It's a good night. Clear. I'm going for a run." The lobby was empty except for Pike and myself and the clerk. Desultory voices leaked from the bar. "Come with me."

"Give me a chance to make some calls."

He nodded. "Meet you out front."

We rode up to our rooms, and I changed into shorts and running shoes and then called Lucy. I told her what had happened with Escobar and Rossier and that there was nothing left to do except wait and see if Rossier would go for it. I asked her if she'd heard from Jodi Taylor. Lucy said, "Yes. And from Sid Markowitz. Sid is saying that they'll sue. I'm not so sure that Jodi wants that, but she sounds upset and confused."

"Did she say anything about Edith Boudreaux?"

"No."

Neither of us spoke for a time, and then Lucy said, "Studly?"

"Yes, ma'am?"

"Ben's going to bed at ten. You could come over and we could neck in the car."

"Pike and I are going for a run. It's been a helluva day."

She sighed. "Just so you know."

"I knew there was a reason I called you."

We hung up and I phoned Jo-el Boudreaux next. I told him exactly what I had told Lucy, and when I was done he said, "Did they go for it?"

"We'll see. Rossier will dig around to see if we're legit, and when he finds out we have something working with Escobar, he'll decide."

"Okay. Then what?"

"He'll call me here. When he calls, I call Escobar. We won't have much time, so you have to be ready."

"I can get my guys in five minutes. Bet your ass on that one, podnuh."

"Whatever."

Pike was waiting out on the cement drive at the hotel's entry, stretching his hamstrings. I joined him, bending deep from the hips until my face was buried between my knees, then sitting with my legs in a great wide V and bending forward until my chest was on the cement. After a day spent mostly driving, and with the tension of dealing with criminal subhumans, it felt good to work my muscles. Maybe I wasn't down about Jodi Taylor after all. Maybe I had merely grown loggy from a lack of proper exercise and was in serious need of oxygenation. Sure. That was it. What's bailing out on a client compared to proper physical conditioning?

Pike did a hundred pushups, then flipped over and lay with his legs straight up against the wall and did a hundred situps. I did the same. The kid from the front desk came out and watched, standing in the door so he could keep an eye on the desk. He said, "Man, you guys are flexible. Goin' for a run?"

"That's right."

"Gotta be careful where you run. We got some bad areas."

I said, "Thanks."

"I'm not kidding. The downtown isn't great. Any direction you go, you're gonna run into the blacks."

Pike said, "I think I hear your phone."

The kid ducked inside, then reappeared shaking his head. "Nah. Must've been something else."

As my muscles warmed, the tension began to loosen and fall away like ice calving from a glacier and falling into the sea.

The kid said, "They say we're one of the top ten most dangerous cities in the country." He seemed proud of it.

I said, "We'll be careful."

Pike said, "Let's get going before I hit this twerp."

We ran south along the street that paralleled the levee, then up the little rise past the old state capitol building and then east, away from the river. The night air was warm, and the humidity let the sweat come easily. I concentrated on my breath and the rhythms of the run and the commitment needed to match Pike's pace. The run became consuming in its effort, and the focus needed to endure it was liberating. The downtown business area quickly gave way to a mix of businesses and small, single-family homes. Black. We ran along a major thoroughfare and the traffic was heavy, so we stayed on a narrow sidewalk as much as possible. The blocks were short and the cross-streets were numbered, and each time we crossed one you could get a glimpse of the lives in the little neighborhoods. We passed African-American kids on skateboards and bicycles, and other African-American kids playing pepper in the streets or tackle football on empty lots. They stopped as we passed and watched us without comment, two pale men trekking swiftly along the edge of their world, and I wondered if these were the areas the desk clerk had been talking about. As we ran, Pike said, "You did your best for her."

I took steady breaths. "I know."

"But you're not happy with yourself."

"I let her down. In a way, I've abandoned her." I thought about it. "It's not the first time she's been abandoned."

A lone running black man turned onto the street across from us and matched our pace. He was about our age, with a receding hairline and ebony skin and the slight, lean torso of a serious runner. Like us, he was shirtless, clothed only in shorts and running shoes, his chest and back slicked with sweat and shining the way highly polished obsidian might shine. I glanced over at him, but he ran eyes forward, as if we were not opposite him, and pretty soon I found that my eyes were forward, too, though I could see him in the periphery. I said, "She hired me to do one thing, and now I'm doing another. She hired me with every expectation that I would protect her interests, but now I'm taking this in a direction in which her interests are secondary."

We ran past a high school and shopping centers, Pike and me on our side of the street and the black runner on his, our strides matching. Pike said nothing for several minutes, and I found comfort in the loud silence. The sounds of our breathing. Our shoes striking the pavement. A metronome rhythm. Pike said, "You didn't fail her. You gave her an opportunity for love."

I glanced over at him.

"You can't put something into her heart that isn't there, Elvis. Love is not so plentiful that any of us can afford to reject it when it's offered. That's her failing. Not yours."

"It's not easy for her, Joe. For a lot of very good reasons."

"Maybe."

The black runner picked up his pace and moved ahead of us. Pike and I glanced at him in the same moment, and we picked up our pace, too. We caught him, matched him, and then we pulled ahead. Our lead lasted for a few hundred meters before he once again came abreast of us. I pushed harder, Pike pushing as one with me, and the runner across from us pushed harder still. My breath was coming in great, quick gasps, the oxygen-rich Louisiana air somehow energizing, the sweat dripping out of my hair and into my eyes, and we ran ever harder, sprinting now, we on our side of the street, he on his, and then we came to a busy intersection and slowed for the light and I turned to the other runner, smiling and intending to wave, but the black runner was gone. He had turned away from us with the cross-street, I guess, and I tried to find him but he was no longer there. We jogged in place, waiting for the light, and I found myself wishing I had called to him earlier. Now, of course, it was too late.

The light changed. Pike and I pushed on, and the miles crept behind us and the night grew late. We came to a park of soccer fields and softball diamonds, and we turned north, running along the western edge of the fields, and then west again, heading back to the river and the hotel. We had been running for almost an hour. We would run an hour still. Pike said, "Are you still thinking about her?"

"Yes."

"Then think about this. You've taken her as far as is right. Wherever she's going, she has to get the rest of the way on her own. That's not only the way it is. That's the way it should be."

"Sure, Joe. Thanks."

He grunted. Philosphy-R-Us. "Now stop thinking about her and start think about Rossier. If you don't get your head out your ass, Rossier will kill you."

"You always know how to end the moment on an upbeat note, don't you?"

"That's why I get the big bucks."

35

Milt Rossier called at fourteen minutes after nine the next morning. First thing out of his mouth was, "I'll go along for twenty-five hunnerd a head."

"Forget it."

"Twenty-two five, then, goddammit, or I'll just leave things the way they are."

I hung up on him. If I had a strong hand, I'd play it. If I didn't, he'd know I was shooting blanks.

Six minutes later the phone again rang and he said, "Twenty-one hunnerd, you sonofabitch. You know goddamn well there's some give. Be reasonable."

I thought my heart was going to come through my nose. "There's more, Milt, but I'm taking it. It's a one-shot, then I'm back home and out of it. After that, if you can screwdriver Escobar out of the extra cash, go for it."

Milt Rossier said, "You sonofabitch," but now he was laughing. One slimebag to another. Just a couple of good ol' boys ripping off each other. "Prima's bringing a load up tonight. That too soon for you boys?"

"Nope. What time?"

"The boat comes in around ten. Prima meets my boy LeRoy at a place called the Bayou Lounge. You know it?"

"Not tonight, Milt. Have Prima meet us at the boat. Escobar and I will meet you at your place at eight. Escobar wants to go in early." If I could get Escobar. If he'd go for it.

Milt said, "Escobar gonna bring the money?"

"Sure."

"Well, good."

I said, "You didn't tip Donaldo, did you, Milt?"

"Hell, no."

"Frank wants him, Milt. That's the deal."

"I said I didn't, goddamn it. If Frank wants to be in business with me he can have Prima's ass in a goddamned croaker sack. I'll gut him and skin him, he wants."

"Good enough. He's looking forward to meeting you, Milt. He's thinking he can run in three loads a week."

Milt Rossier said, "Holy jumpin' Jesus." There were probably dollar signs in his eyes.

"Happy days, Milt."

He said, "One thing, podnuh."

"What's that?"

"You be at the Bayou waitin'. You ain't there, I'll back away from this thing like a mud bug divin' down his hole." Ah, that southern color.

"Wouldn't miss it, podnuh." Now I was doing it.

"Ol' Frank don't show, you gonna wish you had. Milt Rossier don't take shit from any man on this God's earth. You hear where I'm coming from?"

"Loud and clear, Milt."

I hung up and called Frank Escobar. I said, "Donaldo Prima is bringing in a boat of people tonight at ten P.M. Rossier says you can have him. Are you in?"

Escobar said, "Yes."

"He wants to meet at a place called the Bayou Lounge. We'll meet him there, then go to the boat. You have to have the money."

"Don't worry about it."

I hung up and called Jo-el Boudreaux at his home. He answered on the second ring, and his voice was shaky. He said, "Did they go for it?"

"We're on for tonight. Can you get your people together?"

He said, "Oh, Christ."

"Can you get it together?"

"Yeah. Of course, I can." He sounded strained.

"Calm down, Jo-el. The boat will come at ten, but I have to meet him at his bar at eight, and that means your people have to be in position by seven. Are you going to be able to arrange that?"

"Yeah. Yeah, sure. I'll get my guys and have them come over to the house around four, and we'll set everything up."

"I'll be there."

"Hey, Cole."

"What?"

"I appreciate this."

"Sure."

I hung up and phoned Lucy at her office and told her we were on. She said, "Do you think Jo-el can pull it off?"

"There's nothing to it, Luce. When the bad guys are all together with the money and the illegals, all he has to do is arrest them. The trick was in getting everybody together. There's nothing fancy in the bust."

"I guess not." She didn't sound convinced.

I told her that we would be putting it together at the Boudreaux's house at four, and she said that she'd call Merhlie Comeaux and that they would meet us there. We hung up, and then I went next door for Pike. I said, "We're on."

He went to his closet and got the duffel. When he picked it up you could hear the clunk of padded metal. He said, "I've been ready for years."

At three o'clock that afternoon, we went down to the car and drove across the bridge to Eunice.

Three Evangeline Parish Sheriff's Department highway cars were parked on the grass in front of Jo-el Boudreaux's house, and Lucy's Lexus was in the drive. I wondered if the neighbors might think it odd, so many cars, but maybe not. Just a little midweek barbecue for the boys. Pike and I went to the door, and Edith Boudreaux let us in. She smiled when she greeted us, but the smile seemed strained.

Lucy and Merhlie Comeaux were in the wing chairs, and three parish cops were on the sofa. The young black cop named Berry was there, along with the cop named Tommy Willets. The third cop was was a guy named Dave Champagne, who looked like the Pillsbury Doughboy with a pink downy face. Willets frowned when he saw us, then looked away, shaking his head. Still with the attitude. Champagne and Berry were younger than Willets. Boudreaux introduced everybody, and I stayed with the group while Pike went off by himself and stood against the wall. Both Berry and Champagne kept glancing at him. A little tray of Fig Newtons and sugar cookies was on the coffee table, and Edith Boudreaux offered us coffee in fragile china cups. She seemed anxious that we accept, and she hovered at the edges of the room, as flighty as a mayfly trapped behind glass. I thought that, in a way, this might be harder on her than on anyone else. Jo-el said, "I've told everybody that we're goin' after Milt Rossier tonight. I told'm about the illegals and Donaldo Prima and Frank Escobar and what we're tryin' to do. You wanna tell'm what you saw out there?"

I went through it about the towboat and the pumping station and the old man and the little girl, and then I told them about backtracking on Prima to uncover the scam. When I was in the middle of it Willets sat forward on the couch and stopped me. He said, "You saw a damned murder you shoulda come in right away."

Jo-el said, "He had his reasons, Tommy."

Tommy Willets was staring at the sheriff. "Not reportin' a crime is against the law, Jo-el. Jesus Christ, who made this guy the goddamned sheriff?" He shot a glance at Edith. "Sorry, Edie."

Jo-el Boudreaux was looking embarrassed when Dave Champagne said, "Oh, put a sock in it, Tommy. We're gonna finally take down ol' Milt Rossier. Ain't that a hoot?" He was grinning so wide his face looked like a fuzzy pink pumpkin. I looked at Pike, and Pike shook his head. We were making this bust with a Boy Scout troop.

Lucy said, "How is this thing going to be staged?"

I said, "I'm going to meet Milt Rossier and Frank Escobar at the Bayou Lounge at eight, and then we're going to the pumping station to meet the boat. The boat's due in at ten. Prima is supposed to arrive with the boat."

Jo-el looked at Merhlie Comeaux. "How we doin' with this? We clear on entrapment?"

Merhlie nodded. "I don't see a problem, sheriff. It looks clean. We give the state a clean bust with Rossier in possession of cash and a truck full of illegal aliens, and they'll put his name on a double occupancy suite in Angola. I guarantee." He said it *gah-rawn-tee*. Cajun.

I said, "Rossier may not actually take possession of the cash. It could go to Bennett. That's what happened last time."

"Same thing," Merhlie said. "Bennett works for Rossier, and Rossier holds the lease on the land." He looked back at Boudreaux. "I'll wait by the phone. Just lemme know when it's done and I'll call Jack Fochet at state and we'll have ol' Milt arraigned by tomorrow noon. Jack Fochet is a good boy."

Berry was looking concerned. "I know the old Hyfield Oil station. How are we supposed to see any of this if it happens inside there?"

"Prima flags the towboat in from the shore, then they bring the trucks into the building through a couple of barn doors," I said. "They leave the doors open. You won't have any problem. That's how we saw the old man killed."

Jo-el said, "We're gonna be in the weeds, so we may not be able to see what's going on. Maybe we oughta have a sign or some-thin'."

Merhlie frowned. "Well, hell, Jo-el, what do you want him to do, wave a red bandanna? Those sonsofbitches have guns and they like to use them."

When he said it, Lucy sat forward in her chair. "You're going to be with them when the arrests are made?"

"Yes."

She looked at Pike, and then back to me. "Is that necessary?"

"I'm what holds it together. I'm putting Rossier and Escobar together, and they're going to want me with them all the way. Rossier's nervous, and Escobar's only going along because he thinks he's going to kill Prima." I looked at Boudreaux. "Prima isn't expecting Escobar, so when these guys see each other all hell's going to break loose. You'll have to move fast."

Jo-el nodded. "Sure. You bet." He was pale and he kept rub-bing at his jaw.

Willets hooked a thumb at Pike. "Where are you going to be, podnuh?"

Pike said, "Watching."

Willets didn't like that. "What in hell does that mean?"

Jo-el said, "Don't worry about it, Tommy. He'll be there."

Willets stayed with it. "We should know where everyone is. There might be shooting. Be a shame if somebody got shot acci-dental-like."

Pike said, "Don't worry about it, Willets."

Willets frowned, but he let it go.

Berry said, "Where we gonna be?"

Boudreaux said, "We'll set up in the cane with a view through the doors. We'll have to hide the cars off the main road, then hike in. I want you fellas to go home and get your waders. You're gonna need'm."

Willets said, "How much time do we have? I got things I need to do."

Boudreaux checked his watch. "We got about an hour before we have to get in place. That about right?" He looked at me, asking. I nodded, and Willets snorted, disgusted that Boudreaux would ask. Boudreaux ignored him and went on. "I want you boys to change into old clothes, cause we're gonna get wet, but I want everybody in a Sheriff's Department shell parka. I wanna know who's who out there." Boudreaux had brought it to the end, and now he looked at me. "I think maybe we oughta get going. You got anything you wanna say?"

"Yeah. Nobody shoot me."

Berry and Champagne laughed, and everybody stood, moving toward the door. The sheriff went to Merhlie Comeaux, and Lucy pulled me aside. Her mouth was still in the tight line, and she pulled me as far from the others as she could. She said, "Do you really have to be out there?"

"I've done things like this before. Trust me."

Her nostrils flared, and she stared across the room, frowning. "Well, isn't that just great. And what do I get to do, wait here with the womenfolk?"

"If you ask him nice, Pike might loan you a rifle."

She said, "Oh, right," and stalked away to Comeaux.

Pike looked at me from across the room and cocked his head toward the door. I met him there. He said, "You okay with these guys?"

"They're what we have."

He glanced at Willets. "I don't like the dip with the attitude."

"See you on the other side, Joe."

Pike nodded, and I went out to my car and left for the Bayou Lounge.

Years ago, a friend and I booked a package cruise from Tahiti to Hawaii, sailing north. The passage took five days, crossing waters so remote that we were beyond all radio contact with land. As we sailed, the sea grew deeper until, three days out of Papeete, the crew told us that the sonar could no longer ping the bottom. The charts said that the bottom was seventeen thousand feet beneath the hull, but, for all purposes, the ocean was bottomless. No way to know what's down there, they said. No way to call home for help, they said. Here there be monsters.

Great dense clouds grew on the western horizon, towering anvil thunderheads that rolled steadily toward me, filling the sky with the slate-steel color of deep ocean water, water with no bottom.

36

A light rain fell as I parked on the oyster shell lot next to the Bayou Lounge. The heavy cloud layer brought an early twilight that filled the air with an expectancy of wind and lightning. Four or five American sedans were lined up on the oyster shells and, inside, half a dozen guys hawked the bar, scarfing poboys and Dixie beer. The woman with the hair smiled when she saw me and said, "Sugah, I didn't think you'd pass this way again."

"Small world, isn't it?"

"Oh," she said. "It's a lot bigger than we think." A guy with a grease-stained Evinrude cap laughed when she said it.

I ordered a club soda and took it to one of the little tables by the door. The door was wedged open and it was cooler there, but it was a damp cool that made my skin clammy. The Dan Wesson would be picking up a lot of moisture, and I would have to clean it before it began to pit. Of course, if things didn't go well tonight, I wouldn't have to worry about it.

A couple of minutes later LeRoy Bennett's Polara pulled past the door and LeRoy Bennett came in, shaking his hat to get rid of the rain. He was wearing an Australian drover's coat, and he looked not unlike the Marlboro man. Cancer on the hoof. The woman with the hair squealed, "Hey, LeRoy," and leaned across the bar to plant one on his cheek. His face split with a smile and he pawed at her breasts, but she pushed him away like she didn't really mean it. A couple of the good ol' boys at the bar nodded at him, and he shook one man's hand. Old home week with the bar-fly regulars. He got a long-necked Dixie for himself, then came over and dropped into the chair across from me. His eye was still dark from where Joe Pike had hit him. He said, "Where're your spics?"

I said, "I'm here early."

He had some of the Dixie, shooting a wink at the woman with the hair. "Yeah? Well, your spics better show or you in deep do-do."

I said, "LeRoy?"

He was sucking at his teeth.

"Do yourself a favor and don't call them spics."

LeRoy frowned like I was a turd. "That's what they are, ain't they?"

I shook my head. Some people never learn. Some people you just can't talk to.

I said, "Where's Milt?"

"He'll be here."

"I thought he might come with you."

LeRoy pulled on the Dixie. "You jus' worry about your spics." He lipped a Tarryton 100 and lit it with a big steel Zippo. The first two fingers on his right hand were yellow with smoke stains. His fingernails were grimed. He grinned at me and let the smoke leak out between his teeth. Probably hadn't brushed in a year.

LeRoy got up and put money in the jukebox. He finished the first Dixie and got himself a second. While he was at the bar the woman with the hair whispered something in his ear, and he whispered something back. She laughed. It's odd what appeals to people, isn't it? The guy with the Evinrude cap and a heavier guy who walked with a limp went home. I wished I could go with them. The rain came harder, filling ruts and depressions in the shell lot and hammering on the bar's roof, and little by little the remains of day were lost to the night. The parking lot filled with white light two quick times, followed almost instantly by twin booms of thunder, and the guys at the bar applauded. The thunder was so loud and so near that the little building shook, rattling glasses and making the jukebox skip. And they talk about earthquakes.

At two minutes before eight, headlights swung across the door, a baby blue BMW crunched onto the lot, and Frank Escobar came in, the guy with the pocked face holding an umbrella the size of a parachute canopy. LeRoy said, "Well, it's about goddamned time." He was working on his third Dixie and he said it too loud.

They came to the table and sat, Escobar shaking off his coat. "You pick a shit time to do business. Is Rossier here?"

"Not yet."

LeRoy stuck out his hand. "Mr. Escobar, my name is LeRoy Bennett. It's a pleasure, sir, yes it is."

Escobar looked at me without acknowledging the hand or the person. "Who is this?"

"Rossier's stooge."

LeRoy said, "Hey, what the fuck?"

Escobar hit LeRoy with the back of his right hand so hard that LeRoy almost went out of the chair. It was exactly the same move he'd used on his wife. Two of the guys at the bar looked over and the woman gave a little gasp. Escobar grabbed LeRoy by the face and dug a thumb under his jaw. "You see me sitting here?"

LeRoy tried to get away from the thumb, but couldn't. "Hey, yeah. Whatchu doin', bro?"

"If I'm here, where's your goddamned boss? You think I got time to waste?"

Even as he said it more lights swept the open door and you could hear the crunch, even over the jukebox and the rain. LeRoy stood away from the thumb, saying, "That's gotta be Milt right now," just as Milt Rossier walked in.

The woman behind the bar said, "Hey, Milt," but Milt didn't acknowledge her. He saw us at the little table and came over, offering his hand to Frank Escobar. "Frank, I'm Milt Rossier. Lemme apologize if I've kept you, but this rain is a bitch."

Escobar said, "Hey, forget about it. You shoulda seen the drive up from Metairie." He held Milt Rossier's hand longer than he needed to hold it. "I'm looking forward to a fruitful partnership, Milt, but let's get first things first. Where's Prima?"

"Oh, he'll be at the pumping station. You bet."

Escobar glanced at me, then put it back on Milt Rossier. He still had the old man's hand. "I wanna make money with you, Milt, but you have to understand it's personal here, me and Prima. We ain't goin' forward with this until I get this bastard."

Milt was nodding and trying to get his hand away. Escobar's eyes were dark splinters and Milt Rossier seemed afraid of him. "Frank," he said, "I'm gonna bring you right to him." He finally got the hand away. "You ready to do some business or you wanna little snoot before we go? This is my place. It's on the house." Like a guy worth millions wouldn't pass up the chance at a free belt.

Escobar shook his head and stood. He snapped his fingers, and the pocked guy stood with him. "Prima." Talk about one track. You could see his hands flexing, already pulling the trigger. His coat flared when he stood, and you could see a glint in the darkness.

Milt smiled. "Well, hell, let's go do it."

We stepped out into the rain. Milt wanted everybody to go together in LeRoy's Polara, but there were five of us and it would be crowded, so Milt asked if Escobar would mind following us in his own car. Escobar said that that would be fine, and he and his goon hurried to their BMW, anxious to get out of the rain. Lightning crackled again, filling the parking lot with light. Escobar and his thug opened the Beamer's doors, the BMW's interior lights came on, and then two men stepped out from behind the Bayou Lounge. Balls of lightning flashed from their hands, and there was the sharp snapping of autoloading pistols muffled by the rain, and Escobar and his goon fell against their car. The pistols were still snapping when LeRoy Bennett slammed the side of my head with something hard and cold. I went down into the mud and Bennett was over me, hitting me twice more and saying, "Who's a stooge now? Who's a fuckin' stooge?" and then Rossier pushed him away, saying, "Stop that, goddammit, we ain't got time for that! Get'm up."

René LaBorde stepped out of nowhere and pulled me to my feet. Bennett, grinning like his face was split, took my gun and hit me again.

The rain fell harder and no one stirred from the Bayou Lounge.

The two men finished their killing and came to us. One of the men was Donaldo Prima. The other was Evangeline Parish Deputy Sheriff Tommy Willets. Willets looked scared. Donaldo Prima said, "We got that fawkuh good!" I knew then that the good guys were alone at the pumping station. All of the bad guys were here.

I said, "Jesus Christ, Willets."

Willets hit me on the forehead with the butt of his pistol and knocked me into the side of Bennett's Polara. Then Milt said, "Hurry up, goddammit, and get'm in the car. We got a lot of people to kill."

37

Willets put his cuffs on me, then got René to help put me in the backseat of Bennett's Polara. Willets breathed hard as he did it, a torrent of rain running off the brim of his campaign hat, his Evangeline Parish sheriff's poncho molten in the lightning flashes. The lounge's wooden front door was closed, and I thought maybe Bennett had closed it as we'd left. Maybe.

Across the lot, Bennett and a short guy with a heavy moustache loaded the bodies into Escobar's trunk, the short guy Donaldo Prima's thug. Donaldo Prima came over to the Polara and waved his gun at me. "This fawkuh set me up?" His eyes were blood simple from the kill.

Rossier said, "We might need the sonofabitch! *Put it away!*"

Prima pushed past Milt, screaming, "I gonna kill his ass!" When Prima touched Milt, René's snake-fast hands shot out, grabbing and lifting and twisting the gun away. Prima hissed something in Spanish, then said, "Make him let go!"

Rossier made René put him down, and then Prima and Rossier went to Escobar's car with Bennett and the moustache. Willets got into the backseat of the Polara with me, and René stood in the

285

rain. René was wearing a raincoat, but it was unbuttoned and looked as if someone had put it on for him. There was no hood, and the rain beat at his head and plastered his hair. Willets sat with his service revolver in his hand, still with the breathing, staring wide-eyed through the rear window at the group of men in the rain as if I weren't there. The glass around us began to fog. I said, "How much does it cost for a guy like you to sell out, Willets?"

"Shut up."

"I know he paid you enough to keep tabs on the sheriff, but is it enough to buy a night's sleep?"

"Shut up."

"Willets, if you sold your balls by the pound, you didn't get enough to feed a parking meter."

Willets looked over at me, blinked twice, then backhanded me with his revolver. The barrel and the cylinder caught me above the left eye, snapping my head back and opening the skin. There was an instant of blackness, then a field of gold sparkles, and then only sharp pain above the eye. I could feel blood run down across the outside corner of my eye. I grinned. "You didn't think it'd come to this when you sold them, did you? Guys like you never think that far ahead. Only now it's here and happening fast and you're scared shitless. You're in the deep water, Willets, and you oughta be scared."

He wet his lips and looked again at the men in the rain. Scared, all right. "I'm not the guy who has to worry about it."

"Were you in on Rebenack?"

He still didn't look at me.

"That's perfect, Willets. Perfect."

LeRoy and Milt came back to the Polara. Prima went behind the lounge, alone, and LaBorde and the moustache climbed into Escobar's Beamer. The Beamer pulled away, and Willets's highway car came from behind the lounge. We pulled out, and the highway car fell in behind us. No one had stirred in the Bayou

Lounge, and no one had come out to look. All of it had been covered by the rain and the thunder.

I said, "I can't believe you didn't go for it, Milt. Two thousand a head is a lot of money."

Rossier turned in the front passenger seat and grinned at me. His old man's face looked cracked and splintered, and he was holding Bennett's government .45. He said, "Goddamned right it is. You almost had me, you sonofabitch. I woulda swallowed the whole damn hook if Willets here hadn't tipped me."

"Willets isn't the only cop who knows. A lot of people are in it, and Jo-el Boudreaux is going to take you down. The blackmail won't work anymore."

Willets licked his lips. "He's right, Milt. We oughta not play it this way."

Milt said, "Who else knows?"

Willets was licking his lips again. "The guys out at the station, Jo-el's wife and that lawyer from Baton Rouge, and Merhlie Comeaux. Comeaux went home, and the two women are at the Boudreauxs'."

Milt Rossier nodded and grinned still wider. "We'll just round'm up and kill'm and that's that." He said it the way you'd tell someone you wanted pickles on your potted meat sandwich.

I said, "You're out of your mind."

Willets said, "Jesus Christ, that's crazy."

Milt nodded. "We'll see."

Willets said, "You can't just kill all these people."

Milt nodded and asked Bennett if he knew how to get there, and Bennett said yes. Willets was licking his lips every few seconds, now. He said, "Hey, Milt, you don't mean that, do you? You can't just murder these people?"

Milt cocked his head and looked at Willets as you might a slow child. "Son, simple plans are best. What else can I do?"

Willets squirmed in his seat, holding the service revolver limply in his lap. I wondered if I could move fast enough to snake it from him before Milt shot me. Willets said, "But that's three officers. That's Jo-el's wife. How we gonna explain all that? Jesus Christ."

I said, "Hey, Willets, how do you think he's going to explain you being the only one left alive?"

Milt Rossier said, "Oh, that one's easy." Then he pointed LeRoy Bennett's .45 at Deputy Sheriff Thomas Willets and pulled the trigger. The sound was enormous, and the heat and muzzle blast flashed across my face, and Tommy Willets's head snapped back into the seat and then jerked forward, and a spray of red splattered on the vinyl and the door and the windows and me. When Willets's head came forward he slumped to the side and was still.

LeRoy said, "Man, dat was loud as a pork fart, yeah."

Milt reached back and took Willets's revolver and had Bennett pull over. Bennett put the body in the trunk and we went on. I said, "You really mean it. You're going to kill everybody, aren't you?"

Milt said, "Uh-hunh."

We drove to Jo-el Boudreaux's house and turned into the drive, Prima pulling the highway car in behind us. I said, "If you hurt them, Rossier, I swear to God I'll kill you."

LeRoy said, "Save the big talk, asshole. You gonna need it later."

Milt got out of the car and met Prima and the moustache, and together they went to the front door. Around us, the street was quiet and well lit and masked by the rain. Just another dreary southern evening in paradise.

Milt rang the bell, and Edith Boudreaux answered. The moustache pushed past her into the house, and as quickly as that they were bringing Lucy and Edith across the lawn to the highway car. Lucy was struggling, and the moustache had to keep a hand over her mouth. You never expect the bad guys will come to the door. You never expect that they'll ring the bell. When Rossier climbed back into the car, he was smiling. "We'll see what ol' Jo-el does, now. Yes, I guess we will, won't we?" I'm not sure he was saying it to me or to Bennett. Maybe just to himself.

They brought us to the crawfish farm, driving through sequined curtains of rain, and put us in the processing shed. Escobar's BMW was already there, René standing in the rain and mud like some great oblivious golem. When Milt Rossier saw him, he shook his head and made a *tsk*ing sound. I guess you never get used to it. They taped Lucy's and Edie's wrists with duct tape and made the three of us sit on the floor beneath the gutting tables. Rain hammered in through the big, open front of the processing shed, but we were well back and protected. The rear of the place was open, too, and more rain dripped there. Milt and Prima and Bennett gathered together, then Bennett got back into his Polara and drove away. Going to give the news to Jo-el Boudreaux. Edith looked pale and drawn, and Lucy looked scared. After Prima and the moustache finished with the taping and left us alone, I said, "Fancy meeting you here."

Lucy didn't smile. The beautiful tanned skin was mottled, and her nostrils were white. Her eyes moved from Rossier to the moustache to LaBorde to Prima, like something might happen at any moment and in that instant she must be ready or it would be forever lost.

I said, "It's not over. There's Pike, and there's me. I'll get you out of this."

She nodded without looking at me.

"Did I tell you that I'm an irresistible force?"

A smile flickered at the edges of her mouth, and her eyes came to me. She said, "You really know how to show a girl a good time, don't you?"

"Irresistible," I said. "Unstoppable. Able to leap tall buildings in a single bound."

She relaxed the tiniest bit and nodded.

I said, "A moment will come. When it does, I want you to

move back under these tables. You, too, Edith. Did you hear me?"

Edith was as waxy as a mannequin, and I couldn't be sure that she heard me. Then Rossier came over and kicked me hard in the leg, twice. "Shut up that talk!" He tore off strips of the duct tape and covered our mouths.

We sat on the damp cement floor and watched Rossier and Prima and the moustache move around the processing shed, making their plans. René followed Rossier like a dog after its master. Rossier went up to the main house and came back with a couple of pump shotguns and a thin, weathered man with mocha skin. Another thug. He gave one of the shotguns to the moustache and the other to Donaldo Prima. They talked for a while in the doorway, Rossier pointing and gesturing, and then the black man and the moustache went out into the rain. Setting up a field of fire. I worked at the duct tape with my tongue and rubbed it against my shoulder and the gutting table's leg, and it began to peel away.

Milt stayed in the sliding doors, looking out, and in a little bit lights appeared and LeRoy Bennett's Polara came toward the sheds. It wasn't alone. Jo-el's highway car was behind it, but he wasn't coming in with sirens wailing and light bar flashing. He came slow and easy, like he was trying not to make things worse than they were. LeRoy put his Polara on the side of the processing shed, then came inside. He was soaked, but he looked excited. He said, "I got'm. I told'm what you said and they came just like you said they would, goddammit! I got their goddamned guns. I busted their goddamned radio." He was smiling a crazy grin, like we were kids and all of this was some kind of summer-camp game. Blood simple.

Edith straightened to see, and so did I. From where we sat you could see through the wide opening and out to the highway car. Parked in the killing field. Jo-el got out of the near side of his car and stood in the rain, and Berry and Dave Champagne climbed out the other side. I thought I saw a shadow slip from the rear of the car when Berry got out, but I couldn't be sure. Milt Rossier said, "Where's the other one?"

Bennett said, "Who?"

"The one knocked you on your ass, goddammit!" Pike wasn't with them.

Bennett squinted out into the rain. "We couldn't find him, Milt. He's still out in the swamp."

Rossier swatted at Bennett, his face etched hard. "You dumb sonofabitch! I said *everybody*!"

"We couldn't find him, Milt!" Whining. "Hell, we'll get him come light."

Milt Rossier said, "Shit!" then went to the big door and yelled, "Come on in here, Jo-el, and let's talk this thing out!"

Out in the rain, Jo-el yelled back, "Like hell, you bastard. You come out here. You're under arrest!" Boudreaux stayed where he was.

I heard something at the rear of the shed, out where they wash the blood and the scales. Pike, maybe. I worked my feet under me and rubbed harder at the tape, thinking that if things didn't work out I would try to put myself over Lucy.

Rossier yelled, "I got your wife, goddammit. Now get in here and let's talk about this."

Jo-el came forward and stepped inside the door. His side holster was empty. He saw me first, and then he looked at his wife and Lucy. He seemed older and tired, like a man who had run a very long race and had not been in shape for it. He said, "You okay, Edie?"

She nodded.

No one was looking at me. I got to one knee, the other foot beneath me.

Jo-el said, "How we gonna work this out, Milt?"

Rossier said, "Like this," and then he raised Tommy Willets's service revolver. I lunged forward just as Joe Pike stepped in through the back and shot Milt Rossier high in the left shoulder, spinning him around and spraying blood like polka dots across Jo-el. Edith made a wailing sound deep in her throat and came off the floor and into Milt Rossier as if she'd been fired from a cannon. Even with her hands and mouth taped she battered at him with her head and face, her eyes wild and rolling. Rossier dropped his gun and grabbed at his wound, making a high whining sound. René went for Joe Pike, and Pike shot him square in the chest two times, the .357 Magnum loads putting René down on his knees. René tried to get to his feet, and Pike shot him in the center of the forehead. Rossier tried to shove past Edith for his pistol, but I hit him low in the back. Prima fired his little revolver at Pike, but Pike dived to the side. The people outside were yelling. LeRoy screamed, "I'll get the sonofabitch" and stood up from behind one of the gutting tables where he'd run for cover. He aimed his .45 at me, his tongue stuck in the corner of his mouth like a kid trying to color between the lines, and then a tiny red dot appeared on his chest. He looked down at the flicker and said, "Huh?" just before his back blew out and something kicked him across the room in a spray of blood and bone and the heavy crack of a high-powered rifle rocked through the rain.

Donaldo Prima lowered his gun and looked confused. "The fuck?"

Pike rolled to me and used his .357 to bust the chain on my handcuffs. "Del Reyo." When my hands were free I ripped off the tape.

The red dot flickered on Prima's face like a firefly searching for a place to light. He swatted at it, and then his head blew apart and again there was the distant BOOM.

Pike said, "Flash in the treeline. Gotta be two hundred meters."

I said, "Rossier has people outside."

Pike shook his head. "Not for long." His mouth twitched.

There were more booms.

I drove into Edith, pushing her down, and yelled for Lucy to stay under the table. Berry was yelling, too, saying, "Somebody's shooting at us!" Pike shouted for him to crawl under the car.

Rossier climbed to his feet, still clutching his arm, and the dot found him. I pushed him aside just as something hot snapped past and slammed into the wall. Rossier picked up LeRoy's .45, scrambled to his feet again, and lurched out through the rear of the processing sheds, firing as he went. I went after him.

There was one more boom from the treeline, and then the rifle was silent. Behind the sheds, we were hidden. Rossier tripped and fell into the mud and got up and ran on, still making the whining noise. He shot at me, but with all the slipping and falling and the hurt shoulder, the shots went wild.

I yelled, "It's done, Milt. C'mon."

He fired twice more, and the slide locked back and he was out of bullets. He threw the gun at me and ran again, straight into the low wire fence that encircled the turtle pond. In the dark and the rain he hadn't seen it. He went over the wire sideways, hit the mud on his bad shoulder, and slid headfirst into the water. It was a flat silver surface in the rain until he hit it, and then the surface rocked. He sat up, gasping for air, and I stepped across the wire and held out my hand. "C'mon, Milt. Let's go."

Pike and Jo-el came up behind me.

Milt Rossier flopped and splashed, stumbling farther out into the pond. "He'p me! You gotta he'p me!"

Jo-el said, "You're not drowning, you fat sonofabitch. Just stand up!"

His eyes wide and crazed. "He'p me! Please, Christ, get me out!"

The water swelled at the far side of the pond, and I remembered Luther.

I stepped into the water to my ankles. "Get up, dammit. Take my hand!"

Rossier tried to stand but lost his balance and fell backwards, farther out in the pond. I went in up to my knees. "Take my hand, Milt."

Something large moved fast beneath the surface, making a wake without breaking the rain-dimpled plane of the water. Pike said, "Jesus," and fired at the head of the wake. Jo-el Boudreaux fired, too.

I said, *"Take my hand!"*

Rossier made it to his feet, struggled toward me, and grabbed my hand. His grip was wet and slippery and I pulled as hard as I could, but then his left leg was yanked out from beneath him and he was pulled down into the water.

The screaming and the thrashing went on for several minutes, and maybe I screamed as loudly as Milt Rossier, but probably not.

38

Jo-el Boudreaux called in the state, and the state brought its prosecutors and the crime-scene people, and by noon the next morning there were over three dozen parish, state, and federal officials up to their ankles in mud. The rain kept coming, and did not slacken.

After the bodies were cleaned up and the statements taken, Jo-el removed his badge and told the young cop, Berry, to place him under arrest on a charge of obstruction of justice for failing to act against Milt Rossier.

Berry looked at the badge as if it were radioactive and said, "Like hell I will!"

One of the prosecutors from New Orleans shouldered his way in and said he'd be happy to accept the badge. He was a guy in his forties with tight skin and short hair, and he had spent a lot of time walking the area and shaking his head. When he tried to get the badge, Berry knocked him on his ass. A state cop from Baton Rouge tried to put Berry in a restraint hold, but Joe Pike moved between them and whispered something in the state cop's ear and the state cop walked away. After that, the prosecutor spent a lot of time sitting in his car.

Lucy spoke quietly to Jo-el for over an hour, pleading with him not to do or say anything until he spoke with Merhlie Comeaux. Edith said, "Listen to her, Jo-el. You must *please* listen to her."

Jo-el finally agreed, though he didn't seem to like it much. He sat in the front seat of his highway car with his face in his hands and wept. Jo-el Boudreaux was in pain, and ashamed, and I think he wanted to suffer for his sins. Men of conscience often do.

Joe Pike returned to Los Angeles the following day.

I stayed in Louisiana for a week after the events at Milt Rossier's crawfish farm, and much of that time I spent with Lucy. She spoke on a daily basis with Edith, and twice we went to visit.

With Milt and LeRoy Bennett out of the picture, the Boudreauxs could have kept their secret, but that wasn't the way they played it. They phoned their three children, saying that it was important that they see them, and the three daughters dutifully returned home. Jo-el and Edith sat them down in the living room and told them about Leon Williams and Edith's pregnancy and the murder that had happened thirty-six years ago. Much to the Boudreauxs' surprise, their children were not shocked or scandalized, but instead expressed relief that they had not been summoned home to be informed that one or both of their parents had an incurable disease. All three adult children thought the fact of the murder ugly and sad, but had to admit that they found the story adventurous. After all, these things had happened thirty-six years ago.

Edith's youngest daughter, Barbara, the one who was attending LSU, grinned a lot, and the grinning made Edith angry. Sissy, the oldest daughter, the one with two children, was fascinated with the idea that she had a half-sister and asked many questions. Neither Edith nor Jo-el revealed that the child she'd had was now the actress known as Jodi Taylor. Edith no longer wanted to keep secrets about herself, but other people's secrets were a different matter.

Truths were coming out, and the world was making its adjustments.

On the fourth day after the events at Milt Rossier's crawfish farm, I was waiting for Lucy in the Riverfront Ho-Jo's lobby when the day clerk gave me an envelope. He said that it had been left at the front desk, but he didn't know by whom. It was a plain white envelope, the kind you could buy in any drugstore, and "Mr. E. Cole" was typed on the front.

I sat in one of the lobby chairs and opened it. Inside was a typed note:

Mr. Cole,
I regret that I am unable to return the photograph as prom-ised. An associate identified the gentleman, and, as you know, we have acted accordingly. I hope you do not think me small for exceeding the parameters of our association. As I told Mr. Pike, the man with the rifle is always there. Re-grettably, the child remains unknown, but perhaps now there will be fewer such children.

There was no signature, but there didn't need to be.

I folded the letter and put it away as Lucy crossed the lobby. The Ho-Jo door was flooded with a noonday light so bright that Lucy seemed to emerge from a liquid sun. She said, "Hi."

"Hi."

"You ready?"

"Always."

We went out to her Lexus and drove to the airport. It was hot, but the sky was a deep blue and vividly clear except for a single puff of white to the east. Lucy held my hand. She released me to steer through a turn, then immediately took my hand again. I said, "I'm going to miss you, Lucy."

"Oh, me, too, Studly."

"Ben, too."

She glanced at me and smiled. "Please let's not talk about the leaving. We still have time."

I kissed her hand.

We turned into airport parking and went into the terminal, still holding hands, walking as close as two people can walk, as if the most important thing in the world was to occupy the same space and share the same moment. We checked the flight information. I said, "The plane's here."

We walked to the concourse, and I didn't like it much. In a few days we'd make this drive and walk again, only then I would be leaving. I tried not to think about it.

We met Jodi Taylor as she came off the plane. She was wearing jeans and a satin vest over a red top, and she was clearly Jodi Taylor. Not hiding now. The pilot was falling all over himself to walk with her, and a guy in a charcoal suit was trying to cut in on the pilot. She looked nervous.

I said, "Pardon us, gentlemen," and led her away from them.

Lucy said, "How're you doing?"

Jodi nodded. "I'm okay." She didn't look okay. She looked the way you might look if you'd spent the past couple of days with an upset stomach.

A little girl in a Brownie uniform approached. She was holding what looked like a napkin and a ballpoint pen. Her mother had encouraged her. The little girl said, "Miss Taylor, may I have your autograph?"

"Sure, honey." Jodi signed the napkin and tried to smile, but the smile looked weak. Nervous, all right.

When the little girl was gone, I took Jodi's hand. "You sure you want this?"

"Yes," she said. "Yes, I'm sure."

"What about Sid and Beldon?"

Jodi's face grew hard. "I know what I want."

Lucy took Jodi's other hand, and we walked out of the airport.

We brought Jodi to pick up Edith, and then the four of us went to visit Chantel Michot. I had called in advance and Chantel was waiting. There was a lot they wanted to talk about.